THE PURSUIT OF
LEVIATHAN

THE PURSUIT
OF LEVIATHAN

C. D. Baker

ISBN: 1535324813
ISBN 13: 9781535324816

DEDICATION

In memory of my friend and agent, Lee Hough.
Wisdom taught him how to bear life well.

ACKNOWLEDGMENTS

IN HIS LAST days, Lee Hough urged me to keep writing. This book is thus dedicated to his memory as one who endured, and who encouraged me to do likewise. I wish he were here so that I could present him his copy in person. The birthday I chose for our protagonist is not accidental.

Writing is a collaborative adventure, and so I want to express my deep gratitude to a variety of research hosts in Ireland and Jerusalem, as well as to friends in Ukraine. I am in further debt to Dr. Steven Smith for sharing insight and single malt, generously.

Finally, special thanks to my patient editor, Mick Silva of Mick Silva Editing, Portland Oregon. His professional guidance gave this book its final shape; his personal encouragement kept my spirit alive.

A Note on the Story

It is 1658.

Nearly 1,700 years have passed since Jesus of Nazareth changed everything. It has been 1,000 years since the Prophet Mohammed introduced a religion with armies that will swarm over North Africa, the Middle East, and Europe.

In 1354 a young Ottoman (i.e. Turkish) chieftain named Suleiman had a vision while staring at the night sea. The crescent moon appeared to him as a silver ribbon joining Europe and the Levant— the lands cupping the eastern shores of the Mediterranean. The vision enflamed his spirit for jihad, and soon Suleiman led an attack across the narrow strait that separated the two worlds. Victorious, his Turks quickly established a permanent Islamic foothold on the peninsula of Gallipoli—a threshold of the European continent.

In the centuries that followed, the Ottoman Caliphate gobbled up North Africa and the rest of the Levant, even as it swept across Greece and the Balkans. In 1529 it laid siege to Vienna, was turned back, yet vowed to return.

Meanwhile, in 1492 King Ferdinand and Queen Isabella of Spain had celebrated their expulsion of Islam from the west by commissioning an Italian navigator named Columbus to sail away where he happened upon the Americas. Soon the kingdoms of Europe were engaged in a dizzying quarrel over competing imperial and religious interests, eventually leaving Christians especially vulnerable in the east.

By 1642, Great Britain's kingdom of England, Scotland, Wales and Ireland was swept up in a bitter civil war between Parliament and the king. The war invoked the fervor of religious groups within Protestantism. Thousands slaughtered, it ended with the beheading of King Charles I and a brief rule by Parliament under the heavy hand of Oliver Cromwell. However, on 29 May 1660 King Charles II would reclaim the throne and Britain restored to order.

For a time.

In the midst of all this, poor Ireland lay broken in the corner of the British Isles. Her people were oppressed, and thousands even sent into slavery in the New World. Yet Ireland endured in stubborn defiance. Hers was an anvil's strength, one tempered by great sorrow which ironically liberated her spirit from her circumstances. Her legacy remains a powerful reminder of the inspiration that still resides in her enchanting headlands and patchwork greens.

The characters of our story are buffeted by the chaos of these clashing empires. Their rescue follows in the ancient wisdom that seeks to liberate those searching for the deep Love that still imbues all things. May you find that hidden beauty wherever your search takes you. And may you be set free.

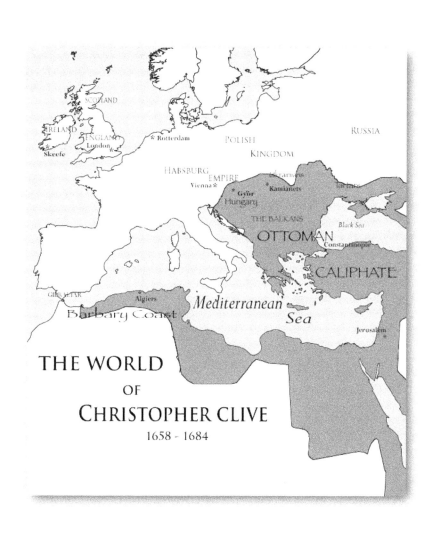

Part 1

1658 — 1661

For all remains as always was
With little yield to what Man does

CHAPTER 1

Midsummer's Day 1658

"SEA MONSTERS?" ASKED young Christopher Clive. "Sounds very Irish of thee." He scanned the unbroken blue line of the southern horizon from his wave-lapped boulder. Still wary, he surveyed the green table-top of the cliff forming the western wall of the narrow sea cove. "I do not fear sea monsters." He returned his face to the black-haired muse bobbing in the cold water at his feet.

"I like tat. Ya shouldn't fear anyt'ing," said Raven O'Morrissey in her lilting Irish accent. The shivering girl licked salt off her blue-tinged lips. "But I tink ya do fear being a nobody like me."

"No, that's not it." Distracted, Christopher glanced behind him. "And you are not a nobody." *By sea or by land?* He was not wary for his sake—English soldiers would not harm him, the grandson of an English baronet. But he had heard rumours of troubles in nearby Kinsale and he worried for the peasant girl now urging him into the water with her sage-green eyes. He then looked to the sea once more and gnawed on his lip. "Methinks I ought not."

"Ya can't ever just *be*," said Raven. "Yer so very English."

Blushing, Christopher struggled for an answer. Indeed, he had been taught to bear life according to the expectations of the empire that had bred him. "I am nearly seventeen. It is not seemly for an English gentleman to just throw off his breeches like a little boy and

3

jump into the water." He looked over his shoulder. "And besides, if trouble comes I need to be ready."

Raven sighed. "Ya suffer a great many burdens." She took a deep breath and sank into the deep blue of her beloved cove.

Christopher fixed his face on Raven's shadowed form as she submerged to curl effortlessly among the many underwater rocks like a seal pup, untamed. Admittedly, the graceful movements of her slender form stirred his blood. Yet, from the very first moment they met six years prior, something else about her had cast a wonderfully troubling spell over him.

As Raven lost herself beneath the waves, Christopher raised his face to feel the warmth of the June sun. He then took a few strides to the edge of a dazzling tide pool where he squatted and dipped his hands slowly into the clear water. He fixed his blue eyes on the rippling reflection of a yet-boyish face framed by a hanging mane of yellow curls. He drew deeply on the salt-scent of fish and seaweed, thinking. *Aunt Comfort says the Breath of the Spirit rides the tide in this place...*

Thus emboldened, he stood and returned to his flat boulder where he removed his waistcoat and folded it neatly on the rock. He pulled his linen half-shirt out of his breeches. He then sat down and abruptly crossed his left boot over his right knee to remove it. But as he did, an inner shadow-voice summoned him back from the brink. "This is beneath thee, for God's sake!"

Resisting the voice's condemnation, Kipper took a determined hold of his boot, imagining his foot no longer separated by his sole from this enchanting world of rock-and-sea. *I want to feel life like Raven does...with bared feet. I want my skin to touch the bottom of these pools; I want to squeeze seaweed between my toes...like she does.*

Christopher Clive thought it all could be so *Irish* of him.

He set his jaw.

He gripped the heel of his boot; he wanted to surrender to the magic of this place—like her.

Raven surfaced with a splash and grabbed the edge of his rock. "Do it Kipper!"

Oh, how he loved Raven to call him 'Kipper.' Christopher pulled harder on his stubborn boot. The hump of the heel yielded and slid over his silk stocking. But as it did, the inner voice hissed again. "A Clive man does not play the fool."

Christopher sat still.

"What is it?" asked Raven.

He shrugged.

Raven furrowed her full brows. "'Tis yer Grandpa."

Defeated, Kipper hastily secured his foot back in its boot. He stood, averting the disappointment in Raven's face. "If my life is to mean anything, I need to be who I am." His voice fell away.

Raven wrinkled her nose. "So who are ya then? You, or who yer Grandpa says ya ought to be." She pushed slowly away from the rock. "He treats ya like yer a dog to be trained. 'Tis why ya live fer approval and know nothin' of love."

Love? "But you don't..." Christopher's voice chased after her as she sank into deep shadows. "I just need to keep watch." Defeated, he pulled his shirt on and slowly fastened the buttons at his throat. Long swells of the rising tide rumbled from deep within one of the many caves pocking the cliffs. *She does not understand what is expected of me. How could she?*

A circling group of seabirds scolded him from above Mitten Rock—a towering outcropping standing in the cove that the elements had carved into the shape of a mitten. "You do not know, either," grumbled Christopher.

From behind, a congress of crows growled within the weedy ruins of a burned out friary tumbled atop a waterside ledge. "Even ye?" *This whole place thinks like she does.*

Christopher ambled toward the ruins where his young horse was grazing alongside the spring that fell through its tight channel to the cove. The gelding was a fine sorrel hunter bred in the Pale and ironically named 'Étalon' by Christopher's grandfather who had presented the horse as a gift. "You understand," Christopher said.

Étalon pawed a hoof hard on firm earth and the lad approved. Yet anxious, Christopher turned his eyes to the hundred-foot cliff that stood against the sea on the eastern side of the cove. Atop, green fields of scythe-ready hay wended in a warm breeze. Still not finding danger, he scratched Étalon's forelock. A pair of stonechats clicked loudly from a tangle of wild raspberry. "Aye, the land. Listen to it, smell it."

He turned to survey the easy heave and tilt of the gentle landscape that rose behind him. Quilt-patched by field and forest, and neatly stitched by wildflowers and ferns, the whole of this refuge belonged to his father and would someday be his own.

"Grandfather says we must rule it, yet Father says we are to serve it," Christopher murmured. He stared at his boots. *So, am I to be conqueror or steward? And what does love matter to either?*

Raven popped to the surface again. Christopher spun about to watch the fifteen-year-old pull herself from the water and on to the flat of a parched-white boulder jutting into the water. There she quickly wrapped herself in a thin woollen mantle. The sight of her sent him leaping over a half-dozen sea-splashed rocks. The panting lad then plopped himself next to her, making every Christian effort to pry his eyes away from her young form.

"Have ya felt the Breath yet?" Raven asked as she rested her head on the warm boulder.

Kipper lay quickly back and watched a slow moving cloud. "A little."

"The monks of former times said ya must open yerself to her." Raven spread her arms wide to the sky. "Tey said she finds ya from beyond yerself, and when she does yer truly free."

"Ever the dream-caster," said Christopher.

Raven folded her arms and wrapped herself in her blanket. She closed her eyes. "Dreams help make hard tings go a bit better."

Christopher lay his head to face her. He wanted to hold her, to nuzzle her neck. "Aye, but a good grip—"

Raven turned her face toward his and opened her eyes, softly. "Gaia says—"

"Gaia? She's mad as a deaf bat. All she does is row her boat from Waterford to Dingle in search of that book."

"Tat book, it holds the great mysteries and is made of gold-leaf and jewels."

Christopher laughed. "Aye. Crusaders plundered it from mystics near Jerusalem and hid it in an Irish cove. The *Libro Mandala*. I've heard the legend."

"Gaia swears it's worth a king's ransom."

"Fie."

Raven sat up, shivering. "Whatever ya tink of her, Gaia is my friend."

Christopher remembered how his father insisted that the old woman was a smuggler and possibly even a spy for Irish rebels. "Friend or not, she's dangerous."

"She's comforting."

"She's chaotic and—"

"Wise." Raven's look was a challenge and he watched as she thought for a moment. "She's wise because she was tended by the living earth as a lost child. When the priest found her he said she was a 'miracle of Creation.' Besides, she loves me."

"Well that is no small thing, I grant thee," Christopher grumbled. "But have a care when near her." He wrapped his waistcoat around Raven, snuggling it under her shivering chin. "And on another matter, might I remind thee that my Aunt Comfort did not teach you to say 'tink' or 'tat' but rather, *th*ink and *th*at. Put the tip of the tongue between thy teeth. '*Th*ink."

Raven looked away.

The conversation over, the two remained silent for a long time. Rogue waves slapped the slated cliffs sending sprays of hissing water into the air. Finally wishing to make peace, Christopher touched Raven's shoulder, lightly. "Tush. I've no desire to fight with thee."

Raven turned toward him.

Kipper took her cool hand. It felt so wonderfully fragile. "We do have an enchanted place here," he said. "It suits thee, and methinks 'tis a good place to dream of happy endings for us all. Aunt Comfort calls it 'Raven's Cove,' just so you know."

Raven yielded. "I like *tat*. 'Raven's Cove.'" She withdrew her hand and held her knees close to her chest. "So, do you believe in happy endings?"

Christopher answered, eagerly. "Of course. All one needs do is bear a proper course—"

"Hey-ho, now who is the dreamer?" Raven said. She studied her cove for a quiet moment. "Yer aunt loves the sea, though I *th*ink she has some hard memories of it."

Christopher pried a white cockle off the rock. "Aye, she does. Grandfather says she suffered a great deal with the Mohammedans who took her away." He checked the horizon again. "He claims that the sea is neither good nor safe, but rather home to all manner of chaos—"

"So yer Grandpa believes in sea monsters!" Raven laughed.

"Well, only the kind a good Navy can defeat," answered Christopher, red-faced. "But he thinks it best for Clive men to ground our boots on what is solid."

Raven wrinkled her nose. "Here's what I tink: Good places aren't always safe places." She paused. "And solid places aren't always good."

She pulled his jacket tighter to her throat. "If ya take up too many of yer grandpa's ways you and I will have some troubles."

Christopher forced a smile. "Well, no matter, I can protect you from monsters of every sort."

Raven raised her brows and pressed her lips tightly together.

"My grandfather gave me a doglock for my grades at Winchester School, and I can shoot it on a line."

"I feel so much better." Raven quickly hid her face in her knees.

Christopher blushed. "You're laughing at me? You think I am not a brave man—"

"I never said such a ting." A small boat suddenly rounded Mitten Rock with a lone figure straining oars toward the cove. Christopher and Raven stood as the old boat rode a long swell, landward. Raven shielded her eyes from the sun. "Gaia?"

The curious pair watched the old Irish woman pull hard against her oarlocks and cut a wake beneath the cliffs. She aimed her boat toward the narrow pebbled beach at the foot of the ruins. "Something's amiss." Raven stood and called loudly as the boat heaved its way past them. "Gaia, what is it?"

CHAPTER 2

SHE'S IN TROUBLE, Raven thought. She threw off Kipper's coat and her mantle. She grabbed her homespun dress from a dry rock and pulled it over her wet shift. "Come on," she cried.

Ahead, the sturdy old woman rammed her little boat into the small landing by the spring. Gaia then grabbed hold of the bow and leaned back, struggling to drag it beyond the tide line.

With her bulky clothing, broad shoulders and confident stride, people might mistake Gaia for a man at first. Indeed, she could back a blushing sailor off the dock with her tongue. Yet, she could also heal a sickly child with a light touch of her crooked fingers, inclining most to consider her to be a lucky charm of sorts—a magical crone standing against the hobgoblins in the Irish shadows.

But what shadows might be looming now? And what of hobgoblins?

"Gaia?" Raven cried as she drew close.

"*Dtriobloid, tá deacracht ag teacht!*" Gasping, she bent over her knees to catch her breath. Long strands of grey hair fell forward from beneath her black felt hat.

"Talk English." Raven tilted her head at Christopher.

"Comes trouble a'plenty to Skeefe." Gaia made her way for the friary ruins.

"What kind of trouble?" asked Christopher.

"The kind tat bids my Raven to hide." The old woman threw off her mantle and reached through a gap in old mortar. She plucked out a hidden bottle of smuggled whiskey and took a long draught, then headed deeper into the ruins.

Raven followed her over burnt timbers and fallen rocks into the shadows with Christopher close behind. Gaia squatted in a dark corner. "Two hours past I seen English soldiers in Kinure—Roche's men out of Kinsale, metinks."

"I knew it!" blurted Christopher.

Gaia's thick grey brows edged to her low forehead like clouds, gathering. "Tey arrested three fer treason, and whipped four women fer yester eve's St. John's bonfires." She took another drink, then spat at Christopher's feet. "Ten yer fine Protty soldiers sang their damned hymns as they sullied the virtue of Mister Ryan O'Sullivan's house."

Oh, not poor Keara, Raven thought. A chill spread through her.

Gaia nodded. "So gerl, ya needs hide in the hills with me, else—"

"But I cannot," Raven said. "I needs warn Ma and Uncle Finn."

Gaia wiped her mouth. "Beggin pardon, but yer ma has more hair ten teat, and Finn's clever. Tey be safe enough."

"My father won't let anything happen to Skeefe," announced Christopher. "He protects his tenants—"

"Yer pa be too weak to frighten a goat." Gaia belched.

Raven watched Christopher puff his chest. "My family is aligned with Lord de Courcey. Roche men would not dare disrespect our property—"

"Tey would."

"They wouldn't."

"Tey would and tey will." Gaia shook a gnarled finger at him. "Even yer Aunt Comfort—may the Holy Virgin bless her—cannot stop them."

Christopher took Raven's hand. She liked the sudden strength in it. "I shall keep them all safe," he said.

"See that ya do."

※

Gaia squeezed her whiskey bottle as Raven mounted Étalon behind Christopher. Watching the galloping horse disappear upslope, she quickly drained it. "Godspeed, deary." She walked to a flat outcropping at the water's edge where she narrowed her black eyes to search the sea. "Leviathan? Have ya come fer us again?" Gaia was no stranger to hard times, yet never cowered to them. On the contrary, she enjoyed the satisfaction of enduring *despite* them. She spat.

She removed her battered hat and raised her face in prayer to the Virgin, the saints and her Christ. "...and Holy Jaysus, keep tat ancient monster chained deep in the sea, at least fer now. Try and get it right tiss time. Amen."

Gaia crossed herself and remained silent for a long moment, eyes closed. She then stretched her arms outward and murmured a benediction on her world:

"All with all, together and forever within the loving heart of
the good Maker.
Mercy for all, peace to all,
And deliverance from the Evil One."

Hat returned to her head, she moved toward the upward path. She thought of Raven and the many hours they had spent in the simple, constant wisdom of the cove. "Tiss has been the delight of m'life." She wiped her eyes.

Truly Gaia had always loved Raven. Perhaps she had seen something of herself in the way Raven melded with earth and sea. Perhaps she admired how her spirit soared freely in the whirlwind. Perhaps it was how Raven could bear the good fruits of love in spite of unyielding misery?

Whatever the reasons, Gaia now feared for her, greatly.

Ready, she made her way to the base of the cliff and began the upward trek along a well-worn sheep path. She dragged herself to the first terrace where she paused to rest. If the English came to Skeefe there would be smoke which she could see from just a little higher. Wheezing, she pressed upward along the cliff's rising rim until she finally reached the broad field at the top. Gaia then stared eastward the three miles to the tiny hamlet of Skeefe that Raven called home. "Oh Christ, me precious deary…"

⊰⊱

Raven wrapped her arms tightly around Christopher's waist and squeezed her bare feet hard against the horse's heaving flanks. Her mind raced with her heart as Étalon strained up the narrow valley toward the Kinure byway.

Raven knew well what her mother and uncle might be suffering. She grit her teeth. She and her family had already endured plenty at the hands of the English. Her father was an Irish rebel who had dragged the family from Donegal to Cork before he died eight years prior when he drowned in the Shannon River during the battle of Meelick. "Hurry, Kipper."

Raven held her arms fast around Christopher as Étalon turned sharply right onto the wagon-rutted byway linking a handful of country houses to Kinsale. Her legs were wet with the foam now covering the horse's sweated coat. As they approached the top of a long rise,

Raven lifted her cheek off Christopher's rocking back and strained to see whether smoke was rising from Skeefe. She groaned. More than a half-dozen black columns were churning into a cloudless sky. "O, Mudder Mary."

Raven held yet more tightly as she felt Christopher lean farther forward in his stirrups. Her mind flew to her Uncle Finn and remembered the long ago day that he had found her sobbing with a dead baby rabbit in her hands. He helped her bury the little thing and then carried her home to the song of a lullaby. She knew Finn's heart well. And so she knew that despite his tenderness, he had never stopped being a rebel no matter his crippling wounds at the same battle that had claimed her father. *Finn O'More, have ya been at some mischief?* Ahead, Raven spotted her secret shortcut, a footpath that she took to her cove. "Turn there."

Christopher reined Étalon hard and then spurred his heaving mount down a fern-swept slope. Steadied by the lurching rhythm of Étalon's gallop, Raven whispered a few prayers. The Protestants may have burned her churches and driven her priests into hiding, but she would not abandon her religion. "...Amen," she said.

Raven held fast until Étalon finally burst from the ferns onto the sandy shores of the bay where the burning village of Skeefe lay. She tumbled off the horse and hiked her dress as she raced through smoke toward her mother's cottage some fifty yards from the shore.

"Ma! Ma! Uncle Finn!"

Raven dashed between terrified villagers and leapt over several bloodied corpses with Christopher urging Étalon close behind. Smoke filled her eyes as blasting heat from burning thatch drove her from side to side. "Ma? Ma? Where are ya?" Arriving at her flame-engulfed cottage, Raven clenched her fists in terror.

"O'er there!" shouted Christopher. He pointed to a thin woman folded in two against a small workshop.

Raven scrambled toward the figure. "Ma?"

Doon O'Morrissey turned and lunged at the sight of her daughter running from the smoke. Sobbing, she embraced Raven. "*O buíochas a ghabháil na naoimh thuas!* O, tank ta saints, above. O Mary...O dear gerl...ya must hide!"

Raven buried her face in Doon's hair until she heard a strained cry. She turned to see Christopher jabbing the air with his pistol at five pot-helmeted footmen in red buff coats now trotting toward them.

"Run, Raven, run!" he shouted.

Face flushed, Christopher reined Étalon sideways to shield Raven and Doon's flight to safety, but now found himself threatening seasoned soldiers of Cromwell's New Model Army with his pointed pistol.

The veterans paused.

"Stay back! I... I am Mister Christopher Clive!"

A young musketeer abruptly kneeled and took aim with his matchlock.

"Nay!" Kipper jumped from his horse and crouched, instinctively covering his head. The musket flashed and belched smoke. Étalon bolted as Christopher felt the ball cut the air close by one side. He lunged for a wall and turned to see the footmen now running toward him with swords and pikes.

Crouching, Christopher squeezed the handle of his doglock and sucked for air. He always kept it loaded but—

The soldiers were within forty paces. *Christ save me! Is my powder dry! Is the flint set?*

From the corner of his eye, Christopher spotted Raven hiding under an overturned cart. He fumbled with his flint and stood upright, pulling back the hammer to full cock. Jaw clenched, he extended his arm and turned his shoulders in line with the on-rushing soldiers. The three-pound weapon became like a hundredweight hanging at the end of his arm. He struggled to hold it straight. *Steady. Closer than ten paces...*

Summoning everything within him, he then took one long stride toward the soldiers. "I warn ye...I am Mister Christopher Clive, grandson of the baronet." He aimed at the padded chest of the one he guessed to be the leader. "Hold or I shoot!"

The man stopped.

Christopher then swung his arm toward the next and then the next, each stopping in turn. "Hold fast! Ye have committed grave harm here. I shall have ye arrested." Young Clive's chest was tight; his throat was closing. Smoke burned his eyes. *Never let it show.*

The pause was tortuous.

A second musketeer dropped to a knee and took aim. "I'll shoot thy pretty blue eye out from here, Goldie-locks."

Christopher tried to swallow. "I am *English* as ye, ye fools."

An officer on horseback emerged from the smoke and calmly commanded his soldiers. "Hold fast."

The men fell still.

He nudged his horse toward Christopher. "Lower thy piece, Mister Clive."

Christopher hesitated.

"Lower, *Mister* Clive."

Christopher slid his eyes from the officer to the soldiers.

The officer moved his mount directly alongside the boy and looked down on him. "Granting refuge to a rebel may suit thy father but it shall not sit well with Baron de Courcey." He wiped smoke from his eyes. "Nor with thy mad grandfather, methinks."

Christopher shifted on his feet. "Rebel?" He lowered his piece.

The officer sniffed and waved vaguely toward the Clive's plantation house that overlooked Skeefe about a mile up-slope from the shoreline. "Aye. We've one in chains by thy father's stable. He'll be bound for Barbados within a fortnight." He looked around at the burning village and abruptly shouted at the unseen faces hiding in the smoke. "*Tá tú tar éis rabhadh!* Ye have been warned. If we needs come back, ye shall each feel shackles, a blade or a ball."

He returned his face to Christopher. "Now, Mister Clive, I suggest you listen more carefully to thy grandfather." The officer then grunted a command and led his soldiers out of the burning village leaving Christopher staring at the pistol shaking at the end of his limp arm.

His stomach roiled and he doubted his legs. As the soldiers trotted away, something the officer said echoed in his mind. *Barbados.* The word lodged in his chest. His father had told him of the terrible fates awaiting the thousands of Irish men, women and children already deported there by Lord Protector Oliver Cromwell. Most were beaten and despoiled in scorching fields of sugar cane just like the black Africans.

Christopher felt Raven's hands clutch his arm.

"Did they harm ya?" she said.

He returned a blank stare.

"They've arrested Uncle Finn!"

Unable to speak, Christopher looked back to the soldiers marching away. What could he possibly do?

CHAPTER 3

CHRISTOPHER SPENT THE next hours running alongside the Irish heaving heavy buckets of water against the fires of Skeefe. The work was futile; the village had been destroyed. At last, he stared sadly into the soot-blackened faces of Raven and Doon. "My father shall rebuild it all. This is my vow to ye."

Raven took her mother's hand. "And what of Uncle Finn?"

Christopher fumbled for an answer.

Doon leaned forward. "The devil with the village. Can ya vow m'brother's return to us?"

Christopher averted her dark eyes. He knew he could never make such a vow. "I shall do what I can——"

Doon spat. "Which be nothin at all."

He opened his mouth but no words came out.

"Go to yer fine house, Mister Clive," said Doon. Her chin lifted.

"But Mistress O'Morrissey, where shall any of ye sleep?" he said.

"Our Irish men will take care of us. We've no need of English." Doon folded her arms.

"We've room enough at the house."

Doon's tone was bitter. "Yer grandfather's in residence with yer pa. Not one of us—not even the dying—would share a roof with tat man, nor he with us."

Christopher knew that Doon O'Morrissey was right about that. He turned aside and whistled weakly for Étalon. "Send a runner if you need anything." He then looked directly at Raven. "I am not my grandfather. I shall help ye all as I am able."

⁓⧉⁓

Exhausted, Christopher mounted his horse and began a slow ride toward his home located in the centre of his father's 600-acre estate that included Skeefe, the cove, and a rectangular sweep of fertile land. Spencer Clive had named his plantation, *Giardín an Croí*—the 'Garden of the Heart.' The name pleased Christopher. He loved every snag, furrow, hillock and softwood of the place.

Christopher also shared his father's hopes for Skeefe to be an example of a more enlightened relationship between English land-lords and Irish tenants. Thus, the village's destruction weighed heavy on his heart as he rode away. He turned in his saddle every hundred yards or so to look again in disbelief at the collapsed timbers and charred remains of what could have been.

Rocking smoothly atop his horse, Christopher began to wonder if his father could actually rebuild the village. He knew that Spencer had already invested a great deal, and his returns had not been encour-aging. He also wondered how anyone could rescue poor Uncle Finn. *If the government finds him for rebellion, he is lost forever.*

Discouraged, Kipper nudged Étalon closer toward his father's splendid house. Soon staring at the Palladian symmetry and air of per-manence looming just ahead, a twinge of discomfort began to course through his body. He turned in his saddle once more. Raven and the Irish would be sleeping under the stars on charred straw tonight while he and his family would be comfortably lounging within a house designed by a protégé of London's famous architect, Inigo Jones.

As if seeing his privilege for the first time, he paused. Scanning the stately stone house and well-crafted outbuildings, he suddenly

19

supposed it was no wonder why he bore the weight of so many expectations. After all, given his father's general frailty, this might all be his sooner than later—a likelihood that pleased his Grandfather Sir Redmond Clive since Spencer had proven to be such a disappointment.

Captivated by the broad landscape and fine gardens, he chewed on the inside of his cheek. *I could do wonderful things for the Irish.* Suddenly both anxious and pleased, he further realized that this plantation would not be his only asset. A deeper legacy was poised to rest on his shoulders, one that had begun with his *great*-grandfather—Sir William Clive—who had been granted the heritable title of 'baronet' from a grateful King James I many years prior. Most of Sir William's many holdings had been passed to Christopher's grandfather who had shrewdly expanded the family's fortune yet further.

Too much to consider at that moment, Kipper blew a long breath through his lips, dismounted and led Étalon to the stables. There he watered and fed the animal, and brushed away clusters of clinging brambles. He gave his contented gelding a final pat and moved to a closet where he removed a spare shirt and breeches, a clean waistcoat and fresh boots. Washing his face, hands and arms in a bucket of fresh-pumped water, he dressed, stuffed his unfired pistol in his wide belt and drew a deep breath.

As Christopher entered the front door of his father's grand house, he found his grandfather staring through the arched Venetian window that overlooked Skeefe and the bay. He took a place just behind the sixty-one-year old. "Terrible, don't you think, sir?"

Sir Redmond snorted. He was a short, stout man with a badger-like face purfled by a long, curly wig. "Imagine. An Irish rebel under our very noses." He turned around and scowled at Christopher with watery grey eyes. "You must realize that the government can make or break this family. Do you think the army would buy grain from my mills if my son's loyalty was suspect? Could I keep bank stocks if my family's integrity was in question?"

Christopher knew that Clive fortunes had been carefully managed during the recent civil war between the King and Parliament. His grandfather had deftly manoeuvred between Royalists and Roundheads, securing profitable contracts from the Parliament soon after King Charles had been beheaded. But no matter which side any Englishman had ever served, Irish rebels were a common enemy to most.

"Our integrity is not in question, sir," answered Christopher. "And Finn O'Neil is no longer a rebel."

Sir Redmond Clive furrowed his brows and leaned forward, setting Christopher back on his heels. "Every O'Neil is a rebel. He'll be charged and sentenced by the magistrate before lunch tomorrow." He shook his head, grumbling. "And then I shall have to fix this mess with the baron."

Christopher had no answer.

Changing course, Sir Redmond blurted, "The captain told me that I ought to beat you with a switch."

Christopher waited.

Redmond then jerked Christopher's pistol out of his belt and looked at it. His tone softened. "This very morning you and I spoke of thy future prospects over pottage and cackling farts. Good prospects, methinks. Superb, actually. Do you remember?"

Wary, Christopher nodded.

Sir Redmond rolled the pistol in his hands and chuckled. He had bought Christopher that particular doglock for its comically fashioned trigger—an upside down baby covering its ears. "The Irish can be assets, but you fail to appreciate why." His tone changed again. "You are ignorant about them like thy father."

Christopher faced the floor.

"Fie. Imagine, my grandson waving his pistol at his own government, ready to die for those bog-trotters." Redmond cursed. "The Irish are to be used, not coddled."

Christopher remained silent.

Sir Redmond stared at the pistol again. "The Clive name needs a *man*, not a fool! And one who can grasp the difference between an Irishman and an Englishman for God's sake."

Christopher's mother, Millicent, sounded from the corner in which she had been listening. She was a heavy, ambitious woman with suspicious brown eyes. "He is smitten by an Irish bitch."

"Of course he is." Redmond growled.

Christopher's father suddenly entered in a nightshirt and slippers, leaning heavily on his cane. Pale as death, Spencer took a seat on a simple wooden chair by the dull light of the front window and said nothing.

Ignoring his son's arrival, Redmond curled a finger at Christopher. "Come close, boy."

Christopher obeyed.

Sir Redmond abruptly pushed the end of the pistol's barrel against Christopher's crotch. "Does that thing have a brain, boy?"

Christopher's eyes widened.

"Nay, it does not." Redmond then shocked everyone by moving the barrel of the pistol from Christopher's crotch to his forehead. "I have had thee groomed from petty school right through grammar school so that you might think with thy *head* at university."

Sir Redmond began tapping the hard barrel on his forehead. "Think, think, think."

Christopher's heart began to race. *Never let it show.*

"This family's fortune needs an educated, properly connected man to direct it. Do you understand?"

Christopher blinked.

"This is why I ordered thy masters at Westminster to use the switch on thee with greater wrath than any other could endure." Sir Redmond nodded as if satisfied with himself. "And it has proven worthwhile. Doctor Selden wrote to me saying that you are 'worthy of Oxford's highest expectations.'" He lifted the end of the barrel away from Christopher's forehead. "Imagine. Oxford's *highest* expectations. This was the year you were to begin proving him right. But now we have this mess of thy father's damned Irish."

Christopher waited.

"You are primed to achieve greatness, unless…" He returned the barrel to Christopher's forehead again, and with his free hand he pulled the pistol's hammer to full cock.

The room fell still as death.

No one dared move.

"Unless…" Grandfather Clive then pulled the trigger. Snap.

Sparks flew from the flint. Christopher jerked with a start. Millicent collapsed into a heap and Spencer cried out.

But the gun had not fired.

Sir Redmond lowered the pistol. He calmly pointed to the touchhole of the flash pan. "Clogged with shite, boy, like thy brains. Could never have fired." Ignoring protests from Spencer, the old man tossed the piece atop an upholstered settee. He pulled a snuff tin from within his vest and looked scornfully at Spencer who was now helping his wife to a chair.

Redmond pinched some finely ground Virginia tobacco between his thumb and forefinger. He inhaled the snuff into each nostril with a violent snort, sneezed, and then returned to Christopher. "As I was saying, you are primed to achieve greatness unless you fail to properly bear thy birthright."

Christopher was trembling.

Redmond put his face close to his grandson's. "You do realize that the captain could have ordered you carved to bits for threatening

Parliament's men? Imagine, the head of a Clive on a pike for the sake of some Papist tart."

Christopher did not answer.

Grandfather Clive wiped his nose with a kerchief. "The captain also said that you stood as brave as any man."

Old Clive's face softened. He stared at his silent grandson like he was suddenly admiring a fine painting. "*That* was music to my ears, and now I've seen the same with mine own eyes. You did not flinch; you stared me down like a lion in the hunt." Redmond pointed a disdainful finger at the puddle of urine beneath Spencer's chair. "Unlike him."

Redmond then steadied Christopher's shoulders with his hands. "So, this is a *good* day, *Mister* Clive! Huzzah! Today you are finally a man. We needs celebrate the acorns in thy sack." He laughed, madly, and then removed two Dutch rummers from a cabinet as well as a bottle of his private *Ron Añejo*. "Perhaps you are not yet shrewd, but a strong spine is a good start." He poured two fingers full of the Barbados rum in each glass, handed his speechless grandson his and raised a health. "To *Mister* Christopher Clive, his many sons to come, and to all whom he shall master."

The baronet laid his eye along his own tipped rim to watch Christopher hastily drain his glass. Satisfied, he swallowed and wrapped an affectionate arm around him. "Listen to me carefully. This world bears heavy. My heir needs be fit, fleet and hard as hammered steel." He sipped some more rum. "You have been born into a fine station, Mister Clive." He pulled Christopher closer. "But to be a great man you must *mean* something. And to mean something you must *do* something. 'Tis why a man who accomplishes nothing is worth nothing." Redmond snorted. "Nay, this is thy purpose. Do not forget it. Take hold of thy life as a man should, and make it worth thrice a king's ransom. Do you understand?"

Christopher nodded.

Redmond released Kipper and began to pace in a slow circle around his grandson, deep in thought. He then refilled his glass.

Christopher sipped the rum, anxiously. *What is he up to now?*

"However, it occurs to me that you may not actually *want* to attend Oxford." Redmond stopped pacing. "Do you?"

Christopher blurted, "Of course, sir."

"Why?"

Why? No one had ever asked him 'why' about anything before. Christopher strained. "The world is changing very quickly. I…I should like to have every advantage."

Redmond approved. "And you are content with Oriental Studies? When you were a child you imagined thyself as a playwright or some such nonsense."

Christopher's passion had always been to put a good rhyme or thoughtful verse to paper, but he understood the obligations of his destiny. "I am content in these studies, sir. They are necessary."

Redmond sniffed, and poured himself more rum. He began to circle him again. "You realize that if you do poorly at university, our competitors shall see weakness and our friends shall lose confidence."

"I do."

The old man stopped. "Good. But avoiding failure in life is never enough. One must overcome. Therefore, you must not piss this opportunity away. Nay, you must *vanquish* thy peers and *astonish* thy professors. Otherwise what's the point? Who should give a shite about an ordinary man?"

Christopher took another drink.

"Supremacy is required for all manner of advantages." Redmond let his words sink into his grandson before moving very close. He then lowered his voice. "A man who stands above all others is awarded greater…shall we say…considerations." He stared into Christopher's face as if to push an idea into his brain.

What is he trying to say without saying? Christopher returned a blank stare until it suddenly occurred to him that he was being offered something. But what? *Would he allow some charity for the Irish, after all? Would he help with Skeefe? With Finn?*

As if to drive the point home, Redmond then added, "We all need to give a little here and there, do we not?"

Christopher was suddenly intrigued. "Aye, sir, we do."

The baronet smiled. "So there he is, no more the boyish priss." He extended his hand.

An unfamiliar feeling fast-filled Christopher's belly. He stood on legs suddenly long in his bucket-top boots. His shoulders lifted. He clasped his grandfather's hand, and as he did a new kind of strength thickened his own. "Vanquish my peers; astonish my professors," he said.

Both men smiled, unaware of what lay in wait for such a plan as this.

CHAPTER 4

———— ❦ ————

9 July 1659

A YEAR AFTER the desolation of Skeefe, Raven finally stole away from the exhaustion that had just begun to lift from her village to find refuge within the summer twilight of her beloved cove. In their raid, Parliament's Roundheads had killed a third of her neighbours outright. Eight fit men, two suckling mothers, an old widow and three children had been shot, stabbed, clubbed or trampled. Despite the best efforts of the physician that Spencer Clive had sent, another five had died from burns within the days that followed. To make matters worse, three entire families later vanished, doubtlessly disinterested in the overwhelming task ahead.

Staring into a sky slowly darkening in the east, Raven grieved for all that had been lost, but most especially for her Uncle Finn now languishing in his faraway hell-hole. So whenever she heard herself complaining, she thought of him suffering on that terrible island and asked the Virgin Mary to forgive her for being weak.

Nevertheless, the nearly seventeen-year-old had endured plenty. Naturally, she had served her determined mother in daily duties with the cow and goats, the fowl, the spinning and basket weaving. But with so many men folk gone, she and other healthy females had been enlisted to help lug timber and thatch for reconstruction, to scythe broad fields of oats, and to stack hay. She had spent damp winter days whetting blades alongside grumbling old men, cutting cords of wood, fishing with the Murrays' boats, or knee-deep in icy water to break oysters from their stubborn beds.

On a sleeting night in the February past, Raven had collapsed with a high fever. Wrapped in thin wool blankets before a raging hearth, the failing girl was rescued from the brink by Gaia who faithfully tended her with herbal soups and her magic touch. Recovered, Sean O'Driscoll strapped her to an iron plough in April which she wrestled as it cut cock-eyed furrows behind a lunging team of garrons. She then spent days spreading seed from heavy sacks.

Her hard work had helped make a great difference and by now Skeefe was nearly restored, as was she. New tenants had begun to arrive and with them came the first hints of hope. This very morning Raven heard her mother whistle a tune, albeit a bit weak. That made her happy and so she now clambered over the flat rocks of her cove with a smile and a song of her own.

Laughing within herself, Raven paused to breathe deeply of the sea-scented air. She was delighted to be alive and in this place. Humming, she sat and dangled her legs in the water, closed her eyes and listened to the music of wavelets playfully slapping the shoreline. Raven sat like this for a very long time, remembering. When she opened her eyes, she delighted in how the rising moon had so quickly cast a luminous haze over her gauzy dreamscape of sea and stone.

After a time, she looked at her hands. Already callused, they were scabbed from repairing the whitethorn fences that the small herd of village cattle had broken down the day before. She wondered if Christopher would want to ever hold them again. Like her, they had become rough and weathered in this past year. She held her hands up to the moonlight. She thought them to be nothing like the tender hands of the young ladies she imagined Kipper admiring in England.

Raven sighed and stood, and then began to amble alongside a cliff, running her fingers along its wet, sea-scrubbed slate as if it were a familiar friend. *Gaia says the Breath will always keep us safe.* She paused to stare into the restful sea, blanketed by a thin veil of mist. *But the Breath did not keep Uncle Finn safe.*

And then she thought of Kipper. She turned landward. *What if he doesn't come?*

But he'd surely know I'd be here on his birthday.

Unless he's too smart fer me now in that fancy school? Maybe he has a gerl in England? Maybe he's forgot me.

She stepped lightly across the boulders that led her deeper into the cove. *The Clives did not lift a finger to save Finn—not even Aunt Comfort. Why?* Suddenly angry, she threw a piece of flotsam into the dark water. *Well, I suppose Comfort is just a woman, but Kipper has ne'er even ask me about him…and two letters in a year.*

Raven's shoulders sagged. She closed her eyes and slowed her breath to the easy rhythm of the night's gentle waves. *Blah, I ought not tink bad tings of people here in tiss place of hope.* She opened her eyes and stared at the first stars hanging low just above the cliff-tops to her right.

Raven then walked quietly to a spot where the sea had bitten a rectangular notch in the centre of a flat rock. The narrow gap offered a short flight of water-worn steps to its pebbled floor about a yard deep at low tide. She loved to sit atop its middle step like a sea-queen lounging comfortably on a water-lapped throne. From there she pondered all that she loved, and once a happy thought or a gratitude brought a smile, she'd search the clear water with her feet for the smooth finger-shaped stones she called 'Joy Stones.' She'd pick one up with her toes and lift it to her hand, kiss it and toss it back to the sea with a prayer or a song.

This evening she climbed into her little throne and plunged her foot to the bottom. Raven felt about and retrieved a Joy Stone, lifted it to her hand wishing luck for her uncle. She then touched the stone to her lips, kissed it, and tossed it as far as she could back to the moon-swathed sea.

She decided to not dwell on Finn's misery—not in this place of happy dreams. Instead she began to think of better days and of dancing. Raven thought of the walks she had taken with Christopher's Aunt Comfort in this very place over the past few years. She smiled. She had no idea why the woman had taken an interest in her, but she had grown to love Comfort and the wisdom she freely imparted. Raven was especially grateful for how Comfort and Spencer Clive had delivered necessaries to Skeefe so often in this past year. Raven reached for a stone, kissed it and gave it a toss.

She relaxed and swung her legs lightly within the water at her throne. She then thought of Kipper riding into smoky Skeefe during the raid to dare the Roundheads for her sake. She smiled and lowered her toes to the bottom again.

The little stone had barely dimpled the surface when the sound of a familiar voice startled her. Turning, she hurried out of her seat and searched through the silver light. "Kipper?"

"Aye!"

Raven clasped her hands and watched him quickstep from boulder to boulder toward her. "O Kipper!" Even under moonlight she could see that he had changed in this past year. He had grown taller and his white shirt hung from broadened shoulders. When he finally stood in front of her she thought his eyes now reflected newfound confidence. "I am so happy to see ya," she said. She thought she might fall into his arms.

Christopher laughed and wiped a finger beneath his high collar. "Aye? And it is so good to see you at last, Raven. 'Tis been so long. I just arrived in Kinsale this very afternoon."

That news pleased Raven. She had wondered if he was avoiding her. She then noticed how his jaw was beginning to square and his nose had become more prominent. "Just look at ya...a true knight of the realm."

Christopher bowed with a flourish. "I am thine, O Irish princess."

Raven pushed her black hair off her fair face and tilted her head playfully. "Is tat so?"

He pointed to the water. "I see you're still tossing thy Joy Stones back."

"I am. What of it, sir?"

"I was hoping to see how many joys you had since I was gone."

"I had a few, but I've not been here in a very long time." She curtsied to the sky. "Those I have were heaved already back to where they will be most wonderfully remembered." She watched his eyes following her lips. Heat rose to pink her cheeks. Giggling, Raven lowered herself into her little throne and picked up another Joy Stone with her toes. She handed it to Christopher. "Now you. Tink of somethin tat makes ya happy, kiss it and toss it back."

Christopher took the little stone and held it to Raven's lips. "Kiss it for me."

She did.

He then put the stone in his pocket.

"What? Tell me ya won't add it to yer pile!" Raven slapped his arm.

"I am building a trove of good things."

Raven wrinkled her nose. "Ya can't make a good ting better by addin more! And hear me, good sir: a man can never collect enough of anyt'ing to build the happiness he seeks. So says yer own aunt."

Christopher shook his head. "Nay, girl. A man *can* build happiness. Such is the way of the world, like it or not."

"Fer all yer smarts, ya have it backwards. Ya needs be happy first, and *then* build what ya can from *that*."

"How?"

Raven laughed. "I've no idea!" She thought for a moment, and then raised her arms over the cove. "But if we spent more time listenin' in tiss place, we may find a clue." She pointed into the horizon. "On some days, storms toss the water hard against the rocks. On other days, pure calm settles it into a place of perfect peace. Gaia says the cove is true because the cove reveals all we were meant to be."

Christopher looked at the cliffs and the rolling water. "I do not know how to let this place fill me like it does thee."

Raven thought for a moment. She then pointed to his boots. "I'm guessin ya won't be takin them off tonight?"

"Nay. They are new and a bit stiff—"

"I say this kindly: The wisdom of this place can't fill us when we are prisoners of ourselves. Yer grandfather's ways weigh heavy on yer spirit. Cast them off and ya'll be free to take off yer boots." She set her finger on her chin, playfully. "Or maybe ya can do it the other way round."

Christopher remained silent.

"Well, enough of that then," said Raven. "Now tell me: are ya still writing yer beautiful poems?"

Christopher looked down. "Nay. Not so much. Grandfather says 'tis a waste of my time. He burns them when he finds them."

Raven's eyes filled. "I am sorry, Kipper. Forgive me, but yer grandpa can be so cruel. The village still talks of yer thirteenth birthday—"

"Father wrote to me that it was a hard year for Skeefe but that things are better. Comfort wrote that you suffered a great deal." He reached a finger to stroke her cheek.

"I swear to you I have seen no more beautiful girl in all of London or Oxford."

Raven nearly swooned. She altered course, shyly. "Thank ya. But happy birthday, Kipper. Ya'd be eighteen now."

"And you shall be seventeen in less than a fortnight."

"I will." Raven hesitated. "Was this a good birthday?"

He nodded. "We had a fine breakfast this morning with Grandfather Clive. What with Cromwell dead and his sons resigned, everyone is happier now...even my father is feeling better. And there is much talk of restoring Charles II as King, so my grandfather is changing churches again." He chuckled. "Anyway, one of the cooks made gingerbread for me, and Sir Redmond shared his special coffee. I did not tell him that I've had better."

Christopher then reached into the satchel hanging from one shoulder. "I bought this in London for thy birthday, but I just had to give it to you now." He handed Raven a small waxed box tied carefully with a striped ribbon.

Delighted, Raven opened the box, unwrapped some stiff paper and stared at several yellow-orange, heart-shaped lozenges.

"Take one."

Raven picked up one of the treats carefully. She squeezed it lightly. It was stiff and a little sticky. She sniffed it.

"'Tis made to be eaten," laughed Kipper.

She nibbled off a piece and her face lit. "Oh, Kipper—" She quickly offered the rest of her piece to him.

He surprised her by leaning forward with his opened mouth and drew the candy from her fingers, slowly.

At the touch of his lips, Raven felt her body rise. Heart racing, she watched Kipper chew. His long blond curls shimmered under moonlight; the breadth of his shoulders and the lean of his hips fired her.

"Do you know what it is?" he said.

Raven kept staring.

"I say, do you know what it is?"

"Em. What does it matter?" She picked another one and held it out for him.

"Nay, they are for you."

She lifted the candy higher toward his mouth.

Grinning, Christopher picked that one off her fingers the same way. He rolled the lozenge about his tongue and then said, "'Tis made of pawpaw marmalet. Pawpaw is fruit that grows by the rivers in the Virginia Colony."

"Well, t'ank ya, Kipper." She snatched another candy and inched a bit closer to him. Raven looked deeply into his eyes and placed the candy atop her tongue, slowly.

Christopher's large hands began to pull her close and she yielded, happily. The warmth of his body quickly filled her. Her breasts rose and fell to the music of his breathing as the sea mist curled about them. Raven trembled, lightly. A long wave rumbled deeply within a nearby cave. Lost in his embrace, Raven felt his breath by her ear. Her limbs went weak. She raised her face, longing to feel his lips on hers. But watching gulls suddenly screeched a scolding from their evening perches, jarring both youths out of the moment.

Frustrated, Raven felt Kipper slowly release her, but she also noticed how his hands lingered around her waist. She waited, hoping, but it was then that she thought how Christopher seemed suddenly uncomfortable.

"I... I am truly sorry about thy Uncle Finn," he said, awkwardly.

Annoyed by the abrupt turn, Raven stepped back and removed his hands.

"I was not able to save him. Can you forgive me?" asked Christopher.

Disoriented, Raven said nothing at first. Her mind filled with unwelcome images of her uncle suffering on that steamy Caribbean island. At last she blurted, "Did ya even try, Kipper?"

"I did what I could."

"Is that so?" Deep within, Raven knew that Christopher had no power to save her uncle, and she knew that he was not entirely like the empire that had bred him. But it had all been so unbearable, and who else but the Clives were close enough to blame? Her mother was still casting dark curses on the Clive name. "It seems to me that yer family abandoned him. How do I forgive tat?"

Christopher stiffened. "By the saints, girl, I just said that I did what I could—I helped my father compose a very risky request to the acting Governor Searle for pardon. And just so you know, Aunt Comfort sent one of her agents there with a bribe."

Surprised, Raven faltered. "Why did ya never tell me?"

"Comfort warned me against giving you false hope. The government has never returned a condemned rebel to freedom."

Raven wiped her eyes.

Christopher took a breath and then reached for her.

CHAPTER 5

RAVEN WITHDREW. "SOMEONE could have told me." She wiped her nose on her sleeve. "Well, I am pleased to hear of yer help." She took a deep breath but dodged Christopher's hand as he tried to stroke her hair. "'Tis been a hard year, Kipper. And I felt like ya abandoned us all. Ya only sent me two letters in a full year."

"Two?"

"Aye. Two."

"I must have sent one every fortnight! I was wondering why you never answered." He took hold of Raven's forearm, firmly. "Bloody Irish Post! Please believe me. I thought of thee night and day."

Raven wanted to believe him. Her heart lifted. "Well, if tat's true, I'll... point my anger at the Irish Post, though ye English operate it."

Relieved, Christopher smiled. "Aye, so they do." He released her arm. Feeling vindicated, he then said, "And just so you know, *I* negotiated my father's loan from a London banker so ye were able to rebuild the village whilst I was at university."

Raven bit her lip. His suddenly boasting tone was grating. "But yer pa increased our rents—"

"Aye, well the loan needs to be paid."

"His increases are heavy."

"Ye cannot live here for free."

Raven clenched her jaw. "Yer English rents make it hard to live at all."

Christopher's voice raised. "You have no idea—"

Raven stepped away and crouched to face a lone starfish clinging fast against a rising tide. "Tank ya fer Skeefe's help...and for yer letter about Finn...but yer family still acts like they own us."

Christopher pursed his lips.

"I understand that my Irish sight isn't always clear. But metinks it is Sir Redmond's ways that are blindin you. He tinks we Irish *are* nothin because we *have* nothin, and on tat account he tinks we are to be used as if we are slaves." She stood. "Hear me: to own nothin is to *not* be owned *by* anythin."

"But—"

"So I ask ya tiss: which of us is really the slave, and which is free?"

Christopher faltered.

"'Tis a plain question."

Christopher opened his mouth and then shut it. He stared at Raven.

"Have ya no answer fer me?"

Floundering, he began to fumble a long string of words about empire and place, about duty and expectations, achievement and reward —even adding an untimely defence of his grandfather. His rising voice rambled on with gathering desperation.

A terrible suspicion then chilled Raven like a December gust. Had the deceits of others finally begun to overtake her Kipper? She could imagine the hissing counsel of brandied breath intoxicating his spirit in the hearths of London. Frightened, Raven's ears closed to Christopher's insistent defence. She begged the saints that her rising fears would be otherwise.

But how could they be otherwise?

She stared at the flailing young gentleman as an inner voice of her own whispered a terrible possibility: what could have been may not likely ever be. *Oh, Kipper.* Raven wanted to weep; she wanted to yell. *They have stolen yer soul.* Nearly panicked, she wanted to pry his eyes open to the darkness she could feel slowly filling him.

Raven wrung her hands. The days they had spent together rushed back, the long afternoons, the talks and walks. All of it was so far away now. Her Kipper was suddenly unfamiliar, snatched away to another place. Watching him through tear-blurred eyes, she thought he now looked ghostly under moonlight. Fearful of all she was losing, Raven finally begged him to stop.

The two stared at one another in silence for a painfully long moment as Raven's mind spun a way of escape. Finally, she clasped her hands together. "It seems that you and I belong to two worlds, after all." She drew a trembling breath. "It is I who have been the fool."

Dismayed, Christopher struggled to answer, but all he could say was that he would talk about this another time—that he was actually late for an evening business meeting at his father's house. He then clamped his mouth shut, awkwardly.

Hearing that, Raven wanted to either dive into the dark water or scream at him. Instead, she delivered her desperate exit with an eerie calm. "I ought tell ya tiss before ya go: The matchmaker of Irish Town says tat a young man is taken with me and...and I'm supposin I'll need an *Irish* husband soon enough. I hope ya understand." The lie fled from her lips with devilish haste.

Stunned once again, Christopher tilted backward and swallowed.

Raven stiffened. She then turned away from his swelling eyes to hide her own, suddenly wondering who she had become.

⊰⊱

24 December 1659

Two opposing pressures had marked the five months that followed Christopher's painful birthday at the cove. On the one hand, his heart demanded that he lament the wound he had suffered. On the other hand, his mind demanded that he suppress everything that interfered with his quest to 'vanquish peers and astonish professors.' To do less would risk the assumed 'considerations' of his grandfather in regard to Raven.

But the heart is not an easy foe for the mind, and Christopher's heart sought Raven as the rhythm of its desire. She had quickened the whole of his spirit from the moment she had first arrived in Skeefe. He was just a nine-year-old boy on that rainy April morning; she an eight-year-old in braids who tumbled out of her cart and landed in a puddle as a gangly tangle, laughing. Kipper had lifted her from the mud, and she had cast an enchanting spell over him with one look of her bottomless eyes.

The spell had never left.

Thus, these past months at Oxford had taken quite a toll on Christopher, and on this Christmas Eve he disembarked his ship in Kinsale exhausted and generally miserable. *What shall I say to her? I never once wrote. But why should I? She said she'd be marrying an Irishman.*

Wouldn't that be best after all?

But how could I ever bear it?

Sighing, Christopher let his weary eyes drift across the ancient town that lay at the north end of its sheltered bay. "This place grows every day," he murmured. The harbour was busy, even on this grey December morning. In past times, Vikings, Normans, and Spanish had sheltered in Kinsale. But now the English—including the Clive Company—worked the town hard.

During the mackerel catch in August or in the high days of October herring, a pilot could barely navigate through the clusters of rocking boats covering the harbour. In all seasons, crates of wine, stones of wool, ox hides and stag, bundles of frize, or salted fish covered the wharves on their way to ports throughout the world.

Relieved to be home, Christopher pointed a steward to his trunk. "Load it in that carriage." He then bought a small loaf of rye bread from a dockside vendor—an Irishman whose eyes belied poverty and sickness. Taking pity, Christopher handed him a sixpence and said, "This is a place where misery mocks sorrow."

The Irishman grunted and turned away.

Young Mr. Clive was right to say that. Kinsale's narrow streets were crowded with prospering shops, warehouses and work sheds, but for many they offered little but hard work and poor wages. They had also been host to morbid scenes of plague and famine, and puddled by the blood of many races. It was here that Irish hope had been turned to tears when they and their Spanish allies met their end by English siege. And once Aguila had sailed his Spanish fleet away, the names of Sheehan, Connell, McCarthy and Walsh were displaced by the likes of De Courcey, Mountjoy, Carew and Clive.

His carriage driver patiently waiting, Christopher Clive's thoughts returned to Raven. *Aunt Comfort now employs her at the house. What if I see her?*

Of course I'll see her!

But what should I say? He grit his teeth and hollered to the coachman. "Deliver my trunk to the Clive House." He tossed the driver a silver groat and then made his way slowly toward his father's offices.

Jostling through the streets, Christopher strained to calculate how he might regain Raven's affections. Though he had never quite sorted out exactly how it was he had offended her that evening at the cove, he concluded that it would be up to him to resolve the matter. "This is a challenge," he muttered. *I have already helped with Skeefe. She does not...nay, she cannot understand me... But Uncle Finn could be an opportunity.* He shook his head. *I understand why father's letter failed. He has no influence. As a baronet Grandfather would have more sway—but I cannot imagine him writing an appeal no matter how well I am doing...*

Before long, he arrived at his father's offices located a block south of Kinsale's busy tollhouse and two blocks from the seawall. After gathering himself for a moment, he took a firm hold of the door's bronze latch and entered with a resolute smile.

"Father?"

At the sound of his son's voice, Spencer Clive jerked his head from his desk and nearly tumbled off his stool. He rushed toward Christopher with the help of his cane. "Hey ho! You are here in time!"

"Aye, barely. The westerlies were harsh." He took his father's hand.

"Let me look at thee." Spencer dropped his cane and laid his veined hands feebly on his son's strong shoulders. "You are fit."

"Thank you, Father. You look well, also." That was a lie, of course, but a charitable one. Poor Spencer had always been sickly, sometimes more, sometimes less, but ever living as if he were dragging his coffin close behind.

"Come, come, follow me," said Spencer.

The pair made their way upstairs to the private offices where they took comfortable chairs, each eager to listen. After exchanging the obligatory comments on weather, politics and the general state of the empire, Spencer leaned forward with a smile. "It seems that thy grandfather approves a Christmas feast this year. He has not said a word about it to me, but I know the servants have been buying a great deal at the market."

"Imagine, approving Christmas!" said Christopher. "I am guessing that he must be quite certain it shall not impede business this time."

"Aye," said Spencer. He was alert and bright. "The government is in turmoil. The King prepares his return. The Roundheads are in disarray and they are surely not going to enforce the ban on Christmas again. They've neither the power nor the heart."

Spencer raised a thin fist to the sky. "Huzzah! Twelve days of feasting and merry-making. 'Tis been a dozen years, methinks. Do you remember how thy mother tried roasting a goose in secret on the first year of the ban? The damned Puritans followed the smell. They sent Roundheads into the house who kicked over the table and threw the goose into the street!" He wheezed a tight sort of laugh. "Her sin cost thy grandfather a contract, so that was the end of Christmas for us all."

Spencer settled into his chair. "But 'tis all behind us now and I see good things ahead with the return of the king, especially for thee. The lawyers are finishing up the details for the great legacy you shall inherit."

His comment made Christopher suddenly uneasy. "And what of you, Father?"

"Me? I am content. I am not strong enough to become Sir Redmond's heir. I never was."

Christopher leaned forward. "But surely—"

"Nay. It is done; it is best. Someday soon enough you shall be 'Sir' Christopher Clive, baronet and heir to a great fortune." Spencer fell quiet, basking in his son's future glory. Staring at Kipper with a satisfied air, he then cleared his throat. "Methinks it a good time to pray two things of thee. Have I thy leave?"

Curious, Christopher nodded.

"Good. Firstly, care for thy mother when I am gone. She is a hard woman but she loves thee, and the Holy Bible requires it of thee."

"I shall, sir."

"Secondly, allow charity to flourish in thy heart. 'Of he who is given much, much is expected.' Can you forswear that you shall not abandon charity?"

"I so swear."

Spencer clasped his hands together. "Good. We need not speak of it again." He left his chair and walked to a cabinet from which he retrieved two cut-glass goblets. "But there is one other thing." He filled the glasses from a bottle of French claret and handed one to Christopher. "I wish to speak of thy grandfather."

Christopher braced himself.

"He is well-intended toward thee."

Spencer eased himself into his chair, stiffly. He continued in a low tone. "Sir Redmond is clever in matters of business and of power, but he is not charitable and he can be very cruel." His hand began to roll the wine in his glass. "Nor is he wise. Have a care what you learn from him."

Christopher did not answer for a long moment. "I understand." He then altered course. "Do you remember the letter you sent on Finn O'Neil's behalf?"

Surprised, Spencer sat back. "Aye?"

"I was very proud of you for taking such a risk. I wish others knew you to be the brave man I know you to be. You have taught me courage and charity."

A twinge of colour came to Spencer's cheeks.

"No doubt the governor rejected it out-of-hand, but did you suffer any penalty for it?"

"Nay." Spencer's voice was suddenly very thin.

"Did grandfather ever learn of it?"

Spencer did not answer.

Christopher leaned far forward. "I am considering asking grand-father to help me find another way—"

"Do not."

Christopher's eyes fell to the toe of his father's boot now tapping nervously. "What's the matter?"

Spencer fidgeted with the head of his cane.

"Father?"

"It is best for you to forget poor Finn," said Spencer. His voice was defensive. "Nothing can be done."

Christopher cocked his head. "Why do you say that?"

His father looked away.

Eyes narrowed, Christopher stood. "Did you not send it?"

Spencer released his breath and hung his head.

"By the almighty Christ—"

The office door burst open with a crash. "The prudes are finally finished!" cried Sir Redmond.

Christopher whirled about.

"No more Calvinists raining on my good times!" Sporting a bright red doublet, a black woollen cloak and a gaudy French cane, Redmond Clive tossed his new beaver hat on to Spencer's desk and shook out his own hair that he had let grow long. "By God, Englishmen shall start living again. Imagine, boys playing ball on the blessed Sabbath without being beaten by soldiers. I love it!"

Redmond ripped a bottle of rum from a cupboard and sneered at Spencer now facing the floor. "What are you snivelling about?" He filled a glass and then poured one for Christopher with a wink. "And the brothels are opening." He reached inside a leather satchel to retrieve a letter. Turning to Christopher he said, "So, how are thy Turkish language studies?"

44

Frustrated by the interruption, Christopher scowled. "I am astonishing Doctor Pococke, sir."

"By the saints, Grandson, that is good to hear!" Redmond threw a letter atop Christopher's desk. "This arrived just now at the dock. Read it to me!"

CHAPTER 6

TEETH GRINDING, CHRISTOPHER broke the letter's seal as Redmond went on. "Our agents began trading with Mohammedans in Falmouth a few years ago, and some months back we negotiated an exceptional sale." He fell into a chair. "I suspect they are not as impressed with it as I am. Go on, read it."

Christopher raised his eyes. "What have you done?"

"Read it *aloud*!" barked Redmond.

Christopher began:

"'Fifteenth Day of Shawwal, 1069

By the Word of Köprülü Mehmed Pasha, Grand Vizier of the Ottomans, and in the name of Sultan Mehmed IV, Son of Mohammad, Hope and Comfort of Mohammedans, Guardian of Jesus' Tomb,

To Sir Redmond Clive of Kinsale, Baronet of the English, Gentleman, Pretender, Fool and Cheat,

I am informed by my faithful and true Agents that the supposed Woolle with which thou hast defrauded us hath already been devoured by Moth and rotted by Mould. Yet, the Gold with which we paid handsomely doth yet remain heavy and bright within thy Strongbox. Said Woollens have been burned and the prompt return of all Payments is now demanded upon thy receipt of this Letter.

The Sultan doth remain ready to offer the Mercy of Allah to all those who repent and make proper Amends. But if this Injury be not remedied forthrightly, may thee and thy Issue be deprived of the false Blessings of thy false God and of all Charity from Allah the Merciful. May ye be stripped of Health, Joy, Wealth and every sundry Hope under the Sun forever and ever. May thy Issue be barren, may thy Land lay fallow, and let it be therefore known throughout the Levant that the Name, Clive, is hereby accursed.

Ibrahim Bakan Effendi, Chief Scribe' "

Christopher fixed icy eyes on Redmond now pouring another rum.

"Well there it is. They found us out," said the baronet. He belched and rubbed his belly.

"Us?" murmured Spencer. "Kipper and I have nothing to do with this."

Redmond cast a disdainful, bloodshot eye at his son. "Yes, *we* shipped the Sultan's army in Hungary barrels of mouldy, moth-ravaged wool." Smirking, he then turned to Christopher. "They shouldn't be in Hungary in the first place." He belched again. "Get a paper and fresh quill. We shall set the heathens straight." He drained his glass. "You shall inform them—in their own hea-then tongue—that we shipped perfectly sound wool and we fail to understand how they blame us for their mishandling, etcetera, etcetera."

Spencer protested, weakly. "But—"

Ignoring his son, Redmond stood and set his empty rummer atop Christopher's desk. "Do as you are told. We turned a liabil-ity into a stunning profit that I've no intention of forfeiting. And undersign *thy* name on our behalf." He rested a heavy hand on Christopher's shoulder. "Imagine, the only man in Ireland who can write to the huggermugger Sultan in his own language. Now, both of you try to find a smile. Tomorrow begins the Twelve Days of Christmas."

⁘

The dawn of Christmas in Kinsale was greeted with a celebration of church bells such as the town had not heard in many years. The rain-muffled cling-clangs echoed wonderfully through every narrow street and alleyway, even finding their way into the large rooms of the square-stoned Clive House bordering the north side of harbour. Over the wall in Irish Town, the Catholics rang hand bells in hopes of the restoration of a moderate English king.

Christopher awakened slowly from his third-floor room. He had not seen Raven, though it had been confirmed that she was in his Aunt Comfort's employ. With her as the first thing on his mind, he dressed methodically, first pulling up silk stockings and linen breeches. He put his arms through a finely woven shirt sporting a pronounced laced collar, and stepped into his freshly polished boots. After donning a green doublet, he reached for a long cloak and a new beaver hat. He held a looking glass to his face and grunted. Still furious with his father in the matter of Finn O'Neil, he plotted when he might finally get him alone and tell him what he thought.

But what would he tell Raven about his father's deception? Should he tell her anything at all? And did Comfort really send a bribe to Barbados or had that been another lie?

Ready now, Christopher trudged down two flights of the wide wooden staircase to arrive in the ample foyer now slightly smoky from a poor draught in the large fireplace of the neighbouring grand hall. He gawked through large, drizzle-smattered windows begging light from the dismal winter's day. Waiting for his parents, grandfather and grandaunt, he helped himself to a few prunes off a silver dish and a cup of coffee offered by the family's middle-aged butler—a dark African named 'Tattie' on account of his love of Virginia potatoes.

Saying nothing, Christopher cast his eyes toward the kitchen in hopes of seeing Raven, but did not. Moments later, the others came down the stairs with servants fussing about them all. Christopher threw a scarf around his neck, stepped outside and barked for the coachman. Before long the Clive family was seated at St. Multose Church.

Nearly two hours later, Sir Redmond led his family back into the house, growling. "By the saints, that flap-mouthed, boil-brained Right Reverend Smythe ought to be thrown into the harbour," he said. "What a waste of time that was...to say nothing of the pitiful gaggle of cowards in the pews. Those foot-licking giglets gawk over their shoulders as if Cromwell was going to come marching in with his loggerheads!"

The joy of Advent had begun.

Still seething, Christopher trailed Spencer up the stairway as the woeful man tried to hurry away to the safety of his room. On his father's heels, he slammed the door behind them both as Spencer retreated to a soft chair against a far wall. Christopher loomed over him.

"You are angry with me as you should be," said Spencer. His face was drawn and pale.

"You let me believe a lie."

"We wrote the letter for Finn, together. You watched me seal it, and you handed it to the messenger with thine own hand," said Spencer.

Christopher waited.

Pale as death, Spencer leaned as far from his son as his chair would allow. "But apparently the messenger could read. Curious about the addressee, he showed it to thy grandfather—no doubt to earn a sixpence."

Christopher seethed.

"Sir Redmond burned it in front of mine eyes and cursed me with every wicked word he could summon. He made me swear that I would never try such a thing again or speak of it to anyone— including thee. If I did, he threatened to have the London bankers call the loan that provided for Skeefe's rebuilding." Spencer wiped his forehead with a kerchief. He could barely speak. "As you probably do not know, it was he who had arranged the loan behind thy back."

Christopher's jaw pulsed.

Spencer reached a shaking hand toward his son's waistcoat and grabbed hold of it, lightly, like a condemned man begging for mercy. "Finn O'Neil is a convicted rebel. The letter could have brought us harm. Forgive me, but methinks this was best after all."

Christopher turned his back, reeling from his father's betrayal and humiliated for the lie he had told Raven. "And what of Aunt Comfort? Did she send a bribe or was that also a lie?"

"Shh!" Spencer stood anxiously. "Who told you that?"

"She did."

"She ought not have." He lowered his voice to a whisper. "Aye, she did do it but to no avail. Thy grandfather must know nothing of it." He pulled Christopher's shoulder around. "I pray thee to leave the whole matter to rest. Say nothing more of it to anyone. Thy grandfather would render vengeance on us all, including the Irish. Can you forswear this to me?"

Christopher grunted. He desperately wanted to bare the truth to Raven.

"Telling the girl would be its own kind of cruelty. It would ease thy conscience but wound her."

Christopher squeezed his fists. He supposed his father might be right about that. He glared into Spencer's gaunt face with a wrath he had not felt before. He then leaned so close that he could smell his father's breath. "I shall think on it."

The Clives spent the rest of that Christmas Day making ready for their evening with the Hopkins of Surrey—a family of influence who shared a lucrative membership with Sir Redmond in the Levant Company that dominated the trade between England and the Ottoman Empire. The ten days following were likewise filled with invitations to dine at ample tables throughout Kinsale.

Spencer's revelation slowly settled into a knot of frustration in Christopher's belly as he endured the days and nights of boredom amongst genteel company. He wrestled within as to whether he should ever tell Raven. After all, he reasoned, she ought not remain deceived with false hopes like he had been. Yet, to tell her would dash any hope at all, as well as further divide her from him. So, with some reservations he decided he'd leave the matter rest—at least for now.

Over these long days, Redmond Clive insisted that Christopher remain by his side to make the proper impressions. Though he suffered his duties with deep resentment, Christopher had come to appreciate that his grandfather had actually made good on at least one 'consideration.' Under normal conditions, Redmond would never have pulled strings for a loan to help the Irish. The money had made all the difference for Skeefe and so Christopher admitted to himself that the old man deserved some credit.

So, Christopher endured. What else was there to do, anyway? Aunt Comfort had already informed him that she had hired out Raven to cater other celebrations, and that it would be best if Kipper did not go searching for her. When Christopher asked why, she answered directly. "The young lady said she is not ready to see you just yet." So, the days between Christmas and Epiphany dragged on until, at long last, they came to their final climax with the Twelfth Night feast that was now upon the family.

The morning of this final celebration, a resigned Christopher waited for his grandfather to arrive in the grand hall of the Clive House. The room was often dreary within its dark oak walls, but today a raging fire from the carpenter's Yule block already brightened its wainscot. In the centre stood a long table beneath a chandelier boasting a constellation of candles. Ivy, holm, and bay added festive colour in generous sprays throughout the hall, the foyer, and the cosy parlour at the far side.

All listened to Sir Redmond clunk his way down the stairway and enter the room. He quickly waved Christopher to his right hand as he took his place at the head of the table. Christopher grimaced as his father was then coldly directed to Redmond's left—an insult that escaped no one. Millicent took her seat alongside Spencer, and Aunt Comfort took her seat at the far end.

Two Irish servant girls hurried to provide a generous breakfast of eggs, various cheeses, a bit-too-jellied brawn, some heavy breads and mustard, all of which was washed down with sweet malmsey.

"Kipper?" said Millicent. She was clutching a pudgy Terrier named Cleopatra.

"Aye, Mother?"

The woman tittered and wiggled a stubby finger for Tattie to come from the shadows. He appeared at Christopher's side with a red velvet hat held upside down. Christopher thought the black butler to look oddly stoic.

Christopher looked into the hat to see several pieces of folded paper.

Millicent smiled, mischievously. "Thy father tells me that you have an interest in charity." She leaned toward Christopher. "Well?"

He shrugged. "What of it, Mother?"

She stroked her pampered dog. "Yesterday I rode by sedan all through Irish Town. You needn't worry, I hired a guard." She took a sip of her malmsey. "I thought to myself, 'this is the final day of Christmas but we've nary a gift for the poor!' So, I searched among the wretches and decided upon five family candidates."

"Candidates for what?"

"For thy charity."

Christopher looked helplessly at his father and then at his aunt, now peering suspiciously at Millicent. "I do not understand," he said.

"I have the names of each family written on those scraps of paper in the hat. You shall pick one and they shall be invited to come and take from the surplus of tonight's feast." Pleased with herself, Millicent smiled.

Christopher shrugged.

Irritated by her son's indifference, Millicent said, "The name 'Clive' needs to ring well in Irish Town. Lady Mountjoy is certain that once the King is restored he shall surely lift the boot off the Irish for a season. When he does, it shall go better for us to be known for a kindness or two."

"So 'tis not really a charity," said Christopher.

"Stop pribbling and just pick a name from the hat!"

Cleopatra growled; Christopher dismissed the mollycoddled dog and reached a disinterested hand into the hat to pluck out a paper. He handed it to Tattie, unopened.

"Do you not care who you have picked?" asked Millicent.

"Nay, as I said, 'tis no charity. The less I've to do with this charade the better." Christopher then stood, bowed to his grandfather and walked away.

CHAPTER 7

———— ✥ ————

"THY MOTHER MADE quite a face when you walked out," said Comfort Clive. Her lips turned upward, slightly. "But sit with me, nephew. The guests shall be arriving soon enough."

Christopher gladly took a seat in the side parlour with his beloved aunt and put his feet atop a hassock. "I must respect her, but that is rarely a light task." He knew that Comfort understood.

Comfort understood many things.

The willowy, grey-haired woman was the younger sister of Christopher's grandfather. As a little girl she had survived an attack of Irish rebels in which her two older sisters had been killed. However, when she was fourteen she had survived something far worse. She had set sail on a ship bound for Bristol when roving Muslim corsairs—pirates from the coast of North Africa—attacked her ship and delivered her into slavery. She spent the next six years enslaved in the bowels of Algiers until the family ransomed her for 1,000 gold sovereigns.

Christopher had heard many rumours of her treatment there. Some said she was a concubine to a sheik, others insisted she had never been despoiled. For her part, Comfort had never spoken of it. Others said that when she finally set foot in Kinsale she simply said that she was 'thankful to Christ.'

"Do you like thine apple-jack, Kipper?" Comfort asked. "I had the cooks add a bit of rosemary this year."

Christopher took another sip and let the sweet-spiced drink roll over his tongue. "Thank you. I like it very much." He watched his aunt study him with a careful eye. She knew him well.

"You have become a fine young gentleman in spite of my brother. However, it is clear to me that you are not happy."

Christopher waited.

Miss Comfort Clive had little time for Sir Redmond. She had always preferred her other brother—Langley—who now lived in London. "Thy father was never strong but I do not blame him for thine unhappiness. He was sickly from his birth. I hope you offer him mercy." She paused to dab her left eye with a kerchief. The eye wept perpetually, some said ever since the day she was set free from the Muslims.

Comfort called into the hallway for almond pudding. She then faced her nephew squarely. "It is thy grandfather who has shackled thee to great weights."

"You and I have both endured many things."

"Aye?" Comfort took a large draught of applejack. "Yet I am happy, and you struggle."

Christopher shrugged, suddenly uncomfortable.

"Why are you not happy?"

"I…I do not think about happiness." He looked at the floor. "I leave that to the Irish."

Comfort wiped her eye again. "Did you know that you are made to be happy?"

Christopher lifted his face.

"Whether aware of it or not, an unhappy man is struggling against the deceits of dark purposes." She took another drink. "Yet, struggling of every sort can prove worthwhile if we allow it. So you do have hope for a real smile." Comfort leaned forward. "Suffering can be used to set us free. I'm quite sure thy grandfather never told you that."

"Nay. He never did."

"Of course not. His counsel is seldom wise." Comfort tapped the edge of her glass. "Redmond trains you for a fruitless quest to acquire something you already have…value. Not feeling valued, you do not feel loved—not feeling loved, you are not happy." She lifted her forefinger to the air. "If you learn nothing else from me, learn this: an unhappy man is ultimately striving *for* love; a happy man enjoys living *from* the love he already feels."

Comfort rose from her chair and took Christopher's face in her hands. "You are already much loved, Kipper Clive. Believe it and be happy; believe it and be free."

Christopher's chin quivered. He fought against the tears.

Comfort released his face with a tender smile. "I pray daily for Wisdom to fill thee." She wiped her eye. "I hope you shall forgive me for that."

As Christopher tried to regain his composure, he watched his aunt move toward a mahogany cabinet. There she pulled open a wide drawer and retrieved a narrow box wrapped in green paper. "I have a final Christmas gift for thee, dear Kipper, and it is not another cravat."

Christopher stood and received Comfort's gift with a mannerly bow. He kept his wet eyes on the woman's face as she sat. He wanted to embrace her. He had always thought her to be the most impressive lady in all the Kingdoms of the Crown. He loved the strength in her movements and the kindness of her voice. He loved the way she wore her hair high but without pretence. He marvelled at how her dignity filled whatever room she entered, and how it was that she could bring a candle to the darkest of times.

"Well, do not stare at me. Open it." Comfort chuckled. She touched a candle to the bowl of her favourite Dutch pipe and drew a glow to its Virginia tobacco.

Now curious, Christopher unwrapped his gift. "A dagger with a dudgeon hilt!" He yanked the glistening blade from its leather-over-wood sheath. He ran his fingers lightly over the razor-sharp single-edge, and then bounced the smooth boxwood grips in his palm. "'Tis beautiful." He examined an etching on one side. "A bird in flight."

Comfort smiled. "Aye, a bird indeed."

Christopher laughed. "I see an owl's face, a swan's neck, an eagle's wings..."

"I commissioned Scully Lynch to fashion it. I thought you'd like an artisan from Skeefe."

"No wonder the bird is a fantasy! He's knackered, but there's no better metal smith in Ireland."

"He loves birds because they are free, and he knows the virtues they each reveal: Wisdom, grace, nobility ..." She dabbed her eye. "Virtues I wish for thee. Now, turn it over."

Christopher proceeded to read the inscription on the other side of the steel blade:

Breathe Deeply Serve Humbly Dance with Abandon

"My grandmother oft' sang me a Cornwall ditty with those words. She urged me to live life this way." Comfort drew on her pipe, eyes smiling. "Are you able to live thus?"

Christopher read the inscription again. *How do I answer her?* Comfort's attention was abruptly taken. He turned his head to see a female servant standing in the doorway with a silver tray, head bowed. "Yer tray, Miss Clive?" He set the dagger quickly aside. His breath quickened. "Raven?"

"Happy Christmas, Mister Clive," Raven said, shyly. She had been cautiously awaiting her Kipper's return from London ever since the very moment she had watched him ride away from her cove on that terrible night of his birthday past.

Taking a deep breath, Raven set a porcelain bowl of almond pudding on the table with something of a crash. She then poured applejack with a trembling hand. She wanted to blurt out that she had been angry and afraid, and so she had lied to him. She wanted to fall at his feet and beg his forgiveness, to tell him how time had melted her anger away. Her eyes moved slowly between Kipper and his aunt. *Don't speak. Not now. Just smile. Don't spill anyting. Smile again.* "I am happy to see ya, Mister Clive," she said. *Oh dear Mary, why did I speak?*

Christopher bowed, awkwardly. "I am the one who is happy, Miss O'Morrissey."

Raven nearly tossed her apron away and ran into Kipper's arms. But the cold-edge of a shrill voice shattered the moment.

"By faith!" Aghast, Millicent Clive filled the doorway of the parlour. Her eyes darted between Raven and Comfort, settling on the latter. "So, you are simply helping Skeefe recover, eh?" Her timber-heeled shoe tapped hard atop the oak floor from beneath the pleats of a high-waisted red gown. Her throat was buried in heavy lace and Raven thought she looked very much like a stuffed Cornish hen dressed for dinner.

Raven could not move. She held her breath as Christopher took a few strides to stand between his mother and her.

"What is thy accusation, Mistress Clive?" said Comfort from her chair. Her voice was steady and hard as a smith's anvil.

Millicent twitched. She strained to look around Christopher's broad shoulders to eyeball the Irish girl. Pointing a rapier-like finger in Raven's direction, she said, "I want her out of this house."

"And what of charity?" Comfort lifted from her chair like a cobra rising from its basket.

Millicent blew up her cheeks. "I've charity enough!" Her small, brown eyes turned on Christopher. "And you! Do not let her ruin this family."

Raven's body began to tremble. Christopher took her elbow, lightly. "She is welcome here," he said. "Enough of this, Mother."

Flustered, Millicent turned on Comfort again. "You hired her against my will."

"I am the lady of this house, Mistress Clive," said Comfort. "And I shall employ whom I wish."

Wide-eyed, Raven watched Millicent flush. The woman puffed and twisted her face into a thick knot. "Well, Miss Clive, you said she would not be working here when Kipper was in residence."

"I said no such thing."

Millicent wrung her hands. "You are encouraging these two in a hopeless...friendship. An English gentleman and a Papist Irish wench! You make a fool of thyself and the rest of us."

She then turned on Christopher. "That scrawny little bitch shall make a laughingstock of thee and spoil the family's reputation. She is not acceptable under any circumstance. This should be clear enough! Are you still a child?"

Millicent abruptly stepped around Christopher and glared at Raven. "At least thy Uncle Finn knows his place." She let the words bite.

Shouting wildly at the whole room, she then said, "I shall be telling Sir Redmond of this. He thinks Christopher is too clever to be so stupid, but now I see this business must be settled once and for all." With that Millicent stormed away, but not before firing a final shot over her shoulder at Christopher. "We expected so much more of thee than *her*."

Raven's chin quivered. She wanted to run. Christopher offered her a sympathetic face as Comfort hurried to lay a kind hand on her shoulder. Tears hung heavy beneath her green eyes.

Comfort stroked her hair. "Millicent Clive is a cruel woman, but she cannot hurt thee, my dear. And Sir Redmond has other matters that concern him. Besides, he has little patience for Millicent." Comfort kissed her on the cheek. "And you shall charm him soon enough." She winked.

Christopher took a firm hold of Raven's hand in both of his. "I am well-pleased that you are here, Raven. I swear that you shall be safe."

Agreeing, Comfort finished her applejack. "Now, I needs beg thy leave. I suspect someone had better keep an eye on Mistress Clive."

Raven curtsied weakly as the woman left the room. Finally alone with Kipper, her heart raced. She withdrew her hand from Christopher's, lightly, and wiped her eyes with a kerchief.

"I am very sorry for my mother," Christopher said. He took a deep breath and self-consciously adjusted his cuffs. "But as for me, I really am happy to see you here."

Raven straightened her apron as Christopher stepped slightly toward her. *Come close. Touch me.* She held her breath.

Instead, Christopher blurted, "So, you have not married after all?"

Her spirits sank. "I did not. I lied to ya back then, Kipper. I was so confused by what ya said and what ya didn't say. I am sorry."

"Well, that's...um, well..." He blinked and rubbed his hands. "What I mean to say is that I am glad and...it is nice to see thee."

His eyes went to the floor.

"Well...em, 'tis nice to be seen." Crushed, Raven paused. "But I best be gettin back to the kitchen now. Enjoy yer Twelfth Night, Mister Clive." She stole one quick look at Christopher and thought he looked very sad. She suddenly wanted to hold him, and yet at the same time she wished someone could slap some sense into him. Raven turned her back. *Maybe if we could just fly away to the cove...*

⁂

By late afternoon, the Clive House of Kinsale was bustling with guests anticipating the Twelfth Night feast. The grand hall boasted a long table now surrounded by milling English gentry and scurrying Irish servants. The hearth roared, keeping the dampness of the waning day beyond the double oak doors of the foyer, as did the heavy curtains draping the windows. The air of the hall was fragrant with roasted meat, wassail and wood smoke. Ale flowed in abundance and sounds of a lute, a fiddle, and a fourteen-string cittern had more than a few dancing through the foyer.

The table fare was what the Clive's guests had expected, though Sir Redmond had demanded his kitchen add a bit more flourish to celebrate the retreat of the Roundheads. Most of the marzipans and candied fruits had already been gobbled up as part of the first course, along with tarts, comfits and baked Warden pears.

The second course was now at hand: a shield of brawn with mustard, boiled capon, and a haunch of venison were being set upon the table to the loud 'huzzahs' of the guests who quickly took their places and piled their trenchers high. An olive pie was in wait, along with a roasted swan and a chine of beef. Later, the much-awaited Twelfth Cake would be presented by the baker presently fussing over a grand display of sugary things being assembled in the kitchen.

Sir Redmond had invited the most influential men of Kinsale to attend this year's feast, so Christopher was not surprised when Tattie announced the arrival of Lord Patrick de Courcey, the twentieth Baron of Kinsale and one of the most powerful men in Ireland. The diners fell silent as he made a dramatic entrance with his young wife on his arm.

Christopher watched De Courcey receive the adulations of others but he would have none of it. He had never forgotten how the baron and his grandfather had shamed him on his thirteenth birthday. Images of that night had troubled him for years, but seeing the baron up close awakened them. He now saw himself in the lamp-lit tavern. He could see his grandfather toss a coin to the waiting hand of a night's lady. He felt her arm around his waist as she pulled him upstairs where she forced off his clothing.

Nausea filled Christopher's belly. He remembered how moments later the mocking woman then dragged him back downstairs by the wrist, naked. He could see her cackling at his boyish 'petty tail and bullets.' He remembered the contemptuous disgust in his grandfather's voice, and how loudly the baron howled along with a drunken knot of their friends. Christopher took a breath. *You thought it was all so amusing, De Courcey. And Grandfather—*

Jaw pulsing, Christopher stood perfectly still as he watched De Courcey step from one admirer to the next. No, he was not about to greet him with a handshake and a false smile. Most assuredly he would not be spending the rest of the feast scraping and fawning over this peacock like his slurring grandfather had already begun to do. This Clive was in no mood for any of it and so he faded into a corner.

Before the baron and his wife were even seated, however, Tattie broke into the hubbub with another introduction from the hall. "I present the Brendan Healy's of Irish Town."

The room fell still once more, only this time it was out of shock. The musicians ended their song, awkwardly. Christopher gawked. His mother's mouth dropped open, then closed and dropped again like a landed codfish. Grandfather Clive looked like he might fall down dead. Indeed, the timing of the Healy's arrival could not have been more terrible for either Millicent Clive or the baronet.

Entering the room with a bold stride, Brendan Healy lifted his clean-shaven Irish chin, and led his red-faced wife, seven defiant sons and three daughters directly across the dining hall to stand before their host, Sir Redmond Clive.

CHAPTER 8

STRUGGLING TO GATHER himself, Sir Redmond shot a searing glance at Millicent, now flushed and fanning herself. His eyes then swept the shocked faces of his guests, resting finally upon the disapproving glare of Lord de Courcey who scowled from beneath his feathered wool bonnet.

Christopher strained to listen as Redmond stammered something about 'unexpected guests,' but Brendan Healy lifted his barrelled chest and spoke over the baronet. "Tank ya Sir Redmond fer the kind invitation to dine in remembrance of Holy Jaysus and the blessed Magi." He then faced Lord de Courcey. "And if ya don't remember, ya confiscated me lands at Kinure fer God knows what cause and handed them to that Protty savage, Captain Roche."

Agitated, De Courcey answered. "What cause? I call it rebellion. I could have hanged thee."

All heads swung to Healy. He held. "I was a friend to King Charles and to James 'afore him. I was no friend to Cromwell, but ne'er raised a sword against him. Ya took me lands anyways."

Christopher was mildly amused at the disaster until his mother slipped away from the table, moved past his dumbfounded father and hurried toward him. He groaned.

Arriving at his ear, Millicent hissed, "The coachman had strict instructions to bring them directly to the kitchen and *after* the party was over!"

"Did you not know the baron had taken the Healy's land?"

Millicent grimaced. "You needs fix this."

"Me?" Grumbling, Christopher thought quickly. He then took several resentful strides forward. "In faith, gentlemen, there seems to be some misunderstanding," he said in a loud but calm voice.

Healy and De Courcey stopped arguing; Grandfather Clive fidgeted in his boots.

Christopher raised a hand over the room. "By thy leave, Lord de Courcey and with sincere sorrow for the discomfort of the hall, pray give me a moment to explain."

The sound of a tumble by the kitchen door turned all heads to see Millicent in a heap.

"As I say, my Lord—and with heartfelt apology—it had been *my* purpose to offer the hand of peace to the Irish on this Twelfth Night." Christopher studied the stunned faces of his grandfather and his guests. *Never let it show.* "Surely, King Charles II shall be soon upon his throne and my family's agents tell us that he is intending a certain, shall we say, *community* of his subjects. To that end, it was my hope that the Clive House might be among the first to celebrate the changing times."

Christopher noticed Lord de Courcey studying him, carefully. The baron then sniffed and offered a slow, unexpected applause. The diners followed.

Relieved, Christopher removed his hat and bowed. "As I say, my lord. With the sincerest apologies."

Grandfather Clive forced a smile and then awkwardly directed the Healy's to the kitchen, growling in Brendan's ear.

Christopher quickly retired to check on his mother now being tended in the kitchen. All well with her, he glanced about for Raven. He found her holding an empty pitcher in a distant corner. He smiled but was distracted by the Healys now being seated along a far wall.

66

He walked past several tittering cooks and reached a hand toward Brendan. "I beg thy pardon, Mister Healy. We are taking small steps on a long journey. Thee and thine are welcome here."

Remaining seated, Brendan answered carefully. "Ya mean here, as in the kitchen?"

"As I said, we are taking small steps."

Brendan then stood and took Christopher's hand. "Was a brave ting ya done." He proceeded to introduce Christopher to his family, including his twenty-year-old son—a strapping black-haired lad named Fallon.

Christopher took Fallon's hand, but when he did a sudden twinge of anxiety came over him. His eyes flew to find his Raven.

⊹⊱⊰⊹

Returned to the dining hall, Christopher's mind remained with Raven in the kitchen. *With that big Irish lad.* His father's whispering voice found him. "You must make thy rounds. Everyone is commending thy quick wit."

Slurred voices from one side of the blazing hearth called to him. "Here, Mister Clive. Over here."

Christopher followed the voices to the faces and he groaned. *Carrew, Mountjoy, De Courcey, and Grandfather.* He hesitated.

"You must," said Spencer. "I understand, but it is expected."

Perspired, Christopher reluctantly joined the old men now guffawing like schoolboys. *Christ almighty. Is Grandfather telling that damned story again?*

"But now he *is* a man," boasted Sir Redmond as Christopher approached. "If I had a spare shilling I'd prove it."

The men roared. Among them was Mr. Wentworth Carrew—a short, stout gentleman from Cork City with a hooked nose and a red-splotched face. He had tipped ale and pawed petticoats with Redmond Clive for more than forty years.

Carrew pulled Christopher close by the sleeve. "Shall we find a Christmas tart for thee? I'd wager she'd not drag you back to us this time!" He belched.

Christopher reddened and pulled his arm free. Wanting to knock Carrew to the ground, he gathered himself and turned to leave.

"Nay, Mister Clive," said De Courcey. "Stay and wassail with us." His voice was commanding.

Christopher held his feet, back still to the men.

"Mister Clive!" De Courcey demanded.

Christopher took a breath and turned. "My lord."

De Courcey surveyed Christopher with a face surprisingly compassionate. He did not demand a bow or handshake. He simply said, "That was then. Time passes." He paused. "Now, allow me to say that I was impressed by how you protected thy mother's foolishness with the Irish." De Courcey took a generous swallow of spiced ale from his pewter mug. "I hear good reports of thee from many quarters. Thy grandfather approves thee. But others agree that you excel in all matters."

De Courcey took another draught and wiped his mouth on a napkin. "I have friends in Oxford as well as London. 'Tis time they make thy acquaintance. Good contacts are the lifeblood of privilege, Mister Clive." He put a hand on Christopher's shoulder. "I have the highest expectations and shall see to it that they are not disappointed."

Taken off guard, Christopher bowed his head.

"Look," interrupted Carrew. "Now *that's* a pretty wench."

Raven's cheeks heated as she faced a host of curious eyes. "Oh dear Jaysus," she muttered below her breath. *Comfort should have told me 'tis a bad idea.* She forced a smile to the guests now gathering. *Do I really need to win Kipper's heart back after all?* Her legs went weak. Did she? She was not certain.

"Miss O'Morrissey?" said Comfort.

Raven swallowed and began to follow Comfort toward the far side of the dining hall. The self-conscious girl was now dressed in a green velvet manteaux and a red satin bodice. A white-laced de Medici ruff graced her slender neck; a red cavalier hat was perched atop her black hair on a sharp angle. She stepped close on Comfort's heels and moved carefully between the quieting gentry.

Scanning every face for Christopher, Raven nodded politely from one guest to the next. *He did seem very happy to see me. Then again, who can know? Blah. Sometimes he's the poet, and other times he's daft about tings of the heart.*

Raven's eye fell on Millicent now scowling at her from a stuffed chair. An unexpected memory abruptly stole into her thoughts. She remembered stealing a rose from Millicent's garden one summer when she was ten. She had presented the rose to Kipper along the beach by Skeefe. Oblivious to the tender feelings attached to the rose, Christopher had simply dropped it in the water to see how far it would float. "He can be such an English *man,*" she grumbled.

Catching herself, Raven blushed all the more. *And where is he?* Still searching, she stood still as death while Comfort took her seat atop a stool with a long-necked French lute in her hands.

There! Raven released her eyes to Kipper's. She thought he looked pleased and she smiled at him. When he smiled back, her fear fell away.

Comfort then said, "A pleasant greeting to all for this Twelfth Night."

Raven turned a shoulder toward Millicent, and then folded her hands at her waist.

Comfort silenced the gathering guests and said, "If ye shall permit, I have firstly chosen a lively little song for this lovely girl to sing." She secured her ebony fingerboard and plucked along her ten pairs of strings slowly, and then more quickly.

Raven licked her lips and turned her face to Comfort. Comfort's toe began to tap and her fingers now chased the strings into a happy tune. The guests began to clap in time. Raven took a deep breath, and when Comfort nodded she began to sing:

"Hi ho we sing this Day of Wise Men and their Treasures
Given to the Holy Childe with Awe and sacred Pleasures.
So happy tap and dancing Feet do we this good Night clatter
And from the Magi learn to sing that Charity doth matter."

Raven sang louder as the fiddler joined in. Her spirit lifted and her eyes flew across her delighted audience.

"…So happy tap and dancing Feet
        do we this good Night clatter…"

Diners began to sing along, and so another round was sung and then another. When finished, Raven curtsied shyly to resounding applause. Relieved, the red-faced girl beamed and turned to Comfort who then bade all to take a moment and a drink.

Comfort wiped her eye on a kerchief and sipped some wormwood wine. She squeezed Raven's hand and whispered, "Perfect, my dear. Are you ready for the next?"

Raven nodded happily and surveyed the room for Kipper. She craned her neck from one side to the other but could not find him among the many faces now crowding close. She then heard Comfort begin to pluck a different tune, one that eased a quiet mood into the room. Abandoning her search, Raven took a deep breath.

The guests slowly settled around the pair, waiting as Comfort's fingers now moved tenderly over the strings of her lute like angels tip-toeing across the tender threads of a loom.

Once again, Raven waited for Comfort's cue. She drew a deep breath and prepared to enter the sober melody.

> "The World abides as e'er she be,
> By there a Field, by there a Sea.
> Yet, Men do strive to fix their Grip,
> The Field by Plough, the Sea by Ship.
>
> But passing o'er such Fools' false Might,
> Like Stars fast-falling in the Night,
> Is Time that mocks the Err to grasp
> Yet mourns for those bound to that Task.
>
> For all remains as always was
> With little yield to what Man does.
> The Joy we seek has always been
> A Gift-in-wait to dance within."

Finished, Raven curtsied as a low murmur of reflection wound about the corners of the hall; generous applause followed. Happy, she received a kiss upon the cheek from Comfort. Her eyes then flew from plumed hats to ale-flushed cheeks to tittering mistresses and to high-collared gentlemen. But before they could rest upon Kipper once more, they fell upon another. She tried to look away but it was then when Raven's heart surprised her.

Blushing, Christopher was thrilled to hear one of his poems put to music—he thought his grandfather had burned them all. He smiled as he listened. *The old man would be furious if he knew I wrote this!* Squeezed between two ladies' enormous hats, he strained to see Raven's lips caress each of his words. His whole body stirred. And when she finished he wanted to run into her embrace.

Happy beyond measure, Christopher now struggled to claim Raven's attention. Waving his hand, he finally escaped the screen of feathers in time to follow the line of Raven's eye. *What?* There, standing boldly by the kitchen door was the handsome Fallon Healy, smiling.

Christopher gawked at the Irish lad and then whipped his head about to find Raven, now being overwhelmed by the polite attentions of her sudden admirers. He watched her carefully, happy for her but suddenly uneasy. Then it happened again; Raven cast a shy eye from beneath her hat—at Fallon.

Murmuring oaths, Christopher spotted his mother smirking at him. She had seen what he had seen, and he thought she looked supremely satisfied. He suddenly realized what his mother had done. *By the saints, she is in league with a matchmaker!* Christopher stormed out of the dining hall and angrily searched for the hat from which he had drawn the 'charity' that morning. Finding it in a corner, he opened the rest of the folded papers and cursed. Each one had the very same words: 'The Family of Brendan Healy.'

CHAPTER 9

5 May 1660

CHRISTOPHER STEPPED OFF the porch at Giardín an Croí to join his father now leaning on his cane and enjoying the warmth of the morning sun. He had been sent home from university on account of an emergency closure caused by threats from a remaining force of Roundheads.

"News is that order is now restored throughout England," said Spencer. "Lambert and his stubborn army are dispersed. I suppose you shall have to return soon."

Christopher nodded. "Very soon." He thought his father looked desperately frail. Every time he had stepped aboard an outbound ship he prepared himself for a final farewell.

"I hate to see you leave, but it is good that the Roundheads are finally accepting their defeat. They must make way for the restoration of the king. Empire cannot advance without good order."

Christopher led his father toward two wooden chairs and a small table set on the deep-green lawn. After helping him to his seat, Christopher claimed his own. From there he stared down-slope at the twenty-nine thatched roofs of quiet Skeefe.

Spencer rested his hands on his knees. "Well, for our part we have given the Irish good order, though I heard a bit too much whiskey was served over Beltane." Chuckling, he said, "What would those wretches do without us?"

Christopher did not answer.

"As I have oft' told you, I remain inspired by the exemplary settlements of former times in places like Kerrycurrihy where Earl FitzGerald taught the Irish useful things rather than crushing them. You should carry on—"

"I know," answered Christopher. "But it seems to me that FitzGerald simply found a different way to *use* the Irish."

"Men are what they are, my son. Motives are never entirely pure. Nevertheless, charity must be kept in view at all times. In March, Molly Leary told me that seven children were desperately ill with the pox. So I sent our physician and now they are well. Thy grandfather thought that was madness, but I told him we are to be Christian stewards of their conquest."

"That was kind, Father."

Spencer blushed. "I am not alone in this cause. Reginald Burroughs has similar feelings you know. I am grateful to have him as a neighbour, though he seems quite taken with the Virginia Colony of late." He looked down the lane. "If he ever shows up today we can speak of it!"

A female servant delivered a silver tray bearing two china cups and a small pitcher. She filled the cups and handed a dark drink to both men. Spencer lifted his cup in the air. "But now, a hearty health to you: My son, the future heir with a charitable heart."

As the men drank, Spencer raised his brows. "I love this. 'Tis a wonderful concoction from the Americas—cocoa, jasmine, vanilla and ambergris." He took another sip. "Reginald says it is from the natives. Just what I need: a tasty remedy for fluxes, consumption, and coughs."

Christopher set his cup down. His mother emerged from the house with her dog, Cleopatra, in her arms. Three Irish servants hurried close behind, one carrying a platter of herb-laced eel alongside a salmagundi covered by anchovies. The second delivered a tray of beverages, and the third a chair. By her blustering gait he knew that his mother was stormy and cross. He groaned.

Arriving red-faced, Millicent said, "Pray tell, where is that vexing Reginald Burroughs' family? They were to come directly from church and they are still not arrived. I must eat something now!" Millicent fell into her chair with Cleopatra held atop her lap and demanded the servants set the food by her side. She then pointed at Spencer. "And we shan't be able to play bowls with *him* very well. I hope you shall remain with us to play, Kipper."

"He can toss a ball," Christopher said.

"He couldn't toss the jack more than a yard." Millicent ordered a glass of a milky drink be poured for her. She took a sip and then spat it out. "What is this bladder-rank piss?"

"It is gorse flower wine," said Christopher. "Doon O'Morrissey makes it and if you knew all the blood lost from her hands whilst picking the flowers you might—"

"Humph." Millicent emptied her glass atop the grass. "She would like to poison us. Pour me buttermilk."

Christopher quickly downed his father's concoction, and then poured himself a glass of Doon's drink.

Millicent stuffed her mouth with salad and then waved at the air as if she were suddenly indifferent to the whole matter. "I suppose you know that Raven is still employed by Aunt Comfort. She and that...um...that Irish lad...What is his name, Spencer?"

"Fallon."

"Aye, Fallon Healy. How could I forget? Thy grandfather hired him to drive the coach and do some carpentry work around the house. Methinks he may train to replace Tattie some day—"

"Enough, wife," said Spencer. "He knows thy game."

Christopher took a bite of eel with his fingers, angrily. He then took another and gulped half his drink.

Millicent stroked Cleopatra's head. "Our Kipper knows what is expected of him." She looked at her son, chewing. "I have heard that you were introduced to a young lady, a nonpareil with good birthing hips."

Christopher drained his drink.

Spencer tapped a finger on his cane. "Ah, is this true?"

"'Twas nothing." Christopher took a spoon from his hat, folded his laced cuffs away from his hands and lifted salmagundi into his mouth. Swallowing, he said, "Lord de Courcey arranged an introduction to Lord Thomas Fairfax with whom I dined for Candlemas. He then made the formal introduction of his daughter, Miss Jocelyn Fairfax."

"A baron's daughter! This is fine news." Spencer tapped his cane on the ground. "Lord de Courcey has most assuredly taken to thy future."

Christopher shifted in his seat. The notion of being drawn under De Courcey's wing both disgusted and excited him.

"And what do you think of Miss Fairfax?" asked Spencer.

Christopher reached for more of his father's chocolate drink, shrugging. Though he resisted admitting it to even himself, fair Jocelyn had stirred him. His mind was now never far from the stunning image of her under candlelight. Her unexpected receptiveness to his tentative interest had been a healing balm for his Twelfth Night wound.

Some might have thought that wound to be a small one and surely unintended by poor Raven. But it was no small matter for Christopher. His friends at Oxford had whispered amongst themselves that the 'tiny sting' had changed him. In truth, Christopher had arrived home for that Christmas at some peace about the prior heartbreak at the cove—he and his friends had eventually concluded that Raven's illogical feminine behaviours had been caused solely by the 'damned Irish Post,' and that she would find her senses soon enough. So he had expected to see all matters set to right—until her ever-so-quick glances at the Irish boy had shattered him.

"Kipper, are you listening?"

Christopher looked at his mother, blankly.

"I said that you surely know what to do now with the Fairfax girl. You are no fool." She sniffed. "You must realize that marrying her would be one of those 'necessary joys' that would advance the family."

Christopher had already calculated the 'necessity.' It was the 'joy' that had him wondering. Yet, the touch of Jocelyn's hand as they danced the dignified sweep of the Pavane had made him genuinely happy.

Millicent ordered more buttermilk and took a large portion of eel. "Now, tell us about the others you've met."

Happy to be done discussing Jocelyn Fairfax, Christopher received some fresh food from a servant. "I had tea with Mister Roger Essington of Bristol. In turn, Essington arranged a supper with Lord de Brucey of Reading who introduced me to the Atwater Lees. In turn, the Lees sent me to Lord Childress of Durham." As Christopher proceeded to recount an impressive roster of introductions, he again felt the strange sense of power that had come over him at the time of each meeting.

And he liked what he felt.

Being welcomed into the hardwood sanctums of England's gilded elite had bestowed a quality of belonging unlike any he had ever experienced. Sipping brandy and picking at oysters midst conversations of empire had been a boost of confidence. Chatting before raging hearths with crystal glasses of brandy had enlivened him. Indeed, this emerging centre had awakened ambition in a way that his grandfather's boorish excesses never had.

Smiling proudly alongside Millicent, Spencer said, "Wonderful! And what of thy studies?"

"I have excelled, Father. Pococke says my Turkish language skills are 'of the highest order,' and I have begun studying Arabic at St. John's College."

"Good!" blurted Millicent. "You shall be able to deal with those Mohammedans masterfully."

"I am more pleased than I can say," said Spencer. "But if you learn Arabic, I suppose you shan't need this." He summoned a servant to bring a box forward. "I was going to save it for thy birthday." He handed Christopher the box.

Opening it, Christopher nodded with approval. "The *Quran* in English."

"Aye, recently translated by Alexander Ross."

"'Know thy enemy,'" Christopher said. "Thank you, sir. This is a most excellent gift. I shall study it with great interest."

Spencer sipped his chocolate. "Now, tell me. How does all this exciting news make you feel?"

Christopher looked past Skeefe, beyond its small bay and into the distant sea. "It makes me feel good. I see a productive course unfolding and I like the thought of it." He then turned his face squarely to his father's. "I shall bring honour to the family, sir. My life shall mean something." Christopher expected his father to smile.

Spencer did not. Instead, he furrowed his brow. "Are you happy?"

Taken off guard, Christopher clenched his jaw. *You and Aunt Comfort?* "You do know that I am not a child any longer." With that, he stood and walked slowly away.

❦

Arriving at the stable, Christopher drew deeply on the calming smell of hay, leather and manure. This world of smooth timbers and tack was a place where he could think. He walked into Étalon's stall with a boar-bristle brush in hand and quietly smoothed his horse's flanks.

Father wants to know if I am happy, he thought and stared at the brush. *How do I answer that?* He picked a thorn from his horse's ear. *Happy chases ambition away like with the Irish. They drink, laugh, dance, and die with meaningless lives.* Christopher started brushing Étalon's flank again. *Blah. I have been happy enough at university.*

The jostling sounds of an arriving carriage caught Christopher's ears, and he walked to one of the six-pane windows overlooking the lane. *They are finally here.* He led Étalon out of the stable and released him into a spring-green pasture, then hurried toward the family of Mr. Reginald Burroughs with a smile.

CHAPTER 10

"KIPPER CLIVE!" SAID Reginald, dismounting. He clasped Christopher's arriving hand with a powerful grip. Burroughs was a winsome English gentleman of middling years whose large estate bordered the Clive's property to the east.

Christopher bowed his head. "Mister Burroughs, Mistress Burroughs and young Oakley, welcome. My parents shall be delighted to greet ye, as am I." He whistled for the stable hand to attend the Burroughs' carriage and horse.

"I beg pardon for our tardiness." Reginald then directed his young wife and son to the house. He removed his hat and shook his shoulder-length hair loose. "So, how fare thee?"

"In my studies? In my health? In my loves?" Christopher smiled. Reginald Burroughs had always seemed like an uncle to him. "In all things I am well, sir."

Burroughs laughed, heartily. "Good to hear it. My travels keep me from seeing thee like I'd prefer, but I am not ignorant of thy successes." He studied Christopher, carefully. "'By faith, you have changed. See, there—a shadow of whiskers." He stepped back. "Look at thee! Broad-shouldered, lean, and tall in thy boots. That blond mane gives thee the look of the quintessential heir of empire." He put a hand on Christopher's shoulder. "Walk with me for a moment before we go into the house."

Christopher followed him to a large ash tree where Burroughs leaned a thick shoulder against the trunk and lit a pipe. "I have been meaning to speak to thee for some time." He scratched at his greying goatee, and then pointed to the distant sea beyond Skeefe Bay. "Look how the horizon is endless and inviting."

Christopher stared seaward. "Aye?"

"You must know by now that I own vast estates in the Virginia Colony." Reginald looked closely at Christopher. "I love the spirit of that place. Indians, trouble everywhere. The opportunities fire my blood."

Noticing the inviting twinkle now in Burroughs' eye, Christopher grew curious.

"You have become a young gentleman of great promise and extraordinary expectations." Burroughs drew slowly on his tobacco.

Christopher shifted on his feet.

"Have you read any of Henry Curtis at university?"

"If so, I do not recall."

"Too busy with mathematics?"

"Aye, and astronomy, theology, philosophy and law. But my specialty is Oriental Studies."

Burroughs grunted. "For all his brilliance, Curtis has never promoted his work well." He drew on his pipe. "Curtis suggests that the New World is a place where traditions are not transported but rather transformed—even *transcended*." Burroughs retrieved a small book from his vest and turned some well-worn pages. "Curtis writes thus: 'A Man hither bound by Place and Station shall be set free by Hardship and Troubles such that beset all Persons in primitive Conditions where undue regard to such Fictions make the survival of Convention IMPOSSIBLE.' So, what say you to that?"

Christopher thought for a moment. "Proper convention brings order, sir. Without order, chaos makes survival impossible."

Reginald Burroughs shook his head. "I lost a small fortune in some chaos with the Powhatan natives, but the loss was worth every pound for the *life* I felt in the struggle!" He searched his little book again. "Here: 'As in the story of Creation, out of Chaos comes that which was deemed by God to be good. Therefore, Leviathan—though a necessary Reality—need not be a necessary Terror.' What say you?"

Christopher was listening, carefully.

Burroughs closed his book. "Now listen to what I have put to memory from him: 'Thus, happy is he who doth scoop Thanksgiving from the Wake of Sea Monsters.'" Burroughs repeated the quotation once more. "Try and remember that." He drew on his pipe. "So, young sir, what if a new order—a *better* kind of order—could emerge from a bit of chaos?"

"Like what?"

"Imagine prospering a safe distance from the likes of De Courcey where a young gentleman like thyself could claim a life in which a man's own wits might earn him his place instead of some proper birth."

"My proper birth serves me well, as does thine."

Burroughs yielded. "You've a bright future, to be sure. I have little doubt but that thy life shall mean something. I suspect you shall gather wealth and power, and in thine old age you may smile upon the knowing that what was expected of thee was properly satisfied."

Burroughs snugged his cavalier hat and leaned close. "But methinks you might discover a greater meaning than any of that. Imagine, England's strongest and smartest leaving this old world to build something fresh."

"So, you are suggesting I go to Virginia?"

Burroughs laughed. "I thought I was being subtle."

Christopher had never considered the Virginia Colony before. He had read of savage natives and of famines, terrible winters, and strife amongst the colonists. But he had also read of forests that spread beyond the imagination, of lush fields and all things new. He recalled a vague memory of his father answering a question about the New World with something about 'the best leaving.' Kipper had assumed his father meant the best were leaving *Virginia* to come home, but it suddenly occurred to him that maybe he had meant it the other way around.

"And take a good woman with thee." Burroughs winked. "Imagine a large brood of Clives claiming a whole new world."

"I have already invested a great deal of time in the company of De Courcey's friends who shall help me *here*—"

"Blah! You are young, strong, and clever like a fox. Take what you can of that…including the Fairfax girl…and sail away." Burroughs drew hard on his pipe. "Listen, we've about 25,000 Englishmen there now and more are on the move. We've blackamoor slaves, good cattle, and more land than the surveyors can measure. I have orchards being planted along the James River and a mile of wild pawpaw trees. By God, boy, the King shall soon be granting favours of estates everywhere."

"I thought you said the old order would not follow."

Reginald Burroughs shook his head. "Not in the same way as here. That is the genius of it. A man can use his connections *here* to boost his prospects *there*, yet once there he shall not bump up against all the rooted corruption that plagues this place."

Christopher's curiosity was now piqued. "Why do you tell me this?"

Burroughs looked at him carefully. "I have known thee since you were a child, Christopher. In thee I see thy father's charity energized by thy grandfather's ambition. We need good men with strength to do great things." He lowered his voice. "I have growing interests in Charles City County and beyond. However, I am not yet able to simply cast off and live there. I need allies in Virginia whilst I hold to my concerns in Ireland and England. Eventually, my heirs shall carry it all over."

Burroughs took Christopher by the shoulder. "Now, pray hear me. I am friends with the same gentlemen and lords to whom you are presently introduced. They are not blind to opportunity either. We can all see to it that thy future in Virginia exceeds anything you might imagine here. In return, I only ask thee to be a dependable friend to my needs over there. We all want happiness, young sir, we just need to make our way to it."

Christopher was suddenly intrigued. *Virginia?* he thought. *And Raven? Could an English gentleman marry an Irish commoner in Virginia... would she be happy there?* His mind began to fly to far places.

Burroughs' dark eyes twinkled. "And you can marry whomever you like. She would not *have* to be the Fairfax girl. She just needs broad hips to give you lots of children." He twisted the end of his moustache. "Some of our men have even married Indians."

Christopher blushed. "My grandfather would not be pleased—"

"Thy grandfather shan't live forever. Just tell me you shall consider what I have said."

❧

As servants brought generous portions of comfits and cakes to the families gathered on the lawn, Christopher's mind began to spin wonderful images of adventure in the New World. *Virginia? Raven? New alliances...new friends...But what use for my Oriental studies there? What about Grandfather?* By late afternoon his distractions caused him some embarrassment at bowls, and so he excused himself to take a walk when a whisper from a servant girl fired his heart. "Raven be at the cove," she said.

In moments, Christopher was riding the wind as he and Étalon disappeared from the roadway and galloped down the fern-edged path to Raven and the sea. Arriving by Gaia's weedy ruins, he leapt off his horse and ran to the pebbled beach where he peered into the sunlit waters for the gliding shadow of his Irish girl. "Where the devil is she?" he muttered. A sound behind him turned his head. "Aunt Comfort?"

Comfort smiled. Her linen gown was soaked and her grey hair dripped free atop her shoulders. "Good day, nephew. You look surprised." Shivering, she wrapped herself in a wool blanket.

"I thought you were in Kinsale."

"Ah well, I've spent a few days rowing about the rocks with Gaia. She shall never give up her quest for that book." Comfort squeezed water from her hair. "I love my time with that woman."

"Be careful with her. You do know she sneaks about Kinure Pointe with heathen rovers and—"

"I know, but she smuggles the best Spanish wine." Comfort laughed. "Besides, being with her is like having a picnic in the centre of a maelstrom—nothing is as it should be, and it is therefore all so much better."

Christopher wasn't amused. "You shall get thyself hung, a Clive woman or not."

Aunt Comfort closed her eyes. "You need to take a deep breath and absorb this place, Kipper." She took a breath of her own. "Better yet, let *it* absorb *thee*." The woman pulled the blanket around her more tightly and continued. "Now, since you were a child I wanted you to ask one question at the end of every day. I fear you have not."

Ignoring her, Christopher searched for Raven from one side of the cove to the other.

"Do you even remember the question?"

"Huh?"

"Are you listening to me?"

"Aye. The question. Of course, 'Where have I seen God today?'"

"Well done. So, look around and answer it."

Impatient, Christopher hurried his eyes over the waves, the rocks, the birds above and the green-capped cliffs edging it all. "His handiwork is everywhere."

"Too easy. Look again."

By the saints!

Comfort decided to help. "There, Kipper. See how that cloud casts a wide shadow over the cove? Watch. The wind shall soon push the cloud away so that the sun can lay sparkles over the water once more."

"So?" His fingers were tapping the sides of his legs.

Comfort laughed. "A sun-chased shadow...it is a metaphor." Christopher's eyes were busy scanning the shallow water-troughs for Raven so she yielded. Pointing to Mitten Rock, she said, "Never mind. She is up there."

Christopher followed Comfort's finger to Raven who was spying the horizon from the flat ledge between the freestanding cliff's closed fingers and its mighty thumb. He smiled. *A mermaid. A sea-fairy, a sprite. Ha, today I see a goddess.* Raven's cascading black hair lay tangled over her shoulders. Her hips held the rock-edge comfortably and she steadied herself with a graceful hand against the coarse stone.

Comfort reached for a canvas bag lying on a flat rock to one side. "I brought us some bacon and beef, a cake and a fruit pastry. I thought

Raven might swim back, but perhaps you can take it to her." She tossed the bag into Gaia's old boat. "I shall row you out, but you'll needs swim back."

Christopher suddenly hesitated.

Comfort set her palm lightly against his cheek. "You think thy grandfather would disapprove of your leaping into the water like a boy, etcetera. Well, of course he would! 'Tis not the sort of thing he expects a gentleman of grand expectations to do. So what?"

She turned Christopher's face squarely toward hers. "Sir Redmond Clive is not wise and so he is not free; he is not free and so he is not content; he is not content and so he is never happy. An unhappy life shall never bear good fruit." Comfort kissed her nephew's cheek. 'Thy grandfather is a bawdy preen, so have a care in what you let him teach thee."

"He just wants to make an English gentle*man* out of me."

"Are you a man now?"

"Aye."

"A man makes his own choices. So make one." Comfort climbed into the boat and waited.

Christopher thought for a long moment, recalling how it felt to stand man by man at the welcoming hearths of privilege in London and Oxford. Indeed, he wondered why he should continue cowering to the whip of his grandfather's vicarious ambitions. *Enough of this.* Defiant, he removed his doublet and folded it neatly on the rock. He sat and put his hands over one boot and yanked it off, crushing the voice within. Clenching his jaw, he pulled off the other boot and then his stockings. He climbed into Gaia's boat and took hold of the oars.

"I am proud of thee, Mister Clive," said Comfort. She wiped her eye. "There are many ways to be a slave, Kipper, but only one way to be free."

Saying nothing, Christopher pulled hard and the oarlocks groaned. He rowed the old boat silently seaward but just before easing it alongside the towering outcropping, he felt Comfort take his forearm.

"Aye," Christopher said. "I heard thee."

Comfort raised her eyebrows. "And?"

"I *am* free." He wiggled his toes.

The woman released her grip with a smile. "Well, we shall see."

Christopher stepped from the boat and steadied himself on the base of the rock that rose nearly sixty feet from the water. Raven's ledge was about fifteen feet above him and she had not yet noticed his arrival. He was about to call to her but decided to simply look at her for a lingering moment. *Virginia with Lady Raven Clive?* He imagined the two of them building a life in that faraway place. His mind's eye saw a dozen children running barefoot in the fields of the new world. Heart now soaring, he slung the bag of food over his shoulder, grabbed hold of the sea-scaled rock and began his climb.

Kipper's grunting and scratching caught Raven's attention. She turned, carefully, and looked below to see him straining toward her. "Kipper?"

He finally eased himself alongside Raven with a proud grin. "Whew." He took a deep breath. "Good day to you, m'lady. I was hoping to find thee."

Eyebrows raised in delight, Raven said, "Good day to ya Mister Clive, man of hope. I like tat. Just be careful what ya hope for!"

"I have missed thee."

"Ya missed me? Mister Christopher Clive of Oxford University missed Raven O'Morrissey of Skeefe?" She playfully slapped his shoulder.

Her touch enlivened him. "I have missed thee a great deal. Have you missed me?" Christopher held his breath.

Raven blushed and twirled her hair around a long finger. "Em, surely I have missed ya, though I've not missed our quarrels."

Kipper thought her tone a bit hesitant. Dare he ask about Fallon Healy?

Raven's eyes dropped to his bare feet. "Hi ho! Yer bootless."

Kipper reddened. "Aye. And I am guessing you are thinking 'at last.'" He stretched his feet forward and wiggled his toes. "I confess, it feels good."

"I'm proud of ya."

He liked to hear that. The two then sat quietly until Christopher opened his satchel to share his food.

Taking some salty bacon into her hand, Raven said, "Yer aunt's as fine a woman as walks the earth. She gives me good work at the Clive House and buys cloth from m'ma."

Chewing on some bread, Christopher nodded. He was still wondering about Healy.

"She is wiser than anyone I know, exceptin maybe Gaia."

Christopher swallowed. "Wiser than me?"

Raven tore a piece of bacon with her teeth. "Especially you." She giggled.

The giggle saved the moment for Kipper. Relieved, he chased Healy from his thoughts and replaced the Irish boy with emerging visions of a distant horizon. It was then when Raven began to hum a tune. Hearing her tender voice melding with the sounds of soft surf, he suddenly wanted to take hold of her and kiss her—to marry her then and there and sail away to Virginia. Instead, he gobbled down a pastry. "Raven…" Christopher struggled for courage.

She faced him, her expectant green eyes fired by the late day sun.

"I want to ask you something." He watched her become still as a deep-forest doe. Christopher licked his lips. *But what if she laughs, or says 'nay,' or...* Fears of Healy returned. He forced his mouth open but a voice interrupted the moment.

"Raven?" It was Gaia standing in her bobbing boat below.

Christopher grit his teeth. *Again!*

CHAPTER 11

"Em...what is it, Gaia?" Raven stood, carefully.

"I needs ya."

"Now?"

"Now."

"But..."

"Finish what ya must with the Englishman. I'll wait."

Christopher climbed to his feet. "She shall be down soon enough!"

Gaia cupped her hands over her mouth. "Gerl, tell the Clive to shut his crumpet. 'Tis *my* cove and I'll do what I wants in it."

"It is not thy cove!" Christopher nearly fell. "It belongs to Clives! Now just go away."

Raven set a gentle hand on his arm. "Kipper, she's old and means no harm."

Ignoring her, Christopher shouted at Gaia once more. "My aunt's down there. Tell her to help you."

"She already rode away."

Raven answered. "What do you need, Gaia?"

"I needs you."

Sighing, Raven raised a hand at Gaia and asked Christopher if he could say his piece quickly.

He hesitated. "I've much to say and it ought not be rushed like this."

"Can ya give me a hint?"

He huffed and sat. "Well, my mind's been flying about a bit today. A picture came to me where we are walking in a cherry orchard alongside a wide river." He gathered his thoughts. "But we are not here in Ireland. Nay, we are there." He pointed into the southwest horizon. "In the Virginia Colony."

"Virginia?"

Heart pounding, Christopher waited.

Raven stared blank-faced into the horizon.

Suddenly embarrassed, Kipper said, "Well, I did wonder if it isn't actually all quite mad."

Raven glanced at Gaia. "Em, can we speak of it another time?"

Christopher now wished he could take it all back. "Like I said, it is a madness of sorts...runs in the family." He laughed, awkwardly, and stood. "But I needs return to school and so——"

"Back to school so soon?"

He nodded and waited desperately for her to say something more.

"Perhaps ya might write me a letter about this idea, then?"

A letter! Christopher forced a smile. "I suppose, as long as the Post can find thee." He reached for his satchel. "But do not think too much on it. It was just a wild notion, a thing not normal for me." Red-faced, he slanted his eyes away from her.

It was then that Raven stood and surprised him. "I like it." She pecked his cheek with a quick kiss and leapt into the deep water below.

⚜

21 July 1660

Christopher Clive stared forlornly through a rain-spattered pane of Oxford University's *Bibliotheca Bodleiana* and into the venerable halls bordering the far side of the college quadrangle. "Do you think she received it? Today is her birthday…I wanted this one to get there in time."

Otherwise distracted, his bulky, ginger-haired second cousin and classmate—Winston Wellington—feigned interest as he scanned a shelf of books. "How old is she?"

"Eighteen." A stray sea gull dipped from the grey sky and swooped low over the walkway below. "I am not sure the Royal Post is improved like they say." Kipper Clive closed his eyes and touched the cheek Raven had kissed. He remembered Raven swimming unfettered through the blue shades of her enchanted cove. He could smell the salt; he could hear her splashing; he could see her pulling herself atop a wet rock.

Such vivid memories had made Christopher homesick for these past two months. But he could not shake the untimely error of blurting his dream of Virginia without regard for how she might receive such a thing so rushed. Images of her flushed face had weighed heavily on him through the festive welcome of King Charles II; recalling how her eyes had averted his had stolen his attention from recent engagements with Jocelyn Fairfax.

Yet her kiss on his cheek had left him with hope.

But why had she not written to him even a single letter? Not even for his birthday. Aunt Comfort had taught her how to write, and she could do so very well.

Had he offended her? Had he made improper assumptions? Was the glance all that he feared it was after all?

"Aha!" Winston finally spotted the book he wanted. "Next to Donne, right where I hid it." Looking warily from side to side, he carefully slid a copy of John Milton's *Areopagitica* into his satchel. "The King shan't be burning *this* copy."

"We could be arrested."

Wellington smirked. "Then we best be off."

Christopher followed his cousin anxiously through the ornate library and out one of the Catte Street doors from which they hurried to the always busy Queen's Lane Coffee House below St. Edmund Hall. There, Winston tucked his contraband beneath a stool and squeezed his belly against a table. He called for a waiter.

The two ordered coffee, a bowl of currant marmalade and wheat bread. Winston dabbed perspiration off his broad face with a kerchief. "So, back to that other business. What did you write to the girl?"

Christopher balked.

"You can tell me."

"Confide in a common thief?"

Winston laughed, loudly. "Nay, not common. I am an *ironic* thief. I have stolen a book on freedom of speech that was to be burned by the King. Do you see the irony in that?"

Christopher shrugged.

"So, I am an ironic thief and you, my friend, are an ironic lover."

"How so?"

"The expectations that *rule* thee demand Jocelyn Fairfax. But, the heart that *leads* thee yearns for the Irish wench. What should be clear is not clear at all."

Christopher stared into his coffee.

Winston reached for some bread. "Truth be told, you are moonstruck over a girl you ought not have."

"Ought not?"

"By the saints, Clive, she is bad for the family business in every way. You know it in that clever head of thine, but thy heart denies it." Winston wiped some marmalade on his bread with an air of assurance that suddenly annoyed Kipper. "But there is another reason why you ought not have her."

Christopher waited.

Winston chewed his bread slowly and then swallowed. "You describe her as an artist's muse, but yours is not the world of an artist. Nay, you are expected to be a *thinker*, yet she is a dreamer... 'tis an impossible blend. You are required to put order to things; she floats. You are taught to seize knowledge; she seeks visions. You are to *do*; she simply *is*. No wonder you quarrel whenever you are together. Nay, she is like fire and you are like a stone; she shall heat thee hot but never light thee." He sipped some coffee, thinking. "Better still, thy world is rock and hers is water; you oppose one another. Do you understand?"

Christopher shifted in his seat. "I do not think this is entirely true—"

"So, Mister Clive, this is why I hope that no fawning letters found their way to her hand. It would not be good for either of ye." Satisfied, he took another sip of coffee.

Christopher scowled. "She can think and she can do…ask my aunt; she taught her well. But she *feels* life in a way that—"

"Listen to thyself," scolded Winston. "You are taught to value the rational in all matters, yet you reject all you know to be true in favour of Raven O'Morrissey." He stood. "She is Irish, she's poor; she is Catholic for Christ's sake. She's unwelcome in our world except to sing a song or serve ale. She is chaotic. The girl's a giglet who teases thee whilst—by thine own admission—she gives her heart to Healy. Which, *ironically*, is actually the one rational choice she—"

"Shut up, Wellington." Christopher stood. "You know nothing."

⊰⊱

After days of pacing, Christopher took leave of his summer studies and cancelled all future appointments with his gentlemen of influence. He hastily scribbled a note of apology to Jocelyn Fairfax and stuffed a leather suitcase for his coach bound for the port of Bristol. Ready, he paused to stare into a small mirror by candlelight. "Is this wise?" he muttered. *But I am already 'vanquishing my peers and astonishing my professors.' I can finish my work later.* He furrowed his brow. *But by the saints, who cares?* "I'm off; this is *necessary!*"

Boarding his coach by dawn, he jostled along dusty roads for the next twelve hours and arrived at dusk in Bristol. The next morning he booked passage on a merchant ship owned by his grandfather that finally delivered him to Kinsale at nightfall on the last evening of July.

Christopher hurried along the fish-scented wharves, passed smoky taverns fast-filling with drunken sailors, and trotted by the Customs House. Ignoring taunts from the King's sailors now taking claim to the town, he circuited the shallow end of the harbour not far from St. Multose Church and rushed through the lamplight to finally arrive at his family's house.

Kipper skipped lightly up the stone steps and hammered the brass doorknocker. His heart beat quickly as he imagined Raven in the servants' quarters just paces away at the back of the house. *Hurry, Tattie! Open the blasted door.*

The heavy door then opened, but to Christopher's dismay it was Fallon Healy in a butler's uniform, bowing and bidding him entrance. "Young Mister Clive? This be a surprise," Fallon said.

"Aye, a surprise, indeed," grumbled Christopher as he brushed past him. "And if you are to answer a Clive door, you say '*is* a surprise,' not '*be* a surprise.'" He tossed his hat to Fallon and dropped his heavy suitcase on the floor. "Where *is* Tattie?"

"He *is* at Giardín an Croí with Sir Redmond."

Christopher strode into the dark house. Few candles were lit and the air was stuffy. He turned to Fallon. "And—"

"She be travellin with yer Aunt Comfort and yer parents."

Christopher did not like the presumptive interruption. "As I was about to ask, how is my father's health?"

"'Tis why tey be travellin."

Christopher scowled. "Where are *they*?"

"Tey be in *an Caoláire Rua* for 'the health of yer pa and the wellness of all,' as yer aunt put it. Ye English would call it, 'Killary Harbour.'"

Frustrated, Christopher threw himself into a chair. "Where the devil is that and what's there?"

"I am not entirely certain, young sir."

Christopher looked at Fallon for a long moment. "You knew how to say it in Irish, so methinks you know something about it."

"I do."

Christopher waited.

The two young men stared at one another until Christopher blurted, "Then tell me what you know!"

The Irishman obeyed, albeit with half a smirk. "Em, let me tink. Em...ah, 'tis west. It seems that gentle persons soak about in seaweed and, by Jaysus, set in sulphurous water fer who knows what—"

"When are they due home?"

"Ah, Mister Clive, none told me."

Standing, Christopher squeezed his fists by his side. "You must have some idea. A day? A week? A fortnight? A month?"

Fallon shrugged.

"When did they leave?"

"Em...metinks...em. I can't be sure of it. I was workin at Sir Redmond's offices fer a time."

Christopher could barely restrain himself. "Mister Healy. When did you begin duties as the butler?"

Fallon twisted his face as if struggling to remember. "Em...em... perhaps a week ago? I can't be sure, what with all the wonderful tings happenin in me life."

Fallon's last sentence was delivered with a bit of a barb and Christopher felt a twinge of fear. *Whatever does that mean? Something about Raven?* He almost asked out loud. Instead, he grunted and stormed away.

⚜

1 September 1660

Christopher raced for the coach now arriving at Giardin an Croi. He had spent the entire month of August alternating between here and the Clive House in Kinsale waiting for Raven to return. Heart surging, he stuck his head into the coach. "Where is she?"

Spencer answered. "Raven asked to remain in Kinsale with Comfort for the night."

Speechless with disappointment, Christopher helped his father and mother dismount the coach as Grandfather Clive came charging across the lawn. "Thy son is a fool! He is a lovesick dolt. I have spent four weeks chasing him to and from his duties at the office. I came here last night to drag him back by the ear! He refuses to do his work. All he does is shoot his pistol and wander about. By God, he only thinks about that Irish bitch."

Redmond turned his wrath on Millicent, hurrying to scoop up her dog. "And you. You were to have that little wench married off 'afore ye all left!" Cursing wildly, he stormed toward back to the house grumbling something about "a new plan."

Christopher gawked. "Married, Mother?"

Millicent hiked her gown with her free hand and hurried into the house.

Christopher followed her, crying. "What are you up to?"

Millicent rushed up the stairs and into a room. She hastily locked her son out. Christopher ran back downstairs and confronted his father still on the front lawn. "Tell me what is going on here!"

Spencer dodged his son's eyes. "Can we speak of it later?"

"Later? Nay!"

"Then can you sit with me?"

"I shall not sit!" Christopher noticed servants loading Redmond's trunks into the carriage for his return to Kinsale. "I am going back with him." He turned his face to his father's. "But you must tell me what is happening."

Spencer leaned heavily on his cane. "It seems—and without my knowledge—that thy grandfather and mother pressed a betrothal of Mister Fallon Healy to Miss O'Morrissey soon after you returned to school. Raven yielded at first since they had made promises to her mother, but she soon expressed reservations to Comfort."

Anger rising, Christopher hung on every word.

"Comfort then announced news of Killary Harbour. So we all went west to soak." Spencer took a tankard of ale from a servant's hand and dropped into a chair. "Comfort said it was impossible for her to leave Raven behind on account that Raven knows exactly how best to assist her and so forth. Obviously, the whole trip was a ploy to allow the poor girl time to think."

"And what has she decided?" Christopher held his breath.

"I do not know. I am not privy to very much." Spencer took a long draught of ale.

Christopher set his jaw. "I am going to see her, now."

Spencer reached an empty hand toward him. "I do know that Raven wants to see her mother on the morrow. Methinks it better for thee to let the girl work through this in her own time."

Christopher withdrew. "She does not even know that I am here! I should go now—"

"If you insist on carrying on like this, you shall either break Raven's heart or forfeit thy fortune." Spencer's voice became uncharacteristically firm. "I do not ask much of thee, son, but I ask you to wait just a bit longer to see how Providence—or Comfort— sorts this out."

Christopher groused. "For all I know, she's decided to marry Healy. That would make thee and everyone else very happy."

"She is smart enough to understand that if she were to marry thee, thy grandfather would surely disown thee. In my opinion, she would suffer her entire life knowing that she exacted such a price. I for one do not wish that on her."

Jaw clenched, Christopher said, "Grandfather would never do that. He would be angry, but——"

"He would disown thee in a heartbeat to save his own face." Spencer leaned his hand atop his cane. "I beg thee to simply wait——"

"And what of thee, Father? Would you disown me as well?"

Disappointed by the question, Spencer's arm went limp. "Of course I would not. My estate is a pittance compared to thy grandfather's, but you remain my heir no matter what."

Kipper stared blankly beyond his father and into the sea. He turned to see Redmond climb into the carriage, grousing something at Tattie who remained behind. At last he turned to his father. "By Christ. I shall wait and see her on the morrow."

CHAPTER 12

IN THE AFTERNOON of the next day, Christopher again raced toward the coach arriving at Giardín an Croí. He flung open the door and looked past his Aunt Comfort to check the inside of the coach.

"You are looking for Raven, of course," said Comfort as she offered him her arm. "We just now delivered her to her mother. Now help me out."

"But I thought—"

"I know." Standing on the gravelled lane, Comfort then took a firm hold of his hand. "We had a late start. Now, settle thyself. She'll be happy to see thee in the morning."

"In the morning?" Christopher grit his teeth.

"Aye, happy...and in the morning." She pointed Tattie to her bags, wiped her eye and laid a second hand atop his, gently. "She must spend some time with her mother."

Defeated, Christopher sighed, heavily, and helped her to the large doors. "But you are certain that she shall be coming?"

Comfort smiled. "Take a breath, dear boy."

Christopher bit his lip. "Is she going to marry Healy?"

Christopher was restless all evening. By nightfall his heart was pounding once more. As he fell into his bed he thought the dawn might never break through his window.

And it did not.

Sometime before midnight he awakened from his shallow sleep to hear Cleopatra growling loudly at the top of the stairs not far from his bedroom door. Kipper sat up, grumbling. He groped about his dark bedroom for a shirt, breeches, dagger and belt. He yanked on stockings and his boots, grabbed hold of his pistol bag and stepped into the darkness of the upstairs hallway. As he did, the paunchy Terrier flew down the stairs, yapping wildly.

Spencer and Millicent emerged from their respective rooms, as did a pistol-bearing Comfort who began to call for Tattie in his first floor room below. The troubled foursome then paused to stare into the murky stairwell, shadowed only by the poor light of a single watch-candle atop the parlour's mantle below. Still growling, Cleopatra began to scratch furiously at the front door.

Christopher withdrew his pistol. "Wait here." He stepped warily down the steps but had only descended about half way when the door suddenly burst open and two men charged through it, shrieking. Startled, he scrambled back up the steps as the dark figures raced for him.

"Run!" Christopher cried. Iron-soled boots pounded up the wooden treads. His mother began screaming. He abruptly spun about and fired his pistol point blank at the first figure now nearly atop him.

Whoom!

The man tumbled backward.

Whoom! Comfort fired over Christopher's shoulder, knocking the second man over the railing.

He fumbled to reload his pistol.

Tattie cried from below, "Back door!"

Belly churning, Christopher charged downstairs toward the sounds of a sudden struggle where he found Tattie thrusting a long pike at two more shadows. Close behind came Spencer who fired his pistol first, dropping one of the intruders. Christopher fired a second round, missing.

Roaring, Tattie then drove the remaining intruder backward with his pike and impaled him against a panelled wall.

Hands trembling, Comfort quickly lit lamps from the watch-candle. As the room filled with yellow light, all could plainly see the baggy blue trousers and tall caps of the intruders.

"Janissaries," groaned Comfort as she deftly reloaded.

At the word, Christopher's body went limp. The Janissaries were the elite troops of the Ottoman Sultan, often accompanying Algerian corsairs on coastal raids. Christopher's mind raced. "Then more must be coming for us. Aunt Comfort, get everyone out of the house!"

Christopher turned to Tattie. He was still gaping at the writhing soldier pinned to the wall. "Tattie, look at me! Take my father's horse and get to James Fort at once. Tell them we have been attacked by Turks and pirates—"

Two more Janissaries suddenly crashed through the front door, shouting. One lunged at Spencer with a curved cutlass, sending the frail man backward over a table. Comfort fired her piece. The Turk fell away. Undaunted, the second soldier charged. Christopher took quick aim and shot him dead.

Christopher whirled about, eyes wide but steady. "Now go, Tattie! Everybody else out of the house; get to the thickets near the road and hide!" He pulled his father upright. "Hurry. And if that dog barks, kill it. Now go!"

"But you—"

"I'll join you later." Reloading, Christopher's face fell upon his mother crouched in a corner. He ran to her and lifted the stunned woman to her feet. "Mother, you must hurry away and hide with Father and Comfort. Do you understand?"

Millicent nodded, weakly.

Christopher then pushed his family through the western entrance of the house and pointed to black clumps lining the night-shrouded Kinure byway. "Get behind those heavy shrubs as fast as you can." He turned his head south, toward Skeefe, and saw flames now licking the sky. To one side a blur of gauzy silhouettes slumped upslope from the village. "Christ save us." With his family hurrying away, Kipper raced for the stable. Once inside he ordered the panicked stable boy to ride hard, east. "Warn the Burroughs'." He then threw a bit and bridle over Étalon's obliging head, swung his leg over the horse's bare back, and in moments began a furious gallop downslope toward Skeefe.

Riding frantically toward the burning village, Christopher soon discerned the blaze-shadowed forms of many men chasing faceless bunches of village folk toward the water's edge. The men were terrorizing the Irish with loud shrieks and the furious pounding of drums. *Raven, I'm coming.* He leaned forward on Étalon's neck. "Go!"

Closer, Christopher finally reined his horse. Careful to remain unseen, he scouted another company of Janissary musketeers strung along the far side of the village. He touched his heels lightly to Étalon's sweated flanks and eased him toward the screen of a low hedge, quickly studying the terrible scene before him. As he feared, the seventy-some souls of Skeefe had been corralled at the beach where they were being dragged aboard shallow-hulled skiffs. *Pirates plus more than fifty Turks*, he thought. *We've two ships-of-the-line in port, perchance...*"But there's little time." Christopher dismounted Étalon and shooed the horse into the darkness behind him. He crept forward.

Now in complete control, the Janissaries finally stopped their intimidating shrieks and drumming, allowing Christopher to hear a commander barking orders in an awkward Turkish dialect of some sort. *He wants them to hurry.* Kipper desperately scanned the beach. *Raven, where are you? What do I do?*

He dashed to the cover of a broken stone wall that ran closer to the beach. Head down, he made his way in the direction of the bay, keeping the wall to his left until he reached its end. There he waited. *What to do?* A column of about a dozen musketeers abruptly appeared trotting toward the village. *Probably ordered back from the house.* Christopher watched them carefully but then spotted the unmistakable glow of fire rising from Giardín an Croí. He muttered a curse.

Christopher returned his eyes to the column of returning soldiers. One was lagging. Fixing on him, Christopher's mind began to race. The company tramped closer and he pressed himself low on his haunches as they finally passed by his screen.

His plan ready, he took a deep, quaking breath.

Kipper's body tensed as he heard the clumsy thump of the lagging Janissary drawing near. *Not yet.* He began to tremble. He wanted to vomit.

In another moment he could hear the soldier's laboured breaths. *Hold.*

Christopher lifted his face as the Turk drew close. He could see a glint of perspiration. *Now!*

Kipper Clive sprang like a panther in the night. Seizing upon the surprised Janissary, he quickly wrestled away his musket, jerked the pistol from his own belt and shoved the end of its barrel into the soldier's mouth. "*Hareket etmeyin!* Do not move!" he hissed.

Wide-eyed, the soldier nodded.

Christopher carefully pulled the man to his knees and set the pistol's barrel on his temple. He then quickly surveyed the beach lying about 300 paces away. Many of the villagers had already been bound and boarded onto the waiting skiffs. He strained to see through the smoke and the orange-cast gloom. *Where are you, Raven?*

Not finding her, he searched for the Janissary commander. A very small man was giving orders by the point of his sword. *There?* Pushing the Turk ahead of him, Christopher strode into the firelight and shouted over the din. "Here!"

The little officer spun about, but a second man pushed past him. He was tall and lanky with long hair flying from beneath a turban. "Wha?"

"Over here!"

"Eh?"

A heavily shadowed knot of men moved closer, straining to hear. The Janissary officer ordered his musketeers to form a line. The tall man ranged a few paces ahead brandishing two pistols.

"Stop! Close enough. *Hayir yakin!*" cried Christopher.

The musketeers took aim as the tall man stuffed his pistols in the sash banding his waist. He removed his turban and bowed, mockingly. "I am Yusef *al*-Mahomet *Rais*...that means 'Yusef son of Mohamet, Captain.'" Grinning he tossed a thumb to one side. "And that's my fine flagship that lay in wait in tha lovely bay." He pointed to the Janissary officer. "And the little fella be Zeki *Karakullukçu*, sergeant of the Janissaries now ready to shoot holes through tha."

Christopher recognized the Lancashire accent. "You neither look like or sound like a 'Yusef.' Methinks you to be a traitor to the Cross, a Liverpudlian-turned-Turk..."

"Yea? Tha hast a good ear." The ship's captain laughed. "I was baptized Richard Crumb of Parkgate, but now here I stand—a true follower of the Prophet, may peace be upon him."

"Well, Richard Crumb, I am Christopher Clive, grandson of Sir Redmond Clive—brother to the living Christ."

"I know who tha are." The man inched forward. "So, what do tha propose here, young sir?"

Christopher shifted nervously. He looked at Sergeant Zeki now inching closer. "Who's in charge here, him or you?"

Zeki answered in a thin voice. "The Sultan hired the rais' ship, so we are partners of sorts."

The captain interrupted. "Enough. Now, Mister Clive, what is tha plan?"

"You must set them free."

"Is that all?"

"Aye."

"Or what?"

Christopher pressed his pistol hard against this prisoner's temple. "I'll shoot thy man."

Yusef laughed. "I'd haply forfeit one man fer seventy slaves. Besides, he is not *my* man, he belongs to the Sultan."

Christopher suddenly heard Raven's voice shouting something. He answered. "Raven!"

"Aye, so there 'tis," said Yusef. He moved a few steps closer. "You love a hoo."

Emboldened by Raven's voice, Christopher said, "Let them go, Crumb. I'll spare the Sultan's man and offer myself as the ransom for the village."

"One English gent fer seventy Irish? Well, let me think. I'd collect $8,000 Spanish fer this bunch, likely more. Would thy grandfadder ransom thee for so much?" The rais moved closer. "Methinks nay."

Christopher tried to calculate.

"But if tha hurry up about it, I'd ransom thee for *one* Irish."

"One? That's madness."

"Tha for one Irish. For this I give thee my vow."

He thought of Raven, of course, but he could not abandon the others. "The word of a heathen is shite."

"Aye? Tell me bout tha hoo." The ship's captain moved closer, still. "Is she a beauty? Has she fair skin? Green eyes? Perhaps a bit too scrawny?"

Christopher was perspiring. *That bastard already knows who she is.* He cast a final, forlorn glimpse at Giardín an Croí now fully engulfed by flames. He tore his eyes away and desperately scanned the boats for Raven. Imagining her stripped naked and probed in the slave market of Algiers was more than he could bear. *Kinsale may send ships in time,* he thought. *But if not...* He shifted on his feet. "I offer myself for *one full boat* that includes the girl."

"I see." Yusef turned to Zeki and exchanged a few words before finally answering Christopher. "We've no time fer hagglin." He pointed to one of the clinker-built skiffs grinding its hull in shallow water. "Tha hoo is aboard that one."

Christopher was so anxious he could barely think. "No tricks. I want her to wave and shout my name."

With a nod from Yusef, the sergeant barked a command and in moments, a dark figure was untied and waving. Christopher listened for her voice. Satisfied, he turned to the captain. "It is she."

Yusef eased forward. "So now wha, Mister Clive?"

Christopher's mind churned. "Set them free, Captain Crumb. I want them safe in the darkness behind me, but I need Raven to come close enough for me to see her face. When they are all safely away I shall surrender to you."

"And how do I know tha won't run away with them?"

"I...I vow it as a Christian gentleman."

"Ha. Good one. But so tha knows, if tha tricks me, I shall kill the other Irish and take me losses."

"Aye. But how do I know *you* shall not betray *me?*"

"I already gave tha my vow as a Mohammedan."

Christopher grumbled.

Yusef Rais said something into the sergeant's ear and soon several musketeers were sent running to the skiff. The boat was hastily emptied onto the smoke-shrouded beach and a cluster of various sized figures began scrambling out of the water.

Nervous, Christopher waited for what seemed an endless time. Finally, he watched the huddling figures rush toward the safety of darkness behind him. *Where is she?* A slender figure abandoned the others and raced headlong toward him. "Raven?" he cried.

Christopher's attention was abruptly stolen by the suddenly tense voice of the captain pressing closer with a dozen high-capped Janissaries. "Now tha see thy hoo's face. Toss down thy weapon and come, else I'll order me musketeers to kill them all."

Christopher's mouth was dry. His legs weakened and his breathing became rapid. He turned his attention from Yusef and strained to see Raven's face. "Hurry, Raven, hurry!"

At last, the stumbling maiden was upon him, sobbing in halting wails.

"Raven…"

The poor girl collapsed against Christopher and clung tightly. "O, Kipper…I'm so sorry!"

"Run, Raven!"

"Now!" shouted Yusef Rais. "Drop the pistol!"

Raven clutched Christopher's arm. "I'm sorry—"

"But—"

A musketeer fired a warning shot. Christopher tossed his pistol into the darkness and pushed Raven away. "Go! Run!"

She stood still, weeping.

"What's the matter with you? Run!" Christopher pushed her again. "Go!"

"Forgive me," wailed Raven. She fell to her knees.

Confused, Christopher gawked, only to be quickly engulfed by the company of soldiers now upon him. He was thrown to the ground, screaming for Raven to fly away.

But no one flew away.

Instead, returning from the darkness behind Christopher were sword-wielding corsairs and a few of their Janissary allies now tossing off their capes and laughing. In their clutches were a dozen Irish women and girls.

"Betrayed!" wailed Christopher. "You bastards! You devils!"

The pirates quickly bound Raven's hands and shoved her past the stunned lad toward the skiffs. "They said they'd kill Ma—"

Kipper struggled against the many hands holding him. He sputtered and spat at Yusef Rais now standing wide-legged over him. "Damn you, heathen!"

"Time for tha to join us, Mister Clive."

A bare-armed Janissary jerked Christopher to his feet and then rammed his belly with the butt of a baton. He gasped for air as soldiers bound his wrists. One plucked Aunt Comfort's dagger from his belt. "The vow of a Mohammedan?" he wheezed. "I should ne'er have trusted a renegade."

"Yea?" answered Yusef. "My *vow* was one Irish for thee. I ne'er pledged otherwise." He then pointed a long finger at a slump-shouldered silhouette standing safely alone at the edges of the shadows. "Look yon, Mister Clive."

Christopher peered into the darkness. "I don't understand."

"Methinks tha knows her. She be Gaia, the crone."

Christopher was reeling. "What?"

"As I said, my vow was to ransom tha for *one Irish*...and there she be."

Speechless, Christopher Clive was then dragged away into a new world, devoured by the woe of Skeefe.

CHAPTER 13

Rough hands bound Christopher tightly by the wrists and dragged him across the pebbled beach. Confused and his mind still whirling, he peered through thick, shadowed smoke at his shouting captors. His limbs felt like soft butter. He teetered his way forward until a sack was thrown over him at the water's edge.

The desperate lad sucked the heavy canvas against his lips. Suffocating, he began to flail against the firm grip of many hands. His head was then whipsawed by punches thrown from alternating fists. He fell forward into shallow water where two large hands held his face against the stony bottom.

Christopher's world went nearly dark until he felt himself jerked upright. He was punched hard in the belly and collapsed against the sea-smoothed hull of a rocking skiff. Someone then pulled the sack off his head and he inhaled volumes of smoky air.

Coughing violently, Christopher was finally struck upon the back of the head by a baton, bouncing him against the boards of the hull. Drifting into unconsciousness, he sank beneath the dark water only to be hauled upward by two sleeveless Janissaries and tossed into the yawning skiff like a limp bag of turnips. He landed atop a tangle of Irish arms and legs, and his world went black.

"Mister Clive? Mister Clive?"

Christopher stirred. He opened his eyes but could see nothing. He felt the touch of fingers drawing him to consciousness and a hush of voices urging him to awaken. Dazed, he tried to sit up. Nausea filled his belly. He rolled and vomited. He was shatterbrained; his ears were ringing and he vomited once more. *Where am I?*

That was the last he remembered for the next hours.

When Christopher awakened, he heard children crying. Bewildered, he stirred, and found himself cramped somewhere within the musty timbers of Yusef Rais' 300-ton ship's sub-structure where he and the Irish had been stuffed like a great catch of June pilchards. He retched. The smell of mouldy wood, human waste and rancid bilge was overwhelming.

Disoriented, he stretched his hands into the blackness to feel nothing but damp planks and the smooth edges of heavy beams. Enclosed in a creaking casket, Christopher began to panic.

"Lay still," said an Irishman. "Ya can't move just yet."

Struggling for breath, Christopher blurted. "Who's that?"

"Paddy O'Sullivan."

The name was familiar and the sound of the man's lilting Irish soothed him a little.

"From Oysterhaven?"

"Tat's right. Nice to set wid ya, Mister Clive. Go easy. Try settin still."

Christopher settled, slowly. His joints began to ache and his head suddenly hurt. He ran his fingers over the large lump on the back of his crown as he tried to recover his thoughts. But the haunting sound of many men chanting from above now filled his black chamber. *"Allahu Akbar...Subhana rabbiyal adheem..."* He covered his ears.

A great shuffling of sorts followed, then another.

"Devils be above us," said an Irish woman from somewhere. "Metinks they're prayin. I seen a picture once."

Another cold wave of terror spread through Christopher's body. He lurched into the blackness of the hold. "What hell is this?" he cried.

"Ease yerself," scolded Paddy. "We're in an Algerian ship and we're not a'goin anywhere just yet. Be still."

Christopher's breath was short; he felt cold perspiration rise all over his skin. The scene at his father's house then rushed to his mind. Images of the beach and the fires followed. "Raven!" he suddenly cried. "Raven?"

Paddy O'Sullivan's hands found Christopher and they pressed on him, lightly. "Be still, laddy."

A voice answered from far away in the darkness. "Kipper?"

"Raven?"

"Here! O Kipper—"

"I cannot see thee!" Christopher pushed wildly against the forest of damp wood around him. He then tried straightening his legs over others. Paddy O'Sullivan pleaded with him to be still. He blinked in the darkness and cried out, "I'm coming, Raven…"

"Over here." Raven's voice was tight. "And I am so sorry."

Determined, Christopher squeezed past grumbling Irishmen and felt his way along wet planking, futtocks, barrels, and over coils of brails. "Where?"

"Here."

Christopher groped like a blind man into another black chamber of some sort where he pushed some heavy crates from his path. Tripping over rope he finally stood upright. "I cannot see—"

"Tiss way, Mister Clive," cried a woman.

Christopher thrashed through the darkness, but then a small door opened from above. Two corsairs ducked through it carrying lanterns. "Mister Christopher Clive," growled one of them.

Startled, he crouched behind two barrels.

"Clive, come out!"

Anxious, Christopher watched the yellow lanterns move aft to forward until finally one of the frustrated corsairs snatched a woman by her hair and jerked her to her feet. He held his lantern close to her face. "Enough of this. Clive come out."

Christopher knew the woman well. *Glenna Murray*. She was mother to five and the wife of a Skeefe fisherman named Sammy. The corsair slammed the woman into a ship's post, breaking her nose. He put a knife to her cheek. "I'll cut her face, Mister Clive."

"Hold fast. I am coming."

The pirate tossed Glenna aside and the pair of them cut a swath out of the darkness, quickly exposing Christopher. The men stormed forward and grabbed him by his shirt. They dragged him out of the hold and up a narrow companionway. They then forced him through the maze of the lower deck, past stacks of cramped bunks and through the galley. "Hurry!" They drove him past the stench of the head, along a coop for hens and up another few steps where they finally threw him onto the main deck now shadowed in the first light of early dawn.

Panting, Christopher climbed to his feet and stood. He strained to gather his thoughts as he watched the grey images of many men scurrying to their duties on all sides. The ship heaved and he spread his bare feet to steady himself. His ears filled with the crash of waves breaking across the bow. His mind quickly organizing itself, he raised his chin and trained his face on the two corsairs.

Though heavily bearded and dressed in Turkish garb, it was plain for Christopher to see both men were renegades from Christianity like their captain. Christopher guessed that one of them was Dutch or German. "Took the turban, eh?"

The Dutchman casually grabbed Christopher behind the neck and punched him squarely in the face. He then put the sharp edge of a short knife against his open throat. "*Ja*, so?"

Christopher wiped a torn sleeve across his bloodied nose. "I look forward to the day when the English Navy hangs thee high."

Cursing, the corsairs shoved Christopher toward a post near the main mast. There the two of them knocked him hard to the ground with batons. One planted his foot on his chest and pressed him to the planking until the other locked the now silent young gentleman's foot to an iron chain.

"You cost us de rape *und* loot we deserved on dat beach," grumbled the Dutchman. "I hopes you pays a high price for dat."

Lying on the deck, Christopher looked blankly at the toes of his shackled foot. Several goats trotted by, one pausing to stare at him for a moment. *They had to hurry off the beach.* He quickly calculated that the raiders must have rushed away because they feared James Fort had been alerted. And they would only think that if they knew his family had escaped. The thought of it brought a relieved smile to his face. He looked upward at the Dutchman in time to see a mallet swinging at him from the corner of his eye.

⫘

As the sun climbed the port horizon, Christopher Clive stirred. Disoriented, he pulled himself upward and rubbed his swollen head, realizing that his hair had been shorn. He then raised his leg against the weight of his shackles and climbed, unsteadily, to his feet. He tried to focus his eyes on the horizon. Straining, he recognized the faint hint of Ireland's ragged fingers clutching the sea. He reached toward the distant headlands with one arm, imagining he might grab hold of the fast-fading shoreline.

The hard tramping of iron-soles on the deck took Christopher's attention. He turned to see a group of Janissaries in baggy blue pants duck hurriedly into a hatch leading below. He quickly scanned

the decks and estimated there to be more than a hundred such soldiers, each armed with curved cutlasses and a few carrying muskets.
Nearby stood the little sergeant from the beach—Zeki—barking
orders. Christopher grumbled. His eyes then fell on another officer
whom he had not seen before. He studied the imposing figure now
pointing from the stern's poop deck. Christopher knew at once that
this man was in command.

A wild pattering of bare feet then caught Christopher's attention
and he turned to watch about forty sailors of every imaginable home-
land running to form two opposing lines. The sailors answered to
Yusef Rais. Seeing the swaggering ship's captain once more brought
a string of curses to Christopher's lips. Yusef was speaking to his
men *Sabir*—a spontaneous language comprised of Turkish and several
other tongues spoken throughout the Barbary Coast. Christopher
strained to understand what he could.

Hearing laughter, Christopher then narrowed his eyes on a pitiful old
man being dragged from the hold by the Janissaries and shoved toward
the waiting rows of corsairs. Sailors and Janissaries alike began to clap
and stomp their feet. He watched carefully as the feeble fellow stumbled
forward. His head was bowed, low. He was bound at the wrists. His fine
doublet was ripped; his shirt hung outside of his breeches and he was
barefoot. Christopher thought him to be vaguely familiar.

Yusef Rais appeared by Christopher's side. "So, I formally welcome tha aboard my *Lebetine*," he said. "She is my lover, my seductive
beauty, my silky siren. See that you respect her."

Ignoring the captain, Christopher kept his eyes fixed on the old
man.

Yusef gulped lemon water from a leather canteen, then whispered into Christopher's ear. "Tha knows him."

Christopher looked harder as the old man stumbled to his knees,
begging. A marine hoisted him to his feet before slapping him across

his face. He suddenly recognized his hooked nose. "Carrew?" He turned his face to Yusef. "But how…"

Yusef Rais tossed his hair over a shoulder. "Watch him run the gauntlet." The captain wiped a hand through his beard and laughed. "'Tis how we lay claim to our rightful share of the spoils."

The soldiers dragged Carrew to the front of the double line where the pitiful man scanned the many shades of faces jeering at him. The laughing corsairs were bearded; most were under turbans. Behind them stood the moustached Janissaries wearing their distinctive *börks*—upright, banded hats with trailing sleeves.

A soldier's flat hand shoved Carrew forward. Carrew took a first step and then a second. A wash of pity came over Christopher. "Go quickly, Mister Carrew!" he shouted.

The old man teetered, faint with fear. Rough hands pulled him upright and pushed him into the taunting corridor. The first corsairs struck him hard, the next harder still. He stumbled ahead. His wigless, bald head was slapped furiously. He was knocked to the deck where he lay for a moment gaping helplessly at the long line of bare feet stomping wildly atop the boards.

Christopher cried to him again, urging him to stand and hurry through. Carrew was jerked to his feet and thrown forward. Pleading for mercy, he ricocheted from side to side as sea-callused hands punched, pinched and pounded upon him. Poor Carrew finally lunged through the opening of his tunnel of fists and collapsed, badly bloodied and weeping. He was hauled away to a far corner where two corsairs tied him with a rope to the first rung of a ratline just above the gunwale.

Christopher whipped his head toward the ship's captain. "I am a Clive, Crumb." The words sounded suddenly pathetic to him.

The captain roared and ordered a sailor to unshackle Christopher. "Exactly, Mister Clive! And for that cause you are to be spared."

Christopher was confused. "I...I am glad you've a bit of sense."

This prompted another round of laughter from the captain. "I've not been to Oxford but I do know of irony, Mister Clive. Soon enough tha shall see it up close." Yusef then ordered two hands to drag Christopher to the ornate poop deck that overlooked the ship's waist from the stern. "For now, tha may keep watch on thy lessers from above."

Christopher was dragged up a short flight of steps to a hand-carved rail supporting the six culverins facing the main deck. His ankle was tethered to a heavy iron chain. Once he was secured, the commanding officer of the Janissaries approached him for the first time.

The Janissary colonel was a huge, broad-shouldered Albanian of middling years with a face disfigured by two vertical scars that dropped from beneath each of his wide-set, brown eyes. He was draped in three colourful layers of ankle-length cotton robes, the outer being blue. His baggy satin breeches were stuffed inside knee-high, yellow leather boots. A sword hung from a black sash, and atop his head sat an ornate börk boasting a tall plume at his forehead. With a wave of his hand he dismissed the other men.

"I am Konstantin-*oğlu* Kasim *Çorbasi*," the giant said in an echo-ing, deep-throated voice. His English was nearly perfect. "I am the colonel of the 27th Battalion of the Janissary Corps. You may call me either 'Colonel Kasim or Kasim Çorbasi.'" He wiped a finger along his thick black moustache.

Christopher eyed the officer warily. Kasim's dark, dead-dull eyes frightened him; his emotionless voice sounded otherworldly. Everything about him was enormous, including his head, and yet he had a quality that blunted his otherwise fearful presence. "And I am——"

"I know who you are. You are the property of the Sultan, no more and no less. I am given charge over thee and thou shalt obey without question or hesitation." The towering Kasim circled his captive in long, measured strides. "Our spies tell us that you speak Turkish."

His tone was exacting but restrained by a hint of reserve, leaving Christopher to imagine that he could have been a professor in another time or place—perhaps of mathematics or another science. "*Evet...* Yes."

The officer studied Christopher. "Good, but I shall ensure I make myself perfectly clear to thee."

Christopher winced.

"You were spared the gauntlet because neither the ship's master nor his men have any claim on thee, not even their usual percentages."

"I do not understand."

"You have no need of understanding."

"But you said..."

CHAPTER 14

As SUDDENLY AS he had appeared, Colonel Kasim walked calmly away leaving Christopher bewildered until noise from the main deck drew his attention. The wretches of Skeefe were now being dragged to amidships from below to face the gauntlet. He strained to find Raven amongst them. *O Christ, don't let them hurt her.*

Christopher groaned as each poor soul emerged into the blinding light. By his father's last count, the village was home to fourteen married couples, forty-four children under twelve, three elderly widows, one old widower, and a dozen unmarried youths. He doubted that any had escaped, unless the Muslims had butchered the elderly on the beach.

Christopher closed his fists as the men of Skeefe were sent through the gauntlet first. They were handled roughly, like Carrew. Some collapsed at once, only to be savagely kicked. He watched Paddy O'Sullivan cover his head and bounce forward from side to side like a bloodied drunk staggering through a tight alleyway.

The women and children were next.

Christopher held his breath, but to his surprise the little ones were barely touched, and if so, their heads were lightly caressed. Some were even given small gifts like brass buttons or biscuits dipped in molasses. Their cowering mothers were treated with equal gentleness. He was baffled.

Then Raven emerged from the hold with four other virgins.

"Raven!" Christopher choked.

The eighteen-year old lifted her face with one arm shielding her eyes from the sun. Her hair was knotted. Her clothing was filthy with the ship's mould.

"O Raven…" Christopher nearly wept. He could see how she was struggling to be brave.

Spotting Christopher's yellow head under sunlight, Raven raised a hand and hailed him, bravely. "Kipper…not to worry!"

"Not to worry?" Christopher's eyes filled. He struggled to answer. "I…I am here with thee!" His impotent bravado earned him more than a few mocks from the crew.

"And I'm here with ya!" Raven cried defiantly.

Christopher could not answer.

A voice surprised him from one side. "*Sen Türk konuşuyoruz?*"

Christopher spun about to gawk at a sun-bronzed soldier nearly as large as the colonel. "*Evet,*" Christopher answered, warily. "I do speak Turkish."

The soldier handed Christopher a wet rag to wipe dried blood from his head. "Do not fear. She is safe."

Christopher stared up into the soldier's face. He thought him to be about five years older than himself.

"Rape of the Sultan's property is not permitted once they set foot on the ship."

Christopher returned his eyes to Raven now passing nervously through the line. Like the soldier said, she was not being assaulted. Instead, the men were touching her with light, even reverent fingers. He waved to her as she cast him a hasty glance before disappearing into a huddle of others gathered tightly against the bulwark.

Relieved, Christopher scrubbed the side of his head, gingerly. "What is your name?"

"I am Mohammed-oğlu Taras, a *yoldaş*—what your army might call an aid—to Kasim Çorbasi."

"So, Mohammed—"

"No. If you speak Turkish you should know it is the father's name that is first. I am Taras, chosen son of the Prophet Mohammed, may he be blessed by Allah."

Christopher studied Taras more carefully. His Turkish was heavily accented and he did not look like either a Turk or a Moor. Instead, he had a large head with wide-set eyes slanted subtly to belie a hint of Hun. He had a strong, broad-bridged nose and a dark moustache. Like the other Janissaries, he wore a sleeveless crimson robe over a white linen shirt; his baggy blue pants were stuffed into high red boots. "You are dressed like a Turk, but you don't look like a son of a Mohammed," said Christopher.

"I was taken from my village by drovers for the Khan when I was eight years old."

"So you were part of the Mohammedans' tax of Christian boys?"

"The father who feeds us...the Sultan...is in perpetual need of recruits for *jihad*."

"They forced you to turn Turk."

"As the Prophet...*salAllahu allehi was salam*...says, the seeds of Islam are in all men."

Christopher noticed the deep melancholy that occupied the young soldier's brown eyes. His words were somewhat stoic and yet personable. "Where was your village?"

"Between the Boh River and the Dniester."

Christopher thought for a moment. "In Ukraine? You are Ukrainian."

"I am a Ukrainian Cossack."

"I studied your people at university. 'Cossack' means 'free man.'"

"Allah has willed me to be what I am today."

"What of your family?"

"I do not know. The Cossacks now fight with the Poles, the Khan raids from the south, and the Russians attack from the east. Perhaps they fled north to Podylla."

"Do you remember your parents?"

Taras lifted his eyes beyond the rails of the ship. "When the drovers came and chose me for Allah's army, my father…being ignorant of this honour…resisted. They cut him open. I still see his eyes rolling back."

Christopher paused. "And your mother?"

"I see her in my dreams."

Christopher waited.

Taras looked to the sea. "She was wise and merciful. She would not step on a bee."

"Brothers? Sisters?"

"You ask too many questions. Enough."

Christopher nodded. "Just one more: What will they do to us next?"

"The scribes count you, check your teeth and squeeze your limbs. They estimate your value and write it all down for the pasha's men in Algiers."

Christopher surveyed the cowering Irish on the deck, hoping to spot Raven. "I swear that I will see to it that you are spared when the Navy hangs the others."

Taras pointed toward the ship's bow. "You should look there."

Christopher followed Taras' finger toward a burly corsair dragging a bare-footed, wobbling figure in a purple doublet from the small hatch of the ship's low forecastle. The figure's head was hidden in a sack and his wrists were bound in front of him. The corsair delivered him to Yusef Rais at the centre of the main deck. By his side were Kasim and Sergeant Zeki.

"Who is the prisoner?"

Taras said nothing.

Two Janissaries hurried toward Christopher, unshackled him and dragged him off the poop deck with Taras following. They pushed him directly in front of the hooded gentleman now cursing at the ship's captain.

"Grandfather?" Christopher was stunned.

Yusef Rais yanked off the man's hood and Sir Redmond Clive stood blinking in the light. His head had been shaved, making him look all the madder. "By God, Crumb, I'll have the King cut thy throat with his own hand!"

"Look here, old man," said Yusef as he pointed at Christopher.

Squinting, Redmond ran his bloodshot eyes over his grandson. "What the devil are you doing on this ship? Where's thy hair, and by God where are thy bloody boots? An Englishman should always stand in his boots!"

"I—"

"Quiet, you fool. How did you let this happen?" Redmond turned to Colonel Kasim. "And you, you moustached miscreant, you puttock. The day soon comes when I shall watch thee and thy heathen Janissaries dispatched by the hangman."

Kasim stared calmly, but Yusef Rais was not amused. "Silence, idiot. For all thy bluster tha was easy for the takin."

Redmond cursed, then glared at Sergeant Zeki. The little man was a Turk with small eyes and a flat nose. "What are you smiling at, mouse? I'll step on thee like the ill-nurtured little malt-worm you are."

Yusef turned to Christopher. "Our spies told us that the baronet would be drunk at a tavern just two streets off the wharf with his crony, Carrew. So, we coaxed the pair of 'em to an alley with some slags, and soon enough they was under canvas in the belly of m'skiff." Pleased with himself, the renegade captain smiled.

Christopher bristled. "Ships are long under sail for us——"

"Aye, Crumb, Yusef…whatever thy cursed name be," said Redmond. "You heard my grandson. The Royal Navy has four ships-of-the-line in Kinsale…"

"Nay, old man. They've but two. And the Admiralty is more interested in Dutch troublemakers in the Channel than in thee."

"Lord De Courcey is my friend. He'll likely be on board himself."

"Enough." With a grunt from Yusef, two men took hold of old Clive and dragged him to the mainmast. "Me men tell me that tha swallowed coins when they snagged ye. Carrew tossed some up earlier."

A large Negro had already lugged a bucket of bilge water up from the hold. He forced his ladle against Redmond's lips. Yusef leaned close. "I suggest tha drink this willingly. Else this Blackamoor might just open up thy belly with a cutlass."

Redmond clamped his lips shut.

The captain shrugged and the black man jerked a short sword from his belt. With a deft motion he sliced through Redmond's doublet, shirt and undershirt, leaving a small gash in his belly.

"Now?" asked Yusef.

Redmond lowered his jaw slowly and the crewman poured bilge water into his mouth. Sputtering, Redmond swallowed, and after a few heaves of the ship he vomited all over the deck. Delighted, Yusef ordered his man to search for coins. Finding nothing, Yusef then said, "Pull off his breeches and tie 'im atop a half-barrel. More bilge down his gullet and he'll shite us a treasure soon enough."

Christopher protested his grandfather's humiliation, earning his rough return to the stern. He was dragged across the deck past bleating livestock and whimpering captives of Skeefe now being returned to the hold. He was then shackled to a heavy iron chain hanging from the aft rail where he was abandoned to his rising fears.

Frustrated, lad faced the sea where he searched desperately for English sails. He clenched his jaw and squeezed his fists. *When the Navy comes for us Raven...* A lone, grey shearwater swept freely by Christopher's eyes and soared into the clear sky beyond the full sails. He raised his face to watch her disappear, but in time his weary eyes settled on the ship's wake falling away from the trough cut by her keel. Remembering Reginald Burroughs' favourite philosopher, he muttered, "Scoop thanksgiving from the wake of this sea monster? Henry Curtis, you are the greatest fool that ever lived."

An urgency in Yusef Rais' voice caught Kipper's attention. He cupped his ear and discerned the captain's primary interest now to be in hurrying. *He's worried. We've ships coming!* Limbs quickly filling with life, Christopher strained his eyes against the horizon in search of sails swelling toward them. *Where? Crumb must have spotted something.* He then looked to ship's masts. Though he was no sailor, he could plainly see that the jib was slacking and its slanted yard could now easily pivot too far, causing the ship to flounder. His heart began to race.

Yusef Rais had seen the same and he was shoving his way to amid-ships where men were now scrambling into the rigging. Shouting at his crew, the captain joined their hands on the thick lines of the jib now slapping against their stays. Urging his robust corsairs to a few lusty heaves, Yusef and his men deftly cut the jib. In moments the huge sail swelled with air. The ship's hull creaked as the *Lebetine* stirred the sea beneath. Others quickly trimmed the mizzen and the large mainsail. The field of canvas snapped taut in the morning's fresh breeze and the ship groaned forward. In moments she cut the waves like the Barbary shark she was.

Disappointed but not disheartened, Christopher slapped the rail and studied the sea. On the boards behind him, skilful sailors were padding about barefooted, and as much as he loathed every Muslim under sail, he had little choice but to yield respect to the elegance of the surging vessel.

Hearing a series of commands, Christopher turned to watch. He correctly surmised that this *xebec*-styled ship had been refitted from an oared galley to a three-winged sailing ship in order to make her more lethal within the dangerous waters of Christendom. Her hull was sleek; her mizzen raked slightly back; her foremast raked a bit forward. Her boasting sails were adorned with red stripes over white canvas. She had a shallow freeboard measured from a low-slung waist that was belted by short bulwarks. Indeed, she was properly fitted to slice the sea.

Now harnessing a strong east wind, the sleek xebec leaned hard to starboard as Christopher searched for oncoming sails. It was then that the sounds of English caught his attention. Previously unseen captives were being dragged from the hold and chained to various timbers along the deck. By their dress and accents he guessed they were gentlemen. "Who are these?"

"Others," answered a passing sailor.

Christopher then shouted to a man just shackled nearby. "You there, who are you?"

"Thomas Roe." His haunted eyes were yellowed.

"Did they take you by ship or land?"

"From the *Ebenezer* in the Channel off Newquay."

"When?"

"Methinks a fortnight past or so." He lifted his face, sallow with hunger and pale with fear.

"And thy family?"

"A wife, down below."

"Do you see her?"

"The women and children change places with us twice a day, between the watches."

"How many of ye are there?"

"Maybe fifty. Some were killed for making noise near Kinsale." His voice trailed away. "When they raided the Irish village we were chained far to stern to make room for ye."

Christopher's blood rose. "I want to see them all hanged!"

Thomas pointed to a wretch chained in Turkish clothes. "He was the master of the *Hawthorne*. He also surrendered his ship without a fight but the heathens raped all the women on his deck and buggered some of the boys—"

"Enough, Thomas. Help is coming, I swear it. I was taken with the Irish off land, but my servant alerted James Fort."

Thomas stared at Christopher with sudden hope filling his narrow face. His long chin began to tremble. "Thanks be to God. What is thy name?"

"Christopher Clive."

"Well, Mister Christopher Clive, I would gladly shake thy hand if I could reach it."

CHAPTER 15

JUST AFTER THE pre-dawn prayers of the following day, the male captives emerged aboards as a flinching column of rags. By seven bells some were unshackled to help the crew scrub the deck of manure, draw water, tend the livestock or coil rope. Eventually, each was given his daily ration of putrid water, a meagre bit of bread, and a spoon of vinegar-soaked rice.

Oddly, Christopher was never sent to tasks. He was simply shuffled between the poop and the tiny forecastle at the quartermaster's whim. And when the men were rotated with the women and children as Thomas Roe had said, he was kept in place.

Watching the women climb out of the hatch, Christopher strained to catch the slightest glimpse of Raven. He studied every slouching figure stepping aboards until he finally exclaimed, "There!"

Christopher gripped the rail of the poop deck and watched Raven inch forward with others to receive her ration of food and water. Hers was a smaller version of a man's ration, but she was then pointed to Janissaries' kettles where she scraped leftover boiled bulger paste.

Dare he cry her name?

Christopher's heart raced.

Raven then glanced upward, licking her wooden spoon dry and searching the raised stern. Unable to contain himself, he cried out, "Raven!"

She stood still as a forest doe.

Kipper waved his arms and shouted. "All is not lost. Tattie raised the alarm—a ship-of-the-line is coming!" A thump on his head knocked Christopher to the deck.

"You are not permitted to speak with her or even to look at her!" Christopher gaped at Zeki.

"If this happens again I will have you both flogged. Taras, too. He is responsible for you."

Christopher's lip curled as he climbed to his feet. "I will enjoy watching you hang, you little mouse."

Zeki clutched Christopher's throat and pulled his face close to his own. "If you were not the property of the Sultan, I would rip out your tongue."

Two days later, Christopher stared into the dawn's fog and waited for the sun to clear his view. *Headwinds. Good.* He thought. *The Navy must be closing.* A corsair spun him around and stuffed a piece of vinegar bread into his mouth. Puckered, he chewed the bread slowly and studied the pirate. *The beast is afraid of something.* A flutter of excitement stirred him.

Eyes fixed on the fog, the pirate handed Christopher a clay bowl of stale water.

"What are you looking for?" asked Christopher.

The black-eyed Moor grumbled. "The night watch thought they heard the monster."

Christopher glanced into the fog. "What monster?"

"The Sarathan—the sea serpent. I have seen it twice. It is an evil *jinn* that seeks to turn us upside down."

Christopher stared into the fog again. *Leviathan.* He spat.

Setting his jaw, the pirate said, "Open your mouth."

Christopher obeyed and was surprised by a delightful fig. He chewed it, slowly.

"The Turks want you in good health."

Christopher paused to wonder about that, then supposed it made good sense for them to treat him well so as to not risk the loss of a generous ransom. He had already calculated what he assumed the heathens had calculated: A prize like himself should be worth upwards of £5,000. *Grandfather would approve a high sum*, he thought. *He could simply affix his name to a letter and that would be that.*

The Moor left Christopher alone at the rail where he spent the next hours gazing into the clearing air. A breeze from the northwest then filled the sails. Christopher cursed. The ship began to cut the water smoothly. He lowered his head. He knew that every passing league made rescue all the more unlikely.

⊰⊱

For the next ten days, Christopher remained at the stern rail where he watched Yusef Rais deftly pilot the *Lebetine* toward the narrow straights of Gibraltar lying some 700 nautical miles from Skeefe. Though other captives waited like hungry dogs along the gunwale to beg leftovers from the crew, Christopher, Redmond Clive and the ever-quaking Carrew were regularly served wheat biscuits, olives, rice, dried figs and even a rare dish of meat cooked *a la Turkeska* in the captain's quarters.

They want to secure our favour because they fear the Navy, thought Christopher one evening. He smiled and took a second helping of roasted goat. However, his confidence was abruptly shaken by what happened as they passed near the mighty Gibraltar.

"Tha, tha, and tha," grunted Yusef. "Get to amidships."

Puzzled, Christopher followed his grandfather and Carrew to the main mast where the captain presented the threesome with bundles of new clothing.

"What the devil is this?" groused Redmond.

"This, old man, is who tha now be," said Yusef. He pointed the clothing.

"Nay." Redmond Clive folded his arms. "I shall not be dressing *a la Turk*. Lord Sandwich is planning to cannonade thy heathen city. That means we have ships a'plenty about this sea keeping watch and making ready…"

Wentworth Carrew blurted, "You see what they are doing, Redmond? They are stealing who we are. First they feed us that Turkish shite to steal our souls from the inside. Now we've these clothes for the outside!"

"Mister Carrew, I think you go too far," said Christopher.

Sir Redmond bristled. "They mean to humble us, boy. But by God when the Navy comes…"

Yusef pulled a sheathed dagger from within his shirt. "I've had enough of thee, Sir Redmond Clive. Either put on tha new clothes… with the turban…else I circumcise thee here and now."

Carrew hurried to dress. Defeated, Redmond Clive donned his new baggy pants, embroidered waistcoat and then pulled a fine silk turban atop his shorn head.

Yusef turned to Christopher and let him see the dagger. "Thy gift from Aunt Comfort."

Christopher stared at his dagger in disbelief. "How do you know that? How do you know her!"

Yusef smiled. "I told thee, we've spies." He tossed the decorative dagger to a sailor with orders to give it to the Janissary colonel. "'Tis property of the Sultan now, like thee. Now get dressed."

⚜

In all these days, Raven endured with few complaints. She thought constantly of Kipper Clive. *Is he well? What will they do to him? Can he save us?* She also feared for those around her. Two had died, several of the children were sick. They were all hungry, thirsty, and lice-ridden. The hold was a hell of damp stench and scurrying rats.

Needing something to distract herself, Raven enjoined the other women huddled around the single lantern now permitted for the Irish in the hold. There she participated in the familiar gossip of Millicent Clive's wardrobe, Redmond's debauchery and Spencer's quiet suffering. She found the triteness of it all to be comforting.

On one afternoon something then happened to bring a smile to her lips and to all the others, save one. Raven's mother had caught the attention of an aging Moor. That day the corsair made a sudden point to grin at Doon as he passed close to fill the lantern with oil.

Doon did not think this to be pleasant attention. "Don't be lookin at me like tat!" she yelled. In truth, Doon was repulsed by the man but her fire only fuelled his passion and so he soon became a constant presence in the shadows of the hold.

"He be in love wid ya," teased Raven a few days following.

"Don't speak of it," said Doon. "The idea disgusts me." She had been through more terror in her life than many, but when she thought of this man's attentions she cringed.

"So, maybe he'll ask yer hand from the captain," said Raven.

"Not anot'er word of it!"

Raven laughed, and when she laughed felt less afraid. "Fine, not anot'er word." She snuggled against her mother, tittering until she fell quiet with her ear upon her mother's breast. It was then she heard Doon wheeze. Raven sat upright. "Ma? Are ya not feelin well?"

"I'm fine, considerin."

Alarmed, Raven studied her mother in the faint light. She had not before noticed the dark circles forming beneath her eyes. "Yer fine?"

Doon nodded, bravely.

Raven looked about the hold at the slumped silhouettes and ran her hand along Doon's arm. "Well, I suppose ya do look fine to me." She forced a smile.

Doon took Raven's hand and squeezed it, lightly. "And you are lovely."

Raven bit her lip. She swallowed against the lump quickly filling her throat. "So, what do ya tink will happen to us, anyways?"

Doon cupped Raven's face in her hands. "Pray to Mary, my dear gerl, for I doubt the English ships are comin." She pulled Raven close against her. "I do not know what comes fer us, but I doubt it is good. No matter what, my love will ne'er fail ya, nor will the Holy Virgin's." Doon kissed Raven's cheek. "And ya must remember tiss as well: a man can force his way upon ya, but he cannot take *who ya be* unless ya let him."

"But—"

"Listen to me, daughter. Yer a special spirit." Doon stroked Raven's hair. "I knows it, Gaia knows it, and Comfort Clive knows it. Yer blessed cove lies within ya…it *is* ya. Bear its beauty against the world and ya'll be no man's slave."

⁂

Feeding the goats amidships, Raven paused to stare into the mid-morning sky. Twenty-nine days had passed since the raid—twenty-nine days aboard a heaving ship racing toward the mysteries of another world. A goat butted her leg and she could only laugh to herself as she looked into its horizontal pupils. "I know. Sorry."

She lay several laps of hay into a trough, then leaned her head against the mizzen mast pretending she was lying next to Kipper upon a sea-sprayed boulder. She closed her eyes and imagined the squeaks of wind-strained rope to be sea birds in her sky. She wiggled her toes and pretended to lift a Joy Stone to her hand. She kissed the imaginary stone and threw it overboard. But when she opened her eyes she felt a fool.

A Janissary was just yards away mimicking her and laughing. Anger suddenly welled within her. Her cheeks heated with a rush of blood. "Damn them!" she murmured. *This is the same sea that rolls into MY cove.* Tears came to her eyes. She stepped to the rail and squeezed it, hard.

The soldier walked past and touched her rump, whispering wicked words into her ear. She stiffened. His touch planted terror within her and terror drove her anger aside. *What is coming? What is going to happen?* Stories had been told in the hold, terrible stories of exactly what happens to Christian women in the clutches of Muslims. Raven began to tremble. She looked desperately for a glimpse of Christopher. Three women of the doomed *Hawthorne* had shared their horrid details. Others told of the children who had been violated in the evillest ways. *Sodomites, demons...*

A cold creep weakened Raven's limbs. Her breathing became short and rapid. She felt faint. Falling to one knee she prayed to the Virgin. "Save us! Save us! Oh, can ya not hear me?"

She opened her eyes to see a huge shadow cast across her. She turned and looked upward to see Taras—the Ukrainian Janissary—standing over her.

Taras offered his hand. "Raven."

Surprised, Raven looked up into his broad face. She thought he had a ferocious kindness about him. She stared at his huge hand for a moment, then took it, lightly. Feeling like a little girl in the grasp of a giant, she stood. "Tank ya, sir," she said with a shy tone.

Taras smiled and nodded. He handed her his canteen filled with fresh lemon water.

Raven gulped nearly half of the water. Embarrassed, she offered an awkward curtsy in thanks.

Taras smiled again.

By the saints above, why did I curtsy? Do their women curtsy?

The Ukrainian turned and walked away. Raven's eyes followed after him until a sudden heave of the *Lebetine* nearly tipped her over. She grabbed hold of the railing with one hand, and then looked across the deck at the hard faces of other women. Raven groaned. *They must think I do him favours.*

A loud curse turned her head. A few paces away a swarthy, heavy-limbed corsair was shoving another sailor. Raven held her breath.

The quarrel quickly turned to deadly earnest and Raven hurried from harm's way. Her eyes swung from one man to the other, and then to the gathering circle of men cheering for one or the other. The pair sliced and thrust their blades, each drawing blood from the other until a final, savage swipe of a blade ended the contest. The victor straddled his victim and raised his blood-smeared weapon to the sun, shouting in triumph.

Sickened, Raven turned away and faced the sea. It was then that Wisdom spoke a truth to her from some deep recess: 'Neither man would yield because neither man *could* yield.' She stared at the dead man being dumped overboard. *Comfort was right; there are many ways to be a slave.*

CHAPTER 16

CHRISTOPHER STARED OVER the larboard rail as the *Lebetine* ploughed through the Strait of Gibraltar and toward the open waters of the Mediterranean. He fixed his eyes on the distant town of Tarifa in Christian Spain, stubbornly hoping that help would yet come.

"Stop fretting about it."

Christopher turned to see his grandfather standing in his Turkish slippers and turban, gripping the gunwale. "You still believe they are coming?"

"Of course."

Christopher was no longer as certain. He looked up at the green Algerian flag snapping in the wind. "The captain assumes he's in friendly waters now."

"Crumb is an arse. And you need to shave."

Christopher lifted his fingers to the patchy new beard that had sprouted on his face. He squinted his eyes toward the west. *Maybe they're following until we are through the straits? And what if Lord Sandwich really is planning an attack? That would mean our ships may be ahead...*

Rescue had been all Christopher had to hold on to for these terrible weeks, that and his sightings of Raven. But standing on the *Lebetine* under a turban and eating meats a la Turkeska had him disoriented. *If not rescue, what?* Christopher tried to swallow. Ignoring his grumbling grandfather, Christopher then faced starboard and scanned the distant horizon searching for hope. Instead, the ragged edges of Morocco's mountains mocked him.

He took a deep breath.

He could only imagine Barbary according to the terrible tales he had been told. And so his mind flew him to chaotic bazaars of wild colours, to the faces of strange peoples, to camels, deserts, minarets and slavers. His breath quickened and he hastily returned his eyes to the fading silhouette of Christian Spain.

⁂

An hour later, Yusef Rais found Christopher still staring at the horizon. "So, Gibraltar is behind and we are sailing happily in our dear lake." He laughed. "Come. We've some business with the çorbasi, tha grandfather and Carrew."

Curious and hopeful, Christopher shuffled behind the ship's captain to amidships where the Janissary colonel was waiting with a grinning Sergeant Zeki and a score of the ship's crew. Redmond Clive and Carrew were standing awkwardly by the main mast.

Yusef whistled and a hatch from the lower deck creaked opened. A few hands reached into the shadows of the companionway and pulled a cowering slip of a woman into the bright of day.

"Raven!" Christopher pressed past his grandfather to watch her emerge on deck, filthy and terrified. His throat suddenly filled. He waved his arms for her to find him. "Raven!" he cried. His belly churned as she shielded her eyes from the sun with her arm. "Here!"

Spotting him, Raven lowered her arm and clutched her hands to her heart.

Yusef waved her forward and in a moment Kipper Clive stood within two paces of his dear Raven. He fixed his eyes on hers as she lost herself in his. The wind tossed her black hair off her face. He wanted to embrace her. "Oh Raven, my Raven——"

"Silence!" Zeki rammed him in the belly with his baton.

With Christopher folded in two and gasping, the captain turned to Sir Redmond. "Tha grandson is taken with this girl who I think should fetch about $300 Spanish even though she is too thin. She'll be a pretty prize when she's had a rosewater bath and fattened. The buyers will have a good time poking her about in the booths——"

"Enough, Crumb!" shouted Christopher. The outburst cost him another baton in the belly. He fell to the boards.

"Dost tha see, Sir Clive? Tha grandson is in love."

"He is a fool."

"Methinks he'd be very happy if tha had a way to rescue her."

Christopher recovered his breath as a light spray of sea water drizzled over the rail.

"Colonel Kasim and I agreed that if tha…the great Sir Redmond Clive…would sign a pledge to ransom the whole of this Irish lot, we'll guarantee their safety in the *bagnio* until thy agents deliver thy gold to us."

Christopher answered. "Of course he shall pledge…"

"Why should I?" Redmond's veined eyes glared.

Christopher gawked. "Because you can."

"Firstly, they belong to thy father, not to me…"

"They do not *belong* to anyone. You are not *selling* them; you are ransoming them!" Astonished, Christopher turned to Yusef. "How much?"

"The price is 15,000 Spanish dollars."

"Grandfather?" Christopher squared himself, scowling. "By the love of Christ, they are God's children…You must believe that." He steadied himself as the *Lebetine* lifted.

The old man scoffed. "They are Irish." Redmond's nostrils flared. "Forget them. Do you not see what these heathens are doing here? They are testing me...us." He pointed vaguely to the west. "Captain Crumb knows that a ship-of-the-line is trailing us through the straits. This 'offer' is intended to earn favour for him when he is captured. In the meanwhile, he wants to humiliate our family by making us beg for the Irish—"

Yusef interrupted. "So, young Mister Clive, it seems the baronet has said 'nay.' Now, let me ask this: If *tha* were the baronet?"

Christopher raised his chin and glared defiantly at his grandfather. "I would sign the pledge on my knees."

Redmond cursed but Yusef smiled. "So, tha hast finally abandoned rescue?"

"Do you see?" barked Redmond. "Do you see how they toy with us? And you jumped into their little game like a brainless toady."

Christopher grit his teeth. "Nay, Crumb. I have not abandoned rescue. But I would sign the pledge and then pin it to thy lips when the Royal Navy hangs thee!" He turned to his grandfather. "And by the saints, sir, what harm would it be to sign such a thing?"

"Christ, boy, I shall never bow to this heathen."

"Bow? Look at you in thy turban."

Yusef laughed. "Now, young sir. As I said, if tha were the baronet—"

"But I am not."

Colonel Kasim took command. "According to our spies, thy grandfather's lawyers have already made thee heir. So if I give thee a pistol you could make thyself the baronet with one shot to his head."

Christopher stared at the stone-faced officer and then at his grumbling grandfather.

Kasim nodded to Sergeant Zeki who pulled a pistol from his sash, cocked it, and handed it to Christopher.

Suddenly confused, Christopher caught Taras' wide eyes watching from a few paces away. He answered the officer in Turkish. "To be clear, Colonel Kasim, you give me permission to kill my grandfather and thus make it possible to ransom the Irish by my own hand?" He spread his feet to steady himself on the deck.

Kasim nodded, dispassionately.

Christopher's mind now whirled. *What is this game?* "But, sir, the Sultan would forfeit a great fortune. My grandfather would fetch a high ransom."

Kasim's hard face darkened beneath his lowering black eyebrows. "What ransom?"

"We both know he is worth $5000 Spanish, maybe more… Killing him would be a great loss…"

Kasim put his huge hand on Christopher's shoulder and squeezed. "Do you remember the name Ibrahim Bakan Effendi?" he asked in English.

Christopher turned white. Nodding, he looked nervously at his suddenly surprised grandfather.

"And do you remember what he said?"

He stiffened. "Aye."

Kasim brushed his black moustache with a sudden air of supremacy. "Bakan said, 'Throughout the Levant the name Clive is forever accursed.'" He bent low. "Hear me well, young Mister Clive. The Sultan shall not be ransoming the baronet. Quite the contrary, he wishes Sir Redmond to die a memorable death, one that cheating infidels shall talk about in their taverns for all time."

Speechless, Christopher looked at the expressionless face of his grandfather.

"So you see," said Kasim. "I am offering thee one chance to rescue the girl you love…and the whole dirty bunch of the other Irish. Otherwise, I think you already know what shall happen."

Christopher stared at his Raven. Her head was bowed; her eyes were fixed on her bare feet. He wanted to vomit.

Kasim tossed his head and an aging Moor stepped forward. "And there is this," he said. "Meet Zuhayr. He hails from an oasis in the M'zab desert. Some say he was born on a rock so that is why his head is flat on one side; others say he was kicked by a camel."

Christopher stared blankly at Zuhayr. The pirate was a toothless Berber with a tangled beard and braided grey hair that hung long from beneath a yellow turban. Smiling, Zuhayr crossed his arms.

Kasim continued. "This man has offered to buy Raven and her mother from the Sultan for $700 Spanish. He says 'the young one for his bed, the hairy one for his garden,' unless you choose to save them."

Raven started to weep and Christopher reached a hand toward her. Yusef Rais slapped his arm away and put a knife under his chin. "Tha has a way to save 'em all, Mister Clive. But until tha do, they'll be no touching the Sultan's property."

Christopher studied at the cocked pistol in his hand and glared at Yusef. *I'd like to put a lead ball between your eyes.* Kasim might be bluffing about Zuhayr, but Raven in the slave market? No!

A picture of the Irish children aboard then flashed in his mind's eye and he groaned aloud. He had heard the stories of the horrors they would likely face, horrors that others from the *Hawthorne* had already experienced. *Can I save them all?*

Christopher turned his back on everyone and took four long strides to the rail where he faced the sea. He breathed deeply of salt air and watched blue water roll gently beneath him. The sun was warm; the air was fresh, but he barely noticed. Eyes fixed on the sea, he hefted the pistol in his hand. The monstrous temptation felt powerfully heavy. *Or I could kill Yusef, maybe Kasim...*

Christopher's breathing quickened. *But to what end?* He strained to find an English flag among the dozens of ships dotting the straits like tiny puffed pillows. *The Navy must have sent help.*

The poor youth's mind wrestled against his heart. *If I shoot Grandfather and rescue comes, then I would have murdered him for naught. If I decline and no rescue comes, Raven shall suffer such terrible—*

"Mister Clive?" Kasim summoned Christopher off the rail. "What say thee?"

Grimacing, Christopher returned slowly to the circle. He gawked at his grandfather who was mumbling something incoherent about the Irish and heathens. "All you have to do is agree to the bloody ransom!" Christopher roared at him.

Redmond blinked a few times. "Never. I shall never cower to these barbarians. I swear this by God and King, and if you—"

"Stop talking, sir," said Christopher. "You are a fool. Did you not hear him? He is *not* going to ransom you. You shall die for cheating the Sultan."

Redmond stared.

"If I kill thee I can save them all!" Christopher was frantic.

"You wouldn't dare."

Exasperated, Christopher stared at his grandfather incredulously. "Why not? You are going to die anyway." He then surprised himself by abruptly pointing the pistol at his grandfather's forehead. "And I suspect you shall die a very cruel death. Why can y'not just sign the damned pledge? I beg thee, sir, push thy pride aside for once in thy life and find some Christian charity!"

Redmond said nothing for a long moment.

Christopher pressed the barrel hard against his grandfather's skull. He watched Redmond's eyes widen and then slant toward the Janissaries now gathering close.

"Nay. They shall not kill me. I am worth a great deal of money. It would be a foolish thing to do. Now lower thy pistol."

Nearly burst, Christopher bent Redmond's head back with the barrel. "What? You are worth *nothing* to the Sultan. Do you not understand this?"

Now sweating, Redmond answered. "The Sultan cannot afford to order my death—"

"Shut thy stupid mouth!" Christopher grit his teeth. His hand began to shake. "Which is it? You say they are barbarians and yet you expect them to think like you think. They shall roast thee alive, or splay thee, or sever thy head, or..."

"Enough." Redmond hissed. "Hear me, boy. You shall not be pulling that trigger and I shall not be signing a pledge for these Irish. That is the end of it."

"Why must you force my hand this way?" Mad with anguish, Christopher swung his head to Raven. His mind again filled with stories of rapine and violation. He returned his face to his haughty grandfather now puffing his chest like a banty rooster. He took a breath and rose on his toes. He clenched his jaw and squeezed his hand around the pistol.

He felt his grandfather's eyes condemning him.

His trigger finger tensed.

Then Raven suddenly cried out. "Know who ya are, Kipper, then do what ya must do."

Christopher whipped his head toward the soft-eyed girl. *What?* He lost himself for a moment. *What? Know who I am? Who am I?* He was no longer certain. He rolled Raven's words over and over in his mind. Struggling, he returned his face to his grandfather's and suddenly remembered something Raven had once said in the cove. *Man of hope. She called me a 'man of hope.'*

His jaw pulsed.

He trembled.

It was enough. Christopher lowered his hand, slowly. He stared at the pistol and returned it to Colonel Kasim, grip forward. "I decline, sir." He looked at Raven.

"Fool," said Redmond. "Clay-brained fool. You could have taken Crumb hostage. Now we are still in this pickle." Christopher turned his back on the baronet as the old man groused after him. "You think I should be grateful to thee? Blah. I expected so much more."

Not answering, Christopher abandoned his grandfather and watched his beloved Raven dragged back to the hold.

"Ya did well, Kipper Clive," said Raven over her shoulder.

Christopher thought her voice sounded suddenly weak. He tried to call after her but he could not speak.

CHAPTER 17

—·❈·—

IMMEDIATELY FOLLOWING CHRISTOPHER'S decision, Kasim Çorbasi ordered two stout Janissaries to strip Redmond to the waist. They then threw the cursing man's slippers aside and put his feet in a looped leather cord that was attached to the middle of a long staff. The men spun the staff so that Redmond's feet were pinched together by the loop. With a grunt, the soldiers then shouldered the staff and lifted the howling old man into the air upside down, leaving his neck and shoulders bent upon the boards.

Sergeant Zeki ordered another Janissary forward with a truncheon. On command, the soldier began to savagely beat the soles of the Redmond's feet. He screamed in agony.

"Harder," commanded Zeki.

Sir Redmond Clive begged for mercy.

"Only the beginning, old man," taunted Yusef from one side. "Tha grandson ought 'ave shot thee dead. Would have been better by far."

Redmond then fainted. He was dropped on the boards, hoisted by the armpits and dragged to the aft hold. Through it all, Christopher had protested bravely until a Spaniard-turned-Turk struck him across the face with a carpenter's mallet. Christopher fell over, nearly unconscious. Taras helped him to his feet and led him to the shade of the bulwark where he now sat.

Christopher touched his swelling face lightly. "I hope they all hang, Taras…every bloody one of them but you," he said in Turkish. "You are not one of them."

"You would do well to abandon hope, Mister Clive, for hope has abandoned you." The soldier pressed a wet cloth against Christopher's bleeding cheek. "They will shackle you here soon enough. Be careful. You have seen but a hint of what is coming."

Christopher stared at Taras for a long moment. "Why are you kind to me?"

Taras plunged the cloth into his bucket and pressed it against Christopher's cheek again. "I am under orders to keep watch over you."

"Why?"

Taras stood. "You must simply submit to what is, Mister Clive."

✦

Taras stepped aside as another shackled Christopher by an ankle to a post. From his place at the stern, the anxious young man stared into the western horizon where he prayed for God's mercy and a fast English frigate. But as the sun eventually cast bright pinks from the edge of the western sea, and as the distant rise of Gibraltar failed from view, Christopher could only hang his head. His mind was now swimming in a swirl of doubts.

Had he chosen rightly? What if no rescue came?

What would become of Raven? Of any of them?

And submit to what?

Images of Raven haunted him. He closed his eyes to see her in the grasp of shirtless corsairs. *She does not understand what darkness is coming for her.* Hatred for his grandfather rose within him and he began to tap his fingers anxiously along the weathered rail. "He could have ransomed them all. He'll be dead anyway…it would have been my gold to give." Christopher grabbed hold of the smooth gunwale and squeezed it with all his might. "Christ above, where are you?"

Christopher remained chained to the rail all that night and all the day to follow, watching the routines of others like an invisible, powerless presence. And through the heat of the next days, Kipper Clive could do no more than doubt his decision, especially when his eyes met Raven's for those few precious moments each day.

Unable to save her, unable to soothe her, unable to do anything other than bewail her entrapment, Christopher slapped the ship's rail with furious force. 'Christ, where are you!' became his hourly lament.

Above, the sails remained full with wind. He thought their stretching canvas to be a mockery of his impotence. "I curse ye!" he shouted. "May ye shred to pieces." He clutched his temples at the sound of the sailors' pattering feet scampering across the boards to hurry them all to the dread-in-wait. "Why did I not shoot that old bastard?" *Hope? Hope is but wasted dreams.*

"Mister Clive?"

"Eh?" Christopher turned bleary eyes to one side where Taras was standing with a cup of fresh water, a biscuit and a lantern.

"You do not look well, Mister Clive. Do you have a fever?"

Christopher shook his head. Fourteen of the captives had died in the past week including Thomas Roe, three women from Skeefe and Scully Lynch—the metalsmith who had fashioned his dagger. He could still see their lifeless bodies dumped overboard like sacks of garbage.

"We will arrive in Algiers today."

Christopher said nothing for a long moment. "How long has it been since you stole us from our rightful homes?"

"Thirty-eight days."

Christopher grunted and turned away from Taras.

"You made the wrong decision. You should have shot your grandfather."

"Crumb and Kasim would have betrayed me, anyway."

"Kasim Çorbasi would have honoured his word. He is a good man." Taras then looked squarely at Christopher. "If you believed that Kasim was true, would you have shot your grandfather?"

Christopher dodged his eyes.

"I thought not." Taras studied him. "Nobody ransoms Irish. Like the Africans, they are doomed to the slavers. Everyone is wagering how much your Raven will bring at the market—"

"The Irish? That has nothing to do with it." Christopher drew salty air through his nose. "Why do you tell me this?"

"You must know the truth so that you are prepared."

"Truth?" Christopher stared, blankly. "And be prepared for what?"

"As a Clive you are yet to be punished."

A cold chill spread through Christopher. "I see. So the Sultan curses the Irish and me for the sins of my grandfather—"

"No. The Irish are simply captured infidels. But you are cursed by his deeds, to be sure."

Christopher rallied to feign courage. His mind raced as he stared into the sea. Finally turning again to Taras he said, "You must know that the Mohammedans are hypocrites. Their book says, 'No bearer of burdens shall bear the burden of another.' Yet the Sultan demands that I bear the burden of my grandfather's sin."

Taras shifted on his feet. "How do you know this?"

"I have studied their book."

"It is *my* Book, too." Taras wiped his moustache with uncharacteristic abruptness. "I will take this to the colonel."

⁙

Two hours later, Yusef Rais ordered Christopher to be shackled at the starboard rail of the forecastle's small deck. Once locked in place, the captain pointed his finger across the bow, beyond the shimmering sapphire water of the Mediterranean Sea and toward the southern horizon. "There, Mister Clive." Christopher obediently followed Yusef Rais' finger to see the hazy outline of North Africa's Barbary mountains. "Soon," said the captain.

Christopher did not answer. How could he continue to deny what lay before him? The weary lad closed his eyes, fearfully yielding to the offensive notion that rescue may not be coming after all. He stood erect in stony silence until the ship's captain left him alone. Then Kipper Clive lifted a frightened face to Heaven. "Was I a fool?"

In response, his ears filled with the sounds of straining canvas and groaning rope as the *Lebetine's* sails swelled in a fresh, morning breeze. From his tether at the bow, he felt the ship rise and fall sharply as the sea raced beneath her keel. He sat down upon the salt-washed boards and buried his face in his hands. "I should have shot him…"

Christopher squeezed his eyes closed and let his mind fly like a soaring bird over the headlands of County Cork, to his Aunt Comfort's parlour, to Giardín an Croí and above the thatched roofs of Skeefe until he landed lightly on the warm rocks of Raven's Cove. There he found comfort in wavelets and seals, in the yellows of Irish gorse and the purples of bell-heather. He tasted applejack on his tongue; his ears filled with the chatter of stonechats and he felt Joy

Stones in his fingers. If only he could take hold of all of it, of any of it. He thought of Raven singing at Twelfth Night.

If he could just seize something familiar to keep him sane in this terrible place.

If only.

And so Kipper sat there on the empty forecastle, undisturbed for two hours until a corsair in the rigging began to cry, happily. Christopher stirred and climbed to his feet. The men of the ship cheered in unison and rushed the starboard rail. Christopher followed their eyes toward a rocky headland rising ahead. His chest felt tight. *We are almost there. But what is waiting? Christ, save us.*

⊰⊱

The *Lebetine* splashed forward, ever forward and toward a collection of ships making way for a common destination. Christopher watched helplessly as Yusef Rais skilfully sailed his vessel toward his home. Ahead, many ships flew flags from Christendom and Islam, all bound to trade without a thought to the peril of the captives on board this xebec. He wanted to shout his name at a passing French ship.

But who would care?

Christopher turned to starboard and studied a heavy, two-masted bark under a Spanish flag ploughing toward the harbour. He then turned to port where a Portuguese merchantman heaved. Ahead two Dutch polacres made way; from behind sailed another European round ship, doubtlessly heavy-laden with goods.

In another hour the *Lebetine* carried Christopher around the Pointe of Pescade where the waters widened. The haggard young man gripped the rail and stared in sudden disbelief at the blue bay now opening before him. Its turquoise waters shimmered and carried his eyes toward a white, triangular city that dazzled upslope against emerald mountains. Gasping at the fearful beauty of it all, Kipper Clive suddenly imagined himself sailing toward New Jerusalem.

If only it were so.

Instead, what lay before him was the city of Algiers—the haughty diamond of Barbary. Walled on all sides, the city had dared Christendom for centuries. It was bejewelled with treasures claimed from scouring land and sea, and home to tens of thousands of European slaves. Christopher gaped at ring of fortresses the city boasted and most especially at the four-level citadel at the end of the breakwater. He groaned.

"The Fort of the Lamp," interrupted Taras.

Hollow-eyed, Christopher took in the forest of masts filling the harbour beneath the fort's watch. He scanned the ships and the white columns of the waterfront, and then the flat hill where another fortress guarded the left side of the bay.

Taras gave him a ladle of water.

Christopher held the ladle limply and surveyed the flat, terracotta roofs of the houses that climbed the mountains. "You think I should have shot my grandfather."

"Now I think you should drink," said Taras. He then pointed to the top of the summit. "That is the Kasbah. It overlooks the world. Now, eat this biscuit."

Christopher stuffed the vinegar-soaked biscuit in his mouth as he surveyed the numberless green patches of rooftop gardens.

Taras surveyed the landscape. "It is a beautiful city."

Christopher stopped chewing. He would not admit it but Taras had spoken truly. Algiers was splendid.

A volley of cannons from Fort of the Lamp startled Christopher. The air thumped and the crew cheered. This was followed by a ferocious retort from the *Lebetine's* batteries. The corsairs cheered again, reloaded, and fired again and then once more.

"We are celebrating a successful raid," said Taras. "This tells the whole city we have booty on board."

"We are not booty."

Taras pointed to the main deck where hatches from below were opening. "They bring the women and children out first. The men stay shackled until the ship is tied fast to the pilings and the rudder is disabled."

Christopher searched desperately for a glimpse of Raven among the woeful prisoners.

"I do hope you can see her before—"

"Before what?" snapped Christopher.

Taras answered gently. "There is no rescue, Christopher."

Christopher stared at the soldier blankly. He had already abandoned hope, but hearing those words spoken struck more painfully than accepting them in his mind. *No rescue.* He licked his lips. He was Mister Christopher Clive, Oxford's student of distinction, heir to Sir Redmond Clive's fortune, a young gentleman of the highest expectations. *This cannot be what is to be,* he thought. *I am destined...* He felt nauseated. *I can still save her...*

Two rough corsairs brushed past Taras, grabbed hold of Christopher's shoulders and jerked him off his rail. He cried out for Raven.

A thin voice answered, "Kipper?"

Christopher whipped his head. "Raven!"

The corsairs twisted his face forward. "Shut up!"

"Raven? Where are you?" Christopher strained against the men's hands. "Raven?" Then for a fleeting moment—for a mere fragment of time—his eyes fell upon her in the centre of a huddle of ragged figures.

He opened his mouth but before he could utter a sound the heathens tossed him wailing through a dark hatch where he tumbled down the short companionway. Christopher whirled about and lunged for light. The hatch immediately filled with the two men and he was thrown backward. Falling on his shoulder, he was then dragged toward a second flight of steps and tossed into the deep hold where his wrists were shackled to iron chains.

CHAPTER 18

FOR THE NEXT two hours, Christopher sat in the black dampness of the ship's belly as she made her slow approach to dockside. He vomited. The *Lebetine* rolled ever so easily to one side and then the other as she slid toward the stable arms of the city's dock. Her hull eventually bumped lightly against the rope-padded pilings of the dock and a chill of dread ran through him. He pictured that final glimpse of Raven's haunted face. Exasperated, tears swelled his eyes. He reminded himself that she was not so far away, that she was standing just a few yards overhead.

In the minutes that followed, Christopher's grief quickly gave way to rage and he began to curse like the men around him. Unwilling to yield to circumstance, his mind began to calculate a new plan of how he might ransom Raven and her mother. *Surely,* he thought, *the Royal Consul in Algiers can negotiate such a simple arrangement. All I needs do is state my case...*

Focusing his anger, Christopher began to rehearse a presentation before the consul. Straining against whispering fears of hopelessness, he rattled his chains and proclaimed, "And so, Lord Consul, the King and Parliament ought—"

"Shut yer mouth," complained an unseen Irishman.

Christopher ignored him and pictured an English aristocrat in a powdered wig, a fine waistcoat and a high-laced collar leaning close to listen with sympathetic ears. So he rambled on about his high station and great worth, and of his innocence in his grandfather's business. "All of this, Lord Consul, ought to prompt a simple mercy for two Irish women."

His rehearsal was abruptly ended when a short column of corsairs rushed into the hold. The men unshackled him and chased him up to the main deck with the other men. Soon Christopher was standing in a long line along the bulwark and searching for Raven in the blinding light. "Raven?" he cried at the sea of persons mobbing the dock below.

"Silence!" A thin corsair in a wind-ruffled shirt slapped him across the face with a bony hand. "They're gone."

"Gone? What do you mean, gone?"

Taras stepped forward and stood between him and the pirate. "She is taken away." The young soldier's face was filled with compassion.

"But I do not understand. Is she not among them?" He pointed to a snaking column of European women being driven along the dock."

"I believe these are from another ship. You must find a way to submit to this—"

"She must be close. Where is she?"

Taras shook his head.

A man approached, an auditor, official looking and dressed in fine robes, curled slippers and a blue turban. He carried a board and paper. "Your name?"

"Raven!" Christopher cried.

A strike on the head returned his attention. "Name!"

Grinding his teeth, Christopher continued scanning the dock. "*Mister* Christopher Clive."

The scribe lowered his quill. "Ah, Christopher *Bey*. Up there, then." He pointed him to the poop deck where his grandfather lay in chains, unable to stand on his broken feet.

"What?"

"Up there! Go up there!"

With Taras close behind, Christopher hurried up the few steps to the stern's raised deck. Ignoring his grandfather, he leapt atop the rail and steadied himself by a hand in the rigging. He studied another group of women on the dock tied to a long rope like a string of fish to a harvest line. He cried her name again.

This time a black-haired girl turned her head.

Kipper waved his arms, wildly. "Raven?" Squinting, Christopher's heart raced. But Raven's face was slapped to one side and the rope-line of captives was jerked forward. He shouted her name again and then once more. "O Christ above..." He leapt into the rigging, frantic to follow the black hair.

At last, she was able to turn her face one final time. Kipper's eyes found hers. "Raven!" For a moment in time Christopher held her in that place, even as she held him.

In that instant, the world around them vanished.

But no sooner had his eyes caught hers than he was yanked out of the rigging by a Janissary officer and thrown hard upon the deck where an iron-soled boot held him fast.

"Nay!" he wailed. "Let me up! Let me up!"

The soldier ground his boot into Christopher's chest. "*Sessizlik!*"

Christopher fought for his legs one last time but he was no match for the soldier who ordered Taras to chain his wrists to the rail of the poop deck beside his crippled grandfather. The soldier then bound his mouth with a filthy, knotted gag.

In the hour that followed, the other male captives were driven off the boat and to the dock from which they would be herded to one of the city's dungeons. There they would await their sale to wealthy Muslims or remain as slaves of the State for the rest of their days.

Muted by his gag, Christopher ached for them. Taras had once told him that most of the State slaves would die aboard galley ships, chained to oars and never to touch the earth again. Others would hew rocks from nearby quarries and drag them to the sea-swept breakwater until they, too, expired from exhaustion.

Christopher stared, helpless, as the poor men were whipped toward the gangplank. He heard the Irishmen begin to sing a song of defiance and his heart lifted for them.

Soon the captives were gone and all that remained on board were a handful of crew and a milling company of Janissaries along with the ship's captain, a well-dressed auditor, Colonel Kasim and Sergeant Zeki. Taras removed Christopher's gag. "It is time."

Blinking, Christopher said, "For what?"

Taras dodged his eyes.

Christopher returned his face to the white-washed city and thought of Jesus' words to the Pharisees. "This place is clean on the outside, but its heart is filth." He grabbed the rail. "And Raven is in the belly of it..."

Redmond then grumbled from the deck boards.

Christopher looked down at the pathetic old man gingerly rubbing his swollen feet. "What did you say?"

"You failed us both. My feet are useless and you stand there snivelling about some Irish bitch."

"You ought shut thy mouth."

"Next time, I do the negotiating."

"There shall be no next time, you old fool."

"I shall offer a huge ransom for the both of us. The consul shall save us."

"They shan't ransom you. I should have shot thee dead."

Colonel Kasim climbed up the steps from the main deck. Christopher thought he looked tired and distracted. Zeki followed with two musketeers, Yusef Rais and a few of the ship's crew. As Kasim approached he said, "You should have shot thy grandfather."

Ignoring his remark, Christopher shook his chained wrists. "I would like to write a letter of ransom for the Irish girl and her mother. The Sultan has no cause against them."

As Yusef laughed loudly, Kasim ran a finger along his moustache and looked at Christopher with sudden pity. He addressed him in English. "The Sultan is not interested in Clive money. That is the end of it."

"As I told you before, thy actions oppose thy Prophet's words. You are punishing innocents on another's account— "

Kasim raised his hand and took a long breath through his nose. "Taras already presented this question of yours. I am impressed with thee, Mister Clive. You read our Scriptures with care, as do I. So I asked the ship's dervish about this supposed transfer of guilt." He paused. "He says you quote this out of its place."

"Of course—the most common escape of religious teachers. But what say thee?" Christopher studied Kasim's stone face. He could see that the man was troubled and he therefore understood him to be devout, perhaps even meticulous in his beliefs.

Kasim switched to Turkish. "*Huzur içinde ol.* Be at peace, Christopher Clive. To be clear, the fate of the Irish is not on account of your grandfather. As Taras told you, they are infidels captured in a heathen land. The Sultan has ordered them to be sold and so I shall sell them. That is the end of it."

Christopher stood, stiffly. "And what of the teaching? Do you agree with your dervish or not?"

Kasim stiffened. "You would do well to stop thinking and simply submit." He took a breath. "Thine Irish girl is being taken to a private chamber in one of the prisons. Women shalll bathe her and the brokers will inspect her. She shall not suffer but she is lost to thee, forever."

Christopher said nothing more.

159

"You may be pleased to know that Zuhayr will not be buying her, though I suspect he may buy her mother."

Christopher grit his teeth. "Allah has ninety-nine names, the first is 'Rahman, 'The Most Merciful.' And thy prophet was supposedly sent to reveal this mercy to mankind. I see this is in your Book and not in your life."

Kasim leaned close. "I have been patient with thee, Christian. You tread dangerous waters here. The Book also says, 'For those who have disbelieved, boiling water shall be poured down upon their head.'"

Christopher scowled.

Kasim straightened his back. "I am surprised you object to assigning the burdens of one to another. This transfer of guilt is something you claim thy Christ does for thee, is it not?" He turned his back on Christopher. "Mister Wentworth Carrew, come here."

Kasim towered over the trembling man. "You are not to be ransomed."

"But..." Weeping, Carrew nearly fainted.

Kasim curled his lips as if the next words had a terrible taste to them. "You shall be set free and sent home to England."

Surprised, Christopher watched Carrew's jaw drop.

"Thank thee, my lord," said Carrew. "But I do not understand."

"First, you have some duties to perform. I have a message you shall sign and personally deliver to thy King Charles with a few gifts. If you fail to do this, our spies shall find thee in Kinsale, Cork, Bristol, or any other city of infidels you waste thy life within and stab thee and thy family in your sleep. Do you understand this?"

Carrew nodded.

Kasim handed him the letter he was to sign. "Read it aloud so Mister Clive can hear thee."

"'For Crimes against Mehmed IV, Sultan of the Caliphate, Protector of Jesus' tomb, Guardian of Mecca, and Keeper of Jerusalem, I, Mr. Wentworth Carrew do hereby present the Head and Hands of Sir Redmond Clive…'"

Carrew balked and stared at Christopher.

"Shall I or shall I not revoke thy pardon?" barked Kasim.

Carrew read on:

"'…the Head and Hands of Sir Redmond Clive to King Charles II, King of Infidels, Liars and Cheats. May these serve as a Warning for any who might offend the faithful Sons of the Prophet, his Name be praised until the Day of Judgment. Justice is delivered by Mr. Wentworth Carrew on this eighth Day of October in the Year of Christ, 1660.'"

Kasim handed Carrew a quill and the trembling man asked, "What do you mean 'head and hands,' and 'justice is delivered,' sir?"

"You shall see soon enough. Now sign it."

As Carrew scratched his name on the letter, Christopher turned a pale face toward his grandfather now lying quietly on the deck. "I am sorry, sir," he said.

Redmond pulled himself up on one elbow. He looked into the sky now fading in the early evening. "Chin up, boy. Keep that Clive chin up! Get home and marry that Fairfax girl. I expect thee to sire an army to avenge this treachery."

Colonel Kasim then commanded several soldiers to drag Redmond down the steps to the main deck where they stripped him naked amidships. His hands were bound behind him and his ankles wrapped tightly together. Howling in pain, he was hoisted by his ankles and hung upside-down again by a loop in the rigging, this time about a yard above the boards.

Kasim led Christopher off the poop and to his grandfather's side with the others. He fixed cold eyes on him. "The Sultan forbids thy grandfather to ever set foot on the soil of Allah's holy Caliphate so he must die on this ship.

"And, on account of thy grandfather's crimes, the Sultan requires two penalties be inflicted on *thee*."

Christopher stiffened.

"As for the first, you are hereby officially declared a slave of the Sultan *until the end of thy days*."

Christopher lifted his chin. "I am no man's slave, sir."

"Huzzah!" cried the upside-down Redmond.

Kasim smiled. "Thy bold claim does not change what is, young man." With a nod, he then bade a Janissary forward with a drawn *yatagan*. He took the curved sabre in hand and touched the razor sharp blade to the skin of his thumb. A tiny trickle of blood quickly ran along the heel of his hand and dripped on the deck. He turned to Christopher.

Christopher straightened his shoulders. *What would he have me do?* He swallowed. *Never let it show.* He waited for a long, agonizing moment as Kasim studied him. He then watched the massive officer turn slowly to Redmond Clive whose face was now purple and swollen. He looked like a boar strung up in an abattoir.

Kasim returned to Christopher. "I should command thee to flay the skin off his back. It would please the Sultan."

Bracing himself, Christopher set his jaw. *Nay. He shall have to kill us both.*

"But I suppose you would just refuse and require me to kill you both," said Kasim. "That would not do."

Christopher exhaled, slowly.

"I am able to show mercy." Kasim returned his attention to Wentworth Carrew. "Come here."

The terrified man scurried close as Yusef, Zeki, and a small group of others gathered.

"It is getting late, Mister Carrew," said Kasim. "Take this sword and drag it through thy friend's throat."

Carrew nearly fainted. "But—"

"Now."

Carrew cast an imploring look at Christopher as if he were asking his permission.

"Do not do this," said Christopher.

Redmond barked at Carrew. "Remember those rebels in County Clare?"

"Aye."

"You've a sword in hand," Redmond said. "Slice these heathen bastards like we did them."

Christopher watched Carrew stare at his blade and then at Kasim. *No, he'll never do that.* He struggled against his bonds.

"But we are not young men in County Clare, old friend," said Carrew. "And these are no half-starved Irish." He took a trembling step toward the old man.

"You are a coward. You could take the colonel and that snake, Crumb, with two swipes."

Carrew did not answer.

"Shite. You always were a fat, fawning toady. Do what you must, but do not call me 'friend' when you slit my throat."

Trembling so violently that he could barely stand, Wentworth Carrew laid the blade awkwardly alongside Redmond's neck, blabbering something incoherent about 'Christ' and 'Heaven's Gates.' He hesitated.

"Nay!" cried Christopher.

"Get on with it, you droning harpy," groused Redmond.

Carrew bit his lip and closed his eyes. Begging forgiveness, he then dragged the curved sword through Redmond Clive's throat. Blood sprayed instantly over Carrew; Redmond gurgled and jerked; his eyes widened and fixed themselves on his poor grandson.

Helpless, Christopher watched the sliding blade exit his grandfather's throat, red-slicked and dripping. Blood now poured upon the deck like water from a wide-open spigot. Redmond's eyes rolled backward and his head tilted unnaturally to one side, severed from his body by all except his spine.

Carrew fainted on the boards.

Groaning, Christopher fell to his knees.

A crewman snatched a crude knife from his sash and proceeded to remove Redmond's head altogether. He tossed it to Yusef Rais like a wet ball. The captain lifted the head by an ear to the cheers of his remaining crew, and then held it in front of Christopher's horrified face. "So, *now* ya'd be the baronet, *Sir* Christopher Clive." Laughing, Yusef sank the head into a deep, wide-mouthed urn filled with preserving spirits. "Tha should have shot him, fool."

Christopher vomited. He turned blazing eyes on the colonel.

"You hate me," said Kasim.

"Do you care, you heartless, heathen shite?"

The officer raised a brow. "We hate what we fear, and so you fear me. That is probably best." He then turned and ordered Redmond's body to be cut down. The headless corpse tumbled atop the pool of blood spreading slowly across the boards.

A crewman tossed a bucket of water over Carrew who was then forced to chop off Redmond's hands with an axe. Carrew could barely lift the blade, but when he finally finished, the hands were added to the urn and a wide cork pressed atop the opening.

Kasim returned to Christopher. "As the rais says, you are now the baronet. It is to be 'Sir Christopher', or as we would say, 'Christopher Effendi.'" He waved for Redmond Clive's body to be wrapped in chains and dumped overboard 'so that it might never ride the tide to touch the Sultan's shore.' He wiped blood off his boots. "Soon you shall learn of thy second penalty, and you shall have another chance to hate me." He stood over Christopher. "However, by *thy* book, Jesus would tell you to love me. We shall see."

CHAPTER 19

——— ❦ ———

CHRISTOPHER WOULD BARELY remember all that followed. The shock of watching his grandfather beheaded and the old man's hands chopped off like parts of a carcass in a butcher's stall had numbed him to his present plight. So he barely noticed as he was dragged off the *Lebetine* in chains. He never heard Yusef Rais bid him a sarcastic, 'fare tha well,' nor did he feel the wads of spit throated at him from a knot of satisfied corsairs lounging by the gangway.

At the dock, Sergeant Zeki released him to the custody of Taras and three disinterested Algerian police who prodded him with batons toward one of the cavernous dungeons that awaited. As Taras followed from behind, Christopher was driven along the same worn stones that tens of thousands of other forgotten Christian captives had trod on their tortuous trail to the slave prisons of Algiers.

The bagnios Algiers boasted were not so different from the other dungeons scattered across the Barbary Coast from Sallee to Tunis to Tripoli, though most observers would have claimed the subterranean *mazmorras* of Morocco to be the most hellish of them all. Nor was Christopher so different from the million other European infidels—and even greater numbers of black Africans—who would eventually be snatched away from shorelines and ships into places like these.

Faceless and nameless in his new world, the otherwise Sir Christopher Clive finally arrived at Algiers' *beylik*—the State slave prison. Still paralyzed by shock, he stared numbly at two massive wooden doors flanked by smoky torches. His guards rang an iron bell and in moments the giant doors were pushed slowly open to reveal candle-lit offices and reeking chambers filled with the shadows of prisoners shackled to dank walls. The stench of the place awakened Christopher's senses.

Suddenly alert, he peered through the thick darkness of a vaulted passage to make out the silhouettes of squat stone arches supporting two tiers of balconies. He stepped carefully forward and listened to the tomb-like silence of the place broken only by an occasional cry or metallic clang.

One of Christopher's guards grunted and pointed him to a desk behind which sat an upright scribe in the yellow light of an iron candelabra. The scribe was a bearded, serpent-faced young man under a massive white turban. "*Naam?*"

"Sir Christopher Clive. I am English, not Dutch."

A guard handed the annoyed scribe a note from Colonel Kasim which he read with rapidly sliding eyes. He then made a quick, official notation of some kind and waved Christopher forward to a shirtless bald man who pushed him against a cool stone wall. Squatting, the smith hammered an iron ring around Christopher's left ankle. Another man then grabbed him and took sharp shears to his head.

Breathing quickly, Christopher was then shoved into another dark hallway where he was given a bundle of something soft to carry and chased deeper into the dungeon. He was finally hurried into a reeking room with scores of other men. There he was ordered to replace his clothing with the contents of the bundle.

Trembling, Christopher pulled on an itchy, collarless shirt, a short waistcoat, a pair of rough, shin-length trousers and thin slippers. He wrapped himself in a wool blanket and then huddled in a corner from which he stared through the damp darkness at the huddled shadows of those others just arrived. *Is Raven in such a place?* A sharp pain gripped his chest. *O dear Christ!* He tried to breathe. *God help her...God help me...*

Before dawn, guards entered into Christopher's chamber and herded him and the others into a long line that led out of the cell and into a gravelled courtyard where a half-dozen blacksmiths waited. Christopher took his turn to face a smith who set a thirty-pound chain over Christopher's shoulder and fastened it to his anklet. By the first crowing of the bagnio's cocks, he limped into a new cell leaning under the weight of his new fetter.

⚜

"Englishman?"

Sitting against a plastered wall, Christopher turned as someone sat himself alongside. A tiny window high above the damp floor cast enough dawn's light for him to see a rough-shorn, bony old man with a hollow face and no teeth.

Christopher nodded, vaguely.

"I am Frederick of Saxony." He handed Christopher a broken loaf of sour bread. "Just arrived?"

"Aye." Christopher was in no mood for conversation. His belly growled and his eyes were heavy.

"They do not feed you so much at first, but you eventually get three small loaves a day. If you are good, they put some vinegar on them. And if you are very good, they gives thee an olive." The German chewed slowly and wiped away a discharge that oozed from one eye.

Christopher looked away.

"Forgive my bad English. What is thy name?"

"Christopher."

"So, Christopher, I am here now five years already."

"Taken from a ship?"

"*Ja.*"

"Bad luck for thee."

"Luck has nothing to do with it. What is, is. I was once a Lutheran minister, but now I am here. My life is what it is today." He gnawed at some bread with his gums. "I tell you, the world is an uncertain place. I am powerless to change yesterday, and I can do but a little for tomorrow. My only true friend is patience."

Christopher closed his eyes.

Frederick snorted a wad of mucus from one nostril. "But I am blessed. I work here in the beylik sewing clothes. Now, open thy eyes."

Christopher obeyed.

"You see my arm? It is crooked from when I fall from a tower cutting rocks many years ago. I am now happy to have a crooked arm. No more work in the quarry. You see?"

"Good luck for you, then." Christopher closed his eyes again.

Frederick smiled. "*Ach.* You English are stubborn." He put a piece of bread in Christopher's mouth, startling him. "Now I wish to give you a different gift. Do you know of Leviathan—the sea monster from the *Book of Job?*"

Annoyed, Christopher nodded. "Of course; the symbol of chaos."

"Ja. I have taught these men to say the word often."

Christopher stopped chewing.

Frederick leaned very close. "Listen to me: accept Leviathan and live; fight it *und* die. This is my gift."

"I do not understand what you are talking about." Christopher shifted on the cold floor.

"Every day Leviathan is near. Chaos, disorder, and absurdities surround us." Frederick laid his hand on Christopher's forearm. "Men who cannot accept this go mad and soon die. If you wish to live, you must accept that Leviathan is."

Christopher shook his head. "I do not accept disorder... or chaos or any of it."

Frederick laughed. "Ja, ja. I understand. We Germans worship order more than you English! But order is an illusion." The German leaned yet closer. "And it is not only so in this place." He squeezed Kipper's arm. "Listen to me, little brother, for I say it only once more: If you wish to survive, you must accept that Leviathan exists, always and everywhere." Releasing Christopher's arm, Frederick offered him a kind smile. "But Wisdom can use this monster to free us from ourselves. You simply must let her."

Christopher looked away. "I do not understand."

"*Wunderbar.* At least you can see your own ignorance; that is a good beginning. Accept that, too."

⚜

Kipper Clive never did see Frederick again. But over the next days he met numbers of Italians and Portuguese, Spaniards and Dutchmen, a few English lads, a host of Negroes, and an old Icelander who had been taken in a coastal raid decades before.

As Frederick had predicted, Christopher's ears quickly piqued to their frequent use of the word 'Leviathan.' Whenever bread was lost or a guard imposed some fool's errand from the Guardian Pasha, someone would bark, "Leviathan." If an olive was granted to an idiot, or a fifty-pound fetter fixed to a 100-pound man, or news of a quarry disaster reached the men, the slaves would grumble, "Leviathan."

Hearing others recognize the madness all about him *as* madness was an unexpected comfort for Christopher. However, it occurred to him that if the world was *actually* mad, how would he survive it without becoming mad, himself?

Unless, of course, he *should* become mad.

Mercifully, the pasha's guards relieved Christopher of his introspection by dragging him from his cell on the morning of his seventh day. They kicked him across the large gravelled courtyard and to the scribe's table by the front door. He waited there, scratching at his lice-ridden clothing furiously. Taras, little Zeki and two other high-capped Janissaries marched toward him.

"We have come to take you from here, Christopher Effendi," said Taras.

The sight of the Ukrainian filled Christopher with such relief that he nearly lunged to hug him. "Taras, *arkadaşım!*"

Taras answered without emotion. "You must carry your irons."

"What is wrong? Where are we going?"

"To another place," said Taras.

Sergeant Zeki studied the English youth with contempt. "You stink."

Without another word, the Janissaries pushed Christopher out of the beylik and into the bright light of the shimmering city where they led him uphill into the terraced neighbourhoods of Algiers. They paused to let Christopher drink deeply of a clear fountain fed by one of the city's impressive aqueducts. Thirst quenched, the wretch stared at the world around him.

Algiers was protected by the corsairs by sea and the Janissaries by land. Thus secure, the city tempted Christopher to imagine being a free man able to delight in her magic. A jewel chiselled into the sun-beaten mountains behind, she boasted innumerable gardens and whitewashed villas. A cascading web of rivulets bubbled cheerfully along her narrow streets all edged by lush greenery. Flowers were abundant and they perfumed the salt air that draughted gently upward from the sea.

Ordered forward, Christopher hefted his fetter over his shoulder and dragged himself amongst the free citizens adorned in colourful robes and silk turbans. Gaggles of women moved past him, shyly. They were dressed according to their religion, covered from head to toe in white burkas.

Kipper's head swivelled from side to side. All about him were the cries of merchants, growling camels, bleating goats and the beautiful melodies of the songbirds that fluttered overhead to red-clay roofs and lush limbs. The power of such beauty lightened Christopher's chains. The splendidly clean air, the laughter of children, and the lively chatter of passers-by crowding the busy streets had smitten him.

He paused in front of another of Algiers' many fountains and stared into the leaping font. A light breeze bent the upward stream enough to send a refreshing spray of tiny droplets to cool his parched skin. Christopher closed his eyes and began rehearsing his speech to the consul.

His captors led him patiently along narrow streets cramped by plastered houses, workshops, tiled mosques and minarets. Over his shoulder, an eager fleet of ships bobbed in the turquoise bay far below. The ships kept the city in plenty with all manner of comforts from the Ottoman's Caliphate, including a regular supply of slaves. His mind turned to Raven and he shifted the weight of his fetter. "O Lord, have mercy on her," he mumbled.

Christopher's guards turned him around a corner and when he did, he stopped short. Just ahead, a dozen black slaves were being beaten into a wagon with such ferocity that he felt as if the whining leather was tearing his own flesh away. "Make them stop," he blurted.

Zeki and the soldiers—excepting Taras—laughed.

Christopher had not seen many Negroes in his time, save Tattie, of course. He had read of them and had been taught by the Right Reverend of St. Multose that 'Blackamoors are children of Ham's curse,' and therefore lesser men. But seeing these terrible wretches, scarred and bleeding, falling faint and kicked before his eyes made him angry. He did not care they were "lesser men'— his fetter removed any difference." Christopher barked at Taras. "Are you not able to make them stop?"

"They are hated more than you," said Taras.

"Why?"

The soldier shrugged. "They are animals, stupid and smelly. They do not bring as high a price in the slave market as whites."

Christopher set his jaw. "They are *men*, Taras."

"The lucky ones are not. They are eunuchs serving the harems of the wealthy. They live well."

Christopher could feel a sickening sensation crawl through his innards. "The Mohammedans are barbarians. You are not one of them."

"Be careful." Taras handed Christopher some figs and some cheese. "Busy your mouth."

Zeki ordered Christopher forward and soon the company emerged at an intersection with the city's primary thoroughfare where Christopher followed the triple-wide market street farther uphill. The steep climb was bordered on all sides by merchants' booths piled high with hides and hemp, produce from the country-side, fish, broadcloth and dyes. Butcher shops and tanners filled the air with peculiar stenches. Candle makers and carpet pedlars stood alongside jewellers, tailors and merchants selling sundry colourful spices from large baskets.

The climb became difficult. Christopher's shoulder and legs ached under the weight of his chains. Spotting a fortuitous bench, Taras nodded for the sergeant to stop. "He needs to rest and we all need water."

Zeki looked up at Christopher. "So, you need a little rest, Englishman? Say it aloud."

Christopher glared at him. Taras had said Zeki was an evil little mole. The sergeant was not a loyal slave like the traditional Janissaries, but rather one of an increasing number of freemen allowed into the sacred corps. As the son of a wealthy Turk in Constantinople, Zeki had joined the Janissaries to advance his reputation and gain influence in the government.

Christopher's jaw pulsed. "I... would... like... to... rest."

Zeki laughed. "No. Say that you *need* to rest."

Christopher hesitated. "I *need* to rest."

With a grunt, Zeki then ordered Christopher to sit in the shade of a dusty tree near the doorway of a brothel while he and two others quickly entered, leaving Kipper in Taras' custody.

Taras fetched a ladle of water from a nearby cistern which Christopher gulped. He scurried away and then bought a dried fish and a strip of goat meat from a nearby booth. Christopher gobbled the food down with two hands and a hearty, "*Teşekkür ederim.*"

Finally rested, Christopher asked, "What do you know of Raven?"

Taras looked away.

"Tell me, please."

"The pasha has ordered all female slaves to the *Bagnio de Galera* near the Marine Gate."

"Is that close to here?"

"It is of no matter to you, Christopher Effendi."

"I want to know more."

"The brokers will parade her three times in the market to get the best price. Her white skin is highly prized and so she will be sold to a wealthy house...perhaps here in Algiers, though I am told there are buyers from Sallee and Tunis. She will be sold tomorrow, converted to Islam, and serve her owner's pleasure as his concubine." The young soldier paused. "It is sad for me to see love come to an end, Effendi, but this is what is. You must submit to this fact."

Christopher nearly burst. Helpless, his chin quivered and his eyes filled. He cursed and hid his face, begging God for all of this to be a terrible nightmare from which he might awake in his bed at Giardín an Croí. Staring at Taras blankly, he tried to lose himself in the sounds of the songbirds around him, wondering whether Raven was listening to the same. *How frightened she must be.* "Taras, how can I get a message to the English consul?"

"We have no business with him."

"But you could take a letter?"

"You have no ink, paper or quill. And I do not have permission."

"But—"

"I would be punished severely."

Christopher looked away.

"Effendi, you really must learn to—"

"No!"

Taras sucked a swallow of water from the brass spout of his leather canteen. "Then no one is able to help you."

Christopher stared into the busy street. The consul was his final hope. *And she is to be sold tomorrow.* He cursed. *How can I get a letter to him?*

Of course, he had no knowledge of how effective the consuls were with the pasha—the mayor. For all he knew, his efforts could get him flogged and thrown aboard a merchant ship in a sack.

Christopher's attention was taken by Zeki and his men as they finally exited the brothel to order the woeful youth forward. They prodded him up the market street for another half-mile and finally to a building within sight of the mighty fortress of the Kasbah rising some 400 feet above the sea. Christopher's mind remained fixated on the consul, even as he arrived at a shaded villa tucked neatly along a narrow street and away from the noise of the souk. Exhausted, Christopher asked, "Taras, if you could find me paper, ink, and a quill—"

"Submit to what is, Effendi."

Not answering, Christopher was taken by the arms and pulled through the gates of the villa into a pleasant courtyard. In the centre was a wide, wooden table, a large-mouthed clay pot filled with water and a small stand holding folded cloth. Several sleeveless, moustached Janissaries milled about a three-legged copper *kazan*—the sacred kettle of the Janissary corps—boiling bulgur and butter into a paste for their singular daily meal.

A lanky Christian priest in a long black robe entered the court-yard from a side room. Christopher looked back to where Taras had been, but he was gone. *What is happening here?*

CHAPTER 20

—— ✠ ——

THE APPROACHING PRIEST had a dark complexion, a black beard, and surveyed the world from behind sad eyes. Kissing the silver crucifix around his neck, he laid a large hand gently on Christopher's head. He prayed in an unfamiliar language and then blessed him with the sign of the cross as he turned away.

A jolt of fear jarred Christopher. *They are going to execute me!* His eyes flew from Turk to Turk. *By strangulation...beheaded like Grandfather...drowned in that pot?* His heart raced. He looked at the linens. *My shroud?* He squeezed his fists. *Never let it show.*

Christopher fixed his eyes on the priest now nodding to a waiting Negro slave. *I shall die like an Englishman should.* He closed his eyes and straightened his back. "Father God, protect Raven and set her free..."

The sound of feet running toward him opened his eyes. He braced himself as the black slave raced forward with a hammer and chisel in hand. Christopher tensed.

With a shout, the slave fell at Christopher's feet and struck his iron anklet, breaking it in two. He nearly fainted in relief. The slave then ordered him toward the bath where two giggling Negresses waited. He walked forward on weak legs, mind spinning.

Bewildered, he let the women undress him, help him into the bath and scrub his body with fragranced soap. They then dried him with plush cotton towels and dressed him in satin clothing. "But why?" he asked.

Clean but still confused, Kipper Clive was returned to the court-yard where another house-slave presented him with a small bowl of hummus and olives before escorting him to a seat beneath a red canopy. There he sat atop a thick cushion with some hesitation. Looking warily from side to side, he began eating. *What the devil are they up to? A bath? Fine clothing? Food?* The air filled with the muezzins' afternoon song of the *adhan*—the Mohammedans' hypnotic call to prayer.

As the soulful song flew from the tops of the city's many mina-rets, the Muslims around Christopher quickly washed their hands and face, and set their prayer mats side by side toward the south-east and the holy city of Mecca. As the men chanted their rhythmic lit-urgy and shifted their postures in unison, Christopher fixed his eyes on the curious Christian priest standing politely to one side. *Why is he here? What did he pray for me?* He set his food aside.

When the Muslims' prayers were over, the priest approached Christopher once again and addressed him in perfect English. "I am Father Paki, a Coptic priest and a slave like thee. I was captured in a raid of my Egyptian village of Geptu a decade ago." He studied Christopher for a long moment before receiving a red clay bowl from another. "Now here, my son, drink this." He held the bowl in front of Christopher's face.

Christopher thought he looked resigned and forlorn. "What is it?"

"Do you have pain?"

Christopher nodded.

"It shall relieve thee of it all."

Christopher hesitated. He stared into a milky, amber liquid and then into Father Paki's face. A chirruping redstart hopped among the branches of a nearby Numidian broom tree, turning his head. His eye followed the rich red plumage of the cheerful bird as it did a somer-sault around a twig. The little comedy turned the corners of his lips upward, if only for a moment.

Father Paki cleared his throat and held the bowl toward Christopher's face.

"I think not, Father."

"Do you think I am here to harm you?"

Christopher said nothing.

"Do you believe that you know what is best for thee?"

Christopher nodded.

"Nay, you do not." Paki stared into the liquid. "No man does." He took a breath and looked at Christopher once again, this time with a pleading gaze. "Tell me: what do you think is best for thee now?"

Kipper watched the bird and thought of Raven. "I am not certain."

"That is a good answer, my son." The priest lowered the bowl and sat alongside the English youth.

Christopher watched the little redstart dash about, freely. He then looked squarely at the weary priest. "You should tell me what is happening here."

The priest gestured with the bowl. "This is best."

Uneasy, Christopher shifted on his cushion. He searched the faces of the Janissaries now encircling him. "You seem certain."

"I am."

Christopher scanned the courtyard. "Taras?"

Taras stepped forward. "Effendi?" His broad face looked looked suddenly strained as if he were shielding a secret. Then Taras nodded.

Christopher took the bowl from Father Paki and lifted it to his nose. He thought it smelled invitingly sweet, like melted flowers with a musty spice. He sniffed it again and detected a slight note of vinegar. "What is it?"

Father Paki spoke calmly. "As I said, it relieves pain."

"Why do you care about my pain?"

"I am a priest."

Christopher turned to Taras again. "Poison?"

"No."

Christopher stared at Taras, then beyond him to the little red-start as it dashed to another limb. *Would it really matter if it were?* He cupped the bowl and took a small sip.

His lips and tongue tingled.

Christopher drank more and his throat and belly quickly warmed.

"And now the rest, my son," said the priest. He lifted his own chin upward, coaxing. A wave of dizziness came over Christopher and he teetered just a bit on his cushion. Steadied by Taras, his head was cradled in the secure hands of the priest. Father Paki then tipped the rest of the bowl's contents into Christopher's mouth and he swallowed.

The nearby bird trilled but Christopher barely heard.

⚜

Three days later, Sir Christopher Clive awakened at the sound of the muezzins' song for noon prayer. He placed his palms atop a comfortable bed of soft sheets. From one side a gentle brush of air cooled him from a shadow waving a large palm over his body.

He tried to remember.

"You are alive, Effendi."

Christopher rolled his head toward the sound of Taras' voice.

"It is I, Taras."

"What happened?"

"*Masha-Allah.* All that is, is as Allah has willed. May his name be praised forever." The soldier's voice fell away.

Christopher then felt a deep ache in his groin. He tried to move but cried out.

"Do not move."

Christopher forced his head upwards. Taras called for Father Paki who came running from the courtyard. The priest entered the room as Taras abandoned Christopher for his prayers. Paki pressed Christopher's head gently backward. "It is Father Paki. You are well."

"Where am I?"

"You are still at my master's house." The priest pressed a firm hand on Christopher's shoulder. "The next days are important, Sir Christopher."

"What happened?"

"I am sorry, my little brother, but the Sultan commanded this."

Christopher winced. "Commanded what?"

Paki took a breath. "He demanded you to be castrated for some crime against him."

The words landed on Christopher so unexpectedly that he demanded they be repeated three times. Struggling to grasp what had happened, he tried lifting himself again, straining against the priest's hand. "This cannot be."

"Be still. Thy wound has been cauterized but you can still open it. If you do, you shall probably die."

Christopher's mind was reeling. He was sick and faint. "But?"

"The orders came directly from the new Grand Vizier, Köprülü Fazil Ahmed Pasha."

Christopher struggled to absorb any of this. "But…" He looked carefully at Paki. "You did this to me?"

Paki took a seat by him.

"How could you do this to me? You are a Christian priest."

"That is true, but I am also a slave."

"But you should obey God first. This evil you have done—"

"This evil is nothing worse than what thy pope does to young boys. He likes them to sing like angels—"

"*My* pope? I have no pope." Christopher lifted his lip in a snarl.

Father Paki tried to comfort him. "Thy voice shall remain a man's voice."

"A man's voice?" He turned his head. "But I am no longer a man."

Paki laid a hand on his shoulder. "Be still, my son." After a time of silence, he went on. "Kasim Çorbasi has shown you mercy."

"Mercy? Christ…"

"It is true. Kasim paid for my services out of his own purse."

Christopher stared helplessly at the ceiling.

"No Mohammedan is permitted to do this work, so they hire Christians or Jews. Most are unskilled butchers who end up killing nine in ten or more. But over the centuries, we Copts learned how to do this better than all others and so our services are valued."

Christopher closed his eyes.

"Kasim paid yet more so that you would sleep. Otherwise you would have been cut wide awake."

I should have shot my grandfather…

"And he ordered that I take thy sack and grapes only." The priest shook Christopher's shoulder lightly to be sure he was listening. "The colonel did not want you to lose thy sceptre, like the Blackamoors."

Christopher reached a hand slowly toward his groin to see if Paki was telling the truth.

"Stop moving. You must lie still as death itself. I am able to save four in ten but you are older than most. Do you understand?"

"I understand that when I am well I shall kill thee."

Father Paki sat back. "That is not a good thing to say. I have cared for thee well. My master's servants and even my wife have bathed thee for these past three days and you threaten me like that?"

"Three days?"

"Three days. And now you are alive again."

"Alive? Is that what this is?" Christopher's mind whirled. He turned his face toward the open doorway and cried for Taras.

The soldier returned from his prayers. "Effendi?"

Christopher stared at Taras angrily. "I trusted you."

The soldier removed his wool cap and bowed his head. "Insha Allah."

"No more about Allah's will." Christopher locked his eyes on Taras' sad face for a long, silent moment. He wondered if this could not all be a terrible dream. He turned his face away and his thoughts abruptly turned to the children he would never have. He groaned within. "Tell me about Raven."

"She has been sold, just as I told you would happen."

Christopher fought the tears. Dare he ask the next question? "To whom?"

"I am permitted to tell you only this: She is now the concubine of a wealthy dye-maker. Kasim says he paid $427 Spanish in loud bidding. Kasim says that is more than an Irishman can earn in ten years."

"Is she still in the city?" Still facing a far wall, the choking lad could barely speak.

"She is gone, Effendi."

Christopher drew a deep breath and faced Taras. "Where?"

"This I cannot say."

CHAPTER 21

Late January in the Year of Grace 1661

FOR THE NEXT many months, Father Paki and his wife, Nena, tended Christopher. Never far from his side stood Taras, and his presence had oddly secured Christopher. Nevertheless, sorrow weighed so heavily on him that Father Paki warned him against his persistent, deep-night lamentations. "They shall steal thy life away," Paki said.

"Good," answered Christopher. Forlorn and heavy-hearted, he welcomed death. The dark skies of winter's rain soothed him. The redstarts' courtyard chirrups annoyed him. Though Nena served him the finest coffee, Christopher preferred sinking into his melancholy with a cup of sour milk and silence.

From time to time he reached for his groin to touch the gruesome void. Groaning, he felt the fool for his dreams of Raven and a family in Virginia. *I should have shot him.*

Christopher's habitual source of joy—memories of the cove—now opposed him. They deepened his agony as they had become reminders of all that had been lost. And so day and night he pressed his fists against his head to squeeze all of it away.

And who would dare accuse him?

What was left for him?

Christopher recalled the words of his dear aunt. 'Where do you see God today?' To that, he released an assault of blasphemies that muted even the birds.

In February, Taras was ordered to sail away with Kasim to duties at the Citadel in Jerusalem where the rest of the 27th battalion had remained quartered. "So you must leave?" said Christopher, masking his anxiety at the thought of it.

"Yes."

Christopher drew a breath through his nostrils. *Why should I miss him?*

"I will pray the mercy of Allah be upon you," said Taras.

Christopher bit his lip. Dismissing the irony, he realized how safe he had felt in Taras' presence. He nodded. "Thank you. You…you have been kind to me."

"Allah wishes us to be merciful to the helpless."

Christopher closed his eyes. *Mercy? Where is mercy? I suppose they all think I should be grateful to Kasim.*

Taras stretched a huge hand forward and Christopher took it. "I will see you again," said Taras. "Accept what is and live."

Christopher could not answer. *Accept?* He'd rather die. He released Taras' hand and looked away.

On a cool March afternoon, Christopher stared into a hand mirror at a rusty-blond beard and nicely trimmed hair. But his joyless face was drawn. "I am so weary." He set the mirror aside and began to walk aimlessly about the Algiers courtyard in his fine wool robes and silk slippers. Refusing to wear a turban, he adjusted a fur-lined fez decorated with a small wooden cross given as a generous gift from one of the Christian Negro slaves.

The chirrup of a stubborn redstart startled him. Christopher spotted the happy bird dash from limb to limb in trees freshly pruned. Watching it, he recalled the etching on his lost dagger and a wry smile urged the corners of his lips. The bird flew close and was joined by an apparent friend—a short-necked bulbul with a pointy crest. The bulbul's trill was comically annoying and the redstart answered with a cheerful chirp. Christopher surprised himself with a broad smile. "You two 'dance with abandon.'"

The smile awakened him. It was his first since the raid some six months prior. Watching the birds at play, a little sonnet then found him. He imagined Raven singing it as he penned the words in his mind.

> *Here's a little Fellow, bold and shrill*
> *Teasing at his Friend with a rasping Bill.*
> *Pray tell the Source of simple Joy that lifts a Bird to sing,*
> *What puts the light in little Eyes and cheerful Chatter brings?*

Eyes suddenly bright, he turned to greet Nena who just arrived with a plate of hummus, olives, and a special loaf of sourdough bread with honey. She was willowy woman with a fair complexion and black eyes. "Would you sit with me?" asked Christopher.

"Of course." Nena quickly took a seat by him. "Thine eyes are so blue," she said. Her English was as perfect as her husband's.

Christopher shrugged and ate some food. He knew that the woman had been kind to him, and that he had not been as gracious as she deserved.

"The Mohammedans live in terror of the Evil Eye, you know," Nena said. "They believe some people have the power to steal another's well-being with a simple glance. The Jews fear it too, and a few Christians. Blue eyes are thought to be the most dangerous."

Christopher stopped chewing. "Perhaps I ought to have stared the corsairs out of Skeefe."

Laughing lightly, Nena turned her attention to a honeybee climbing over the white petals of an iris brushed with a hint of bright yellow and violet. "I would like you to look at him, Mister Clive."

Christopher followed her eyes.

"The bees are free…free to serve, and the loving sun opens the flowers for them for the sake of life. I think of their honey as sunshine in a jar—a sacred gift."

Christopher watched the bee rummaging through the flower.

"So, when you taste honey you should always think of light and of love." Nena slowly laid a thin finger alongside the busy bee which stepped atop it. "Such a gift ought not be taken for granted." Nena looked carefully at Christopher. "Without light and love, neither trees nor men are free to bear fruit."

The drone of the city's muezzins suddenly sounded as they called the faithful to pray. Ignoring them, Christopher studied Nena. *Beautiful and wise.* Suddenly curious about her, he asked, "Is life difficult here for you?"

"My husband and I are slaves, but we do not suffer. Free Christians are heavily taxed and treated sometimes harshly or sometimes kindly according to the whims of the pasha."

"You have been a slave all thy life?"

Nena shook her head. "I was born free in Ottoman Egypt." She brushed a spider off her arm. "But our village rebelled and thus justified the Turks making slaves of us. Otherwise, their religion permits them only to take slaves from newly conquered territory. This is why they expand their Caliphate."

Christopher listened, turning his attention to the tops of the trees sway in a light breeze. "What if you converted to Islam?"

"Our lives would be better." Nena wiped some bread through the bowl of hummus. "We Christians are feared. The Mohammedans live in constant dread of a new crusade, so they are always anxious about us." She took a bite and chewed, thoughtfully. "But my husband is a man of genuine faith. He would never convert to a false religion that shows mercy only to its own."

Watching her carefully, Christopher thought her to possess an elegant beauty ripened kindly by time. When she spoke, her lips lingered upon each word as if they tasted as sweet as the intentions behind them. In some ways she reminded him of Aunt Comfort. *Would she help me find a way home? Dare I ask?* He ate some hummus and then said, "Nena, could I ask something of thee?"

Nena waited.

"I need paper, ink and a quill." Christopher held his breath. He knew his plan had risks, but how could he simply remain in this place? And what of Raven?

"Why?"

Christopher leaned toward her. "I want to appeal my plight to the English consul. It is my only hope."

Nena did not move. "My son, thy hope is not in this—"

"I must try."

The patient woman folded her hands on her lap. "The English consul is exiled at the moment."

"Exiled?"

Nena nodded.

"Well, in time he shall return and—"

"Perhaps, perhaps not. The pasha is fickle."

Christopher's mind raced. *I must do SOMETHING.* What did the Sultan intend to do with him, anyway? Would he be sent to the Hungarian frontier? Some forgotten redoubt in the desert?

And how could he ever search for Raven as a slave?

Determined, he said, "Then I should like to write an appeal directly to the Sultan."

"You wish to ask for thy freedom?"

"Aye." Christopher stood. "But it is also on account of another. I want to be free so that I can save—"

"A young woman?"

"Her name is Raven. She is an Irish girl whom the rovers also captured."

Nena's eyes filled. "Thy dreams are very bold."

"I cannot imagine her a slave." Christopher turned his face away as a lump filled his throat. "But I must first be free."

Nena remained silent for a long moment. She wiped her eyes. "A letter from thee could be seen as insolence of a high order. Any involved could be punished, including my husband on account of my part in it."

"I understand," he said. "I am asking much."

Nena stood and began to pace slowly about the courtyard, pausing to look at some flowers. She picked a white bloom and held it to her nose. "When I confront a difficult decision, I have learned to ask myself the only question that really matters: 'What does love look like in this?'"

Christopher waited.

Nena handed Christopher the flower. "With God's help there may be a way. I am friends with the wife of an Alexandrian who does business with the whole of Barbary. For a fee, he may be willing to put thy letter in the hands of a low minister perhaps in Tunis or even Sallee. From there it could be passed up. This would take much longer but it would be safer."

Christopher's heart leapt. "Would you do that?"

Nena stared at the hopeful young man. "Yes. For love's sake. Now let me see how we can make this work."

That same evening Christopher leaned over a desk under candlelight and wrote his plea in perfect Turkish:

10 Rajab, 1071

From the miserable Hand of Sir Christopher Clive, Infidel, unworthy Slave, and treacherous Fool,

To the honourable Mehmed IV, Sultan of the blessed Caliphate, most excellent Son of Mohammed, Guardian of Mecca, Sword of Allah,

With Body and Spirit afflicted by thy proper Justice, I write to beg Pardon for the Crimes of my wretched Family, even as the Prophet Mohammed offered the Forgiveness of Allah to the infidel Meccans who had slaughtered his beloved Wife and his good Uncle. Thankful for mercies I have already been shown, I humbly beg yet more because Allah's 'Mercy encompasses all Things.'

For the Crimes of my Family I offer no Excuse. I pray thee be satisfied with the Wrath already visited upon Sir Redmond Clive, and the removal of the Fruit of my Loins so that the Name, Clive, is forever forgotten and thereby accursed in accordance with thy prior Decree.

I now humbly entreat thee for my Release so that I may return to my Home and spread a good Report of thy boundless Mercies. May the magnified Name, Mehmed IV, be thereby forever remembered in the Halls of Europe for his Forgiveness of this contemptible Creature.

Christopher Clive, Slave

Christopher read and re-read the letter several times. Grumbling for playing the scraping wretch, he stared into the small mirror once again. Almost twenty, he suddenly thought he looked twice his age. His face was drawn, making his nose look longer than he remembered. *And what if Nena is right? What if their mercy is reserved for believers?* Sighing, he returned to the table. *I could convert...or maybe I could just say I converted.*

The idea troubled him. *How could I become one of those who have enslaved my Raven!*

He folded the letter slowly and then sealed it with a small puddle of yellow beeswax. "I shall not sink that far. God's will be done."

⚜

A Janissary appeared at Father Paki's courtyard on a warm day in late April with orders to transfer Christopher uphill to the citadel near the Kasbah. "Why?" complained Christopher. *Did someone find the letter?* A cold chill spread through his limbs.

The orders caught Christopher, Paki and Nena unaware. Faltering for words, Christopher said, "Thank you for thy good care." He looked into Nena's eyes and knew that she feared exactly what he now feared.

"God be with you, Sir Christopher Clive," said Father Paki. "I shall come see you."

Christopher nodded, then turned his face to Nena. "You showed me what love looks like," he said. "May love always protect thee."

Within the hour, Christopher was stripped naked and locked within a small cell. There he sat on a three-legged stool where he struggled against the panic rising within. Unfortunately, Taras was away with Kasim in Jerusalem, Sergeant Zeki had been assigned as his temporary keeper.

Zeki threw open the cell door and stood in the doorway with a shy dog on a leash. He kicked Christopher off his stool. "This is what we do to our lessers." He began to beat the dog furiously with his baton. The creature yiped and strained on the leash as the flat-nosed little Turk continued the beating.

Heat rose to Christopher's cheeks. He clenched his fists. "Stop it!"

Zeki kicked the dog and released it to run away. He then turned blazing black eyes on Christopher. Without a word, he struck Christopher across the side of his head, knocking him to his knees. "I hate all infidels, but do you know why I especially hate you?"

Shielding his head with his arm, Christopher shook his head. *Is this about the letter?*

Circling like a predator, Zeki slapped his baton into his own hand. "An Englishman murdered my mother when I was a boy in Constantinople." He struck Christopher twice along his shoulders. "Yet, there you were at Paki's enjoying honey and wheat bread in silk robes."

Christopher crouched on the floor, arms parallel across his face.

Zeki swung a ferocious blow against Kipper's forearm, and once the arm dropped, he struck his cheek. "Obey me and live."

Crying out, Christopher rolled to one side. Zeki's baton landed on his back. He slowly stood.

Zeki struck him across his shin and he staggered forward but did not fall. He stared hatefully at the red-vested Turk.

"The dervishes say, 'beat the dog and tame the lion,'" shouted Zeki. "I should have shot you in that stinking Irish village, eunuch." He then rammed Christopher in the belly with the end of his baton.

Gasping, Christopher folded over. *Do nothing. This is not about the letter...*

Zeki then hit Christopher across the side of his knee, dropping him to the ground. "Evet! That is where you belong, dog."

The groaning young man stared at Zeki's scuffed red boots and the hem of his white tunic.

Zeki then laid the long baton hard across the side of Christopher's head and he fell flat to the ground where he struck him again Christopher clenched his jaw.

Zeki thwacked him once more, and then again and again. "And we should have had our way with that Irish girl—"

"No more!" Christopher leapt to his feet and punched Zeki on the jaw with a desperate fist. Shrieking, he struck him again, knocking Zeki against a wall while shouting months of suppressed rage. "Bastards! Heathen bastards!"

Christopher's cries immediately caught the attention of the guards just outside his door. They rushed into the room and threw the raging Englishman against the stone wall where they beat him senseless.

CHAPTER 22

CHRISTOPHER AWAKENED CHAINED by both wrists to a damp wall deep within the State beylik to which he had been returned. Father Paki dabbed his brow with a rag, then wiped a tear from his own eye. "I have sent word to Colonel Kasim but you must know that a slave who strikes a Turk is to be put to death."

"I do not care," answered Christopher. "Not anymore." He knew that his moment of wrath had cost him dearly.

"However, the rule is a *kanun* of the Sultan and not *sharia* law, therefore it is subject to some negotiation. But I am especially concerned about *this* Turk. Zeki's father is a prominent judge in Constantinople, and he is an ambitious little man who wants to take Kasim's rank—"

"As I said, I do not care... not anymore."

Paki shook his head and checked his surgery. "You are fortunate to have healed so well. But you do not understand the punishments the Mohammedans impose. You could be sunk in wet concrete. You could be hung on one of the hooks outside the Gate of the Stream to die slowly. You could be hanged, impaled on a stake, beheaded—"

"I submit to it all," said Christopher calmly. "What is, is. And Leviathan is what is. The world is darkness and I have been a blind fool."

Father Paki sat back.

"Chaos, disorder, call it what you will."

"I know what it means." Paki stared at the tiny candle lighting the cell, thinking. "You go too far, my son. Firstly, chaos is not *all* that is." The priest leaned forward and laid a hand on Christopher. "It is important that you understand this."

"I do not wish to speak of it any longer."

"Then you *are* a fool." Father Paki's tone was suddenly hard. "And fools are slaves to their foolishness. Do you wish to die a slave?"

Christopher refused to answer.

"Until you are wise you shall never be free."

"As I said, I submit to the world as it is. Allow me this simple peace."

Paki heard guards coming. Grumbling, he quickly unrolled a cloth that he had hidden in his robe. "My wife sends this for you." Inside was a small loaf of bread sliced open and filled with honey. "She said you should remember the bees." The priest lifted the bread to his swollen lips. Christopher opened them and lay his tongue out to receive the blessing. At the taste of Nena's honey he began to weep.

❦

On a steamy day in mid-July, Colonel Kasim stormed into the beylik with Sergeant Zeki and Taras at his side. He was taken to Christopher's cell where he unleashed a torrent of curses at the shackled youth. The twenty-year-old Clive was too weak to answer but the sight of Taras drew a faint smile to his lips. Father Paki's weekly gifts of smuggled bread and honey had kept him breathing, but he had lost so much weight that he now hung by his wrists like an awkward skeleton.

Kasim paced in a tight circle. He then shouted in English. "Because you are the property of the Sultan, the pasha did not have you executed. Thus, it fell to me as thy overseer to seek the counsel of the new vizier. He is a violent, ruthless man who now must punish us *both* for this!" He slammed his fist into his palm. "After the mercy I have shown, you strike my sergeant?"

Christopher whispered something, keeping his eyes on Taras.

Kasim drew close. "You cannot say that you are suffering on account of another's crimes now."

"Masha-Allah, as Allah wills," whispered Christopher.

Kasim roared in frustration and slapped the frail young man ferociously. "Do not ever mock the true religion again." He turned his back on Christopher and snapped at Taras. Switching to Turkish he barked, "Tell him."

Taras stepped forward. "First, the battalion's imam testified that the Prophet...blessed be his name...taught that men should be judged by their *intentions.* After that, the colonel's lawyer argued that in acting to defend your life, you *intended* to protect the property of the Sultan. Thus your life should be spared."

Christopher grunted.

"After much hand-wringing, the unhappy vizier agreed and ordered you to be punished severely but not executed."

"I do not care."

"You should." Taras then called for a smith waiting in the corridor with irons and tools. Changing subjects, he whispered. "An English fleet is approaching."

Christopher shrugged.

"King Charles has negotiators in the city but our agents believe your Lord Sandwich is planning a bombardment."

Christopher looked away. "It does not matter to me, not any longer. Raven is gone and I am not even a man."

The smith released Christopher from his shackles, but then fastened an iron fetter to his ankle and draped its heavy chain over his bony shoulder. Scowling, Zeki then dragged Christopher out of the beylik with Taras, Kasim and three city guards.

"Prepare yourself, Englishman," said Zeki.

Saying nothing more, Kasim exited the prison and marched away, leaving Christopher in the custody of the others.

Struggling to keep his balance, Christopher teetered downhill and toward the harbour now bustling with men preparing for the English attack. Delivered to dockside, Christopher was finally given some clean water which he gulped. Duty done, the city guards left. Sergeant Zeki then grumbled something and walked away. Taras quickly fed Kipper a handful of raisins, soft goat cheese and a small loaf of coarse wheat bread.

Christopher trembled as he stared at a large galley with two towering lateen sails. On board, slump-shoulder slaves were chained to their benches. The reek of the unwashed oarsmen filled the air. Their one-hundred sweeps lay still in the turquoise water, protruding from the gunwale like thin bones strung along the spine of a great fish. Fearing the worst, he stopped chewing.

The galley was a slim, low-riding *kadirga* that had battled the Venetians for nearly twenty years—including a recent skirmish that had left her men exhausted and her bow slightly damaged. She was manned by a Turkish crew of thirty-five, a company of Janissary marines and 500 naked Christian slaves roasting under the North African sun.

Christopher was not unaware of the infamy attached to such ships as this. *I am to be chained on that!* He trembled all the more. After all, he had read that once chained to a bench few moved for any reason other than death. The French, Spanish, and Italians had filled their own galleys with Muslim slaves and so it had always seemed perversely fair to Christopher that the Ottomans would pack theirs with Christians. But the inhumanity before him took his breath away. He remembered reading that 20,000 Christians sank to the bottom of the sea chained to Turkish galleys in the Battle of Lepanto decades before. His legs went weak.

A dark-skinned smith smelling of garlic then appeared from nowhere alongside Zeki and deftly released Christopher from his fetter. Laughing wickedly, the sergeant immediately shoved Christopher toward the galley. "Take a good look at this; it is the final home for many a Christian." He spat into his face and ordered Taras to take the quaking Englishman aboard.

Saying nothing, Taras wrapped a huge hand around Christopher's bony arm and steadied him as the pair walked up the gangway of the galley. Once arrived at the rail, the ship's one-eyed barber took control of the trembling Englishman. He shaved Kipper's head with a long razor, stripped him completely naked and then ordered him to a starboard bench near amidships. There he was squeezed between two stinking men of the five who shared a narrow, four-foot bench.

Numb with dread, Christopher watched Taras fade away. He sat his bare arse on a thin padding of wool covered by a rotting sheepskin stained by the defecations of others. His sweated, snow-white skin pressed tightly against the slippery, salt-ulcerated shoulders of each neighbour. Beneath him sloshed a disgusting slurry of sea water, urine and human feces.

A crewman jerked his left foot from under him and fastened a chain to the iron ringlet still wrapping his ankle. His right foot was then placed flat on the stretcher—a board nailed on the edge of the bench in front of him against which he'd press his leg while pulling at the huge oar.

Christopher's head went light and his skeletal body began to lean against the slave to his left.

"*Levati*," muttered the wretch.

Christopher forced himself upright and looked at his neighbour. The slave was an Italian with lifeless brown eyes and a skull-like face void of teeth. His protruding ribs grotesquely scalloped his torso.

A shirtless Moor under a turban then ordered Christopher to wrap his hands firmly on the forty-foot oar. He began screaming in his ear. "When you hear the boatswain's whistle, lift yourself against the stretcher, throw your body back and pull the sweep with all your might. Then do it again and again until the whistle blows. Stop and you are whipped." The growling Moor stuffed a piece of wine-soaked bread into Christopher's cracked mouth.

Disoriented and barely able to sit up, Kipper swallowed slowly and wiped his palms gingerly along the mighty oar. The wood felt smooth to his touch. He looked at fifty pairs of identical oars along each side of the ship.

Christopher then stared into the stern. There, ornate quarters sheltered the captain and special passengers, including Kasim who was now staring into the galley beneath an enormous cap replete with a tall plume. Christopher followed the colonel's gestures as he drank from a tiny cup and nibbled on food under a green canopy. He then spotted Taras stepping quickly along the centre aisle.

"Taras?" Christopher moaned. "Taras? For the sake of Christ..."

Eventually spotting him, Taras stopped. "This is your punishment. You live or die as Allah wills."

Christopher stared at him. "I shall die, then. But this suffering..."

The soldier stared at the wretch sadly. "Evet. It is possible you will die, but I think not." He then hurried forward to join a handful of marines gathering atop the forecastle.

The hope of the ship's rais was to slip out of the harbour and hurry beyond the reach of the approaching English fleet. Though a warship, the galley's shallow hold had been hastily filled with some precious cargo from faraway places, including salt hauled by camel from Taoudenni, several crates of books bound by the scholars of Timbuktu, and a select group of terrified young female slaves from Dagomba.

Just before the afternoon song of the muezzins, the galley was ready. With sea birds crying from above, the ship's master nodded to the boatswain who blew his silver whistle. At the shrill blast, the galley slaves came alive like fearful dogs. Christopher's heart began to race. He followed the movements of his neighbours as best he could.

Facing the stern, each man quickly pressed his unchained foot hard against the stretcher board and took firm hold of his long oar. Each lifted from his seat in unison with his fellows and—with many moans and curses—all pulled mightily on their sweeps until their bare arses collapsed atop their benches. They then leaned forward to raise the great paddles, only to lift their bodies and heave once again.

The boatswain controlled the pace from his place next to the captain. Two lesser officers prowled along the centre aisle with long whips. One was amidships, the other at the bow. When seeing a man begin to fail, these officers would strike the slave harshly.

The ship had barely left the harbour when Christopher felt his first blow. He cried out. "Christ have mercy!"

The man hit him again.

Christopher strained against his leg and heaved, then sat and leaned, and heaved again. For the next hour, he struggled to keep the methodical rhythm of the men on either side. Groaning, "Christ," he gasped for air as the oar rocked forward; he then grit his teeth as he rose up to pull it back again.

The sun above blazed hot against his tender skin and the shimmering water just yards away offered little more kindness than an occasional spray. Over the next five hours he slowly fell into a hypnotic state. His body obeyed the cadence of his fellows the best it could; his mind numbed into some nothingness, awakened only by the occasional sting of the whip.

Evening fell and a little breeze finally began to fill the triangular sails above. The boatswain blew his whistle and the slaves collapsed forward on their oars to keep them from dragging on the sea. Christopher thought he must be dead; he would have wept but did not have the strength.

As the stars emerged in the cloudless sky above, a crewman stuffed bread into Christopher's mouth and someone followed with a ration of stewed beans. He then guzzled a measured amount of water and was abandoned to sleep slumped across his oar.

Somewhere in the night, Christopher slid off the oar and slipped from his seat. Cursing, his neighbours kicked him away from their legs, leaving him to lie chained in the disgusting slurry of the scupper as a cramped tangle of a man. Unconscious, he did not wake to the first call to prayer, nor to the boatswain's whistle that followed soon after. This prompted a furious assault against him by an officer. He was jerked atop his bench, whipped and repeatedly slapped but did not respond until a bucket of seawater was thrown over him. At last, Christopher stirred, only to collapse across his oar, helpless.

CHAPTER 23

CHRISTOPHER AWAKENED IN the low hold of the galley, shivering and chained to a timber. Delirious, he thought he heard the distant voices of women speaking in a strange language. The sound of it frightened him. He covered his ears and turned his body into itself as if he might hide. He retched on the reek of feces and urine that had slicked over his skin. He fainted again.

When he awakened, he listened to the voices once more. Wide-eyed in the black hold, he clutched his hands together like a mad man. "I am in hell...in hell." He began to jabber and the voices stopped. "I am in the belly of Leviathan." Terrified, he clawed at empty air and hissed for the spirits to leave him alone.

Hours passed. Christopher alternated between terror and numbness, even as the ship heaved forward according to the alternating strokes of her suffering oarsmen above. From somewhere in the darkness, an unseen hand suddenly forced a meagre bit of mouldy bread into his mouth and poured a thimble of water over his sun-blistered lips before vanishing. At long last, however, a friend arrived following a small candle through the hold.

"I have been worried for you, Christopher Effendi."

Christopher stared into the little light, then lifted his eyes. "Taras?'

"It is I."

"O thank Christ."

Taras gave him a generous draught of clean water and some bread.

Christopher drank and chewed, and then began to weep. "I am so afraid."

"Of course."

"I hear voices. Who is here with me? Demons?"

"There are no jinn here, only Blackamoor girls. They are in chains in the stern. You are safe."

Relieved, Christopher nodded.

"The rais wants you at the oar again in the morning. Kasim has agreed."

Christopher gasped.

"Kasim showed you mercy because he agrees that the Prophet—blessed be his name—did not intend for a man to bear the burden of another's crime. But this attack on Zeki is *your* burden, alone."

"I cannot survive the bench."

The soldier placed a fig into Christopher's mouth. "Some men ride the bench for fifteen years. You did not last one day."

Christopher struggled to chew his fig.

"Do not be ashamed. When the drovers tied me to my captor's saddle, my mother said to me that no man is able enough to overcome all things."

Christopher tried to answer.

Taras placed another fig through Christopher's bleeding lips. "You are too weak to row and you are also too weak to resist the order." Stoic, the soldier stood. "Do not let the fear of what you cannot do rule you."

As the galley ploughed forward under the late night groaning of her oarsmen, Christopher wrestled within himself. Somewhere in the hold, a score of African girls hummed soft songs in their shackles. *Am I any different than those poor wretches?* He took a trembling breath and then another. The song of the slaves slowly comforted him. *But I was supposed to be a great heir, a gentleman of promise, a conquering prince...*"

Clinging to the damp timber at his side, Christopher began to consider all that had brought him to this place. He eventually shook away the images of his grandfather's head in Yusef Rais' hands. *There are greater powers than us, Grandfather.* He thought of Raven and yanked pathetically at the chain tethering his ankle to an iron eye. He yielded. "I cannot save her." He set his spine against the timber and let his rump sag to the damp decking. *There it is then; this is who I am.*

Christopher breathed slowly over the next hour, inhaling recollections of the man he was supposed to be—and exhaling them all with deep resignation. As he did, he sobbed, wiped his eyes with the heel of his hands and then whispered to the two angels he now saw standing before him.

Too weak to stand, Christopher reached a limp arm toward them. "Can ye save Raven?" The angels looked compassionate. "Can ye?" He waited, respectfully, then asked, "What of the Blackamoors? Can ye save them as well?"

Christopher held his breath, hoping. "Hello?" *Perchance they could take us all to Virginia?* The very thought of Virginia summoned his heavy eyes to close, and a vision of wide rivers and virgin forests filled his mind. Étalon was galloping beneath him; Raven's arms were wrapped tightly around him.

The ship pitched and Christopher returned. Virginia gone, he stared peacefully into the darkness of the hold. His angels were gone, but an unexpected sense of calm filled him. His tongue tasted of honey. He licked his lips and he smiled.

⚓

Just before dawn, Christopher yielded his frail body to the crewmen who dragged him from the hold. Spitting on him, they chained his leg on the larboard side between two sour Frenchmen in the void created by a Spaniard who had died in the night. Saying nothing, he sucked on salty, damp air and fixed his hands to the oar. He set his free foot obediently on the stretcher and waited for the whistle and the lash.

Merciful rain pelted the ship for that day and the next, and a stiff westerly breeze kept the triangular sails filled, thereby keeping the rowing to short intervals.

However, the third day was dead calm and even though the galley was now far beyond the reach of the English fleet, the boatswain's men struck writhing backs ferociously.

On this day, the sun began to roast the suffering oarsmen again, and by dusk Christopher had nearly expired. He touched a light finger to his blistered skin. He could feel blood leaking along his back from too many stripes. He tried to scratch at his itching legs now infected from the filth splashing upward from the scupper. A freshly lit lantern on the stern caught his eye. Groaning in pain, Christopher raised his head to receive a sympathetic glance from Colonel Kasim.

Just after the noon prayers of the next day, two Janissaries marched along the centre aisle and ordered Christopher's chain be removed. Too weak to speak, Christopher watched numbly as an angry crewman obeyed. A voice from one side found him. He squinted his eyes to see the naked body of a towering man now waiting at the end of the bench. "Taras?"

The muscular Ukrainian stood bravely. "Allah wills you to live."

"But…" Strong hands took hold of his armpits and legs. "Taras, I…"

As he was dragged from the bench, Taras offered an ankle to the smith. "Do not be ashamed, Christopher Effendi. No man can overcome all things."

Christopher tried to answer but failed, even as Taras took his place on the bench. Carried away, he writhed at the jarring screech of the boatswain's whistle. The snap of a whip on the flesh of a nearby slave made him retch.

Kipper Clive began to weep.

⁂

Sixteen days later, the galley dropped her anchor in the small harbour of Jaffa on the coast of Palestine nearly forty English miles west of Jerusalem. Jaffa had been destroyed centuries before in the wake of the Crusades and left in disrepair to prevent another invasion from Christendom. The once busy harbour was now nearly deserted, but it was the closest port to Jerusalem and Kasim was impatient to return to the rest of his men garrisoned there.

Two pairs of callused hands dragged Christopher from the hold and taken past the poop deck where Taras was dressing gingerly under a canopy. Christopher tried to speak a word of thanks but could barely open his lips. He was then carried to a dockside Christian hospice where sisters bathed him, dressed his wounds and fed him a salty broth.

The next day, a smith fastened a light, ten-pound fetter to his ankle. A Turk tossed him jackal-hide sandals and a fresh linen robe. By dawn he stood in the column making ready to begin the three-day march to Jerusalem.

Waiting quietly for the journey to begin, Christopher watched a soldier mount a camel and raise the Janissaries' standard—a half-green, half-yellow forked flag that bore the image of a soup kettle. A second standard-bearer mounted his rising camel and lifted the flag of Kasim's battalion toward the blue sky. The flag of the 27th displayed six black canons crossed like 'x's' on a yellow field. All things in order, the battalion band then struck up a Turkish martial tune. *March? I can barely stand...*A ferocious command from Kasim startled him. He took a breath. The Janissaries shouted in unison, and Christopher took his first step.

Within the hour, Taras came alongside Christopher and handed him a canteen. "You survived, Effendi."

Christopher guzzled a draft of water, then looked at Taras for the first time since that moment on the galley. "You need not ever call me 'Effendi,'" he choked. "As I have said before, I am no 'Sir.' Not any longer and never to you." He shifted his fetter. "I saw God that day; He was in your mercy. *Baraka Allahu fika*, may Allah reward you."

Embarrassed, the soldier looked away.

"They whipped you?"

"A little."

Christopher studied the man. "Why did Kasim approve your relief of me?"

Taras wiped his moustache. "The sons of Islam are charitable."

Christopher said nothing for a long moment. He took a slow drink. *Mercy and misery dwell as one with these people.* He then asked, "Was Kasim born a Turk?"

"No. He is Albanian but raised as a Turk. His father was an Orthodox priest."

"He was taken in the tax of Christian boys, like you."

Taras nodded. "His mother cut his face so the Turks would not want him. But they took him anyway and crucified her. His scars keep him from the honour of palace duties. She should have submitted."

"So, like you, he was first a Christian— "

"We are both what we are, today."

207

The men fell silent and continued their eastward march past cotton fields filling the flatlands around the approaching city of Ramallah. Between them sprouted a few vineyards and fruit orchards. It was a more pleasant land than Christopher had expected.

"What happened to the African girls?" asked Christopher.

"They will be sold in Constantinople. They will submit to Allah and serve the desires of their masters."

"And what of charity?"

"It is charitable that they are young and beautiful. It is charitable that they will be dressed in silk and drink cool water in the shade of their master's villa."

"Like Raven." Christopher's tone was suddenly bitter.

"You must release her. If you do not, you will go mad."

⧖

11 August 1661

In the afternoon of the third day, the column crested a difficult summit and Christopher shielded his eyes to scan the scene before him. There, tucked into the lion skin of the Judean hills, he found the sandy-white blocks that formed the high walls of Jerusalem. The lump filling his throat surprised him. He surveyed the distant stone terraces, domes and pointed minarets. "It is beautiful," Christopher muttered. "And He was here, in this very place…"

Two hours of silence passed until Kasim's column finally arrived at the Jaffa Gate almost one full year since the raid on Skeefe. Christopher followed obediently as Kasim commanded his men forward through a crowd of clamouring travellers. Looking from side to side, he listened as Taras explained that infidels were barred entrance without a proper escort and the adequate fee.

Christopher thought there to be about one-hundred or so loitering angrily about and waiting impatiently for a variety of consuls or chaperones. *I'd like to tell them that they don't have it so bad!*

"The city is on constant alert for Crusaders," said Taras. "That is why that man is being arrested for not unbuckling his sword. Others are being questioned as spies."

Christopher said nothing, but simply tramped forward on weary legs as Kasim led them through the gate, past crowing merchants, and to the fortress located close by along the centre of Jerusalem's West Wall. Weary but awestruck to be inside the Holy City, Christopher marched within the middle of the column in his Turkish shirt and trousers, leaning hard to his left under the weight of his fetter.

Arriving at the gate of the Citadel, he waited silently as Kasim then prepared his men. Christopher studied the fortress with a curious eye. It was enclosed by an irregular rectangle of huge blocks that formed an outer curtain defensive wall. Surrounded by a moat, it contained the soldiers' barracks, numerous offices and storehouses, two mosques, and several courtyards.

Taras pointed to the garrison's five massive towers overlooking the city and the western horizon. "From here we can defeat the world," he said.

Christopher grunted. "I suppose you believe that. The same would be said in London."

Kasim finally ordered his men inside the fortress. Christopher obediently marched through the outer gate of the garrison's eastern portal, then over a fixed wooden bridge and through a second gate flanked by a receding niche leading him under a pointed arch into a primary courtyard. Once inside, he and the 27th battalion stood in wait alongside the battalion's bronze kazan. A mighty 'huzzah' was sounded and the band struck up a lively march.

Christopher marvelled at the integration of power and beauty in this place, but his awe was soon interrupted by a rough hand across his head, directing him into a small workshop where a smith waited with tools in hand. In moments he was relieved of his fetter.

Burden lifted, Christopher was then led to a clean cell at the base of one of the Citadel's towers where he was locked away with a handful of angry pilgrims imprisoned for untold violations. He rubbed his ankle. *Now what is coming for me?*

CHAPTER 24

FOR THE DAYS that followed, Christopher rested on a comfortable
wool-stuffed mattress, was escorted to the garrison's latrine in due
times, fed well and properly watered. His body began to heal; his
mind began to clear. However, in his recovery he now struggled
against a persistent melancholy which Taras attempted to relieve with
simple kindnesses like freshly picked grapes or a summer date.

On his twelfth day in the cell, a guard delivered Christopher to a
courtyard where Taras met him without a word and led him through
the coolness of a shaded stone stairway into Colonel Kasim's office.
With Sergeant Zeki watching carefully from one side, Kasim finished
a drink of some kind, took a bite of bread and rose from his desk.
He stared at Christopher from his black eyes and said nothing for a
very long while. He finally removed the plumed, white börk from his
immense head and wiped his brow with a blue kerchief.

Christopher shifted, uneasily.

Leaning his rump against the front of his richly oiled, cedar desk,
the colonel crossed his yellow boots and spoke—this time in English.
"Everyone in my world is unhappy. Are you unhappy?"

Christopher shrugged.

Kasim received a small cup of thick Turkish coffee from a servant. The aroma filled the room. He sipped it, slowly. "You understand that you are destined to be the Sultan's slave until the end of
thine days?"

Christopher said nothing.

"You may convert to Islam if you wish, but this shall not free thee. Nothing you can do shall ever free thee. Nothing you can do can free the girl. Nothing can save the other Irish."

Christopher did not react.

Kasim swatted a fly. "I am commanded to assign a second keeper to you who serves as thy daily guardian. I have chosen Taras. Zeki is not happy about it, though this honour comes with a great weight."

Relieved, Christopher nodded.

"Now hear this plainly: If you even *attempt* escape, Raven shall be taken from her master and executed. This was a condition of her sale and I want this to be perfectly clear."

Hearing 'Raven' startled Christopher. He raised his eyes.

Kasim leaned his head forward. "Secondly, if you were to *succeed* in an escape, I am to be stripped of rank, pension, and deprived of all personal wealth. Further, Taras would be sentenced to a galley for ten years. Do you understand this?"

Christopher nodded. "I understand." *These penalties are severe.*

Kasim studied him for a long moment. "Good." He moved behind his desk and sat atop a wide-armed chair, one hand-carved in Persia. He dropped a date into his mouth. "Now, to the other unfortunate matter: You should never have struck Zeki, even to save thine own life."

Kasim swallowed, slowly. "The vizier's punishment was satisfied by thy time at the oar. You should praise Allah for his mercy. However, because you were improperly supervised, *I* have now been fined heavily by my superiors—ten Dutch gold pieces to be precise. That is the value of a small herd of Arabian horses."

The colonel took another date. "Further, my sergeant correctly argues that the battalion was insulted by thy brash actions. Therefore, on behalf of all my men and myself *I* must now punish thee in some fashion." He paused. "Zeki wants you executed, of course; others want you to be beaten severely or at the very least, humiliated. They even took a vote in the barracks."

Christopher stiffened.

Kasim leaned forward and returned to Turkish, glancing sideways at Zeki. "But I believe a *symbolic* penalty is in order." He sipped some coffee. "Therefore, I order you to be tied to an unsheltered post at the Eastern Portal for twenty-two days and nights in order to contemplate your crime. This is one day for each of the years that the Prophet…blessed be his name…received the words of the Quran from the archangel Gabriel.

"Further, at each of the five calls to prayer you will recite each of the Six Articles of our true religion."

Secretly relieved, Christopher listened in silence.

"You will then spend sixty-six days as a servant of the battalion, attending to my men's daily demands. This is the holy number of Allah the Merciful." Kasim released a long breath and his shoulders relaxed.

Staring at Zeki, he switched back to English. "Once this matter is behind us you shall begin thy duties as my personal scribe. I own an olive grove and presses in Nazareth, I deal in cotton cloth from my fields near Ramallah, I wholesale soda ash for soap, own herds of camels and goats near Damascus that I shear for camlets, and I import rare spices from the desert.

"I move all of these products through agents in Cadiz, Alexandria, Constantinople, and even Venice and Ragusa. I have a villa by the Galilean Sea in Tiberius. So you see, Sir Christopher Clive, I am no mere soldier. I intend to spend my late years in comfort."

Christopher was impressed.

Kasim took a bite of a Turkish biscuit. He then drank some more coffee before folding his arms. "Since you speak English, Turkish and some Arabic, you shall also tend to my commercial interests as a translator, especially with the Levant Company. You shall write correspondence on my behalf to the infidels of thy miserable islands or to my superiors in Constantinople, and do any other duty for which you are able."

Kasim set his jaw. "You shall live in a small apartment just outside the garrison where I shall have guards rotated. This is to be thy life, Christopher Effendi. I suggest you submit to it, for it could be far worse."

⁂

After the muezzins' call to the dawn prayers of the day following, Sergeant Zeki, Taras, and two Janissaries took Christopher Clive to a tall pole in the middle of the courtyard just beyond the Eastern Portal. He was ordered to remove his shirt. One of Turks then pulled his arms around a well-greased, fifteen-foot cypress post and bound his wrists with leather cords. Mocking the crucifixion of Jesus, a sign was then nailed over his head that was written in Turkish, English, and Hebrew: *Disrespectful Crusader.*

Threatened by a long, punishing cane, Christopher was immediately forced to recite Islam's *Six Articles of Faith.* To Zeki's chagrin, he recited each perfectly, thus avoiding a strike.

For the hours that followed, Christopher bore the insults of passers-by and an occasional tossed egg or wad of spittle. The sun was hot and his limbs ached. But compared to the horror of the galley, he was grateful.

On the second day, Christopher noticed a Catholic sister standing nearby praying from under a small sycamore tree. As the first Muslim prayer ended, he fixed his eyes on her. She was short, stout, and draped within the black and white folds of her habit. He began his recitation: "We believe in one God, Allah." He spat.

The soldier struck him for spitting.

Christopher arched his back in pain, cursing. He went on to the second. "We believe in unseen beings."

"Evet." The old soldier grumbled. "Now the third."

"We believe that Allah sent prophets into the world."

By the dawn prayers of his fourteenth day, Kipper Clive's back was welted with a few stripes from the cane, and his shoulders were blistered by the sun; feces ran down his legs. But he remained thankful for what mercies had found him, including the kind face of the Catholic sister.

When Christopher finished his first recitations of the day, Taras faithfully ladled water to his lips from a wooden bucket and then emptied the bucket over him. He then untied him for his allotted rest, fed him some bread, olives and a small cluster of freshly picked grapes. "Kasim's mercy has infuriated Zeki," said Taras. "He plots day and night against the çorbasi."

Christopher lay to one side and stretched his aching limbs. "What can Zeki possibly do to Kasim?"

"Zeki has family at the Sultan's palace who can work magic."

Six hours later, the muezzins began their song for the *dhuhr* prayers. Christopher locked his gaze upon the sister and began his recitations. He missed part of the third Article and received a vicious strike. Cursing, he went on to the fourth, carefully. "We believe that… Allah gave… sacred Scriptures to his Prophets.

"The fifth is we believe there will be a Day of Judgement."

Christopher's mouth was parched. "The sixth: We believe that Allah's decree is supreme in all things." He was too dry to spit.

With Christopher done for the second prayer of that day, Taras tossed a bucket of cool water over his head again. "Soon this will be over." He glanced at the sister now walking briskly toward them. He set a second bucket near Christopher. "Mercy can be found in every day." Christopher slid to the ground as Taras walked away.

The woman arrived at Christopher's side and chased off three mockers who had thrown garbage at the Christian. She looked down at him and smiled. The sister had a round red face and a small nose. Her tiny eyes twinkled from beneath full brows. Defiant wisps of black hair edged the white wimple pressed against her full cheeks. "I hope ya can forgive me, but my superior forbade my approach until today. She said she had to pray about it... dried up old sow."

At the sound of her musical Irish, Kipper's heart lifted.

The sister dipped Taras' ladle into the bucket. "Drink tiss."

Christopher sucked at the water splashing over his lips. "Bless thee, nun," he muttered.

"Don't bless me, curse the Mohammedans." The woman gave him another drink. "And I am a *sister*, not a nun. Ya must be a Protty, else ya'd know tat nuns stay hidden; sisters serve."

"Thanks be to God for you, whatever you are."

"Drink." She held her nose. "And by the saints, ya stink."

Christopher took a drink, then another and another.

The sister reached into a satchel by her side. "So, m'name's Mary. What else could it be?" She shoved a wedge of cheese into Kipper's mouth. "I am a Dominican sister on pilgrimage from my work at the bottom of the Kingdom of Poland." She then read the sign over his head. "'*Insulting Crusader*.' I like the sound of tat."

Christopher swallowed. "My name is Christopher, Christopher Clive. But call me 'Kipper.'"

Mary stooped and pushed more cheese into his mouth. "Englishman. Too bad."

He stared at the sister and chewed.

"So, I'm guessin if ya turned Turk it would have gone a bit easier fer ya?"

"Aye, perhaps, but then they would have circumcised me." He forced a smile from his bleeding lips.

Sister Mary howled. "Indeed, ya wouldn't want tat. Now, tell me. What did ya do to earn tiss insult, Kipper Clive?"

"I punched a Turk."

"Ha! Well done, boyo. Tat's de best ting I heard all day." Mary fed him a biscuit. "But ya don't look good. How many more days?"

"Eight."

Mary then studied him, carefully. "My pilgrimage is over in a week."

Christopher wished she could have stayed with him forever. "So you know, I was no friend to Cromwell." He looked longingly upward into the sister's face. *I see God today, Aunt Comfort.* "I love the Irish."

Mary smiled. "I believe ya." She leaned close. "Have ya ever been?"

"I live in County Cork!"

"Ah, County Cork. Never been, but I hear 'tis magical. I was born in County Donegal. 'Tis wild." She leaned closer to him. "You've an Irish lover, do ya not?"

Christopher nearly burst. "Aye, 'tis true!"

Sister Mary chuckled. "Of course it is. I t'ought I seen her in yer eyes. Keep believin fer her, boyo."

He struggled to his feet, nearly weeping. "Must you leave?"

"Indeed I must. I cannot save every puppy, ya know." She took a breath. "But ya can trust tat big Taras fella."

"How do you know?"

Mary laid a hand on Christopher's forehead. "Everythin is not as it seems, Englishman. Now, may the Lord bless ya richly fer not turning Turk. Ya'd be proof tat as long as a man has a breath, he has a choice." The sister stared quietly at Christopher for a very long moment. She then wiped a tear from her eye. "Islam means 'submission.' Did ya know tat?"

Christopher waited.

"Indeed it does. Do not be submittin to the darkness, boyo, not ever."

"I was told that submitting to the chaos is necessary."

Mary narrowed her eyes. "Who told you tat shite?"

"An old slave said chaos is, and I must accept it to live."

Mary pursed her lips, thinking. She fed Christopher a dried fig as she furrowed her brow. "Em…metinks ya did not hear him quite right. 'Tis true we needs accept tat bad tings lurk about." She then took Christopher's jaw in one hand and gently squeezed his face. "But *acceptin* is not the same ting as *submittin*." She kissed his cheek. "'Tis an important difference, so get tat straight in yer head, boyo."

Sister Mary found one more biscuit in her bag. "And by the saints, Kipper, don't suffer big notions too much. Jaysus wants to see ya smile from time to time." She nibbled a bit of the biscuit. "After all, chaos is not the *whole* truth of the way tings be." She set the biscuit lightly into Kipper's blistered mouth. "Tis why we can't save every puppy, and yet every puppy has hope."

Christopher bit down on his biscuit. Inside was a generous swipe of honey that squeezed out over his tongue. His mind flew to Nena. He swallowed, slowly, letting every precious drop of sweetness lift him. "Light and love," he murmured.

"Eh?"

Christopher's mind spun. "Light and love…they exist together against the darkness." A smile urged the corners of his lips. "Father Paki was right; Leviathan is not *all* that is." He smiled, weakly.

Mary narrowed her eyes. "Leviathan?" She then embraced Kipper's stinking, waste-stained body and held him for a long time.

Ignoring the jeers of passers-by, the woman put her hand on his heart. She lifted her eyes and lost them in his. "Now hear me well, boyo: You were born to be light and love yerself. Believe *tat* and the world will change before yer eyes."

Life pulsed through Christopher's body.

Sister Mary then walked away to draw another bucket of water from the well. She returned to Christopher and offered the ladle to his lips. When he finished drinking, she proceeded to pour cool water over his head. "Now I leave ya with tiss final ting: Yer misery is not all bad."

Christopher stared into her face.

"Yer struggle seems to be against the cursed Mohammedans, but 'tis really against the chains tat bind ya in here." She tapped a finger on his chest. "Tat struggle is Wisdom's war to set ya free. 'Tis why the blessed Psalmist said, 'He who is a sower of tears will bear a harvest of joy." Eyes filled, she placed a tender kiss on his cheek and walked away.

PART 2

1675- 1684

The Joy we seek has always been
A Gift-in-wait to dance within.

CHAPTER 25

9 July 1675

LIKE A WAVE rolling weakly across a windless sea, the fourteen years that followed his arrival in Jerusalem passed slowly for Christopher Clive. He remained trammelled to heartache, yet these many years proved to also be merciful. Like Taras, Colonel Kasim treated him more kindly than any slave could have expected. The officer's continued grace had reinforced Christopher's long-held suspicion that an echo of Christian charity had survived somewhere deep within him, perhaps reverberating some early word of truth given to him as a child.

As promised, Kasim had given Christopher the position of scribe for the colonel's affairs and he had quickly risen to become his chief secretary. Therefore, Christopher had spent most of his days at Kasim's office inside the Citadel, or writing within his modest second-storey apartment atop a silversmith's shop just outside the Janissaries' barracks.

Owning nothing, Christopher was nevertheless well fed, dressed in fine Ottoman attire, and given access to an impressive library. Spared the horrors of many other slaves, Christopher was appropriately grateful for his lot and his gratitude made space for him to rest in a fragile joy from time to time.

Taras had remained Kipper's second keeper for all these years and so the two had grown close enough for the Janissary to perpetually worry about him. Taras repeatedly reminded him that simple submission to his state of being would be less painful. "Abandon false hope, my friend. Just let it fly away. *This* is your life. Do not die from a thousand neglects." To which Christopher never failed to answer, "My life may be as it is today, but it is not as it must be tomorrow."

The baronet's words were bold, yet in his inward parts Kipper Clive knew that his endless bondage meant he had no idea what his life could be on any given morrow. So, his other companion for these many passing years had been a distressing infirmity of purpose.

Thankfully, Christopher had been richly blessed on four occasions by visits from Sister Mary who returned to Jerusalem from time to time as a favoured pilgrims' guide for the Polish elite. Christopher and the sister spent hours in deep conversation, usually joined by Taras who was always overjoyed to see the greying sister—a curious response that did not escape Christopher's notice.

Despite all of this, Christopher was not without his treasures. Memories of Raven were more precious to him than the gems filling Ottoman strongboxes throughout the city. Visions of her soulful smile sent him to pleasant dreams by night and soothed his spirit by day. Sitting alone at his desk, he would sometimes catch himself staring blankly at his quill, smiling, only to scratch out a few verses of a poem that he imagined her someday singing before the great hearth of the Clive House in Kinsale.

On this July morning of his thirty-fourth birthday, Christopher sat on the grass of a small shrine in the Muslim quarter of the city under a fruited fig tree reflecting deeply on what was and what might be. He was smoking his ceramic hookah alone and considered the many years that had passed since the raid on Skeefe. He could hardly fathom how it was that he had remained a slave for all this time, and how he was likely little more than a beloved memory for what family yet remained in Ireland.

Christopher sighed. He stared into the quiet water of a clear pool by his side. He could see how his face had aged. No more the naive boy of English privilege, he had become worn as a captive of others. Kasim had curiously permitted his bold mane of golden curls to remain despite its defiant pronouncement. And his clean-shaven jaw still set squarely against all things Muslim. Yet his blue eyes had lost most of their shine and his sun-dried skin had begun to wrinkle at the edges.

For the past hour, Christopher had doodled charcoal sketches or captured the words of a poem. Eventually, he looked up at a tempting summer fig dangling from an overspread branch just over his head. He stood to snatch it when he heard a familiar voice.

"Happy Birthday," Taras approached offering a modest grin. The muscled veteran handed Christopher a folded cloth filled with sweet cakes and olives, and a canteen of pear water. Taras' courageous service in recent wars with the Venetians and his successful encounters with rogue Bedouins had advanced him through the battalion's ranks. The almost forty-year-old was now Kasim's second-in-command—his *Aşçi Usta*—the 'master cook' in the Janissary's odd culinary theme, or what Christopher understood as a lieutenant-colonel.

"Another birthday and somehow I am still here." Christopher received the bundle with a smile and opened the cloth to remove a cake.

Taras removed his cap—a gold banded börk with a red conical sleeve falling behind. "You English are stubborn."

Christopher chuckled and took a bite. "Perhaps a little. Can you sit with me?"

Taras folded his robes behind his baggy pants and sat in the grass across from Christopher. The soldier was still Spartan in many respects, but more than a decade of friendship had softened him.

Admiring Christopher's sketches of passers-by, Taras said, "You should draw Zeki and then write a poem about Satan."

The two laughed, loudly.

"So, Zeki was promoted after all."

"Yes. He went from our 'scullion' to our 'cook'...a captain."

Christopher shook his head. "You should create a rank of 'garbage collector' for the likes of him."

"He fought hard on Crete. But the truth is that his family at the Palace put a great deal of pressure on Kasim."

Christopher pursed his lips around the hookah's *sipsi* and drew on his pipe. The fragranced tobacco smoke hubble-bubbled through the water bowl, followed the curves of the embroidered hose and filled his mouth. He released it slowly and studied the large Cossack. Taras had become well-seasoned by his soldier's life. His hands were thick and callused like a mason's. His clean-shaven jaw jutted forward like a battering block; like his hair, his moustache was greying. With his colourful uniform and his hints of Hun, Christopher thought Taras to look like the hero of an Oriental fable.

"I hear the Sultan is fighting against a tough new general of the Poles," said Christopher. "Kasim says he is a hard man." He handed the amber *sipsi* to Taras, now pulling off his yellow shoes.

"His name is Sobieski. I think we should remember it." Taras drew on the pipe. "As I once told you, it is likely that my grandfather took my family northwest to a place called Podylla. It is where my mother was born." Taras took another long draw on the bubbling pipe, then splashed his hand in the cool pool. "I say this because Podylla is ruled by the Poles for now, but Allah will soon add it to the Caliphate. Sobieski will not like that."

The two then spotted an obese Sufi dervish walking by, deep in thought. The teacher wore a close-fitting cotton *kufi* on his head and loose blue robes. He had tiny eyes set close to the bridge of his small nose. Christopher and Taras both knew him from his lectures on mystical teachings at the coffee house where more traditional Muslim imams often debated him.

Christopher called out, "Stop thinking, Doctor Ozan. Enlightenment comes from love, not knowledge."

The Sufi whirled about. "Christopher Effendi! You interrupted me."

Christopher laughed. "*Astaghfirullah*."

"You should not speak of Allah at all, Christian, and he will not forgive you."

"As Allah wills."

Dr. Ozan shook his head and walked away.

"Be careful, friend," said Taras. He stood to pick a fig from the tree and sat again. "You laugh, but our corps remain closely tied to the Sufis, perhaps now more than ever."

Christopher shrugged.

"You cling to your spirit of rebellion."

"I am what I am today." Christopher smirked.

Taras drew on the tobacco and released a thick cloud of smoke, thoughtfully. "Kasim is pleased with you. He says you are a brilliant negotiator. You should be happy about this."

"I expected to be doing business for my own assets, not those of another."

Taras said nothing for a long moment. He looked carefully at his friend, now scrolling meaningless loops of charcoal on a scrap of paper. "You remain a captive of her memory for all this time."

"Of course."

"Many years have passed, Kipper Clive. You should set yourself free."

"Free? Who is free? Even you are a slave."

"Freedom is an illusion. We are all free and yet we are all slaves."

"Doctor Ozan has taught you well."

Taras remained silent for a moment. He then said, "If a man has a choice, he is free."

Christopher picked up an olive and then dropped it back into the cloth. He then reached for a cake. "Ah, I see it now. Yes, you are correct. I am free to choose between an olive or a cake."

"You mock me, but to have *any* choice is to be at least free in part."

"Then I am not free enough."

"So you do admit to having *some* freedom?"

Christopher pursed his lips. He then burst into laughter. "Fine! If that is freedom, then I am free indeed. Allah be praised."

"We do not lack freedom; we lack choices." Taras stood. "Now wait here. I have two gifts for you."

In less than a half hour, Taras returned with a brown, leather-covered box, a basket of food and a perspiring Dr. Ozan. This time, Christopher stood to greet the round dervish with a polite English handshake.

Ozan then placed his hand over his heart. "Peace, mercy, and the blessings of Allah be upon you."

The Sufi proceeded to collapse awkwardly upon the dry grass in order to sit partially crossed-legged in front of Christopher and alongside Taras. The Muslim monk reached into Taras' basket and retrieved some bread, cheese and a dried date. "We are all on a journey, but I am told that you are lost, Christian."

Christopher narrowed his eyes at Taras.

Dr. Ozan then recited two lines from one of Rumi's ancient poems:

"'I do not care if you are dead,
For Jesus is here and wants to resurrect somebody.'"

Christopher furrowed his brow.

"You think you are dead, but I am here to give you an answer. Like the prophet Jesus, we are all part of the great struggle toward Divine Oneness."

Is that what the struggle is about? Christopher doubted Ozan had struggled very much in his lifetime. His hands were soft and his clothes were expensive.

"You must learn how to be one with the Love that lies at the heart of all things," said Ozan. "Then you will have peace."

Christopher's mind raced to Raven's Cove and the Breath that had filled that place with love. The Sufi's notion was tempting. "In this we agree, but Mohammedans only offer love to those who submit to the teachings of the Prophet. You kill the rest or enslave them. I call that evil."

Dr. Ozan wiped his forehead with a silk kerchief. "Evil is an illusion."

Christopher thought for a long moment. He was not unfamiliar with Sufi teaching. He had also spent hours in conversation with Christian monks, especially Irish monks. "God is love. This I believe," Christopher said. "And God is at the centre of all things. However, evil is not an illusion. Ask the men on the galleys."

"We could play with words, Christian. I tell you this plainly: the illusion of evil can be shed from the world through the disciplines of enlightenment." The dervish placed an olive into his mouth, content in his wisdom.

Christopher shook his head. "Your reach exceeds your grasp, teacher. Evil exists, and men are not made to overcome it in their own power." He glanced at Taras.

"You are partially correct, my son. Illusions cannot be shed by *unenlightened* men. But the disciplines of enlightenment release the divinity that *is* us." Now very pleased with himself, Dr. Ozan popped a date into his mouth. "This is the deep wisdom that lies beneath all true religion."

Christopher tapped a finger on his chin, thinking. "So, deep inside you believe you are a little god." He took an olive of his own. "Then what say you to this:

"I am sacred but not divine.
I am one with all things, and yet I am a particular man.
I walk alone and yet surrounded.
I am born to bear and yet be free.
I have knowledge and know little.
My God is beyond the stars,
And yet He has touched the earth."

Grumbling, Dr. Ozan struggled to his feet.

Christopher smiled. "I see." He stood with the Sufi. "Let me tell you what I think: You sages of 'true religion' are lost within yourselves. You are blind to your pride. Thus, ignorant of your ignorance, you attempt to overthrow ignorance. So you defeat yourselves like men attempting to breathe more air without exhaling."

Dr. Ozan's eyes bulged. "Christopher Effendi, you shall never be free. I will waste no more breath on you."

"I am already free. My struggle is for choices."

Watching the Sufi master disappear, Christopher then reached into Taras' basket and retrieved some sweet bread. He sat down, chewed slowly and then swallowed a long draught of pear water. He re-lit his exhausted pipe and glanced at Taras, certain that something was troubling the soldier. "I did not intend to insult your dervish."

"No, it is not that," answered Taras.

Christopher drew deeply on his water-pipe and released a fog of fragrant smoke as he handed Taras the *sipsi*. "I know you are trying to help me."

Taras sucked on the pipe and blew rings of smoke into the evening air. "I thought you were lost. You are not as lost as I feared."

"No, I *am* lost. I do not know who I have become, and so I do not know how to hope. This causes me great anguish, especially in the night."

Taras studied his friend. "You are not as lost as you think. And you are still becoming." He picked at some grass. "Did you *ever* know who you were seeking to be?"

"When I was a boy I thought of myself as an heir of great promise...whatever that was supposed to mean."

"Who told you this?"

"Everyone." Christopher ran his fingers through his hair and tossed his mane to one side. As he did, he noticed the deep distraction in Taras' dark eyes. It was then he realized that Taras was engaged in a struggle of his own.

"I wonder if the boy inside wanted to be something else," said Taras.

Christopher shifted his rump. "I do not remember thinking about it. Nothing seemed so complicated then. I was to *be* what I was to *do*." He paused. "But what of you?"

Ignoring the question, Taras plucked two overhead figs. "These taste like fruits, but few know that a fig is actually a flower." He tossed Christopher one fig and then bit into his own as he sat. "Few know the man you actually are...even you."

Kipper rubbed his fig clean, eyeing Taras carefully. "You have become wise."

Brow deeply furrowed, Taras studied his friend for a very long moment. "Perhaps I have been wrong all this time." He looked at the fig tree. "We have always been *who* we are. What can change is *how* we are."

Surprised at the soldier's comment, Christopher carefully considered his words. He chewed his fig, slowly, and said nothing more until deep shadows began to cover the grassy shrine.

A quick gust of wind stirred the tiny pool and Taras broke the reflective mood. "Enough of this. I have another gift." He handed Christopher the narrow, leather-wrapped box still setting to one side. "Kasim sends it to you."

Curious, Christopher received the box, opened it, and retrieved several scrolls, three fine quills and a sealed jar of black ink. On the bottom was a small bolt of cotton cloth in which was wrapped a half dozen charcoal sticks. "I do not understand."

"Kasim thinks you are happiest when you are writing your poems or drawing your pictures. The çorbasi has his duty toward you, but he has always wanted you to be happy. I do not know why but perhaps you remind him of someone."

Surprised again, Christopher stared at the gift.

Taras stood. "I will tell him you are grateful."

CHAPTER 26

CHRISTOPHER WAS LONELY, sometimes desperately so. It was true that Taras had become a good friend, and his other guards were generally friendly enough. He had learned to enjoy the company of various merchants, Christian monks, a few imams and a rabbi. By now he had become well-known throughout Jerusalem, was welcomed into coffee shops and regularly invited to smoke in the souk with groups of men gathered atop stools.

But Kipper Clive yearned for more.

The truth was that despite his mutilation, he craved the touch of a woman. His persistent melancholy and his obsession with memories of Raven had kept these natural desires at bay for long stretches of time. But of late his heart had been so empty that his longings urged him to be ever bolder.

Of course, Muslim women were out of reach for a Christian male. In fact, were Christopher to touch one—even by accident— he would likely suffer death. These women were guaranteed their private modesty by high walls or heavy lattice-work that surrounded their living spaces. When venturing beyond the confines of their homes to visit graves on Thursdays or to shop the souk on market day, they remained covered from head to toe by loose-fitting cloaks with sleeves large enough to hide even the skin of their hands. Their faces were veiled, opened only by a slit through which their eyes might view the horizontal world of men. But that world dared not include infidels. Therefore, Christopher was forbidden to even speak to them.

However, lately the city had Christian females in abundance—pilgrims with whom Kipper delighted in engaging conversation whenever possible. This awakening passion had Colonel Kasim smiling when he summoned Christopher to his office on a cool December morning.

"That is why your guard must follow thee to the Christian quarter every day," said Kasim in English.

Christopher blushed.

"I am told you watch for pretty Christian females and then write them quatrains and couplets."

Indeed, Christopher had been enjoying the company of English women by the Church of the Holy Sepulchre. The feminine sound of their voices stirred him. Their occasional shy flirtations piqued his manly instincts and he delighted in writing them short poems. He shrugged.

Kasim sipped his coffee. "There is a brothel not far from here. Ramadan is over, so it should be open."

Christopher shifted, uneasily.

"You are ashamed of thy castration. I assure you, those women only care about the coins you toss them."

"That is not the point."

Kasim set down his coffee cup. "At least you are no longer lost in memories of the Irish girl."

"I shall never forget her, Kasim Çorbasi." Christopher set his jaw.

"You should." Kasim dismissed Christopher's guard, then stood and walked to the small window at one side of his desk. He cleared his throat. "I have served the Sultan for thirty years. I have scars on my body from Bedouins, Venetians, Bulgarians, Cretans, and Russians. I have no interest in bloodshed anymore." He turned to Christopher.

"Like you, I long for the company of a woman… and I also do not mean the sport of a brothel. I would like to have a wife."

Curious, Christopher waited.

"Therefore, I am considering my retirement so that I might marry."

"Why retire? I thought Janissaries have been permitted to marry for a long time."

Kasim nodded. "This was a concession to the weak among us. The Eleventh Article of our sacred *Kanun* says we are not to marry until we retire. I choose to follow this tradition.

"The ebbing tide from our rule of faith is slowly destroying the corps. I wish nothing to do with this and I have taught Taras the same. Better to walk away than be a part of our destruction." Saying nothing more for a moment, Kasim returned to his chair and took a deep breath. "You have managed my affairs well. I am wealthy enough to live happily. But I do not wish to live alone." He motioned for Christopher to sit. "I think you understand."

"I do."

"I shall soon recommend Taras for command of the 27th. I am quite sure the supreme *Yeniçeri Ağasi* shall approve this promotion. Of course, the general discourages retirement. He would prefer that I die in battle so that my estate goes to the battalion without being reduced by a few years of leisure." Kasim looked suddenly troubled. "Our defeat at Khotyn has led to great troubles with the Poles. Sobieski is pressing us along the Ukrainian frontier. I do not wish to enter combat in that place."

Christopher waited.

"Hence, more interest in retirement." Kasim then brightened. "Now, hear me. There is a barren widow about thy age named Elif. She is the daughter of Hasan Pasha *ibn* Ahmad and the sister of Husayn Pasha—once the governor of Jerusalem." He smiled.

"Her father had many wives and concubines, and eighty-five sons! As you probably know, the imams prefer us to have no more than four wives." Kasim sipped his coffee. "Therefore, it is said that he enjoyed this world but is now being punished in the next." He laughed. "Elif's husband was slain by Bedouins on his only pilgrimage to Mecca."

"Your face reveals thy love for her."

Kasim brushed his moustache with a light finger. "Love? I only saw her one time as she hurried past. Though she was covered, something in the way she moved left an impression I cannot escape. I am told that she is available and I think to myself, why not? But I must convince her brother. He prefers to invoke the levirate, but none of the brothers or uncles want a barren woman."

"So you have no idea what she looks like?"

"Her form seemed nicely curved beneath her garments."

"Maybe she is a shrew? Maybe a lioness—"

"I do not believe so. I heard her singing within her veils and I thought an angel must be close." Suddenly embarrassed, Kasim tapped his fingers on his desk. "Now, I need you to deliver a message to her brother." He handed Christopher a sealed envelope. "This is my proposal. It outlines the advantages of my station, my assets and my plans to live at my estate near Tiberius which I am pledging as my *mahr* for her. This is a generous dower." He shifted in his seat. "But I need something more. Her brother has the final authority over her, of course. However, one of the house servants told me that he is willing to consider *her* wishes. The servant also says that she is a lover of living. Therefore, I think she would prefer a man of feeling."

Christopher listened carefully. Kasim had always been something of a mystery to him. The enormous Albanian had ordered grandfather Clive's decapitation as if it were a casual deed. He had sent men to dungeons with a disinterested wave of his hand. Just two years prior he had hung three Christians by the Jaffa Gate on suspicion of evangelizing Muslims. And yet, he had also treated Christopher with patience and kindness over these many years. He handed money to beggars with a smile, and he once went out of his way to defend a groaning camel against the brutality of a driver.

"Are you listening?" said Kasim.

"Aye. Is there something you wish for me to do?"

Kasim removed his börk and wiped his grey hair with a huge hand. "I am told that women all across the Caliphate are smitten by a poet named Karacaoğlan who happened to fall in love with a girl also named, 'Elif.' His words are simple, like me. And his heart…" Kasim shifted again. "I would like you to write a poem for my Elif and deliver it as my gift. And I want this whole matter settled before the Feast of Sacrifice. Can you do this?"

Christopher sat, wide-eyed. *Write a love poem for the colonel?* "Aye."

Kasim smiled. "I knew you could. And something else. I needs thee to gather a purse full of symbols as a gift."

"Symbols?"

"You are a poet; you can think of things. You know…like a hard stone for my reliability. Like that." Kasim then placed his hand on his heart. "*Teşekkür ederim.* I thank thee. Allah be praised." He eyed Christopher. "This is a matter that requires thy discretion. Now go and write something."

⋈

Weeks later, Christopher stared at a blank sheet, grumbling. He closed his eyes and imagined Elif. *I do not even know the colour of her hair! I guess she has brown eyes? All I know is that she likes to sing and loves living.*

He stood and paced, then sat on a woollen carpet in his room and closed his eyes. Silence settled him. For a half an hour he listened only to the breath filling and leaving his chest. At last, he moved to his desk and dipped his quill in ink.

When he was finished, Christopher set down his quill and read the Turkish lines to himself several times. As he did, images of Raven filled his mind's eye and he whispered, "Raven, hope of my hope..." Kipper laid his head on his arms.

⚬⚬⚬

On a pleasant, mid-February afternoon, Christopher and his guard arrived before the arched camel-gate of Husayn Pasha—Elif's brother—with a letter and an embroidered purse. The gate had a smaller man-door. To one side of the man-door hung a brass bell with a shiny hammer. Christopher took a breath as his guard rang the bell.

The door was immediately flung open by a servant—a menacing Negro eunuch dressed in colourful layers of expensive silk robes. Christopher introduced himself and asked to see Husayn.

In moments, a stout, ageing Turk arrived to bid Christopher entrance into his spacious courtyard. Leaving his guard at the door, Christopher stepped inside where he heard a loud scurrying of feet from the plastered balconies above. He caught a glimpse of giggling women disappearing behind screens.

The two men exchanged courtesies and Husayn ordered trays of food and drink. He then bade Christopher to sit on a red velvet cushion placed atop a stone bench. "I have never allowed an infidel into my home before this day. *Astaghfirullah*...may Allah forgive me." He stared at Christopher with hard eyes.

Christopher sat quietly and received a cup of tea and a plate of prunes, almonds and goat cheese. He watched a little bird hop about.

"I am told that you are neutered."

Christopher stopped chewing. He nodded.

"Good. Then you are at least not a real man." Husayn relaxed. He gestured to his eunuch who hurried up the stone steps. "I have already received the contract of dower from Kasim Çorbasi. But now you have something else?"

"Evet."

Husayn settled into his cushion. "First, tell me about Kasim."

Christopher stopped chewing again. "I... I am just a messenger—"

"Tell me."

Perspiration quickly gathered at the edges of Christopher's scalp. He had not expected to vouch for his master. "He is a good man."

"And?"

"He is a furious warrior. He loves music."

Husayn leaned forward. "Is he a true believer?"

"He is devout."

Satisfied, Husayn tossed his head toward a curtain. It was then that his sister, Elif, emerged from the shadows alongside the eunuch. Husayn motioned for her to stand before Christopher.

The tall, slender woman moved toward Christopher with an elegant modesty. She was dressed in a blue velvet jacket that fitted her neatly atop a green silk gown of many folds that fell to the ground and obscured her feet. Her hands were kept within ample sleeves. Her face was hidden behind embroidered veils attached to a white head-dress. With a nod from her brother, Elif released the golden brooch which held her veils.

At the sight of her face, Christopher nearly collapsed. "Raven?"

"What did you say?" barked Husayn.

Christopher stared into Elif's face. Her eyes were sage green and made all the more magical by the heavy kohl outlining them. Her hair was black and her skin was fair. His body trembled. Nearly his own age, Christopher could only stare at the woman standing before him.

"What is the matter with you!" scolded Husayn. He ordered Elif to cover her face.

Christopher kept his eyes on hers. *I must make her speak.* He put his hand on his heart and said, *"Assalamu 'alaykum."* He watched Elif slide her eyes to her brother. His mouth went dry. *Speak. Let me hear thy voice.*

At last, the woman answered, "Wa 'alaykum assalam."

Crushed, Christopher closed his eyes and took a deep breath. *What a fool I am.* He turned to Husayn. "With your permission, I will tell Kasim of her heavenly beauty."

Husayn grunted.

Hands still trembling, Christopher reached for the purse he had brought. "I am commanded to present gifts from Kostandin-oğlu Kasim Çorbasi, son of the Sultan, protector of Jerusalem, sentry of Al-Haram."

Husayn grumbled and told Elif to sit by his side.

Christopher presented the purse to him. "Inside are tokens of my master's affection." He could barely pry his eyes away from the woman.

Husayn dug through the embroidered pocket with his pudgy fingers and began to retrieve its contents. The first thing he lifted was a small pearl.

Christopher cleared his throat. "May I address your sister with the words of Kostandin-oğlu Kasim Çorbasi, a man who loves the beauty of creation—"

"Yes, yes. Get on with it." Husayn waved his permission and handed the pearl to Elif.

Christopher turned to the woman. "With this know that you are a fine treasure."

Husayn muttered. He then retrieved dried flower buds that dissolved at his touch.

"You are my flower but I do not lock your life away."

Husayn pulled out a braided wire of gold and silver.

"You and I belong together as Love and Wisdom, entwined."

Husayn grunted again. He pulled out the final items—two black olives. He handed them to Elif.

"My two eyes: they seek only you."

Christopher could see Elif smiling behind her veil. "And now this:" He presented Husayn the written copy of his poem still sealed in its envelope. He then stood and recited it, slowly, enchanted by Elif's attention:

"Elif of Jerusalem, daughter of Allah
Beloved one of dreams, the joy of each Sura.
Elif of the Caliphate, singer of songs
Dear lamb of my heart, for thee do I long.
Elif, friend of warblers, night lark and dove
Grant me thy hand, for thee do I love.
Elif, hope of my hope, desire of my desire,
I pledge thee my strength, my fortune and fire."

When Christopher finished, no one said a word. He pried his eyes away from Elif's to see several veiled women with children by their sides leaning over their railings. He then faced Husayn whose stance revealed satisfaction, perhaps even pleasure.

Saying nothing, Husayn tossed his head to the eunuch. The slave motioned for Christopher to follow him out of the courtyard and toward the door where he cast a final look at Elif. His heart had melted; his mind was whirling.

The eunuch shoved him into the street with his guard and slammed the door behind him. Kipper stood still, savouring every moment that had just passed. His guard waited patiently, but finally nudged him back into the lively life of Jerusalem's busy streets.

Christopher barely noticed the sounds and colour now pressing him on all sides. Perhaps it was the spirit of Raven he had just felt; perhaps it was the tender smile in Elif's green eyes; perhaps it was the soft way she took her seat. Whatever the reason, Christopher suddenly attached his heart to Elif like a wing to a butterfly. *If I could only soar over these walls with her.*

But soon an unexpected wrath began to supplant his ecstasy. Christopher's stride lengthened; his pace quickened. *Slave. I am a slave, a castrated slave.* He glanced at his dispassionate guard and tears of frustration filled his eyes. He cursed Kasim and paused in an alley-way to gather himself.

Within the hour, Christopher entered the Citadel and found the colonel pacing in an open courtyard, anxiously.

"And?" Kasim blurted.

Christopher could barely utter a sound. *"Allah's will be done."*

"Why do you say that?"

It was the first time Christopher had ever seen fear in Kasim's face. He was glad to see it. "I thought Allah's will should be invoked for you."

"Yes, yes. But tell me what happened."

"I presented the purse of gifts to Husayn and offered your words for each gift as he handed them to Elif. Then I handed him the poem."

"And? And? Did you see her? Did you see Elif? I told Husayn you were a eunuch; I thought that might give him a way to let you see her face for me."

Christopher stared at his master, coldly. "Yes. I did see her."

Kasim hung on every word like a schoolboy listening for a good word. "And?"

Resentful, Christopher nobly forced the truth to his lips. "She is as beautiful as any woman I have ever seen."

CHAPTER 27

SIX WEEKS LATER, Taras ducked into Christopher's small office with a satchel and a smile. "Kasim Çorbasi is singing today."

"I am glad he is happy."

Taras paused. "You do not seem glad."

Christopher shrugged.

"Husayn Pasha has betrothed his sister to him. They will be wed after the coming Ramadan…this year that is near your Christmas." Taras was beaming. "Your poem must have been magic."

"Good for him."

"What troubles you?"

"Nothing."

"Kasim sends you another gift." He handed Christopher the satchel.

Opening it, Christopher stared at several documents. "I do not understand."

"Today the colonel grants you his trust."

Confused, Christopher waited.

"In two hours you are to deliver these documents to English agents of the Levant Company at Ismail's coffee shop."

"And?"

Taras offered an uncharacteristic smile. "And you are free to go there *without a guard*."

Christopher was stunned. For all these many years he had never been permitted to step out-of-doors without at least one Janissary on his heels.

"He trusts you. That is his gift."

The surprised Englishman stood. *Walk freely?*

Taras stiffened. "But you do understand what would happen—"

"You would be sent to the galleys and Raven would be executed." Christopher could feel Taras' eyes probing him.

"The Sultan would hunt her until the end of days," said Taras.

The soldier's unusual choice of words did not escape Christopher's sudden notice. "Why would he have to *hunt* her?" He eyed the suddenly faltering Ukrainian. "You know something. Tell me."

"I know that trust is a gift that must never be abused." Taras fixed his face hard on Christopher. "Now go."

⟨⟩

Christopher's mind whirled as he stepped quickly into the mottled stone maze that was Jerusalem. *'Hunt her down?' Has she escaped?* He smiled at the thought of Raven slipping away from her captors. His feet nearly floated on the air as he elbowed his way through the Arab souk crowding King David Street. A spice merchant barked from behind pyramids of yellow saffron. On every side, brightly coloured vendors' booths were squeezed against one another from which shouting peddlers pressed unsuspecting Christian pilgrims with cheaply made brass or poorly woven cloth.

If she had escaped, she would have surely been recaptured by now.

But he would not have mentioned 'hunted' if she was already recaptured.

Christopher slowed his way through the souk. *Could she have found a way home? Could she have stolen money for passage?* He paused to take a deep breath. The air was filled with the smells of dusty canvas, roasting goats and urine.

In some ways, Jerusalem had not changed greatly from the times of Jesus and the Romans. Yet, the tile-roofed city had slowly become ever more Islamic over the centuries. She was now something of an exotic admixture of blocky houses, smooth Turkish domes, distinctive archways and pointed minarets all gathered into a sandstone collage neatly framed by massive rock walls.

Typical to other Islamic cities, Jerusalem's religious communities co-existed, but they did so with careful separation among four quadrants. To Christopher's left was the Christian quarter, evidenced by extravagantly adorned churches—most notably the Church of the Holy Sepulchre marking the spot of Jesus' crucifixion.

To Christopher's right was the wall shielding the Armenian quarter that was home to those persecuted for their distinct Christian orthodoxy rooted faraway at the eastern edge of the Ottoman Empire.

The comfortable Jewish district and its expensive shops and pleasant homes lay farther ahead. However, Christopher now hurried toward his meeting in the Muslim quarter which lay in the northeast quadrant. There his eye had always been most pleased. Ottoman architects knew exactly how to employ the sun and the moon to cast light and shadow over their vaulted roofs and latticed balconies to create a transcendent harmony that quieted his soul.

Finally arriving beneath the immense shadow of the famed Dome of the Rock mosque, Christopher's mind reeled. *I pray this is all true! Imagine, Raven free!* Panting, he entered the popular coffee shop of Kemal oğlu Ismail, once a whirling dervish—a Sufi monk given to the meditation of circular dance. "As-salam-u-alaikum," he said to Ismail.

The Turk smiled, broadly and opened his arms. He kissed Christopher on the right cheek. "Wa alaikum assalam wa rahmatullah."

The short-legged proprietor had curly grey hair and a kind face. "Why are you here, Christopher Effendi?" He wiped his thick hands on his dirty apron and waved a cloud of potent *tömbeki* smoke away from his face. "I have not seen you in a very long time."

"I have a meeting with English businessmen." Christopher looked about the shop crowded with blue-robed Sufi brothers of the nearby shrine. They were busy yammering and smoking their bubbling water pipes. Not seeing the Englishmen, he said, "Your patrons seem upset."

"Do not give them a thought," said Ismail. "An imam from Damascus scolded their lodge last evening. He shouted that the world is a place to serve Allah through obedience to outward laws. Doctor Ozan answered that the world is a mere bridge for our inward journey.

"The imam then accused the brothers of having dark spirits of the jinn distort their minds. Ozan answered that the imam's outward religion is but a grape and Sufi wisdom is the wine. So it went for more than two hours. You see, Christopher Effendi, this is why I abandoned the Path and now just sell coffee."

Christopher laughed.

Ismail winked and ordered his busy young son to prepare a fresh pot. "And bring a plate of *siron*." He then offered Christopher a corner couch. "But come and sit! I am so very happy to see you."

"The colonel has kept me busy with meaningless things."

"Nothing is meaningless. Even one drop joining the sea has meaning."

"You still seek my enlightenment." Christopher grinned.

Ismail then looked about the shop. "Where is your guard? I should feed him."

"Kasim now trusts me to walk alone."

Ismail raised a brow. "This is good."

Christopher shrugged. "I have no human guard, but I have another watchman that has no mercy whatsoever." Suddenly bitter, Christopher reached for a pastry. "Kasim guarantees my trust by a threat."

Two Christian gentlemen then entered the shop. "Where is the secretary for Colonel Kasim?" said one, loudly.

At the sound of English, Christopher's heart leaped. He stood and quickly found the speaker—a tall man in a knee-length, red doublet over a frilled shirt, and a pleated cravat. Christopher hurried toward him and his companion. "I am he. I am Christopher Clive, the colonel's secretary."

The surprised Englishman removed his hat and shook hands with Christopher, cautiously. He was middle-aged with a narrow face, a thin moustache, and an unhappy scowl beneath a flowing French periwig. "I am Mister James Barrington, chief solicitor for the Levant Company. And this is Mister Charles Fry, my assistant."

Christopher turned to Fry—a younger, doughy-faced man with a goatee who was similarly dressed except for the addition of puffy trousers affixed to his knees with bunches of ribbons. Christopher invited the men to sit atop embroidered ottomans setting haphazardly by a small mahogany table. His Turkish pants and silk shoes made him suddenly awkward. "I am happy you found this little shop—"

"It was far from easy," grumbled Barrington as he studied Christopher. Perspired, he removed his doublet and bade his assistant do the same. He wiped his face and neck, and then began with a few forced pleasantries as he settled atop his cushion. "You may be interested to learn that the world at home is changed. London suffered a terrible plague almost exactly ten years ago." Barrington swatted a fly. "Nearly a quarter of the citizens died." He wiped his neck with a kerchief. "And then we had the Great Fire that burned for four days. No doubt you've heard about it."

Fry went on to update Christopher on the current state of the English throne, the war with the Dutch and the removal of all Catholics from public offices.

Formalities dispensed, Barrington abruptly changed course. "Now to be clear, you are *Sir* Christopher Clive?"

Surprised, Christopher's eyes swung from Barrington to Fry and back to Barrington. "You know of me as 'Sir?'"

Barrington leaned forward. "You are the grandson of Sir Redmond Clive and the son of Mister Spencer Clive?"

Christopher's heart pumped. "I am." As if anticipating the next question, he blurted, "I was taken captive from my father's estate in County Cork—"

"We know. But we did not know you were alive." Barrington grabbed a pastry off the half-empty plate. "Is there nothing to drink in this heathen hot-box?"

Christopher motioned to Ismail.

Charles Fry looked at Christopher sympathetically. "You attended Oxford with thy cousin, Mister Winston Wellington. He has been granted thy seat at the Levant Company."

Christopher listened, carefully. "How do ye know so much?"

The two gentlemen exchanged uncomfortable glances. Ismail interrupted with jars of a thin apricot compote and a pot of coffee. He ladled the coffee into three small cups and scurried away. The brew was syrupy and fragrant with the aroma of finely ground beans enlivened by cardamom and nutmeg.

Barrington took a sip of coffee and nodded in satisfaction. "Superb." He removed a tin of snuff and sucked a pinch into each nostril. Sneezing, he wiped his nose with a silk kerchief and then studied Christopher. "News of thy story has travelled far." He tried the apricot compote and approved. "Now, by thy clothing it seems you have turned Turk. But you are clean shaven. So, tell me first whether you are a Christian or a Mohammedan."

Christopher did not like Barrington's suddenly demanding tone. "Are you a Christian, sir? One can never be too sure. Perhaps you are a Jew?"

James Barrington scowled. "I am a Christian and so is Mister Fry. Are we done with this game?"

"You began first, sir. But to answer thee, I am a Christian."

"And you are a slave."

"So the Sultan says."

"Would it not go easier for thee if you turned Turk?"

"I do not like the notion of fasting for a month, and I imagine circumcision to be a distasteful inconvenience."

Barrington's face opened with a grin and Fry laughed out loud.

The tension relieved, Christopher answered plainly. "Despite my circumstances, I remain true to the Faith, sir." He took a long drink of his compote. "But before we do the colonel's business, you would do me a great kindness to tell me what you know of my family."

Nodding, James Barrington took a breath. "I served thy grandfather whilst he was a member of the Levant Company. He was also a friend to my father and so I gave heed to thy family's travails." He nibbled on a pastry and reached for a piece of goat kabob just presented by Ismail's son. He then looked directly into Christopher's waiting face. "The whole of the Kingdom is aware of the cruel death of Sir Redmond." He shook his head. "Talk of Sir Redmond's head and hands in that pot was fodder for many an ale-house evening."

Christopher looked away.

"Nay, do not be ashamed, sir," said Fry. "Fie! That miserable, puking Carrew is the one who ought have despised himself. All of London hated him. He was imprisoned at Newgate for his part in it and not a soul in the city grieved when his charred body was found in the prison after the inferno."

Barrington leaned toward Kipper with thick eyebrows now furrowed with curiosity. "The heathens did something horrible to thee as well, did they not?"

Christopher dodged his eyes.

Barrington sat upright and tapped his fingers. "Some years ago, a low-level minister near Constantinople delivered a strange letter to the English consul, one intended for the Sultan and written in perfect Turkish—by thy hand, sir.

Christopher waited. *So it never made it.*

Barrington continued. "I was in residence serving as solicitor to the consul at the time. Thy letter was read aloud. I remember well the reference to the removal of the 'fruit of thy loins.'" He paused. "Did these miscreant heathens castrate thee, sir?"

Christopher said nothing.

Barrington slammed his hand flat atop the little table, spilling all three cups of coffee. "Christ almighty! What evil is this!"

Ismail scrambled to wipe the table, and ordered his son to bring fresh coffee and a new plate of kabob. In that moment Christopher noticed three Janissaries pressing their faces against the shop's window at Barrington's outburst. Given the thick tobacco smoke Kipper could not be certain but he thought one of the men to be Captain Zeki.

Barrington and Fry went on to lament the misery of the Christian slaves held throughout the Levant. "Methinks they shall snatch away a million of us 'afore it is over. But when judgment finally comes for these savages you shall be vindicated along with thy grandfather."

Christopher stared into his coffee. Lost for a moment, he murmured, "'My fingers have touched the prickly and the tender; my tongue has tasted both honey and herb.'"

Barrington glanced at Fry. "With pardon, this is all beside the point. You asked about thy family."

Christopher fixed his eyes on him.

"I cannot say it any other way: I do not have good news for thee." Barrington cast an uneasy look at Fry. "Thy grandfather's estate is in miserable dispute. You were…are…the heir, but thy letter was the only proof of your surviving the voyage. It is believed by most that you are now deceased. The court has not known what to do."

Braced, Christopher nodded. "Why is my father not appointed as trustee?"

The men exchanged glances again. This time, Fry answered. "I am sorry, but Mister Spencer Clive is deceased for many years. His assets are held in escrow for the benefit of thy mother pending a resolution to thine own status."

Christopher's eyes filled. "How did he die?"

"I do not know, though I believe it was soon after thy capture."

"And my mother?"

"The last I knew she lived with her brother in Bath."

Christopher turned to Barrington. "You have more."

"Aye. As I say, thy estate is in disarray."

"Who opposes my interests?"

"Thy cousin—Mister Winston Wellington recently of Bloomsbury by London. Also the Crown."

"And who champions my cause?"

"You have a grandaunt," said Barrington. "She picked a fight from Ireland."

Christopher smiled inwardly. "Aye. Miss Comfort Clive."

Barrington nodded and sipped his coffee. "She is a brawler who swears by Heaven that you are alive. Her solicitors have been torturing Wellington for years. She even led three hundred persons to petition the Crown on behalf of all the captives in Algiers. The effort was fruitless."

"What do you know of her now?"

"Very little. However, I do believe that Wellington granted her use of the Clive House in Kinsale since it is said that she spent her entire trust on thy account."

Christopher cursed. "Wellington *granted* her use? This is an outrage." He squeezed his fists. "Is she well?"

Fry answered. "Here is the rub, sir. With respect, I answer that Miss Clive may be mad. Wellington is using this to support his claim."

"She is eccentric, but not mad."

"I fear that her behaviour in the court has not served her well, and—"

"We know nothing more." Barrington sipped fresh coffee and wiped the crème from his moustache. "Do not take offense, Sir Christopher, but thy present plight does not bode well for thy estate."

Fry then whispered, "But surely we can negotiate thy freedom."

Christopher shook his head. "Nay. The Sultan has declared me to be a slave until the end of my days. It is a matter of personal offense, and so all efforts otherwise shall prove fruitless."

Fry leaned very close. "Perhaps we can help you escape. We leave for Damascus in less than a week, and shall sail home from Beirut soon after. You could be in Kinsale before the buttercups bloom."

Christopher's face brightened with an idea. *IF she is free...* He took a deep breath. *But if not...* "Nay. I am in a complicated predicament—"

Barrington answered in a hushed tone. "Nothing thy escape cannot remedy."

Hands flat on the table, Christopher leaned very close to the two men. "Ye both would be surprised. But firstly, I hereby authorize ye as my solicitors. Do we agree?"

Both men nodded.

"Good. Now, set my escape aside for now. No matter the cost, you must locate a woman named Raven O'Morrissey. She may yet be a slave somewhere, or perhaps she is in hiding, or—"

"An *Irish* woman?" Barrington scowled.

"What of it?"

Grumbling, Barrington stuffed his mouth with goat meat. However, Fry answered in a sympathetic tone. "Where would we begin?"

Christopher reached for his satchel and withdrew paper, ink and a quill. "With my aunt. I will write her a letter that explains everything. See that it is delivered to her as quickly as you can, and then do exactly as she says."

CHAPTER 28

CHRISTOPHER CHEWED HIS lip as James Barrington and Charles Fry hurried out of the coffee shop door with his letter. In it, he had informed his aunt of Raven and her possible escape, of his location, his health and spirits, and of his predicament. *'Do not attempt to rescue me, or to ransom me,'* he had written. *'I only want to know that our Raven is discovered and is safely returned.'*

Closing his eyes, he thought, *Aunt Comfort shall know exactly what to do. And if I remember rightly—*

"Christopher Effendi," Ismail shook his shoulder.

"Eh?"

"Soldiers are searching the Englishmen."

Christopher leapt to his feet. "By God, no." He pushed past the shop's patrons and leaned carefully into the doorjamb. Just yards away, Captain Zeki and two other Janissaries were rifling through the gentlemen's things. Barrington was protesting, loudly, as a soldier dumped his documents upon the street. Charles Fry then shouted as another Janissary stripped him of his doublet.

Zeki snatched the coat and shoved his hand into a vest pocket.

Christopher paled.

Zeki jerked his hand out and in it was the letter.

Christopher spun away from the doorway and laid his back flat against the wall. He breathed, quickly. He grit his teeth. *Zeki shall use this against us all.* Panic rose. He peeked once more into the street. Both Englishmen were now stripped to the waist. Their shoes were removed and Barrington's wig had been tossed to a beggar. Piled around the two men were their clothes, various documents and sundry jewellery. Coins had been spilled from their purses. Loose tobacco scattered along the street.

"Effendi," whispered Ismail. "Are they Crusader spies?"

Christopher pitied the terrified Turk. He would be hanged if the city's pasha believed the coffee shop was a meeting place for spies. "No. Of course not. They are only lawyers."

"But why——"

"Go about your business." Christopher turned his eye to the street once more where Barrington and Fry were now naked and being bound by the wrists. *But that fool Zeki cannot read English.*

Just then, Zeki charged into the shop waving his pistol. "Christopher Effendi. We have you now." He held the letter close to Christopher's face. "A secret message for your Crusader king." Zeki grabbed Christopher by the shirt and dragged him into the street.

"You have nothing," Christopher said. "Let me read it to you."

One of the Janissaries quickly laid a cutlass under his throat. A crowd began to gather close. Zeki laughed. "I am no fool. You could read what you want."

"It is a love letter, Captain. Nothing more." Christopher pointed to the trembling Charles Fry. "I wrote a love letter on his behalf." He folded his arms and laughed. "I would like to see you stand before Kasim Çorbasi when it is translated." He turned to the crowd. "He will be mocked for a generation."

The people howled.

Zeki hesitated.

Christopher remained silent. *Never let it show.*

But Charles Fry could not bear another moment of this. He fell to his knees and began blathering.

Zeki faced the poor Englishman, smirking. "I do not understand a word this fool is saying, but I never saw a man do this for a love letter." He tossed his head to his men, and scrambling hands quickly bound Christopher's wrists.

That same afternoon, Colonel Kasim dragged Christopher by the hair out of the Citadel's dungeon and into a courtyard, screaming. To one side strutted Zeki; to the other walked Taras, head down. Red with rage, Kasim shoved Christopher to the ground. "I give you my trust and now this! Do you have any idea what you have done?"

Christopher said nothing.

Zeki laughed. "Love letter? More like secret code to me."

Kasim kicked Christopher in the ribs and then again in the belly. "You have betrayed me."

Christopher laid on his side, groaning. Kasim bent over him. "I treated you like a son!" he sputtered. "Now you will have to be punished...again."

Christopher peeked out between his forearms. "I did not betray you. I only want Raven to be safe."

Zeki bent low. "Yes. And if your Raven was ever safe, you would flee."

"That is not it," protested Christopher. He climbed warily to his feet and pleaded with Kasim. "I would not risk you or Taras being punished on my account. Never. I so swear by Christ." His mind flew.

"Read the letter again. You will not find a single word asking for help in my rescue. Not one. In fact, I told her to *not* attempt a rescue of me."

Kasim slapped Christopher across the face with the back of his hand. "Any exchange is considered an attempt at escape. Do you think we are idiots?"

Christopher choked. "Taras, you must believe me. Do you think I would have you sent to the galleys?"

Taras stood near, stone-faced.

"Kasim?"

The colonel stepped close. Towering over Christopher, he answered, "It does not matter what you say." He held the letter in front of Christopher's face. "This is what matters."

"But—"

"Enough!"

Christopher wiped blood from his nose. "My intentions violated nothing that was forbidden."

Kasim fixed his dark eyes on Christopher. "You are a fool to believe that."

"Then I am a fool."

Kasim motioned for two guards. "Jail him with the others."

⸙

Christopher was locked within a plastered cell deep inside the Citadel where three figures stood in the dim light of a high, tiny window. As the door was locked behind him, he strained to see. "Barrington? Is that you?"

"Aye. You have put us in a terrible state, Sir Christopher." He could barely speak.

"Is Fry with thee?"

"Over here."

Christopher walked toward Charles Fry squatting in the shadows like a terrified child. His arms gathered his knees together as if he might be safer in a ball.

"What shall they do to us?" Fry asked.

"I do not know. But I am sorry for ye both. Ye were trying to help me."

James Barrington slid his back along the wall until his rump found the stone floor. "You could have warned us that passing a letter was a crime."

Christopher grit his teeth. The man was right.

A third voice murmured from another side. "If they judge ye as spies, ye shall all hang...or worse."

Christopher faced a young, bearded man emerging from a black corner. He quickly assessed him to be in his early twenties, seemingly healthy, and—judging by his voice—robust. His dark hair fell along his shoulders in curls like Christopher's own.

"I am George Carteret of Charlestown in the Massachusetts Bay Colony." He bowed, revealing a large ribbon in his hair.

Christopher clasped his hand and introduced himself. He then said, "These men are not spies."

"Nay? But they did attempt to pass a letter."

Christopher waited.

"There it is," said Carteret. "The Mohammedans are terrified of a new Crusade and so they interpret all things in the most imaginative ways. No doubt they believe the letter is filled with codes."

"This was a simple letter from me to my aunt."

"Why did you not send it by a common courier?"

"I am a slave."

George Carteret shook his head. "I see. Well, I am sorry for that. This makes matters all the worse for the three of ye. I have seen

Christians executed in the city for far less. Many have been hung, some beheaded, others impaled—"

"And you, sir?" asked Christopher.

"I entered the city with no passport or chaperone. Now I am waiting for the consul to vouch for me, but that ill-bred toady is on business in Alexandria. So here I sit."

Barrington and Fry were visibly shaken by Carteret's words. Barrington spoke first. "Can we not insist on a hearing? By Christ, I am a solicitor for the Levant Company!"

Carteret shrugged. "If ye three be charged with spying, then ye have little hope."

The two lawyers groaned, woefully, and turned away.

Christopher shook his head. "Nay. The only crime in this is mine own. The letter is interpreted as my attempt to clear the way for my escape. It is all very complicated."

"Was it for thy escape?"

"Nay. I was trying to save someone."

"A woman."

Christopher nodded.

"It is always a woman." Carteret looked at the three sympathetically. "I have no fear for myself. My only crime was not having proper paperwork at the gate. But ye? I shall pray for ye without ceasing."

Seven weeks later, Taras and two soldiers arrived at Christopher's cell and bound his wrists. They then dragged him to a small office cut into a narrow hallway nearby. To one side stood a low table and a squat chair. They pushed Christopher's back flat against the blue plaster. "Do not move," ordered Taras. He then dismissed his men and stood alone with Christopher. He removed his cap and set in on the table. Then, after glaring at Christopher for a very long time, he said "I am angry with you."

"Listen to me, friend—"

"Do not call me 'friend.' I have been your fool for all these years."

"I did nothing to betray you or Kasim."

"You have given Zeki all that he needed to wound the colonel. I am injured as well." Taras grew increasingly agitated. He began to walk around the dingy room with quick strides. "I have told you over and over to submit to what is, and yet you do not listen!"

"I only meant to—"

"You meant to encourage your aunt to rescue the woman. In so doing you would shed the Sultan's threat. Zeki has argued to the magistrate that this was the first part of your plan of escape—a plan that Kasim and I failed to anticipate. Can you not see this?"

"I can. But it is not so."

Taras clenched his fists. "You think I am a fool?"

"No. I swear by my very soul that this was no plot for my escape. I would not betray you to save myself." Christopher stood still as stone as Taras bent over to press his face close to his. Not flinching, he surrendered his eyes to Taras' penetrating gaze. *How do I convince him?* Christopher's mind returned him to Taras' noble sacrifice on the galley. *I shall never betray him. Not if it costs me all that I am. I have come to love you, brother.*

Taras blinked, slowly. He withdrew his face and released a long, sad breath. "I have seen your spirit. Your word is true." He stepped away. "But Zeki seeks your execution and Kasim is powerless to stop him."

Christopher's mouth went dry. "A judge may not agree."

"I do not know how to help you." Taras shook his head. "Can you accept that what you did was foolish?"

"My heart blinds me. I still love her, Taras, and I think of her every moment. But I love you, too. I would never send you to the galleys. Not even for her. This remains my pledge."

Taras withdrew a short dagger from within the folds of his cloak and cut the rope binding Christopher's wrists. "Sit."

Christopher sat cross-legged on the floor as Taras took a seat on the chair. "I should tell you something."

Christopher fixed his eyes carefully on the soldier who now set his large hands flat on his knees. He thought he looked suddenly anxious.

"Kasim Çorbasi resigned this morning."

Stunned, Christopher answered, "But why?"

"Zeki's family pressed the Palace to arrest Kasim. But Kasim is a partner with Kara Mustafa—the Grand Vizier's second-in-command—in a company that provides gunpowder to the Cebehane armoury. Mustafa persuaded the vizier that Kasim should only retire and pay a fine to the battalion. So despite your foolishness, Kasim is safe."

"I feel sick. He has been so good to me." Looking up, he asked, "And what of his betrothal?"

"Elif's brother has cancelled it because of the dishonour."

Christopher bit his lip. "And what of you?"

"I am demoted to captain."

"And Zeki?"

"As of today he is promoted to çorbasi."

"No!" Christopher cursed.

Taras' face turned suddenly hard. "You fail to ask about yourself! Your situation is perilous."

A clammy chill spread through Christopher's limbs. He licked his lips.

"I expect you to be hanged within a fortnight."

A twinge of panic swept over him.

Taras let the news rest for a moment before he continued. "Zeki's case is strong. I do not know what defence can be offered."

"But hanged?"

"It is not for me to say. Allah's will be done."

Growling, Christopher stood. "Allah's will!" He began to pace.

Taras stood. "Be still. I have more to tell you before you die."

Nauseated and anxious, Christopher sat slowly.

"Kasim commanded me to keep a secret from you for a decade." Taras wiped his broad face with a large green kerchief. "However, my tongue is no longer ruled by Kasim."

Christopher's eyes widened.

Taras returned to his chair, slowly. "Raven was rescued about nine years ago."

The news landed on Christopher's ears with such force that the slack-jawed man could only gawk.

"We know little about it other than a corsair bought her from her master and then disappeared."

Christopher tried to clear his mind. "A corsair? Then she is not rescued; she is simply the slave of another—"

"Her original master said that he was paid a huge ransom and that she was being taken to Ireland."

"Ireland!" Christopher's chin quivered. "O dear Jesus! Can it be? Can it truly be?"

"Under torture, her master confessed that he was paid $2,000 Spanish."

Aunt Comfort? Christopher's mind was racing. *But she has no money...and she had to first find her*—He lunged to embrace Taras. "Thank you. If I die, I die in peace."

Taras peeled his grasping arms from around his shoulders.

"Do you know where she was?"

"She was a concubine for a dye merchant's small harem on the island of Jerba."

"The Land of the Lotus Eaters," mumbled Christopher. "Do you know if she had children?"

"I would expect so, but I do not know." Taras bound Christopher's wrists again. "Now you must go back to your cell. We will soon learn of Allah's will."

CHAPTER 29

FOR THE NEXT week, Christopher, the two solicitors and George Carteret languished in their dark cell. During that time Christopher thought of little else than Raven. Like the rise and fall of an ocean swell, his soul filled with relief for her only to sink into a deep trough of yearning. *She is in Ireland. To be there with her! Instead, what shall they do to me here in this low chamber of hell? Hang me like Taras says? Behead me? Crucify me?*

"Are you listening?" groused Barrington.

"Eh?"

"You are thinking about her again. How do *we* get out of this?"

Christopher had no good answer. "When we stand before the pasha I shall bear witness to the truth. It is all we have."

Barrington scoffed and Charles Fry whined something from a dark corner, but Christopher's attention was suddenly with Carteret who was whispering to someone through the door. He shuffled closer.

Carteret turned, smiling. "Finally. I have been waiting to tell ye a plan."

"What are you talking about?" snapped Barrington.

"I have a plan." Carteret bade them all close. "Two weeks before ye came, I helped others escape. I could not tell ye until now—"

"What the devil are you talking about!" snapped Barrington.

"I bribed a guard—"

"With what?" asked Fry.

James Barrington was suspicious. "Methinks you are up to something."

"I take offense to that, sir."

Christopher raised his hands. "If you escape and are caught, you would likely hang. Why risk it for a passport offence?"

George Carteret winked. "I did not say that I had a plan for *my* escape."

"Whatever do you mean?" blurted Barrington.

"He means that he can arrange *our* escape for a fee." Charles Fry was shrewd.

Carteret nodded. "You are correct, Mister Fry. I dare no escape for myself. The consul shall release me eventually. But hear me. I am losing a fortune every day that I am not conducting my business out there." He waved his finger at the door. "Therefore, I needs do some business in here." He lowered his voice. "So I charge a fee for this service."

"What were you whispering about at the door?" asked Fry.

"The guard arranged thy escape with a caravan that leaves for Damascus at dawn. He is a cousin of the caravan's master."

Barrington remained suspicious. "How do we pay thee?"

Carteret reached inside his cloak and retrieved scraps of paper, a stained quill and a small bottle of ink. "With a promissory note. Your signatures guarantee payment."

The men were uneasy.

Barrington blurted, "No guard shall accept a promissory note for a bribe."

Carteret dug into his codpiece and retrieved gold coins. "Mohammedans do not search men's loins. They fear being accused of sodomy." He smiled. "I speak enough Turkish to communicate with the guards." He then opened up a folded paper and revealed the promissory note two escaped Poles had recently given him. "I bribe the guard with my money, and you give me a promissory note for my future payment." He then turned to Christopher. "You look troubled. Do you not trust me?"

"Why did you not tell us this before?"

"I was waiting for news of the right moment, else ye would have been all the more anxious and pestering me."

Fry studied Christopher. "What's wrong?"

"I do not know if I can do this."

"Why the devil not?" blurted Barrington.

Christopher closed his eyes and imagined Raven sitting in the web of Mitten Rock, facing south and longing for him.

Angry, Barrington grabbed Christopher by his Turkish shirt. "They are going to hang thee as spy for writing a letter in secret codes. And by that reckoning they shall hang Fry and me as well."

Christopher shook his head. "Nay, the charge against me shall be an attempt at escape."

Barrington released him. "So what? I do not intend to be hanged, chained to a galley or rot in some dungeon for any reason. Now you listen to me: In less than two months you could be home with her."

Christopher tried to swallow. *The Sultan would send Taras to the galleys.*

Carteret held out his pen and paper. "My fee is £200 per man. Are ye ready?"

Fry laid a hand on Christopher's forearm. "What say you?"

Christopher looked up. "I cannot...I—"

"Christ, Clive." James Barrington stared at the anxious Englishman. "As thy recently appointed solicitor I have decided that you have suffered too much to make a sensible decision." He snatched the paper and quill from Carteret and scribbled a note for £600. "I am signing my name on behalf of the Levant Company; payment is guaranteed for the three of us." He tossed the note to Carteret and then turned to Christopher. "We are all *Englishmen*! By God, I shan't leave thee behind."

Christopher protested. "Nay. Go yourselves, but I...I cannot—"

"Now is thy only chance to return to the woman you love," said Fry, kindly. "Abandon whatever fears you may have and cling to this."

Christopher's heart raced, wildly. *She is home. To be with her in the cove...to touch her hand...to hear her voice...to begin again.*

Barrington was less charitable than Fry. "Damn thee, Clive! You are the reason we are in this pickle. By God, you speak the heathen's language. We need thee!"

Carteret tucked the promissory note inside his vest and tapped lightly on the door.

⚜

Before daybreak, the hinges of Christopher's cell door squeaked and the low voice of a guard murmured. "Come quickly. You must hurry."

Christopher had not slept a moment. Now faced with the open door, he needed to make a decision. Barrington and Fry crept into the blackness of the unlit hall where the guard waited.

But Taras...Yet this is all my fault. He felt Carteret's hand pressing him into the open doorway. Christopher clenched his jaw. *What do I do? Taras? Raven?* He gaped at the desperate Englishmen trembling in the dark corridor. *They are helpless...*

Christopher yielded to Carteret's hand.

The Janissary guard whispered for all to crouch. Christopher licked his lips. He could hear two soldiers speaking some distance ahead. Their voices then faded down a different corridor.

"Come," said the guard.

The four scampered forward like rats through a black tunnel until they came to a short flight of worn steps to their left. They climbed down the steps and squatted before a wooden door upon which the guard pressed.

Christopher's belly churned.

The door opened to a large courtyard. The Turk leaned forward and turned his head from side to side. The Citadel was a complex of facets that provided defenders enfilading fire in an attack. For the escapees, these angles provided heavy shadows and screens.

Seeing nothing, he waved the group forward in a mad dash. Bent over, they raced beneath the fortress' thirty-four towers and hundreds of loopholes toward a final portal—a low, shuttered hole in a short wall.

Panting, the guard pushed the shutter open and peeked carefully into the relative obscurity of a distant alleyway. "Now." He ducked and waddled to the far side. Each man then climbed through the small opening in turn.

Out, Christopher sprinted behind the Turk and in another moment found himself pressed against a short wall at the edge of Jerusalem's Christian quarter. "Barrington? Fry?"

"Aye," they whispered as each arrived.

The unseen trio of escapees waited for their next command. The Turk pointed into the dark maze of silent streets. "Follow me to New Gate."

"Why there?" asked Christopher.

"It is the safest way out."

"Then where?"

"I take you to Jaffa Road. My cousin is waiting."

A dog barked, startling Christopher. "How do we know?"

"You must trust me."

The guard then crept forward, leading the Englishmen carefully through the narrow alleys of the sleeping Christian quarter on a jagged, middle path between the city's wall to their left and the Church of the Holy Sepulchre to their right.

Christopher looked up. The eastern sky was still dark but was about to yield to the first shades of morning grey. "We must hurry," he said. "The muezzins—"

"Yes, yes." The Janissary increased his pace as the giant silhouette of the Citadel disappeared behind a screen of black domes and flat-topped roofs.

Christopher's face flushed. With each hurried step a new voice within began to challenge him. *Taras. You cannot betray Taras. Stop. Turn around.* He muttered a curse. *Taras to the galleys? Is this who you are?*

But Raven.

Could he ever tell Raven what he had done to Taras?

Christopher breathed more rapidly. He swung his eyes from right to left. From behind he heard the panting breaths and the padding bare feet of James Barrington and Charles Fry. *I must save them.*

They can save themselves.

But they need me.

They do not need you now.

Christopher stopped.

"What are you doing?" whispered Barrington. "Hurry."

Christopher bit his lip. His mind spun images of Raven in a crimson bodice and a bird's-eye hood, looking like the Christian pilgrims sporting the latest fashions in the city's souks.

He then saw Taras chained to the unyielding bench of a galley. He heard his blood pumping through his ears. "Nay. I am going back. You are close enough."

"What!" hissed Barrington.

Christopher squeezed the gentleman's forearm and laid a hand on Fry's shoulder. "Godspeed to the both of ye."

Against the hushed protests of the Turk and the gaping Englishmen, Kipper Clive then turned and stared into the darkness behind him. *God help me.* He took a breath and left his dumfounded fellows behind.

In moments, Christopher was pattering atop the sandstone alleyways. *Hurry...hurry. Faster.*

A cock crowed.

The muezzins...any moment...

Christopher rounded one corner and then the next. He leapt over a clutter of baskets and a sleeping donkey.

Faster. Faster.

He lowered his head and sucked for breath. His chest rose and fell; his limbs burned. He brushed past a sleepy Christian monk, knocking the surprised man against a wall. *Almost. Almost.*

He struggled to remember the whereabouts of the small shutter in the wall. *There? Nay, there?*

Clenching his teeth, Christopher strained to see. Suddenly, the muezzins began to whine their first call to prayer from the minarets stabbing the pre-dawn sky. *Nay!* He raced toward the angled walls of the Citadel, begging his Christ to point him to the portal. Torches began to cast their yellow light from the musket loopholes dotting the walls of the fortress. He ran beneath them, hard.

There? Desperate, he spotted a dark patch against the grey stone. *Aye!* Christopher raced for the shutter. He pressed his fingers against the bare lip of wood and pried it open. Sucking for air, he climbed through the small portal and into the maze through which he had escaped. He took one moment to compose himself. *Think. Think.* His eyes flew about. *There.*

His keen mind now retraced his earlier steps. Around this wall; now over to that; under that window. *Hurry. There.* Ahead stood the door that would lead him up the short steps and into the corridor.

Christopher dashed for the handle.

He yanked.

The door did not yield.

Jaw set, he yanked harder until the door flew open with a loud crack.

By now, the fortress was awake and the Janissaries were assembling for prayer. Christopher scampered up the stone steps, turned right and raced along the dark corridor toward his cell. He heard men grumbling from a side room. Ignoring them, he rushed forward. *Almost. Almost.*

Voices behind him grew louder; the yellow cast of lantern-light filled the hollow of a side hallway. "There!" Christopher pushed the cell door open and stepped inside. "Carteret?" he whispered.

No one was there.

"Carteret?" *Where the devil...*

Footsteps drew near. Christopher retreated to the back of the black cell and he sat in the corner. His heart thumped, wildly. He cocked his ears to hear keys unlock the neighbouring door. The guards said something about bread. Christopher strained to hear a response. He heard none.

He held his breath. *Where is Carteret? Am I in the wrong cell?*

The guards passed his door and entered the next.

Why not open this door? Christopher had barely finished his thought when the hinges creaked. A guard stuck his head casually into the cell, but upon seeing Christopher he cried out. He called for another and the two men burst into the room with lanterns held high.

Christopher sat still.

The shirtless soldiers waved their lanterns. "Why are you here?"

Christopher stammered. "Why am I here?" *How would these two know I shouldn't be here?*

Both men jerked their pistols from their sashes and pointed them at Christopher. "Why are you here?"

"I... I was arrested."

"Why are you not with the other two?"

Two? Christopher's mind spun. *They are not counting Carteret. They must be part of this.* "I do not know what you mean."

One of the soldiers lifted his lantern high. When he did, Christopher noticed his company tattoo was the same as Zeki's. Another guard then grabbed Christopher by the throat and threw him against a wall.

"I... I know nothing about anything. I was sleeping. When I awoke I was alone. I thought the guards took the others away."

Cursing, the soldier shoved him to one side. He whispered something and then led the other guard out of the cell.

Christopher stared, trying to calculate what had just happened. *Carteret and Zeki; what the devil are they up to?*

273

CHAPTER 30

"AND YOU ARE certain of this?" asked Taras.

Inside of his cell, Christopher faced Taras and three Janissaries from Taras' own company. "Yes."

"I blame myself," said Taras. "I never took account of that other Englishman." He turned to his fellows. "You must say nothing of this."

His men nodded. As with all Janissaries, company loyalty came first.

Turning to Christopher, Taras continued. "Misters Barrington and Fry are officially escaped."

Christopher was relieved for them.

"Why did you not flee with them?"

"Escape was never my plan."

"Were you tempted?"

Christopher nodded.

Taras stared at his friend. His lip twitched and he took a breath. "George Carteret is known here as George ibn Mohamet—an English pirate who claims he converted to the true religion.

"He is known to take coffee with Zeki. Kasim suspected him of causing troubles."

Christopher's jaw pulsed. "If they are working in league, the escape enriches Zeki, too."

Taras strained for a plan. "We must find Carteret," he said. "He will be playing cards or taking a boy at the Daniel brothel in the

Christian souk. Otherwise he will be sipping coffee at Tayyib's shop by the Damascus gate. These are his favourites."

"Or he may have fled," said Christopher. "The morning guards would have already warned Zeki that I am still here."

Taras barked orders for his men to send riders east on the Jaffa Road and north toward Damascus. "Tear every caravan to pieces and find this man. He is a young, healthy Englishman…long dark hair and beard, and he wears a ribbon on the back of his head. Go!"

Taras stared at the wall as he calculated his next move. "Or he may still be in the city. I must move quickly."

Within a half-hour, Christopher hurried alongside Taras through Jerusalem's streets with three trusted Janissaries. As planned, they went first to the Daniel brothel—a popular destination filled with slave girls and boys captured from everywhere between the Balkans and the interior of Africa.

Not finding Carteret there, Taras dusted his blue breeches and white sleeves as if to discard the disgrace of the place. "Effendi," thundered Taras. "To the Damascus Gate. We must find this man *now*."

Christopher and the Janissaries rushed to Tayyib's coffee shop standing alongside the busy gate. Taras immediately ordered his men to block the door as he led Christopher inside. The two scanned the faces of the surprised patrons.

"Look carefully. Every face."

Christopher nodded. He stepped deeper into the shop. Most were old, but one man's back was turned. Squinting, he waved Taras forward. Through the thick tobacco smoke Christopher spotted the shape of a flattened ribbon atop a mass of curls. "There!"

Taras charged forward and yanked the hunched patron off his cushion. "Carteret." He slapped him across the face once and then again. Lifting him by his hair, Taras then shouted to the silent patrons. "Identify this man."

Men from four corners answered, "George ibn Mohamet."

❧

Weeks passed before Christopher fell on his knees before Taras. "And you are certain?"

"You are released from all charges." Taras folded his arms, equally relieved. "Kasim argued that your refusal to escape with the others proved you never had an intention of fleeing. As you know, *intention* is the key to our justice.

"He reminded the council that your help in discovering Zeki's ring of criminals was of immeasurable worth." Taras threw the cell door open. "Consider it another birthday present."

Thin and stinking, Christopher hurried through the door. "And what of Kasim and you?"

"With Kasim exonerated, Elif's brother has permitted the wedding to go forward. The colonel is happy as a morning lark. He will enjoy his retirement."

"And you?"

Taras led Christopher down the corridor and into the bright light of the autumn day. "I have been promoted. Imagine, Mohammed-oğlu Taras Çorbasi, commander of the holy order of the Janissaries' 27th Battalion." Taras grinned. "And I have been appointed your official keeper for the Sultan."

Christopher could hardly believe his ears. "I am pleased beyond words, Colonel." He walked with Taras across a courtyard. "And Zeki?"

"The men voted to have him and his men strangled and dumped in the Salt Sea. Instead, the agha stripped them of all assets, cancelled their pensions and banished them from the corps. They will spend the rest of their lives in disgrace."

"And Carteret?"

"Already beheaded. Now, get a bath."

❧

January 1677

It was a chilly day when Christopher was summoned to Taras' office in the Citadel. "Yes, Çorbasi?"

Dressed in folds of fine cloth, Taras stood tall in his yellow boots. Perhaps it was the outrageously tall plume attached to the front of his already high cap, but Christopher thought him to be more immense than even Kasim. "I received this." Taras handed a letter to Christopher who quickly read its contents.

"So Kasim is happy with Elif. That is good to read. But exactly where is Podylla? And why would he recommend the agha send the battalion there?"

Taras stared through his small window into the courtyard below. One hand tapped his thigh, nervously. "If you travelled straight east from Vienna you would come to Podylla about half-way to Russia."

Christopher thought for a long moment. "Where your grandfather wanted your family to flee?"

Taras turned. "Yes. In those times, the Ukrainian people in that place were under the Poles and safe from the Khan's raids. Just five years ago, Allah willed these lands to come under the wing of the Sultan. As you might imagine, King Sobieski wants it back." Taras removed his hat and wiped a huge hand through his greying hair. "The provincial garrison at Kamianets must be reinforced."

"But why you? Why the 27th?"

277

Taras sat. "Zeki's lust for vengeance is unending. Kasim warned me a month ago that Zeki's family conspires for my exile into some honourless duty. They first plotted to have us transferred to protect the pilgrims' routes to Mecca. That is horrible service. So Kasim went to Constantinople to negotiate with Kara Mustafa who just became the new Grand Vizier."

Christopher was confused. "What does this have to do with Podylla?"

"It was the best Kasim could do for us."

Christopher eyed Taras carefully. "I am sorry, Çorbasi, but I think you are hiding something."

Taras looked away.

Two months later, Christopher marched with Taras' 27th battalion out of Jerusalem on a dusty journey through Palestine toward the port city of Haifa. In the fore of the 300-man column was Taras atop a large camel. The battalion's horse-tail standards and the wagon bearing the sacred kazan were right behind. Somewhere close was the battalion imam—a Sufi dervish who taught the men each Friday.

Some distance in the rear, Christopher wiped dirt from his eyes. "I'd like to ride a camel, too," he muttered. As secretary, he was considered the superior of lesser men, but assigned a place near the centre of the line. He looked over his shoulder to see a long column of smiths, dung-haulers and farriers. He then leaned his head into the shoulder of the road to admire the perfectly ordered ranks of tramping, red-booted warriors ahead. The Janissaries were not unlike the holy orders of Christian knights. Committed to their religion with a fervour exceeding ordinary Muslims, the corps understood itself to be the sword of Allah in a world of jihad. Thus they marched with purpose.

Christopher soon began to lose himself in the rhythm of it all. The martial tunes of the *mehterân* helped him and the whole of the long column move forward in a measured cadence. Bass drums thumped the air; the whining emotion of the *zurna* uplifted his heart and the clash of cymbals stirred his limbs.

More than anything, however, was the surge of joy he felt each time he reminded himself that his Raven was *free*. Christopher laughed out loud.

A breeze pushed a cloud of dust away from his face and he drew a deep breath through his nose. The air smelled of sweated horse-flesh, of camel droppings and leather. He thought of Étalon and wondered what had happened to his beloved horse.

Pretending he was a bird, he soared overhead in his mind's eye and considered the unlikely situation he still faced. Before long he composed a song to the meter of the drums and wrote it as he marched:

Journey on this Journey
Step by Step and lightly so,
For thy End is unknown.
Perhaps seeming lost, you linger
For a Time
Unable to turn or return
To familiar Places
As Mystery beckons thee ever forward
Where Emergence lies in wait.
And so let Sofia unfold thy Destiny
By Faith in that unseen Heart

That beats within Light and Love
To move thy Feet, Step by Step,
And lightly so.

Christopher returned to the earth and laughed out loud. "Lightly so? I am mad, indeed."

He then watched sea-birds hurry west. He released a sigh, thankful to at least be free from the clench of Jerusalem's walls. He cast his eyes across the wide Palestinian plain, delighted to be absorbed into an expansive horizon. And so he marched forward, expectantly— step by step and lightly so.

Arriving in Haifa, the battalion was quartered by a host garrison for two weeks, after which the men boarded two heavy 'round ships' captured by the Ottoman Navy from the Portugese some years before. Upon seeing the high boards and rigging, Christopher shouted for joy. He doubted he could have borne the horror of passage on a galley.

Aboard ship, Christopher was granted permission to bunk in Taras' quarters at the stern and alongside the captain's own. Though cramped, he was kept busy by day in writing correspondences, reports, and taking inventory for the colonel and the battalion's quartermaster. By night, he sketched soldiers, sailors and the ship.

Memories of times aboard other ships did not escape him and he occasionally awoke late in the night sweating in fear. Once he dreamt that the *Lebetine* was sinking and he was chained in the hold with the Irish, unable to save Raven or himself. In another night's dream, the ship pitched hard to port and he smelled excrement as it sloshed over his bare feet as it had on the galley. He awoke and ran to the rail where he vomited.

Other than such night terrors, the thousand-mile journey from Haifa to the Straits of Constantinople passed without troubles.

Of course, Taras' officers had broken up several inevitable brawls amongst bored warriors, and two Janissaries had died from fevers. The springtime seas were gentle, however, and gulls screeched happily overhead. Only once did it rain and that was as they passed among the white-bleached stepping-stones of the Greek islands dotting the sapphire Aegean Sea.

Without misery to distract him and with salt-scented air to intoxicate him, Christopher invested a great deal of time walking the boards under starlight where he lost himself in memories of Raven. The woman had never been far from his thoughts of course; time had not stolen her from him. He loved her, it was true, and he longed for her. Yet, time had enabled him to acknowledge the reality of what was, and to be eternally grateful for her rescue.

So Kipper Clive thanked his Christ that she was safe, and prayed that she was happy in her beloved Ireland. He hoped she could set aside what terrible things she must have endured in the harem of the Arab. He reasoned that his Aunt Comfort had endured similar horror and may have helped Raven defeat the power of lingering agonies.

He surely wanted that to be true.

He also wondered whether she thought of him from time to time. Christopher liked to think so, but he was also oddly content to imagine her now married to Fallon Healy. Kipper thought that would be a gentle destiny for her, and he wanted nothing more.

C H A P T E R 3 1

———— ⚜ ————

"THERE." A TURKISH sailor pointed ahead. "Hellespont."

Christopher stared over the bow rail at a notched horizon. Ahead lay the Dardanelles Strait connecting the Aegean Sea in the west to the Sea of Marmara in the east. He recalled studying this place in grammar school. But seeing first-hand how the narrow, winding channel had once protected Christian Europe from the expanding world of Islam gave him new respect for the importance of this place.

"Three hundred years ago," grunted the sailor.

"Eh?"

"Three hundred years ago the armies of Allah crossed over for Allah."

Christopher nodded. He knew that was when the armies of Islam established their foothold in Europe. Staring over the rail at the peninsula of Europe to his left, he considered the significance of that loss. Once north of the straits, the Muslims had swept over the rest of Thrace, Greece, the lands of the Bulgarians, Romanians, Hungarians and now Ukrainians.

The ships finally docked at the port of Gallipoli. Disembarking, Christopher wobbled onto solid earth from the gangway.

Taras hurried past. "We have about fifty days of marching ahead. Maybe more."

Christopher grumbled.

"But first we wait for supplies."

The resupply of Taras' 27th battalion took nearly a month, during which Christopher was directed to a small tent near the colonel's own on the grassy parade grounds of Gallipoli's garrison. Unlike their counterparts in Europe, the Ottomans took great pride in clean encampments and Christopher was impressed. He was particularly pleased that they abhorred dung heaps or towers of rubbish. Instead, the battalion's camp was quickly arranged into good order and even fragranced with incense. Fine tents of silk or brocaded canvas created an exotic city of broadcloth and pennants. Impressive horse-hair standards identified various companies, and a gold-gilded flag waved in easy summer breezes by the colonel's comfortable tent.

Supplies eventually arrived and Christopher logged the inventory as the battalion hurried to prepare their departure. Camels and wagons were soon heavy-laden with munitions, deadly trench muskets, curved bows, baskets of quivered arrows, *yatagans*, war axes, grenades, and halberds. A Bulgarian artillery detachment joined the 27th. Christopher recorded sixteen battering guns that fired five-pound balls, and a dozen small calibre bronze pieces. He also noted eight *balyamez* cannons—four-wheeled long-range guns that shot a destructive one-hundred-pound ball.

Why all this? Something big is afoot.

Despite delays and the inefficiencies of the huge Ottoman war machine, the 27th was finally ready to move on the first Wednesday of June. Appearing preoccupied, Taras trotted by Christopher on a regal bull camel. He was an imposing, behemoth of a soldier. Dressed in new robes and surveying his men from beneath his high-plumed börk, Christopher thought him to be utterly invincible.

"Did I say fifty days, Christopher Effendi?" Taras shouted.

"Yes."

"Make it seventy." Taras tapped his baton against the hips of his mount and lurched away.

⁂

The artillery slowed the column to a pathetic pace through the long days that followed. No number of lively marches by the band or severe demands of the çorbasi could urge the procession beyond eleven miles per day.

Christopher trudged along at a comfortable pace, leaving behind the tulips of Edirne to wind across a green countryside of beech and Bosnian pine. Ahead lay the flatter ground between the Balkan Mountains and the western shoreline of the Black Sea.

Still suspicious of the battalion's mission, Christopher finally stood at the shores of the mighty Danube River. *Dare I ask Taras what this is really about? And what troubles him so?*

For the next weeks, the 27th pressed northward along a Roman built highway through Wallachia and the lands of the Romanians. As Christopher followed the hypnotic tramping of boots, he reflected on the immensity of the Islamic Caliphate. Stretching from Morocco to Constantinople, it continued along the eastern shore of the Mediterranean Sea and spread over Greece and the Balkans. To the east its borders circled the Black Sea; in the north it had snatched parts of the Ukraine and the Kingdom of the Poles.

But they want more, he thought. *What would a mosque look like in Vienna? In Kinsale?*

"Almost," grunted a wheel-rite. "We are almost there."

Christopher was weary. Nearly seventy days of marching now brought the column through the tip of Moldova and to the sweeping banks of the Dniester River.

The colonel approached from nowhere and dismounted, barked at a few junior officers and walked toward Christopher. "We wait for ferries."

Christopher thought Taras looked haggard. He had recently heard him groaning alone in his tent late in the night, and now he suspected something was wrong. "I am glad for a rest," Christopher said. Taras' clothing was torn and filthy; he had uncharacteristically allowed grey stubble to rise on his face. "Are you well?"

Taras stared at him for a long moment. "Why do you ask?"

Christopher shifted on his feet. "I know you."

"You do not know me as you think you do."

Taras did not answer his question and Christopher did not press. The 27th crossed the Dniester and marched through the early September heat to finally arrive at Kamianets—the capital of the Ottoman province of Podylla.

Christopher was astonished as the battalion entered the city. Wide-eyed, he looked ahead at his destination—a grey-stoned, fairy-tale castle perched high atop the cliffs overlooking a tight loop in the Smotrych River. To one side, three round towers with conical witch-hat roofs stood watch with pennants fluttering. To the other stood three squat, four-roofed towers.

"Allah took this place from the Poles for us," said a harness maker now marching alongside Christopher. "Look around you. Mere men could never conquer it."

Soon, Christopher crossed the narrow bridge that connected the city to the castle, and within a few hours the exhausted army was busy unloading wagons and organizing itself in its new garrison.

Christopher was assigned to a small apartment furnished with a small bed and one cushion. His sparse office was located near Taras' own. In it he found a small, cherry wood desk and stool, a floor cushion, and a cabinet with ink and paper. On one wall was a small mirror.

An unshuttered window gave him a view of the courtyard below. To one side of the green square stood a nice pear tree; to another lay several vegetable gardens. He leaned out of his window and drew deeply of air scented by the nearby forests of the low mountains ringing the city. No longer surrounded by a horizon of sandstone and dusty scrub, Christopher smiled. His world was alive with lush green and rich soil, clear rivers and soft rain.

※

The Year of Grace 1682

For all of his relief in having been returned to a more familiar landscape, the next five years passed more slowly for Christopher than had the prior decade in Jerusalem. The city of Kamianets was small, the garrison was in good order, and Leviathan had not made a show for a very long time.

Christopher had plodded about his days as a man bearing a great weight. "So this is my purpose?" he asked himself one lonely afternoon. He walked across the bridge and looked into the deep canyon below. "Has my life been spared for this?" He spat and watched his spittle fall to the cramped river below. Gone were his secret hopes for the miraculous; fantasies of a Christian crusade, laughable. He took a deep breath and stared at the sky. "Why do I even bother to awaken each morning?" He closed his eyes until he thought he heard someone whisper. "Eh?" He turned but so no one.

The words were repeated, deep in his spirit. *Because you are loved.*

Christopher turned his head from side to side. But he knew the answer had not come from outside.

A picture of the cove flashed before him and Raven, his Raven, diving down once again into the gentle waves. *Oh why did I not follow her into the water?*

In these lonely years, Christopher spent many nights atop the castle's parapets gazing at the stars over Podylla wondering about *her*. He asked himself whether she loved him, or ever had loved him. He wondered if she ever thought of him.

But on one winter's new moon he suddenly realized that memories of his Raven had become repetitive and had lost much of their prior energy. Fear jolted him. *Her memory is fading! She is like the light of a receding candle!*

He was then jolted again. *Have I become a fading light within her?* He hung his head and groaned.

Deep melancholy returned.

It was true that his sinking heart lifted when he was free to depart into his world of poetry. He had composed nearly one hundred pages of verse that he had stuffed into his cabinet. But the only other source of interest for Christopher in these years had been the odd behaviour of Taras. Since the day the battalion had arrived in Podylla, Christopher thought him to be preoccupied.

Was it the long list of duties Taras had in refitting the fortress defences? Was it the need to keep his men on alert? Maybe it was the demands of other battalions now propping up the frontier. Christopher worried that it could be on account of the rumours of a coming jihad against the Habsburgs of Austria—rumours that agitated Taras.

Christopher recalled how the colonel had once complained bitterly of the cruelties inflicted across Podylla when it was first conquered not so many years prior. It was then that General Kara Mustafa had flayed his Christian captives alive and sent their stuffed hides to the delighted Sultan as trophies. Maybe Taras now feared such atrocities would soon become expected of him in an invasion of the West.

Perhaps all of this was true, yet Christopher remained convinced that something else had been out of kilter in Taras' life. Not only had he seen him pacing the parapets in the night, but he had also noticed how he had disappeared on many occasions. This fact had also prompted a great deal of whispering amongst bored soldiers. Most of Taras' troops assumed he had taken a Slavic lover for which they saluted him. After all, none would have blamed him—the beauty of Ukrainian women was a topic of discussion around every company's kazan.

But Christopher was not convinced, and so he had probed Taras for some hint of this mystery. Initially, Taras dismissed his queries, but he then rebuffed his persistence and finally threatened Christopher with a rod. That was enough for Christopher to abandon any further questions, and had left him to watch time turn with an increasing sense of dejection.

⚜

9 July 1682

Christopher stood before his mirror to mock the image he had grown weary of seeing. On this—his forty-first birthday—he held a small, single-edged razor in his right hand. *Look at the fool.* Christopher lifted his face to the ceiling. *You are a very quiet Father in Heaven. I have not betrayed thee. Can you say the same?* With his left hand he then grabbed hold of the flowing curls hanging atop his left shoulder. He laid the edge of his razor beneath the curtain of faded hair.

"Christopher."

Startled, he whirled about.

Taras ducked through the low doorway of the office and removed his hat. He pulled his curved sword from his sash and set it alongside his pistol on the crowded desk. "What are you doing?"

Embarrassed, Christopher set his razor down. "I have no idea."

Taras picked at some brambles sticking to his sleeves. "I have known you for twenty years. You spend too many hours looking within yourself. You must look beyond yourself to find yourself."

"You are studying with the dervish again."

Taras grunted and sat on a tall cushion across from Christopher. He placed his huge hands on his knees. "In all our years you have not betrayed me."

Christopher thought Taras looked deeply troubled, even anxious.

"Kasim once told me you are 'a lost man of deep feeling locked in a shell of ruined expectations.'"

Christopher had never quite put it that way to himself, but as he rolled the words over in his mind he thought they made some sense.

Taras laid two fingers along his moustache. "It was once black like the soil of Podylla. I am now forty-five years old but I feel much older." He took a deliberate breath. "I have studied with the Sufis but I have not become wise. The dervish tells me that I am too busy to be wise." He crossed one boot over the other. Leaning against the wall, he continued. "I am burdened with a secret. Like all secrets, the weight gets heavier each day."

Christopher remained quiet.

"Kasim warns me that Zeki has spies in the artillery companies. He reminds me that discretion is my most trusted friend. You are the next most trusted."

Christopher nodded.

"The rumours of invasion are true. Kasim writes that the *tuğ*— the standards of the Sultan's war monster—are not yet displayed at the Palace, but that Kara Mustafa is coaxing the Sultan to invade. Kasim says the vizier lusts for Vienna. If this happens the Poles would come to the aid of the Austrians since Sobieski lives to drive Allah out of Europe."

"When?"

"Soon. The Sultan has already made alliances with Protestant Christians to fight with us against the Catholics. Some Ukrainians may join us to fight the Poles. It is all very complicated and many lives will be lost."

"Is this your burden?"

Taras stared at Christopher for a long, silent moment. "Only in part." He leaned forward and furrowed his thick brows. "I am now worried more than before for the safety of two people who live outside of the fortress."

"Just bring them in."

Taras shook his head. "One is Catholic; one is Orthodox. You see how the Christians are treated inside the city. It will be far worse when the invasion begins. But beyond the walls the Tartars will slaughter or enslave all they can. So I have a dilemma."

"Who are they?"

Taras shifted in his seat. "Their presence would be very awkward for me."

"I do not understand." Christopher's mind raced. *Who is he talking about?*

Taras hesitated.

CHAPTER 32

"BEFORE I TELL you who they are, you must vow that you will try to convince them to either flee or convert," said Taras. "One is very stubborn and they are both devout in their own ways."

"Why would I want another Christian to convert?"

Taras flattened his palms on the desk. "After the mercies you have received, you still refuse the peace of Allah for yourself and others."

Christopher stood and folded his arms. "I am the slave of the Sultan, but remain faithful to my Christ."

"He has not been very faithful to you."

Christopher scowled. "Because I do not betray you, do not think that I accept this world of forced prayers and jihad. I honour you because you offered your life for me on that galley…like my Christ. But do not ever expect me to turn Turk or to urge others to follow your blasphemies."

Taras stepped close and towered over Christopher. His jaw pulsed. "Be careful, infidel. I love you as a brother, but do not insult the true religion."

Christopher locked eyes with the colonel for a long moment. His defiance enlivened, he said, "The sultan has taken my birthright, my manhood and my destiny, but he cannot take my faith. I am free enough to keep this choice."

Confounded, Taras squeezed his hands into fists. "I have treated you with mercy—"

"And I have denied all my joy to protect you. Do not expect me to surrender my soul." Christopher threw himself into his chair.

Taras stared at the hard-eyed Englishman for a very long time, mouth twitching. He exhaled. "It is true. We have taken everything from you, yet here you stay." The soldier wiped a hand through his hair. He placed his thick forearms against the wall above his head and leaned on them, thinking. There he remained in silence for almost a quarter hour, eyes closed. He then took a position in front of Christopher's desk where he stood wide-legged with his hands crossed behind his back. He took a deep breath. "Forgive me, Christopher Effendi. I forget your sacrifice for me."

Surprised, Christopher said nothing.

Taras relaxed his shoulders. "You asked who they are. One of them is my mother."

"Your mother?" Christopher stood.

"Yes, her name is Nadia. The other is Sister Mary."

Stunned, Christopher paused before blurting, "Sister Mary... from Jerusalem?"

"Yes."

Mouth open, Christopher walked to one side. "But how—"

"Soon after my capture as a boy, my mother fled to Podylla."

Christopher opened his mouth to speak but Taras raised his hand. "The Dominicans of Letychiv sponsored members of Sister Mary's order to help poor Catholics in Kamianets. On their way, they found a singer in a meadow. Thinking the singer was an angel, Mary's superior bought that very meadow for their hospice. The singer was my mother."

"*Your* mother and *my* Sister Mary?" asked Christopher.

"Yes."

Astonished, Christopher returned to his seat and dropped his forehead into his palms. "This is a great surprise—"

"Mother and Mary quickly taught one another their own tongues. Soon they spoke of me. Then Mary was sent to accompany Polish wives on pilgrimage to Jerusalem where she sought me. This was about a year before your capture—"

"But how on earth did she—"

Taras sat atop the cushion. "After prayers one Friday afternoon I heard a Catholic sister shouting my name. Surprised, I answered, 'What do you want?' She fell to her knees and asked me questions. After I answered, she hugged me. I was uncomfortable." He stifled a laugh. "She then sang me a message from my mother. And she gave me this gift."

Taras retrieved a small wallet from which he withdrew a leather cord tied to a small, lime-wood icon of Jesus on the cross. Jesus' head was encircled by a golden halo; his mother, Mary, stood close, praying. He dangled the icon before Christopher's face. "My mother said I should this should remind me of two things: First, she would always love me, even as Mary loved Jesus. And second, Jesus showed how suffering can be used against itself to set us free."

Taras stared at the icon for a moment. "She is a good woman and Jesus was an important prophet." He hid it away. "So began my friendship with Sister Mary."

"Did Kasim ever know about her?"

"Kasim knew everything. This is why he used his influence to have us transferred here."

Christopher struggled. "So, when I was tied to the post you already knew Mary."

Taras nodded.

"I do not know what to say."

※

The summer's dawn was misty and warm. Taras and Christopher led two horses through the castle gates and across the city's recently refortified bridge. They climbed into their saddles to ride along the highway leading north.

Christopher had not ridden a horse since his glorious gallops across the wild countryside of County Cork atop Étalon, and so the rhythmic stride of his gelding and the warmth of the animal's flanks on his legs brought a smile to his face.

Enjoying the songbirds of daybreak, Christopher drew a deep breath through his nostrils. The air smelled of sweet cut hay and dew-damp foliage. Long stands of hornbeam and oak lined both sides of the quiet highway, as well as an occasional clump of hazel, buckthorn and scrubby bilberry. The morning's rising mist swirled amidst the foliage, and Christopher lost himself in all of it.

The road paralleled one of the numerous clear streams falling south toward the Dniester River. As the sun rose higher, the mist evaporated and the view opened into a pleasing, upland landscape of well-watered fields and small forests. Like Ireland, this green land had been a place of continual healing for the perennial suffering of her people, and Christopher enjoyed its balm.

Within two hours, the pair rounded a wide curve and came to a white-plastered building under new thatch. A host of women and small children in colourful clothing were busily about their day.

"We are here, Christopher," said Taras. The excited man dug his heels lightly into his horse's flanks and trotted to a small stick gate. The pair dismounted and handed their reins to a young, red-headed Ukrainian woman. She was dressed in a beautifully embroidered blouse and a green wraparound skirt. Christopher was smitten.

"Over here," said Taras. "Follow me."

Waving to the woman, Christopher hurried to keep up with Taras' long strides. Arriving at the long building, the Janissary was met with familiar smiles and Christopher was eyed with great curiosity. His curly mane attracted admirers who giggled and trailed him from a shy distance.

Taras ducked through the doorway and spread his arms. An old round woman in a crimson skirt released a shrill laugh and fell into his arms. Taras kissed her apple-cheeks and then turned her toward Christopher. "This is my mother, Nadia."

The woman stepped away from Taras and folded age-spotted hands over her heart. She smiled, kindly. Her head was covered in a green scarf from which white hair hung in a long braid over the shoulder of her multi-coloured blouse. Her eyes were tiny and sparkled like blue jewels. Her face was red and jolly; her skin was wrinkled like a raisin.

Christopher bowed like the English gentleman he was. "My lady."

Nadia stepped boldly toward Kipper and seized his arms with her strong hands. She strained upwards to kiss his cheeks.

Red-faced, he bent low and obliged her. He then took her hand and kissed it, bringing a round of titters from the on-lookers crowding the low doorway. Christopher studied Nadia for a long moment. He thought her to be magical.

Nadia smiled, revealing two sets of pink gums. She then laid her right palm on Christopher's heart and began to sing. As she did, Kipper stood still, suddenly enchanted. He did not understand her Ukrainian, but the soft touch of the old woman's hand on his breast and the sweet melody of her blistered lips lifted his spirit.

He wished this angel could have sung to him forever.

When Nadia finished her song, she spoke with slow, deliberate words. "I once sung tat song for my boy, Taras."

Christopher raised a brow. "Tat?" A voice came from behind. "Ha, boyo!"

Christopher whirled about to see Sister Mary rushing toward him dressed like a Polish peasant. He lunged.

"Holy Jaysus be praised!" Eyes wet, Mary embraced him, kissed his cheeks and then took a firm hold of his hands. "Ya look fit and well...and old."

"Aye." Christopher said with a chuckle. "Time has its way with us." He most certainly knew that time had taken a toll on dear Mary. The sister had aged quite a bit in the nine years since he had last seen her in Jerusalem. Now in her late fifties, Mary had endured a great deal of suffering in this place.

According to Taras, war, rebellions, and slave-raids were never far from her door. Much of her spirit had been drained away by her love for the women and children whom she had salvaged from starvation, rapine, widowhood and homelessness. "It is so good to see thee. Tell me everything."

"I am a bit weary." Mary released Christopher's hands and hurried toward a cabinet to retrieve some cheese and bread. "Of eight sisters who began here, only one remains exeptin m'self. The Mohammedans murdered two fer no cause. Dear Katherine—my original superior—died from old age under an apple tree, bless her soul. On one of my pilgrimages, three were taken into slavery by a roving band of feckin Tartars. Curse tem to hell."

She set a plate for Christopher and Taras. "Taras has kept our little family safe. We are now twenty-nine women and children; Poles and Ukrainians under the same roof; Catholics like me and Orthodox like Nadia. We plant gardens and tend orchards together; we sew, weave, make baskets and pottery to sell in Kamianets for our taxes. But ever since the Turks took Podylla, the monastery in Letychiv sends no money."

"Who protects ye?" asked Christopher.

"A good God…and the Virgin, of course." Mary crossed herself.

"Right. But what about—"

"You mean who *really* protects us? All we have is two old gardeners with axes. The Mohammedans don't let us keep arms. T'anks be to Christ for Taras. He comes by often and keeps us in good supply. But he needs be careful, else the pasha might wonder why he protects a Christian poorhouse."

Christopher looked across the rows of straw beds. "You give them hope, Mary."

She blew a wisp of grey hair from her face. "We all have hope, boyo. We just don't all see it. Now, ya must come with me."

Sister Mary and Kipper Clive left Taras to visit with his mother. They walked atop the black Podylla earth toward an orchard of clustered cherry trees. Along the way, Mary chattered on about the cabbage harvest and the remaining rows of red beets. As they skirted the apple grove she paused. "We had a wet spring but a dry summer; the apples will be sweeter fer their sufferin. 'Tis the way a strong tree bears good fruit."

Christopher smiled. He knew she would never stop teaching him. Ahead, he could now see many hands reaching into properly pruned cherry trees.

"Now Kipper, fruit requires work." Sister Mary abruptly rolled her sleeves and hurried ahead to join the others.

Soon Christopher's hands were stained with cherry juice; his baggy Turkish trousers were scuffed from climbing into the trees and his silk shirt was torn. By the end of the day, he had made many a friend among the women and children. A little girl ran to him with a bunch of white spirea flowers in her grasp.

Kneeling, Christopher received the gift. "Thank you."

"*Chronić nas*," she answered with a smile.

Christopher laid a hand on her head as Mary's voice came from behind. "She says, 'protect us.' She is a little Pole. Now I needs a drink." She led him toward a water barrel and a ladle.

After Mary drank, Christopher drained his ladle quickly and then another. A group of women gathered around him. The more adventurous ones began to reach for his curls.

"So, I'm guessin ya like tat," said Mary as she slurped a second round of water.

Christopher blushed.

"Ah, well. So it is." Mary dropped a cherry into her mouth. "Let me know when ya've had enough."

Christopher slowly pulled the fingers out of his hair and gently pushed the women away. "Aye. No reason to make a spectacle—"

"Too late." Mary tossed her head to one side where Taras stood at some distance with his fists on his hips. "Look at him. He's jealous." Mary laughed. "Are ya hungry?"

"Very."

"Good. Come along then." Mary led Christopher along the tidy rows of the cherry orchard back toward the house. "Nadia will be sure everyone is well-fed. She is planning a good borscht, heavy in cabbage and beets but with some fish the gardeners caught this morning. She'll have bread, of course—the Ukies worship it. And the Poles will make something with a lot of cream and eggs."

Wanting to delay their departure just a bit longer, the sister then plopped herself on the ground and rested her back against a cherry tree. "So, what ails ya?"

"Eh?"

"Ya heard me. Taras says in these past years yer feet fall heavy."

"That would be very painful in the slippers the bloody Turks make me wear—"

"So, there it is. Those bastards still rule yer heart."

Christopher suddenly wondered if that were true. He picked a piece of grass. "Nay. They never did."

"But look at ya. Last I saw ya in Jerusalem ya had something of a smile." Mary picked a cherry off the ground and nibbled the meat off the pit. She then held the pit up to Christopher's face. "Look at tiss little ting." She bounced the pit in her palm. "Cherry pits are stubborn...like ye English. Unless they be broken down by awful cold they'll not grow.

"But tat's a good ting. It keeps the little sprout safe until the cold winter's passed." She offered Christopher the pit.

He squeezed his hand around it. "Aye. You're telling me to be patient; that the barrenness of my present life is protecting me for a coming Spring." An unexpected lump filled his throat.

Mary pinched Christopher's cheeks, playfully. "Yer a smarty."

"'Tis been a very long winter."

"But Wisdom warms ya."

He shrugged.

"Taras says you have become wise, and I'm not surprised to hear it. Wisdom rules the day if we just let her." Mary chased a fly from her arm. "But I don't know very many wise persons who have not endured terrible winters." She looked at Christopher carefully. "Wisdom is breakin ya into the man ya were meant to be."

He lowered his eyes. "I have no idea who that is."

Mary thought for moment before pointing a crooked forefinger at the branches above her. "I'm guessin tiss tree has no idea what sort of tree she is." Mary reached for a forgotten little cherry. "But *we* know by tiss." She handed the cherry to Christopher, then took Kipper's long locks into her hands and pulled his face toward hers. "Let Wisdom continue to fill ya, boyo; Let the Maker's love find ya, and ya'll be free enough." She kissed him on each cheek, marked his forehead with the sign of the cross and whispered a prayer before taking him by the hand to Nadia's kitchen.

CHAPTER 33

—❦—

LONG AGO SISTER Mary told Christopher that 'God changes the world every day, yet on some days he changes it more.' Neither of them knew that 6 August 1682 would be the first day of a change that would affect the history of the world for centuries to come.

Christopher and Mary had spent that particular day strolling along rows of late cabbage sprouting eagerly under the summer sun. But in Constantinople the gardeners of Sultan Mehmed IV had planted something rather different. They had dug a trench in front of the Imperial Gate of the Sultan's Topkapi Palace. In this trench they planted seven thick crimson poles that suspended regal cascades of black horse tails. Capped by carvings and gilded in gold leaf, these standards were known as the caliphate's tuğ and when they were thus displayed, the world understood that Allah's Sultan was about to launch a campaign against someone.

On that day, even the Palace's most intimate consorts did not know exactly what Mehmed IV or his Grand Vizier—Kara Mustafa— had in view. It had been rumoured that the Sultan and his vizier had different appetites, the former content for a small helping, the latter a feast. The fare, however, was expected to be some portion of the lands belonging to the Austrian House of Habsburg.

King Leopold ruled the Habsburg's grand empire that occupied the very heart of Europe. His army provided Christendom's sword and shield against the expanding Islamic Caliphate.

In better times, Leopold's Catholic Kingdom included all of Hungary but by now the Ottomans had bitten off about two-thirds of that region. Recently, more had been nibbled away by a pesky Protestant rebel and unlikely ally of the Ottomans named Count Imre Thököly. All that was presently left of Hungary for Leopold was a narrow swath of land that included the city of Györ. This city seemed to be the Ottoman's target. If taken, the Sultan's massive armies would be poised to strike Vienna and well-positioned to take the whole of Western Europe.

From all corners of the Caliphate, men were now being sent ahead to prepare the roads and bridges between Edirne and Belgrade where the invasion's first encampment would be centred. Thus, Taras received urgent messages to improve his defences in Podylla with an eye toward any encroachments by the menacing Poles. In so doing, he would be defending the Sultan's flank from any manoeuvre from the north.

Accordingly, the bitter winter of 1682/83 was spent in the busy work of preparations. Messengers raced in and out of Taras' office demanding reports, inventories and recommendations, all of which kept Christopher busy. The Sultan, his harem, and the main body of the army—including most of the Janissary battalions—had wintered within the comforts of Edirne. From there the vizier boasted to the whole world of having offered the Austrians' peace in return for Györ. Leopold had naturally refused, and so the Sultan now replanted his tuğ so that they faced Hungary plainly—a sign that officially declared all the rumours to be true.

The armies of Allah were about to invade the heart of Europe.

⁘

5 June 1683

An exhausted messenger arrived at the castle of Kamianets. He handed the çorbasi two sealed messages in the courtyard, one from

302

the agha of the Janissaries and the other from the Palace. Curious, Christopher watched Taras move anxiously to one side and first crack open the seal of the Sultan.

Christopher edged closer as Taras' eyes narrowed. By the way his brows furrowed beneath his high hat, Christopher knew he was reading the Palace letter very carefully.

Taras stuffed the letter deep within his robes and opened the message from the Supreme Agha.

He looks tense, anxious, Christopher thought.

When Taras finished reading the second message, he stood still as death. His swarthy face was grim. He then ordered Konstantin—his ruthless second-in-command—and Christopher to follow him.

Once inside his office, Taras slammed the door behind him and threw his hat to one side. He tossed his weapons from his sash and grabbed a large map from a honeycomb of scrolls on his wall. He unrolled it across his desk. Placing his palms atop the map he looked squarely at Konstantin. "The Sultan has handed Kara Mustafa the *şancaki serif* and is therefore now our Commander-in-Chief." He stared at the map. "Units from every far-flung province of the Caliphate are in Belgrade—one-hundred-thousand warriors of the Prophet... blessed be his name."

The colour left Christopher's face.

"So it begins." Taras' dark eyes scanned the map. "Most say Mustafa lusts for Vienna."

Christopher turned to see Konstantin's round face red with excitement. The Bulgarian lifted his face and recited from the Quran. "'I will cast terror into the hearts of those who disbelieve. Therefore, strike off their heads and cut off every fingertip.'"

Christopher chewed the inside of his cheek.

Taras pointed to the map—specifically to Kamianets. "Our spies tell us that the Poles want to take back Podylla at all costs. They have registered many thousands of Cossacks to fight for them. The vizier is willing to forfeit the north of the province, but not this city or the Dniester Valley to our south."

His thick finger tapped the map. "If the Poles cross the Dniester, they control the coastal plain. This would make for constant threat from the rear and cut off support from the Khan's Tartars. Therefore, we are to withdraw our forward troops at Proskuriv and more heavily fortify Kamianets."

Konstantin raised his fists. "We shall 'fight with them until the only religion left is that of Allah.'"

Christopher leaned over the map. "But if Mustafa attacks Vienna, Sobieski would move westward to support the Austrians—" He caught himself. *Why am I helping?*

Taras grunted. "Then we would be ordered west. Regular army units could defend Kamianets." He ran his fingers along the map. "Advance siege cannons and culverins are already moving forward to Buda. Mustafa will send the Tartars ahead in a wide wheel of destruction." He looked at Konstantin. "For now we wait and prepare our defences. Go and inform the men."

Christopher waited silently as Konstantin dashed away. Studying Taras, he feared the worst.

Finally, Taras turned to Christopher. "Bloodshed and horror as you have never seen is coming. The Tartars will spread themselves far. They will rape and butcher their way through Podylla on their way west. My scouts already reported hearing their mastiffs hunting slaves."

A shudder passed through Christopher.

Taras studied his map again. "The chaos will drift south, toward us. I could bring Mother and Mary here, but if our 27th is ordered to Vienna they would be in very great danger." His eyes swept across his map. "No, they must go somewhere else." He pointed to a Polish controlled city northwest of Kamianets. "There. They should flee to Lviv. They would be out of the Tartars' reach."

Christopher followed Taras' finger.

"Its heart is Ukrainian and Sobieski keeps it safe. Mother would do well there."

"How long a journey?" asked Christopher.

Taras measured the distance. "Mostly valley highways. I say a fortnight."

Christopher wiped sweat off his face. "Then they should leave at once."

"It may already be too late. Our garrisons are pulling back. The Tartars—"

"Allow me to escort them." Christopher stood upright. "I would return within a month."

Taras walked away from the desk and stared into the courtyard below where Konstantin was presenting the news to his cheering men. "The Quran teaches us to be ruthless with unbelievers. We are not to 'love our enemies' as Christian liars claim Jesus taught." He turned. "Therefore, my men complain about my merciful treatment of you. Imagine if you never returned."

Christopher objected. "The women need me to protect them."

"Konstantin demands I have you flogged in front of the men from time to time for minor offenses, like when you belched whilst walking past our Friday prayers last autumn."

"Too much cider—"

"That is not the point!" Taras began to pace, angrily. "You forget that you are the Sultan's slave. The men see you help yourself to my food as if we were equals. You thought it was funny to hide my slippers outside the mosque. You wink at Muslim women when we walk together."

Christopher lifted his chin. "Your Sultan has violated your own teachings and has taken everything from me without any cause other than my grandfather's insult. Now you complain about a belch and a wink."

Taras leaned his two strong fists atop his desk. "Do you understand how great a burden you have been? For twenty years you have had power over me. If you fled I would have died on a galley ship; if you died, I would have been stripped of wealth. If I treat you well my men despise me." He clenched his jaw. "I have loved you and I have resented you."

Surprised, Christopher said nothing.

"And now there is this." Taras retrieved the letter from the Palace and threw it at Christopher.

He read it quickly, shifting on his feet. The colour left his cheeks. The dispatch ordered Taras to deliver Christopher to the capital in chains where 'the Clive will suffer more appropriately for his family's crimes.' "But—"

The weary Ukrainian threw himself into his chair and pointed Christopher to a stool. "Zeki's spies in the artillery have doubtlessly reported my mercies to the Palace." His face hardened. The secret of his mother had been a heavy weight; war was looming, and now this. Taras studied Christopher for a long moment. "My orders are clear. They come from Allah's Sultan. I cannot appeal them."

Christopher's heart quickened.

Taras folded his hands on his lap. "It is not for me to judge the justice of any of this. I am expected to obey." He stared out of his window, thinking. "Allah's will be done."

Suddenly anxious, Christopher blurted, "That is a convenient place to hide."

Taras said nothing.

The Palace in chains! Christopher stood. "You see how submission makes no room for wisdom?"

"Stubbornness makes for even less." Taras fumbled with a glass paper weight.

"This is all very convenient for you. Once you send me away you are free from my burden."

"I do not choose this!"

Christopher scowled.

Taras pressed his fists atop his desk. "You are forever a stone in my sandal!" He threw the paper weight through his window and grabbed hold of Christopher's shirt. He slammed the surprised Englishman against a wall, roaring, "Do not judge me, Christian! You do not know my heart."

On the dawn following, Taras ordered Christopher to accompany him to the parade grounds. There he surprised everyone by sending a selected handful of artillery spotters out of the castle, supposedly to reinforce a small redoubt positioned on a highway just below Proskuriv.

Watching the gates close behind them, he turned to Christopher. "Zeki's spies are on their way." He wiped his moustache. "I suspect the Poles will make short work of them."

Christopher said nothing.

"Now, come with me."

Christopher entered Taras' office and obeyed a command to sit at his table. *So now he prepares me to be sent away next.*

Taras settled at his desk and remained quiet for a long moment. "You will write the following message to the chief scribe of the Sultan."

Christopher swallowed. Saying nothing, he dipped his quill in black ink and poised its tip above a clean paper.

"Inform him that I am unable to comply with my orders at this present time."

Christopher looked up.

"Write that I cannot spare the needed escorts, and in my opinion the journey to the capital would be too dangerous under our circumstances. The Sultan's property would be thereby put at too great a risk."

Restraining his relief, Christopher scratched his quill across the paper. Dipping for more ink, he now regretted yesterday's anger. Finished, he handed Taras the letter who read it carefully.

"Good. Seal it and have it sent." Taras then looked out the window. "Do not think too much about it." He folded his hands behind his back. "Now, leave me in peace. We have greater troubles upon us."

Christopher paused at the door. He turned. "Thank you."

Taras stiffened.

Christopher fell silent, but remained poised in the doorway. "What of your mother and Nadia?"

Taras turned. "What of them?"

"I had an idea."

Taras wiped his face with a kerchief and pointed Christopher to a cushion.

"We agree that the women should not travel to Lviv alone. But could your own soldiers not escort them to the frontier? They could keep watch nearby until Polish scouts found them."

Taras grumbled. "Two problems. First, why would my men do this? Second, the Poles could abuse the women, too."

Christopher thought. "To the second: some of the women *are* Poles, and Sister Mary is Roman Catholic like the Poles. She would threaten their souls."

Taras considered the point.

Christopher regarded him. "How many men would it take?"

"No less than six. But as I said, why would they do this?"

"You tell them that the Ukrainian women are your spies."

Taras did not answer at first. He tapped a single finger on his chin, deep in thought. His black eyes then revealed the faintest smile. "That could work."

The pair soon rode hard to Sister Mary's hospice. Without time to tarry, Taras summoned his mother and the sister from the fields and explained the plan. He then informed them that he would send six Janissaries and three wagons of provisions to them on the morrow.

"You cannot delay," said Taras. "Load what you must and take every person with you. Most importantly, you must choose three or four of the Ukrainian women to pretend they are our spies. I will have my men seek them out and discuss a plan."

Mary objected loudly, of course. At one point she stamped a foot for which Taras scolded her. But dear Nadia listened, patiently. She finally took Mary's hand and pulled it to her own heart. Her face puckered with a smile. "Do as my son says, Mary," she said. "Good tings will happen."

Nadia turned to Taras. "Now show me," she said.

He obediently retrieved his icon. Nadia proceeded to hold the image of Jesus to her lips and she prayed. She then bade Taras to kneel. As he did, she took his large head in her two small hands.

At the touch, Taras felt a surge of feeling, one he had not remembered since he was a small boy. His throat began to thicken. He clenched his teeth.

Nadia kissed his cheeks and lips. "Remember your vow to me: 'protect the weak and love the unlovely.'" She then pressed the icon deeply into Taras' thick palm as she pronounced a benediction over him. "Бог любить вас; зміцнюйтесь через випробування; нехай плід ваш буде добрим."

To another side, Christopher and Mary watched, quietly. Mary translated Nadia's blessing: "'God loves you; Let suffering teach you; Bear good fruit.'"

Christopher thought it was something Comfort might say. He faced Mary squarely as a melancholy dread began to spread through him. "I shall not see you ever again, shall I?"

Her eyes released small tears. "Why do ya say tat?"

"I just know it."

"Come with us to Poland. From there ya could make yer way fast to Ireland—"

"A very long time ago you told me to be light and love in a dark world. Abandoning Taras would be neither."

Mary took his hand. "Yer a good man, Kipper Clive. But I had a dream not even a week ago. It was of Ireland, and I saw ya in tat good place. I felt good when I awoke." She squeezed his hand. "Ya needs to believe, boyo."

"Was I alone?"

"Ya were. I am sorry to say tat."

Christopher's face fell. "Then what's the point of it? Besides, it was but a dream."

"Aye, but a dream." Mary then took both of Christopher's hands in hers. Her speech began to falter. "I prayed to the Holy Virgin tat she might get God to speak even just one word on yer behalf. Fer when God speaks, mighty tings happen."

Christopher smiled. "I shall imagine just such a word."

Taras' voice caught Christopher's attention. Time did not allow the sort of farewell that either man would have wanted. Christopher gently released Mary's hands from his own. "I love thee, woman." His throat was swollen. He held her by the shoulders and kissed her forehead with lingering lips. "Godspeed."

Sister Mary then commanded both men to kneel side by side before her. She blessed them with a bold prayer, and finished by waving the sign of the Cross over each of them. "*In nomine Patris, et Filii, et Spiritus Sancti…*"

The men stood. Taras summoned the horses from the gardener's hand. He then pulled four bags of coins from his saddle and turned to Mary. "Keep these hidden in different places. It should be enough to buy or bribe your way to safety. You know the plan?"

Lost for words, Mary nodded. She gave Taras and Christopher a final hug. "God's will be done."

Christopher mounted his horse, wondering what God's will might look like in the storm fast approaching.

CHAPTER 34

———— ⚜ ————

14 July 1683

TARAS WAS PACING the castle courtyard when the Janissary escorts of
Sister Mary's hospice finally returned to Kamianets. A sergeant and
his corporal dismounted. "Çorbasi?"

Taras whirled about. "Yes?"

The sergeant spoke. "The Christians have been delivered to a
Polish patrol as you commanded. We sent them into a meadow where
we could watch from a ridge. The Poles gathered them up quickly
and took them away."

"What arrangements did you make with the spies?"

"Three Ukrainians told us their husbands were killed by Poles
so they hate them. They showed us how to read the embroidery on
their blouses. One kind of stitch means that the Poles are planning an
attack; another means all is quiet. A third means they must speak to
us. On the new moon they will leave a blouse behind a certain birch
tree."

"Good," said Taras. "Pray Allah keeps them safe. Casualties?"

"None." He hesitated. "The little old one kissed all our hands and
sang us a song."

Taras held his smile. "Did the Catholic sister give you any
trouble?"

"She is not a very nice person."

Taras pursed his lips. "*JazakAllahu khair*—may Allah reward you."

The sergeant bowed, but then struggled. "Forgive me a thousand times, Çorbasi. The men think you were protecting a lover, or that this was a favour to the Englishman. I am to ask you for the truth of this."

Taras scowled. "This was about placing spies in the north. Tell the men if I had a lover I would want her close and not in the bed of some Pole. As far as the Englishman, he is the Sultan's slave. My duty is to keep him alive. Do not mistake my treatment of him in any other way."

The sergeant released an anxious breath. "One more thing."

"What!"

"There is a rumour that the Englishman was ordered to the Palace—"

"That is a lie! Now, no more talk." Taras reached into his purse and retrieved some silver coins. "Here, take this as a bonus for you and your men. Get some rest."

As his men disappeared, Taras exhaled. He sat on a bench imagining his mother blessing the Janissaries. Smiling freely, he fell prostrate on the grass to offer his thanks to Allah. "*Alhamdulillah!*"

Finished, Taras stood and hurried to tell Christopher the good news. He found him flirting with some Cossack women on the bridge. "Christopher Effendi!"

Christopher whirled around.

"Leave them."

Christopher walked quickly to Taras. "You have news?"

Taras gave him the sergeant's report in a hushed tone.

"You have done a good thing, Çorbasi," Christopher said. "And three Ukrainian spies with secret stitching? I should write a song about this."

The very same day, an urgent message was delivered from Buda informing Taras that Kara Mustafa had begun a bombardment of Vienna. The 'Golden Apple' of Europe was being softened in preparation for 'Allah's great avenging' of the Caliphate's humiliating defeat in that same place some 150 years before. The message further revealed that King John Sobieski of Poland had subsequently abandoned all plans to invade Podylla in favour of supporting the Austrians.

The message went on:

'Our Turks, Arabs, Berbers, Greeks, Armenians, Ukrainians, Kurds, Negroes, Serbs, Bulgars, Magyars, and Tartars approach the thin walls of the trembling city. The unbelievers have seen the edge of our swords and feel the terror of our artillery.

The riders of Allah have slain thousands throughout the whole of the surrounding countryside. The terrified infidels have burned their own suburbs and have withdrawn behind pitiful fortifications soon to be razed by powder and fire. Their emperor has fled, leaving the defence of his pitiful city to inferior subordinates. Kara Mustafa now views the jihad in comfort from his pitched palace in the centre of our encampment.

Your 27th battalion is hereby ordered to immediately support the rest of the Janissary corps. Your haste is demanded.

Ibrahim ibn Hussein, scribe of the Agha'

"What of Kamianets?" Christopher was breathless.

"Bulgarians and Romanians will replace us." Taras was flushed with anticipation. Taking long strides, he began barking orders at his junior officers. Munitions needed to be piled into wagons; cannons needed to be rolled from the castle's walls and gathered on the highway behind heavy horses.

"We've a dozen brass culverins," answered Christopher to a question of inventory. "And seven nine-pounders ready for travel."

Taras surveyed his scampering men. "We will be supplied with grenades, trench guns and more ammunition in Buda. From here we take bows, axes and pikes—"

Another messenger galloped into the castle. He dismounted and raced toward Taras. Looking up from the message, Taras barked, "Regular army units will relieve us in two days. We leave tomorrow."

By nightfall, Christopher found the courage to ask a troubling question. Entering Taras' busy office, he waited to one side until the last of the colonel's junior officers had presented their reports.

All others dismissed, Taras motioned for Christopher to come close. "I know what you will ask." Taras took a long drink of water and wiped his hand through his greying hair. He threw himself into his chair. "Sit."

Christopher obeyed.

"You will come with the battalion. Otherwise, one of Zeki's agents will cut your throat."

Christopher waited.

"You remain as my scribe, but you will remain far from the battle." Taras rapped his knuckles lightly on his desk. "I see how you toy with the women at the market, but I know you will always want to be with Raven more than life itself."

"If you are wondering whether I would try and flee in the chaos, I will not. Any joy of Raven's touch would be ruined by the cruelties visited upon you. Day and night I would see you chained to a galley. To betray you would be to destroy whatever sort of man I am, and Raven would be left with a shadow."

Taras listened carefully. He then leaned forward and said, "You are an uncommon man." He folded his hands. "But it is my wish that you escape in the chaos of what is coming. I will report that you were killed and the Palace would never know."

"But they could find out and then—"

"Yes, yes, of course." Taras shook his head. "I know your heart and I am grateful. So I say this to you: Pray for my death."

Christopher blinked. "I will not."

"My death is your liberation, Christopher Effendi. It sets you free from the authority of your conscience."

Christopher furrowed his brow. "I do not like this talk."

"I do not care. I could die for a lesser cause than the freedom of a good man."

Christopher's eyes welled.

Taras leaned back. "That is the end of this. Whatever happens in Vienna is according to the will of Allah. You will obey me in all things; you will not counsel me without my permission or interrogate my thoughts. Do you understand?"

Christopher nodded.

Taras relaxed. "Good. Now, get some sleep. Tomorrow we begin a journey like no other."

⚜

Christopher and the 27th battalion followed the Dniester River toward a pass in the rugged Carpathian Mountains that opened to a road leading southward to the Tisza River valley. From there they crossed the Great Hungarian Plain and finally arrived at the city of Buda lying on the west bank of the Danube downstream from Vienna. The Janissaries had pressed nearly thirty miles a day for a fortnight and Christopher arrived exhausted.

As expected, the expedition was heavily resupplied in Buda from munitions and material moved forward from the Sultan's base of

316

operations in Belgrade farther to the east. To the already impressive train was added more wagons loaded with hundreds of iron grenades, sheaves of arrows, crates of muskets, sharp *kilij*, trench guns, and caissons of powder for the miners still busy trying to undermine Vienna's defences. Christopher wondered how the Austrians would ever be able to defend themselves against such an invasion.

After two days, the band of the 27th struck up a dignified tune to launch the six-day march to Vienna where the largest invasion force to ever gather in Europe was engaged in heavy combat.

Christopher was quickly caught up in the rhythmic tramping, the cadence of the drums and the sense of sheer power sweeping over the countryside. Marching in time, he realized that he felt a certain affinity to the men around him. *I know so many by name, yet they enslave me and they hope to kill my brothers-in-Christ.* He spat. *But when I eat bulgur with them, or laugh at their jokes, or sing their songs, I like them. They fear death, as do I. They love their women, as do I. They love their God, as do I…* He lowered his head and pressed forward.

Morale ran high amongst the Janissaries, and they marched quickly past the conquered city of Győr to cross the frontier of the Habsburg's empire. However, wagon trains of wounded began to appear from the west and Christopher's ears quickly filled with troubled murmurs of the soldiers watching them pass.

Later that same evening, a column of teamsters heading east paused to rest, and they leaked information that Christopher was eager to learn. It seemed that Vizier Kara Mustafa had incorrectly assessed Vienna to be something of a thin-shelled walnut that could easily be cracked open and its digestible interior devoured. But his elite troops—his Janissaries—were being massacred day after day.

Wrongly assuming an easy victory at the walls, Mustafa had ordered tens of thousands of Tartar cavalry to scour the Austrian countryside instead of supporting the siege. In their wake, unde-fended villages were left burning and citizens raped, slain or carried into slavery atop the wild ponies of the Tartar bowman.

⸙

5 August 1683

Arriving at the Caliphate's siege encampment, Christopher gaped at the scene before him. An Oriental city of exotic fables lay sprawled across the landscape in the shape of a huge crescent. Orderly and beautiful with its colourful pennants and Persian lines, the Ottoman camp was a broadcloth of canvas and silk, all ruffling in the breezes that brushed the gentle slope descending to Vienna's stubborn walls.

Unable to tear his eyes away, Christopher continued to stare in disbelief. Domed palaces, crescent spires and elegant silk mosques rose amongst thousands of steep-pitched tents housing the soldiers. Huge herds of camels and horses grazed within wide stockades; countless goats and sheep covered the green of stick-woven folds. The air was fragranced with incense, the mood was bright.

Taras had informed him that space for the 27th was reserved in the centre of the encampment, near the Grand Vizier's staked pal-ace—an elegant maze of Chinese silk and rich brocade divided into chambers for dining and various other pleasures. Christopher's eyes found the palace, but his ears suddenly cocked to the unmistakable rattle of musket fire at the city's walls.

Heavy cannonades began to thump the air. Voices then turned his head. An ornately uniformed brigadier of the Janissary corps and three juniors stepped off their camels and shouted a series of anxious instructions to Taras who immediately sent Konstantin and two ser-geants scampering away with orders.

"Christopher!" Taras shouted. "Follow me!"

Christopher ran with his secretary's satchel into the officer's tent. Inside, the brigadier opened a map. "There. We have concentrated our main assault against their south-western wall. The city is protected by a complicated series of pits and ravelins. We have lost thousands of men to their obstinate general."

Christopher kept to one side, ears piqued. The officer went on to describe the city's commander—a wiry forty-six-year-old named Count Rüdiger von Starhemberg.

"He is as clever a fox as I have ever fought. His engineers turned Vienna into a porcupine."

Amused at the description, Christopher leaned forward to follow the officer's finger on the map.

"He has a series of impaling defences here, here and here. We've lost hundreds of men and animals on his skewers!"

Another officer jabbed his finger at the map. "They've trenches and pits there, in front of the walls for their musketeers who are protected by a network of heavy ravelins."

Taras cursed. Ravelins were triangular outworks that deflected cannon balls and provided an asymmetrical field of fire. As he offered a suggestion, Christopher noticed a bead of perspiration slide down Taras' cheek and drip on the map. *Is he afraid?*

"We have thrown waves of men at all of this and they lay in heaps," groused the brigadier.

Another slammed his palm on the map. "When we get close, we are either blown to bits by Austrian grenades, or dragged into their trenches by long hooks and axed." He turned to Taras. "You'll see the heads of our brothers staring back at you from the heathens' staves."

Taras lowered his heavy brows. "What about our sappers?"

"They've had some success excavating an advancing line of trenches for our musketeers, but at a high price."

The tent fell silent as the officers stared at the map. Finally, Taras asked, "Do we have good news at all?"

One officer grunted. "We've a thousand miners digging underground and their explosions have heaved the earth up. But Starhemberg's pikemen drive us out every time." He looked squarely at Taras. "We need fresh troops."

To all this news, Christopher's mind began to race. *If Taras is killed—*

"The 27th will support an assault tomorrow," said the brigadier. He pressed a smudged finger on the map. "There. The miners will set off explosions just after dawn." He stood upright and faced Taras. "Your men will charge into the gaps."

Taras nodded, grimly, turned, and led Christopher out of the tent. The two men stared silently at the furious centre of the combat line some 500 yards away. Flashes of muskets and clouds of smoke obscured the carnage. "We are ready," said Taras.

CHAPTER 35

CHRISTOPHER SAID NOTHING as the battalion's whirling dervish led the 27th in their prayers just before dawn of the next day. Taras surveyed the men about to enter combat. Head and shoulders above every one of them, the huge Ukrainian raised his fist to the heavens and cried, "Allahu Akbar." In unison with the ranks, he then led a recitation of the first *Sura* of the Quran:

> "'Praise to Allah, Lord of the worlds; the compassionate, the merciful! King on the day of Judgment; You only do we worship, and to You do we cry for help. Guide us on the straight way, the path of those to whom You have been gracious— with whom You are not angry, and who do not go astray.'"

With the eastern sky softened by a hint of grey, Christopher ran his eyes along the ranks of men prepared to die within the next hours. Many shouldered muskets; some held bows. Most carried pistols in their wide sashes; all had daggers, yatagans, or small axes for close combat. Their baggy pants fluttered over leather shoes. Their eyes remained fixed and steady beneath their upright caps except for one cadet who scratched nervously at his moustache.

Knowing most of them, sorrow began to weigh on Christopher. *And yet most of them hate me.* He tore his eyes away and looked downslope at the yellow glow over Vienna, wondering about the men who would die in that place on this day. *All of this death, and here I stand, safe in Turkish slippers. What kind of man am I?*

The sounds of forward musketeers crackled; a thundering volley from the city's cannons answered. Taras climbed atop his camel. Long robes fell from his wide shoulders and draped over his yellow boots. His tall cap and feathered plume rose high above his head. He waved a hand for the band to begin playing.

Christopher caught his eye. *Will I see him again?*

Taras offered a proud smile. Fist in the air he cried over his men, "Allahu Akbar!"

"Allahu Akbar!" they answered.

Christopher felt a chill. *Who could defeat them?*

With a grunt from Taras, the advance began beneath his approving eye. Then, as the last company passed, he urged his camel close to Christopher with his baton. "Remain near my tent and assist the quartermaster. I will send you messages as necessary."

Christopher nodded. *He is a huge target. He cannot survive this.*

Taras leaned downward and lowered his voice. "If you learn of my death, flee at once." He then sat upright in his camel's saddle. "A man is what he loves, Christopher Effendi. The things you love have revealed your heart. Be at peace."

Christopher paced all that day and the next, and the two weeks that followed. Taras returned from time to time, weary but spared the horrors so many others had suffered. He spoke little, simply reminding Christopher before each return to the front that he must be vigilant—ever ready to flee.

Christopher struggled to think about that. He busied himself with inventories and help for the wounded when he could. Endless columns of wagons passed through the camp, those of the 27th pausing briefly for his accounting before groaning toward the hospital tents or the cemetery.

In spite of heavy losses, however, news arrived that the 27th had helped collapse a primary outer defence of Vienna. Learning of this, Christopher climbed into a hospital wagon to deliver water. "So, some success?"

"Yes," reported a wounded Turk. "But we cannot break through! That heathen Starhemberg fills the infidels with the power of the jinn."

Christopher helped him drink.

"We broke through to a dry moat, but they do not yield."

"What of Taras?" asked Christopher.

"Allah protects him. He stands in the front and his robes are shredded with ball. But he does not fall."

Christopher hurried his count of the wounded and dead before dismounting the wagon. He glanced about the busy encampment. Thousands upon thousands had died from the wet-work of Christian canister, axes, musket balls and arrows. *How many more? How does Taras survive this?* He took a drink for himself. *Do I want him to?*

⚜

23 August 1683

Christopher spotted Taras trudging upslope with a column of threadbare, exhausted soldiers trailing behind. "By Christ," he muttered. He ran to help the staggering man.

Falling into his large tent, Taras waved a bloody hand at Christopher and threw himself upon his straw mattress. Christopher lifted a canteen to his lips, then rushed into the neighbouring cooks' tent to fill a plate with bread, cheese and some freshly roasted lamb.

"Eat," Christopher said as he returned. He looked into his friend's empty eyes now peering at him from the deep hollows into which they had retreated. Christopher wrapped a bandage around his hand and cried for a doctor.

"I am to lead the next assault," said Taras. His voice was weak.

Christopher bit his lip.

"Have you heard of the complaints?"

"No."

"Many of our brothers have served their forty-day obligation under Allah. Yet Mustafa refuses to relieve them." Taras took some lamb and chewed, slowly. "We will not be blessed for his disobedience."

"You should rest—"

Taras lay on his back. "Take an accounting of my men."

Within two hours, Christopher returned to report that the battalion had been reduced to 140 able-bodied soldiers—less than one-third of its original strength. The rest were buried or wounded.

Lying flat on his back, Taras shook his head. "I cannot crack this walnut with one-hundred and forty men." Christopher helped him sit up. "Last night I dreamt of many things." He reached a hand toward Christopher. "What I saw did not surprise me."

"What did you see?"

Saying nothing more, the exhausted colonel dressed. He laid a large hand on Christopher's shoulder, turned, and led the survivors of the 27th back to the siege trenches.

On the evening of 27 August, Christopher spotted a spectacular display of rockets bursting over Vienna atop the flame-silhouetted steeple of St. Stephen's Cathedral. Rumours had abounded that Pope Innocent XI—himself a rabid enemy of the Ottomans—had poured his treasury into an army of Christian princes now likely to be coming in relief of the city. Christopher wondered if the rockets were not a signal for them to hurry. He was aware that the cavalry and dragoons of the Austrian emperor's son-in-law—the French Duke of Lorraine—had already engaged the Turks some distance to the west, blocking columns of Ottoman infantry from supporting the Tartars in their raids.

Perhaps these Frenchmen were now riding hard for the city?

Spies had leaked information to the camp that the Elector of Bavaria had promised 11,000 men in relief, the princes of Franconia and Swabia another 8,000 German footmen. It was rumoured that 10,000 Saxons were enroute with artillery. Even Scots mercenaries were reported to be coming. But the greatest fear for the Muslims was the prospect of King Sobieski and his terrifying hussar horsemen charging from the north.

To all of this Christopher responded with mixed feelings. Imagining Christian armies chasing Kara Mustafa's Muslim horde out of Europe made him nearly giddy with hope. Realizing that this probably meant the death of his friend made him sorrowful. He did not like the confusion of it all. "God's will be done," he muttered.

Christopher stared at the sky. He knew that if the city's rockets had been a signal, the vizier would need to press yet more desperately against the stubborn Starhemberg. Wounded soldiers had told him that the Austrians were able to seal every gap within an hour of the miners' explosions. They reported how it was that the defenders pulled chains across gateways and doors, and how they could quickly throw up ramparts of rock and broken timber. Wherever a stave could be pointed, a stubborn Austrian jammed one into place. Vienna was a scarred, ravaged, and stubborn porcupine.

As Christopher expected, Kara Mustafa raged about the encampment the next morning demanding his assault escalate to yet more ferocious proportions. He had lost patience with the Janissaries and—as Taras had feared—had boldly overruled their forty-day expectations. Everyone was ordered to the walls.

⚜

4 September 1683

Christopher languished about the nearly empty camp. Almost any man who could fight was thrashing in the death pits at the base of Vienna's battered walls. All that was left in the tent city were some cooks, wounded men, a few guards and a heavy pall of dread.

Christopher kept close to Taras' tent, dodging the eyes of wounded veterans viewing him with increasing suspicion. Several told him that he was Jonah in their storm—he needed to be cast away.

In the mid-afternoon, a loud explosion at the walls turned Christopher's head. It was followed by the distant shouts of thousands of men rushing toward the breach. Christopher gripped the canvas flap of his tent and stared through clouds of distant smoke as he imagined Taras and his beleaguered 27th engaging a Viennese counter-attack of pikes and musketeers.

"Heads are being cleaved," grumbled a one-armed Turk to one side. "So should yours."

Christopher scowled. He listened carefully to the prattle of musket fire. Within an hour the front fell quiet. *Starhemberg held.*

At dawn, a column of wagons rumbled upslope from the city again. Christopher waited with canteens and his ledger.

"Look what I have," cackled a teamster as he reined his horse. Tied in his wagon was a trembling prisoner in a grey-white coat and cowering under a wide-brimmed hat. "We dragged him out of the gap and interrogated him." The teamster lifted his yatagan and waved it at Christopher. "We think he has more to say, but after he does..."
He swiped his sword through the air, laughing.

Christopher looked into the young Austrian's colourless face. "*Gott sei mit dir—*"

The teamster interrupted, "He told us that we've killed most of them—eight thousand men. Even more infidel women and children have died, and Starhemberg is sick." The teamster snapped his reins. "Soon we'll have them all."

Christopher tore his eyes away from the prisoner. "The colonel is well?"

"He is protected by Allah."

Two days later, the earth shook from two more explosions set off by the miners. Christopher looked from his tent to see smoke rising to the left of the prior assault. Again, he heard the distant cries of the Janissary charge as they poured murderous salvos of arrows, artillery, and musket fire against determined defenders. *How does anyone live through this!*

He watched flashes of musket fire and heard reports of distant cannon. But within an hour, the sounds subsided and Christopher knew the assault had again failed.

That night and on the night following, Christopher spotted rockets over the steep, forested ridgeline west of the city known as the Kahlenberg Hill. Seeing them, he now knew what the vizier's war council had already known: the relief armies were indeed coming and they were close. He now knew why wounded Tartars were appearing. *They are being driven out of the west. Mustafa shall have to pull regiments off the walls to defend the rear.* Heart pounding, he thought, *If I can slip away now... but exactly how...*

The rockets also gave spirit to the exhausted Austrians. The next morning, Christopher took a spare eyeglass from Taras' tent and watched the city celebrate the nativity of the Blessed Virgin Mary. He could see priests and altar boys serving the Host to the desperate men on the walls. During the lull he could hear the faint sounds of singing drift in an easterly breeze.

The celebration was more important to the defenders than Christopher knew. Emperor Leopold's grandfather had declared the Virgin Mary to be the Sacred Commander—the *generalissima sacrale*—of the city's struggle against the Muslims, thus inspiring the whole city to special prayer and devotion.

Desperate, Kara Mustafa ordered another savage assault that same day. Again, the city held.

At nightfall, Christopher felt eyes upon him. Fear was fast-claiming the encampment. Tens of thousands of the Sultan's men had fallen, yet Vienna had somehow held. The Turks were feeling cursed, and he was an unbeliever walking freely in their midst.

Moving toward his tent, Christopher wondered whether Taras was right? Had Mustafa's arrogance cost them the favour of Heaven? The imams and dervishes still urged the exhausted soldiers to keep faith; the black flag of the Prophet—the *sancak-ı şerif*—still stood tall alongside Kara Mustafa's headquarters. Yet a foreboding sense of ill mingled with the smell of death that permeated the encampment.

"You must be happy," scowled a Turk.

Christopher turned his face away.

"The Crusader armies are coming." The Turk leaned close. "But you will not live to see them."

Christopher ducked into his tent, mind racing. Dare he feel hope?

CHAPTER 36

THREE DAYS LATER, the morning broke under heavy clouds and a wind-swept rain. Ordered off the front-line, Taras stumbled into his tent, cursing. He threw off his drenched cloak and collapsed on to the ground.

Christopher scampered for fresh water as he rushed through mud, past rearing horses and bolting camels. Everywhere men roiled about in confusion. Returning to the tent with a clay pitcher of clean water, he found his friend on his knees. "Taras?"

The giant of a man turned his blackened face toward Christopher. His eyes were blood-red. "The battalion is reduced to thirty-six men." He clenched his fists. "If we could have breached the walls yesterday we would have slaughtered every unbeliever and claimed the city for Allah. But now…" He guzzled his water. "An army of forty-thousand Christians is coming from the west. Maybe more."

Christopher said nothing. The patter of rain atop the canvas grew louder.

Taras' body trembled. He bled from wounds on both arms and one leg. His hands were swollen; his moustache was matted with blood. The exhausted man gulped more water. "And Sobieski is surely coming from the north with more." He wiped his mouth across a torn sleeve and dragged himself to a cushion. "What day is this?"

"The eleventh of September."

Taras took another drink. "History will remember this day." He listened to the confusion beyond the walls of his tent. "Today is the high tide of Allah's Caliphate. Tomorrow we begin to fall away."

Christopher watched tears fill his eyes. "Let me find you some food."

"Make sure my sons are fed first."

Christopher obediently hurried to the cooks' tent where bakers were running armloads of bread to the battered men now collapsing into their tents. Content the men were being cared for, he ventured farther into the camp in search of meat or cheese, olives or anything that might lift Taras' spirits.

Once tidy, the once splendid encampment had been reduced to muck and disorder. The latrines had been abandoned and the air reeked of septic and of death. Wounded men lay strewn about in the mud, unattended; their festering wounds blackened by swarming flies.

Food was scarce as the wagons from Hungary had slowed to a trickle. Christopher gaped at a company of Janissaries brawling in the rain. "Leviathan has come," he muttered. Unable to find anything other than bread to feed the colonel, he returned soaking wet.

"The men are eating what they can, Çorbasi."

"The vizier has proven himself to be an arrogant fool." Taras covered his head with his hands. "He vowed that the army would be feasting within the city by now. Instead of reinforcing us, he sent too many west to ravage the unbelievers. Our wagons are filled with fair-skinned virgin slaves instead of meat and vegetables." He wiped bloody spittle from his mouth. "He disrespects Allah's forty days of service. Our cause is lost."

Taras chewed a bite of bread, studying Christopher. "It is soon time for you to flee." He smiled, weakly. "Sail to Ireland. It gives me joy to imagine it."

"But—"

"The way of escape will appear when the time is right."

Christopher sat on a silk cushion. "As long as you live—"

"Live?" Taras laughed, wincing. "No. I command you to flee, Kipper Clive. I am going to die."

"You don't know that."

"But I do. I had another dream. I was defending the blessed black flag when I suddenly felt nothing but bliss." He pressed a bandage against a leaking wound. "Two hours ago I was ordered to join the Albanians in the defence of the flag. You see? My dreams are true."

A lump filled Christopher's throat.

Taras took another drink and tore a large bite of bread from his loaf. "Now listen to me carefully. In my dream, the sun was setting when I die. So, it must be that the Christians will not break our lines until late in the day. Hide here until then."

Christopher ran a hand through his hair. "But the lines may hold."

Taras shrugged. "My dream says they do not."

Christopher remained silent.

"Do you understand?"

Christopher nodded. *Is it true? Is this really happening?*

"Good." Taras reached for a large blue satchel with a wide strap that he had tossed atop a bench. He opened the leather satchel and retrieved a broad-brimmed black hat pinned up on one side, a pair of filthy leggings, badly scuffed shoes and a long, grey-white coat with wide, blue cuffs. "From one of the prisoners we beheaded."

Christopher gawked at the blood-stained collar.

"When the time is right, put it on. The chaos will give you cover."

Christopher's mind whirled.

"Are we agreed?" Taras tone was abruptly firm.

The two men stared at one another as a torrent of rain now crashed over the tent. Christopher could barely imagine leaving Taras Çorbasi. "Yes."

"Alhamdulillah. All praise to Allah." Taras took a satisfied breath. He pointed to the eyeglass. "Keep watch on this battle as best you can. But beware of those around you."

Taras then walked to his walnut strongbox sitting beneath the map table. He retrieved a hidden key and squatted to unlock the iron-strapped chest. He pushed the heavy lid up to reveal a canvas bag containing a variety of gold and silver ducats, some Spanish dollars, a few Dutch guilders and some Algerian bucus. "This will help you get home. Keep it hidden until you are ready." He dropped the coin bag into the empty blue satchel and set it to one side.

"I—"

Taras waved him to silence. He then rummaged to the bottom of his strongbox and retrieved a large bundle of papers tied by twine. He handed Christopher the papers. "I took these from your office in Kamianets. These are your writings."

Speechless, Christopher received the bundle with two hands.

Taras eyed him, carefully. "What we love is revealed by the fruit of our lives." He pointed to Christopher's bundle. "Your writings are fruits. When you forget who you are, read them."

Christopher's chin quivered. He nodded.

Taras returned to his strongbox and removed a homespun cloth wrapped around something. "I should have given this to you long ago."

Christopher received the cloth and unwrapped it. Inside was the dagger that his Aunt Comfort had presented to him on Twelfth Night more than twenty years prior. Jaw sagging, he removed the blade from its sheath and ran his fingers slowly over the smooth, boxwood grips. He slid his forefinger lightly over the razor sharp edge. Staring at the bird-in-flight etching on one side, his eyes welled. Christopher looked at Taras in amazement.

"Turn it over. I have always wanted to know what the words say." Christopher translated the inscription.

"'Breathe Deeply; Serve Humbly; Dance with Abandon.'"

Smiling, Taras thought for a moment. "You have surely been a deep breather, Christopher Effendi! And you have served humbly." He leaned forward to speak. His broad face suddenly filled with emotion. "Now it is your time to dance with abandon."

Taras reached within the folds of his robes and withdrew his hand to reveal the icon from his mother. "In all the earth, this is still my most valued treasure." He stared at it for a long while before struggling to speak. "In the dark nights… after battle I would kiss it and… hold it close. I do not think Allah is offended."

He looked carefully at Christopher. His bloodshot eyes were wet and swelling. "I do not want a scavenging Crusader to find it on my body and toss it to some whore as his trophy." He handed the little image of Jesus to Christopher. "Wear it around your neck. Remember how this Jesus overcame suffering."

Hushed, Christopher received the icon respectfully. He stared at it lying in his hand. What could he say? Oh how he loved this man. Christopher hastily hung the necklace around his neck.

Taras turned suddenly grave and dried his eyes across his sleeve. "One last thing: The Sultan will have Mustafa strangled for this catastrophe, but that will not be enough to cover his shame. He will swear vengeance on all Christians everywhere." He laid a huge hand on Christopher's shoulder and squeezed. "The day comes when Zeki's family will remind him of you, and he will send agents to kill you."

Christopher stiffened.

"The Sultan has many spies. They will find you in Ireland or in London or anywhere you go." Taras removed his hand. "You may be free, but you will not be safe in any of your days."

Christopher set his jaw. "We are not born to be safe; We are born to be free."

⟡

12 September 1683

Lighting a candle, Christopher helped Taras off his bed for pre-dawn prayers. Neither man said a word until Taras was ready to leave.

"From here you can see some of the battlefield," said Taras. "The trenches at the walls are all but abandoned. All of our strength is now at the rear." He groaned a little and rubbed his knees. "Stay near and keep an ear for messengers. After they report to the vizier they always share news with the cooks to get extra bread." He hefted two pistols in his hands and set them in his sash. He pointed Christopher to a third pistol lying on the desk. "Keep it loaded. When the line breaks, you must put on the Austrian uniform and hide yourself. Once the Christians overrun the camp, hurry west."

Christopher understood. He reached a hand forward. Taras pulled him into an embrace.

"I am at peace, friend," said Taras. "Today you begin your dance." Saying nothing more, he turned and ducked through the tent.

⟡

As if Heaven were smiling that morning, shafts of sunlight pierced the fleeting clouds. Christopher stared at his feet, certain he could feel the earth beginning to tremble. From the hills to the west of Vienna, an avenging army of Christ's Kingdom was coming.

Just as Taras had predicted, the first messenger arrived at the cooks' tent at mid-morning and reported that French dragoons and a regiment of Saxon footmen were holding at the flanks, but some 65,000 Christians were on the move.

Within the hour, Christopher heard a distant cheer from the city's walls. He crept out of his tent and aimed his glass in the opposite direction. He gasped. A French army was advancing downslope toward the Ottomans under a huge white flag boasting a crimson cross. *It has begun.*

For the first hours of the battle, Christopher sat silently against the centre pole of Taras' tent. Eyes closed, he listened to the incessant crack of musketry and the thump of cannon. The cries of war from both armies echoed in a wide crescent arcing the western landscape. He could hear the Muslim's hypnotic chants of 'Allah, Allah.'

"And where is Taras?" Christopher left his tent and searched for Mustafa's position with his glass. Taras would be guarding the vizier and the Black Flag. "There." Mustafa had pitched a scarlet tent close to the front and planted the flag of the Prophet as a rallying point for his anxious army now wavering on the plain.

Returned to his tent for the next two hours, Christopher paced. *Taras' dream said late in the day...*In the distance a great cheer suddenly rose from the hillsides. Christopher cocked his ear wondering if the feared Poles had finally arrived to reinforce Lorraine's French army. He crept toward the cooks' tent and listened for news.

Nervous messengers blabbered about King Sobieski assembling his cavalry. Christopher hurried to one side with his eyeglass. He swung it along the line of the Ottoman's front, then searched for

Mustafa again. "There." The vizier was standing atop his velvet chair and swinging his arms, wildly.

The ground began to tremble once again. He aimed his glass at the Christian infantry now tramping steadily forward. Behind them, gleams of light reflected from the lance-tips of 20,000 cavalrymen poised to strike. Christopher's scalp tingled.

Within the hour he glanced at the sun and guessed it to be about four o'clock. *Soon. Soon.* His breath quickened. He crouched low. "But when…"

The earth began to shake. Men scampered from all sides. Christopher lifted his glass one more time and when he did, his mouth went dry. The Polish cavalry was advancing through gaps now offered by the infantry. At the fore rode King John III Sobieski atop a huge stallion and under a feathered, high-crowned hat. Behind, his winged hussar horsemen were massed in their draping leopard skins.

As the hussars' pace quickened, their high-arced wings of feathers rose over their broad shoulders, rustling. Awed, Christopher could not look away.

A messenger ran close, crying that Mustafa was retreating from his forward position. Christopher kept his eye fixed on the advancing Poles.

Sobieski's hussars cantered closer, closer, and closer still to the nervous Ottoman line. They advanced downslope with increasing speed like an avalanche beginning to tumble. Sobieski then stood in his stirrups, aimed his royal mace directly at the Turks, and gave the order to charge.

Watching breathlessly, Christopher flinched. In a single motion, the hussars lowered their lances, leaned their horses into a gallop. "*Jezus Maria ratuj!*" The earth shook beneath Christopher's feet so severely that he felt his silk trousers flutter. "My God," he gasped.

As Sobieski's cavalry neared the trembling Ottoman line, the wind lifted their feathered wings higher, filling the air with the sound of a great whirring. *Heaven's army has come!*

The shimmering blocks of hussars roared forward, faster and faster toward the helpless footmen of the vizier. The ethereal sound of wind-wound feathers rose ever louder, terrifying Christopher but most especially the Ottoman soldiers now braced. In moments, however, the rising whirr gave way to the crash of lances as the cavalry of the Christ collided with full force into the shields of the Prophet.

The Ottoman line shuddered.

Christian infantry quickly swarmed behind Sobieski's hussars, shouting the name of their Saviour and falling upon the Ottomans with fury. The Muslims held for a mere moment before collapsing. Vanquished, they began to flee the field in disarray.

Christopher gawked, then dropped his eyeglass. "Now!"

CHAPTER 37

SCAMPERING INTO HIS tent, Christopher ripped off his Turkish clothing. An artillery shell exploded just yards away. Debris blew through the tent, partially collapsing it and knocking Christopher backward. Coughing, he recovered himself quickly and crawled through heavy smoke.

He dressed into the Austrian's uniform, tied his shoes, pressed his wide-brimmed hat atop his head and secured his dagger in the wide belt snugging the long coat to his waist. He grabbed the blue satchel loaded with coins and his writings. He slung it over his shoulder as musket balls popped through the canvas.

Ducking, he clawed about for the pistol Taras had left him. He found it tangled in a blanket. More musket balls snagged through the canvas, popping and zipping. Christopher dropped to the ground where he lay flat as his mind raced. He then crawled out of the tent. Before him the encampment was in the grip of Leviathan. Terrified men ran from all directions. Fires were raging. Corpses lay everywhere. *What to do…*

Gritting his teeth, Christopher hesitated. *What of Taras?* He strained to look in the direction of the vizier's position. The smoke was too thick. He wiped his burning eyes. Another artillery shell exploded nearby, heaping mounds of rock and earth atop him. Covering his head, his ears filled with Taras' voice. "My duty is to die well—yours is to live well."

Enough. Christopher lifted himself into a crouch, secured his satchel and rushed into the chaos.

⚜

The sun setting, Christopher found himself sliding amongst burning tents within an orange glow of smoke and flame. He wheezed. The air was filled with the sour smell of burning wood and canvas, mixed with terrible wafts of burning flesh. He snatched a scarf off a dead Turk and covered his mouth.

For all the glory of their prior cries for 'Jesus and Mary,' great numbers of the victorious Christians were smiting the wounded Muslims with hatchets and pikes. Still burdened for Taras, Christopher crept toward the now abandoned tent palace of Kara Mustafa.

In the glow of the fires, he could see that no Janissary had been left standing there or anywhere else. He stepped over the corpses of the 27th and of the Albanian guard who had perished in the defence of the missing vizier. *Taras is most likely dead or captured.* Christopher finally crouched behind an upset cart to gather his thoughts. He correctly reasoned that Mustafa had escaped, and so he settled in the hope that Taras had somehow fled with him.

Such hope would have to be enough. He turned toward the bloody plain stretching upslope to the west. *It is time to go home.*

Christopher made his way across the violated plain under the night's sky. Thirsty, he moved among the dead to retrieve a canteen and then some bits of bread or smoked fish. He finally sat carefully against the broken wheel of an artillery piece and drank, deeply.

He heard a merry tune of trumpets and kettledrums drifting from the distant walls of Vienna. Relieved at many levels, suffering at others, fearful at yet more, Christopher listened until the paradox of merry-making within the stench of death was too much to bear.

He covered his ears. *What does all this mean? What is coming next?* "Christ, what is this madness?" Confounded and afraid, Christopher pulled the brim of his Austrian hat over his ears and folded himself within himself. "Leviathan," he muttered.

Cold, he understood that he was utterly helpless, like a finger-worn pawn in a grand game of chess. In his overwrought state, he stared at the silent stars above and began to pray. But he abandoned his prayer quickly and closed his eyes instead, quietly acquiescing to the inevitable mystery that overwhelmed him.

Perhaps he was too weary to supplicate.

Perhaps he was too weary to bother; his God seemed so terribly silent.

Or, perhaps he feared to invite his Christ into that moment. After all, where had he been all this time? Had he not abandoned him to the *Lebetine*, to Paki's knife, to the galley and to more than twenty years of slavery?

Had his Christ not allowed Raven to be swept away into the harem of a grunting Muslim?

Fighting anger in his smoky hide, Christopher coughed. He could not grasp any of it, but he decided he would dare not pray. He had learned to endure that which he could not control, but he had concluded that there was something dangerous about his Christ. And so he pulled his blood-stained collar close to his skin, leaned hard against the tilting cannon and waited for the sun to rise.

⚜

Daybreak arrived with a light kick on Christopher's leg. The forty-two-year old former slave awakened with a start. Facing east, he squinted. "Eh?"

A young, round-faced Bavarian priest crouched low. "*Hallo?*"

340

At first startled, Christopher sat up. "*Hallo? Who the devil are you?*"

The priest smiled, revealing the bloody stumps of broken teeth. That, plus musket holes in his black robe suggested he had either fought in the battle or had been close at hand. "*Ach, Engländer.*"

Christopher nodded, cautiously.

The Bavarian motioned for Christopher to stand up. "*Aufstehen.*"

Christopher obeyed.

The priest looked him over, feeling his limbs for broken bones. Nodding, he then reached into a bag at his side and handed Christopher a caraway pretzel which Christopher stared at, curiously. Saying nothing more, he beckoned Christopher to follow.

He did and soon was striding quickly across the terrible plain of death and into the foothills of the Kahlenberg. There the pair traversed ditches, rough earth, more bodies of Muslim and Christian alike and finally entered a vineyard. They followed broken rows of white grapes along a south-facing slope until they marched over a small rise to arrive at a camp of about thirty blue-bonnetted Scots licking their wounds and laughing.

The priest delivered Christopher to the captain—a blustery, flush-faced fellow with a broad-axe. "*Engländer,*" said the priest.

Christopher bowed, anxiously. *Bloody stupid priest. Why did he bring me to Scots!*

The captain stood to study Christopher's broad-brimmed hat and long coat. "Englishman in an Austrian uniform." He then looked covetously at his pistol and poked at his satchel. "Hoo are ye?"

"Christopher Clive." He quickly assessed the man and his curious soldiers now gathering close. They were young. He thought the captain to be about twenty-five. He inwardly prayed that they were not Catholics, else they might cleave him in two where he stood.

"Whaur ar ye fa?"

Christopher struggled to understand his thick brogue. "Ah. Kinsale."

"So whit's yer here fer?"

He thought quickly and spun a quick tale. "I speak Turkish. I was hired as a secretary for the Austrians." He pointed to the blood stained collar of his long coat. "But, it was a bit difficult in there for us all—"

The Scot snorted and silenced Christopher with a raised hand. "Enough, old man."

"Old man?"

"Aye? Look at yersel."

Christopher supposed the Scot was right.

As the Leslie Clan circled him, the priest began tearing pretzels apart and handing them to the soldiers as if he were offering the Sacrament. The men began laughing at the Bavarian. Christopher suddenly remembered that the Scots' blue-bonnets placed them in the lowlands, thus most likely Presbyterian.

"Thank ye fer the food, priestie, but keep yer Pope, ya fool bastart," shouted one.

Relieved, Christopher seized the moment. "Aye. And keep thy Holy Virgin."

The captain approved. "So, yer no Papist?" He wiped his nose. "Yer kirk?"

"Aye. Calvinist."

Again, he approved with a nod.

"And what is thy name, sir?" said Christopher.

The Scot picked at caraway seed in his teeth with a broken fingernail. "Ah am hoo ah am."

"We are comrades in a great victory. I have a right to ask thy name." Christopher set his jaw.

The captain smiled. "I like yer spunk, Chrissy Clive. Ah am Fergus Leslie, captain." He dug at his tooth again. "Did ye fight wid Cromwell in yer time?"

"I was too young."

Fergus sniffed. "I suppose. So whit kinda of man are ye?"

"Why do you ask?"

"You'll be wantin us to lead ya back, won't ye?"

"Aye."

"Then tell me whit kind of man ye be."

Christopher stared at the Scotsman, blankly.

"If ye canno' answer me, ye canno' come with us."

Christopher took a breath, thinking. *A man is what he loves.* He cleared his throat. "I am a *free* man, sir."

"Guid. Whit else?"

He struggled. "I am a poet seeking wisdom?"

The Scot raised his bushy red brows and laughed, loudly. "Sounds *Irish* of ye."

Christopher shifted on his feet.

Fergus studied him. "Ah believe ye be once a rich man. So, 'ave ye coin?"

Christ, they are going to rob me. Christopher stiffened. "Some."

The Scot pulled a knife from his boot.

The blood fell from Christopher's cheeks.

"Guid." Fergus proceeded to dig at the stubborn seed with the point of his blade. "Bastart Dutchy priest pretzel." He spit the seed away. "Ye look a fright, Chrissy Clive." He put his knife away. "We'd not be pannin ye, but fer a price we'll see ye safe to Rotterdam."

Christopher cast a look at the priest now ambling away. "And how much is a fair price?"

Fergus listened to his men now barking outrageous fees. The Scot wiped his nose again, thinking. "Ah forbid ye slow-walkin. And ye canno' trouble us in any way. Yer English tongue grates our ears, so keep yer flapper shut."

Christopher nodded.

"Faerstly, $150 Spanish or the like of it in other coin in advance. Fer two, ah take the pistol when we leave ye at the dock. Finally, ye must write a poem fer each man's wee hen awaitin by Aberdeen." He spat. "Wha say ye?"

Relieved, Christopher said, "Aye. We have a deal."

The Scots delayed their departure for another week while they joined the thousands of others scavenging the dead and pilfering the Ottoman encampment. The delay was good for Christopher. Feeling more secure, he spent the first three days searching for Taras amongst the doomed captives and among the thousands of corpses still lying about.

The only hint of his friend that he discovered was a single yellow boot near the tent palace. Holding it, Christopher thought it to be the right size and in the right place, but other Janissary officers wore yellow boots as well. He set it aside and continued his fruitless search. With birds and wild animals tearing corpses apart, he doubted he would even recognize Taras even if he could find his body.

Around him, huge wagon trains of booty began to form on the plain. Everything from ropes to pitch, grease, iron, copper, bows, hand grenades and fuses, muskets, swords, and every imaginable stock for siege had enriched the Habsburg emperor and his allies. Individual soldiers and the half-starved citizens of Vienna searched ravenously for Turkish stores of food, but did not find the abundant larders of flour, butter, coffee, and sugar they expected. Christopher looked away as they butchered camels and horses.

A captive Turk told Christopher that the defeated army of Kara Mustafa had slipped away. "Probably to Buda," said the man.

"Do you know Taras Çorbasi?"

"No. Janissary?"

Christopher nodded. He stared at the man's bound wrists.

"I am in the regulars."

Saxon guards dragged the man into a cart. Christopher looked across the battlefield one more time. *I must leave Taras to his fate*, he thought. "God save him."

He then made his way to the Danube where he paid two women to scrub his clothing. There he sat under the September sun atop a warm, flat rock and within a wool blanket staring at the mighty river. He reconsidered his fortunes.

His spirit somewhat refreshed, he nibbled on a strip of salted pork. "By God's teeth, the taste of pig!" He then lifted a canteen to his lips. It was filled with an early white wine called, '*Sturm*' by some for its stormy bubbles. Swallowing, Kipper smiled broadly and lifted his face to the sun.

Heady from the wine, his spirit eased and his body warmed atop the smooth rock. Christopher lay back and stared at the clouds moving eastward. He closed his eyes and imagined his Raven. *Older now. Maybe grey? Maybe a little wider?* He chuckled. *Aye.* He pictured her green eyes and heard her voice, singing. His breath quickened and he sat up. *But is she still waiting for me? Did she marry that bastard Healy?*

Christopher then pictured Raven swimming in her cove, curling among the deep rocks and surfacing with her laugh. A chill ran through him as the fog of chaos began to lift. "And I am free to find her. I am truly free."

As if surprised by this otherwise obvious truth, he stood. *I must hurry to Kinsale. I'm sure she must be there...unless Healy took her away? Maybe to Cork?* He darkened at the thought of that.

A little greenfinch chirped by Christopher's leg and he watched it bounce around, snatching bits of something from the rock. The forked-tail bird paused, offered a gentle 'tooeep' and a 'chup,' and then throated a sweet, melodious twittering song as she circled away. *Surely I can find her. If Aunt Comfort is alive she will know...But as long as she is happy...Is she happy?*

His ear was then caught by the rhythmic slap of the river's wavelets against his rock. He stared at the water rolling along the shore and then lost himself in the greater sound of the surging river. The wind rushed through the ancient oak behind him; its weary branches groaned. He thought the tree rustled his name and he spun around. Amused at himself, he closed his eyes and heard his own heart beating. "Music," he whispered. "A fine concert, a fantasia; as sacred a prayer as I have ever heard." He kneeled on the rock. "Christ above, help me home."

CHAPTER 38

21 September 1683

SIR CHRISTOPHER CLIVE took the first steps of his long journey. Chin up, faith partially restored and filled with anticipation, the former gentleman of Kinsale prepared to enjoy all that had always been his—love and liberty.

As he and the Scots began their march north-westward across the breath-taking countryside of the Austrians, Christopher found his companions to be an agreeable and even loveable lot. He thought them second only to the Irish in storytelling, and nearly as direct in their speech as the Germans.

The clan found German beer to be a suitable lubricant for their incessant quarrelling and brawls. In spite of that, they shepherded Christopher safely through the rustic villages of northern Bavaria, past the timber-frame farms of Saxony and over the gentle hills of Hesse. By the time he entered the flat land and wide sky of the Low Countries, Christopher had learned to enjoy their hearty songs sung to the steady rhythm of their tramping feet.

Christopher was eventually able to comply with his obligation to write a song for 'each man's wee hen awaitin' by Aberdeen.' The variety of descriptions the Scots had offered about their lovers meant the task was far more difficult than Christopher had initially expected, primarily on account of the men's dialect.

One described his wife as 'a bit glaekit but guid-hearted enough;' another was a 'scunner with a neeps head;' a third was 'peeley-walley and round as a quick-turd.' Then again, some of the men were plain spoken—like the spindly lad who described his wee hen as 'mammoth like a shite-fed pumpkin.'

The men loved the songs Christopher wrote for them, and they practiced their own melodies to pass the time. But they learned to love Christopher, as well. He had revealed the truth to them about his life, and they listened to his stories of captivity in awe. They considered his many insights carefully, and surprised him one evening by applauding his wisdom.

Christopher objected to the affirmation. "I am not yet wise," he insisted. "I am only a seeker of wisdom."

To which one answered, "Nay, Chrissy Clive. We see who ya are. A man *do* as he already *be*." Christopher considered the man's rebuke and then smiled. "It seems Wisdom has found thee as well." And so it had gone for six weeks.

The band finally arrived at the docks of Rotterdam on a cold Thursday morning in November where the clan decided to follow Christopher aboard the first ship outbound for London—a 600 ton English merchantman aptly named, *Patience*. The next morning, the men crowded aboard the sloppy three-master which followed the tide into high seas where the wind howled against her masts and heavy autumn rains slanted into her drenched canvas.

Christopher was bunked in cramped but private quarters at the ship's stern. It turned out that Fergus had told the ship's captain about his suffering past, prompting some charity. For themselves, the Leslies joined sixty other passengers quartered below where they were jammed between stones of Dutch butter, wheels of cheese, and sundry stocks destined for sale in England.

Grateful for some privacy, Christopher relished the fact that his liberty was, in fact, real. *To London!* The notion of walking free in the city of his people made him laugh out loud for joy.

Yet as darkness settled over the ship on that first night of two, his solitude invited him to turn inward where he began struggling to comprehend all that had happened. Avoiding everyone, he read and reread his own writings to reflect deeply upon a life that had strayed so far from the expectations of his youth.

Staring at the walls of his shadowy berth on the second night, he wept bitterly for what was lost. And yet his single candle reminded him of light and love, and so when the ship's bell awakened him on the third morning, he was both drained and yet refreshed.

Lying still, Christopher felt the *Patience* heaving gently beneath him. He sat up slowly and smelled the salt air soured by heated pitch. He poured himself a glass of stale ale and leaned his back against the damp wall. "What would you say now, Grandfather?"

Christopher stood upright and made his way aboards where he narrowed his eyes into foamed water rushing along the dark hull. He tapped his fingers along the rail. *Leviathan.*

It seems even you have a master.

Gulls cried above the masts; the sea hissed below as the bow crashed forward. *Aye, Wisdom*, he thought. *It has been Wisdom all along.* Christopher let the sounds and the smells of the ship absorb him. *I have ne'er been alone. And I have been loved.*

Indeed, Wisdom has fed me from her many baskets. He closed his fists. *May I bear her well and become the man she thinks me to already be.*

A sailor's song took his thoughts. Soon tapping his foot to the rhythm of the sea chantey, he laughed out loud. His mind quickly turned to England and he wondered what he might first do when he set foot on her green land.

Should he run along the docks at Billingsgate in search of a quick frigate to Kinsale?

Should he restrain his racing heart and settle matters in London with his solicitors? After all, he was nearly out of money. Perhaps Barrington and Fry had properly negotiated his estate? *Or did they abandon me?* He returned his forearms to the rail.

As the *Patience* finally eased into the tidal tug of the Thames, Christopher rested his eyes along the passing English countryside. *I cannot delay...not for long. Raven! She is in Ireland. Is she waiting? What shall she think of me?* He considered his mutilation and set his jaw. *I am what I have become, and can do nothing to change it.* He squeezed the smooth rail. *And she is whatever she has become. I love her no matter anything. I pray she feels the same.*

Nay, I shall not fear.

At dawn on the fourth day, the *Patience* docked and her passengers disembarked. Christopher followed his Leslie compatriots to the gangway and across the gap to gather on the busy wooden wharf. Crowds of hawking merchants pressed close. Hearing it all in English spread a broad smile across Kipper's face, and so he bought a small cake—a ginetoe—from a young girl selling treats to passengers from a baker's cart.

A hand on Christopher's shoulder turned him around.

"Did ye buy any fer us?" asked Fergus.

Laughing, Christopher dug deeply into his nearly empty bag of coins lying at the bottom of his blue satchel and flicked the little girl a Hungarian ducat. "'Tis enough for each man standing here, missy."

The Scots gathered round and soon the circle of them were chewing on the lemon-ginger treats. Fergus looked closely at Christopher. "Tha has no' enough coin fer sailin home?"

"I thought I did but I am not so sure. Maybe enough to take a coach to my cousin's home…if he is still living where I think."

Christopher then presented his pistol to Fergus according to their arrangement, only to have it returned with a grunt. "Ah do no' want yer piece, Chrissy Clive. Ah only want ye safe in the wings of yer Irish swan. 'Tis wha ye belong." The Scot reached his hand forward and Christopher grasped it with two.

"I thank thee, Fergus Leslie," said Christopher. "And I pray thee and thy brave lads a bounty of blessings. May we meet again." He then looked at each ruddy face now staring back at him from the circle. "I hope thy hens enjoy your songs, men. Ye sing them like true choristers."

Chortling, each man then took Kipper's hand in turn to offer a heartfelt farewell. In the parting, Christopher's throat thickened as he wished each a 'guid life and Godspeed.'

Saying nothing more, Fergus squeezed Christopher's shoulder and turned away.

Christopher sadly watched the clan vanish around a building. With a sigh, he then hefted the blue satchel at his side, secured his pistol, checked his dagger and pushed the Austrian hat atop his head. He withdrew Taras' icon from within his shirt and kissed it. Ready, he turned and walked along the busy dock in search of a coach bound for the upstart suburb where his cousin was said to live.

⚜

Sir Christopher Clive stepped from the coach and placed his worn shoes flat atop the newly cobbled streets of Bloomsbury—a fashionable and rapidly growing neighbourhood situated slightly north of Westminster and west of the City of London proper.

Following directions, he hurried through the puddles of a late November rain to stand before the elegant, brick house of Winston Wellington. He hesitated. In their days at Oxford, Christopher had always liked the mischievous boy. But now he expected Winston to be different. Living here suggested he had accomplished much in his life. That is, unless his good fortune had come from Christopher's own inheritance. *But does it really matter, after all?* He shifted on his feet. *Does it? Should it?*

Christopher pulled his collar close and yanked the brim of his soldier's hat low over the bridge of his nose. He climbed up five stone steps and wrapped his knuckles on the pecan-stained oak.

An old butler invited Christopher into a candlelit foyer and a fine dining hall with an ample hearth now burning brightly. He took a seat near the fire where he warmed his chilled body for some half an hour. *I shall not judge him until he has a chance to speak…*He suddenly appreciated simply being in England. *Nay, I shall not judge him at all. Unless…*

Finally, a rotund man dressed to near perfection in wide green breeches and a long sleeveless waistcoat entered. A cascading periwig of white curls covered his head, and he sported a thin grey moustache. "Christopher!"

Standing, Christopher removed his hat and took four long strides to receive Wellington's outstretched hand. "It is good to see thee, Cousin."

"I am speechless! More than twenty years." Wellington studied Christopher's dirty clothing and pointed him back to his chair. "You must be half-starved." He ordered his cook to prepare an early meal and to provide some bread, jam, and cheese. Studying him from head to toe, the gentleman fumbled for words. "I hope the fire has warmed thee." He poured a glass of Madeira for them each.

With a careful eye on Wellington, Christopher took a sip and let the island wine warm his belly. "Again, I beg pardon. I had no means to warn you of my arrival, or even of my status."

"I confess that it is a shock, but a welcome one." Wellington adjusted his laced cravat and took a drink of his own. His wife, Emily, appeared in a low-cut, red manteaux. She was a wispy, plain woman with a suspicious face and grey hair.

Standing, Christopher bowed as he was introduced.

Formalities over, Emily advised her husband that the food was coming and that a bed was being prepared. Turning to Christopher she said, "How long do you plan on remaining with us?"

By her tone, Christopher suspected she hoped his visit would be brief. "I should very much like to board passage to Kinsale as soon as possible. However, I fear I have little choice but to organize the affairs of my estate." He glanced sideways at Wellington. "So...perhaps a fortnight?"

Emily curtsied and vanished into a dark hallway.

"I apologize for my wife," said Wellington. "She is out of sorts."

Christopher cleared his throat. He had a great deal to discuss with this man. "Firstly, I need to know of my family, Winston. I have heard nothing for a very long time."

Wellington swallowed a large gulp of his Madeira. "Aye. Misters Barrington and Fry found me in London immediately upon their daring escape from the heathen Turks. They told their story and thine at the club to men most troubled by it all. Thy grandfather's end was monstrous."

Christopher nodded. Images of Redmond hanging headless from the *Lebetine's* rigging still haunted him.

Wellington's eyes unconsciously drifted to Christopher's crotch. "To learn what they did to thee..." He shook his head and looked away.

Christopher now pressed. "How did my father die?"

"His heart failed him soon after the night of thy capture."

"And what of my mother?"

Wellington pulled a snuff-tin from inside his coat. He diverted his face and refilled his wine. "I regret to be the one to inform thee, but thy mother is also deceased."

Christopher recoiled. "Deceased? When?"

"St. Michael's Day, three years past. I am very sorry. She was mad, you know. She lived with her family in Bath and she was discovered drowned in a hot spring there."

Christopher stared into his caramel-coloured wine.

"I am truly sorry."

The two sat in a respectful silence as Christopher watched the fire. He finally asked, "And our aunt, Comfort?"

"As of Martinmas, she lives in Kinsale. But I fear she may be mad as well."

Christopher fumbled with his drink. *He would say that…*"I've little doubt that my mother was mad, but Aunt Comfort? We both know better." He took a deep breath. "Can you tell me of the Irish girl I so loved."

"Ah, thy dear Raven O'Morrissey. I am very sorry…truly…but I've not much to tell. I think Comfort wrote of her once in a letter but I would need to find it. I do not think Comfort imagined her to be any of my concern."

"I see." Christopher took a sip of wine and shifted in his seat. "Now, secondly, what of my father's estate? Was my mother well cared for in the end?"

Wellington nodded. "Soon after thy father's death—and on account of thy absence—Millicent successfully claimed the rights of escrow to thy father's modest assets for her own care."

"As she should have."

"Aye. Her brother was named as trustee on her behalf. He wisely sold off the Irish plantation to thy neighbour—Mister Reginald Burroughs. The rest he gathered into a London bank.

"Thy mother drew from that account until her death, but there has been no official reckoning."

Christopher sat thoughtfully for a moment. "Now this: what is the status of my estate?"

Wellington raised his hand and shook his head. "By faith, I am too weary to explain it all now. We shall speak of it on the morrow, and I vow you shall not be unhappy." He took a snort of his snuff and sneezed.

"I should prefer to discuss it presently." Christopher felt his cheeks heat. *Let's get on with this.*

Wellington shook his head. "Nay. It is all far too complicated."

Christopher stared at him. *Is he preparing a lie? But what if he is? What does the estate mean to me now?*

"Well then. Allow me to be a good host. We shall feed you some snacks and then put you in some comfortable dining attire."

Perchance it is better to wait. Christopher yielded. "But on the morrow—"

"I promise," said Wellington. "And I swear to you that you shall not be disappointed. Now, we cannot have thee strutting about London dressed like an Austrian footman. Tomorrow I shall have my clothier come by to arrange a fresh wardrobe." He looked at Christopher's hair. "You've still the curls, but fashion dictates we shave them off and set a respectable wig atop that noggin. What say thee?"

<hr />

Christopher finally lay in his bed to spend the night staring at the ceiling. He set thoughts of his estate aside and grieved his parents. He had already known of his father's death, of course, and he had suspected his mother might have followed by now. Yet somehow hearing that both his parents were in their graves had left him feeling especially alone. He clung to the hope of Aunt Comfort's well-being, though he estimated her to be somewhere in her mid-seventies.

As might be expected, however, thoughts of Raven kept him in a state of frustration. He sat up in bed, heart-pounding. *What did Comfort write of her? Did she say whom she married? DID she marry?*

He hated to imagine her as another man's wife, yet he had always wanted her to be happy. He then pretended that she hadn't, and he thought how wonderful it might be for him to marry her along the sacred shores of Raven's Cove. He smiled—until he remembered. *Would she be truly happy with half a man?*

Christopher lay on his side. "And Burroughs owns the cove." His heart exhausted, his mind then returned to matters of his estate from which his necessary resources would come. He calculated that his grandfather would have left him a great fortune. *But has Winston stolen it? His father was not this wealthy...*

The next morning, Christopher took a seat at a table covered with a solid breakfast of porridge, eggs, bacon, bread, and an assortment of puddings. Before he could press his concerns, Emily insisted that he tell his story.

Ignoring her, Christopher turned to Wellington. "Can you not first tell me of Raven? Did you find Comfort's letter?"

Wellington shook his head. "I am very sorry, I did not. It was written many years ago. But, if I recall, Comfort wrote something about 'the Irish girl whom Christopher loved' finding her way home as 'if by magic,' or the 'plots of angels.' Aye, methinks those very words were used. But that is all that I have in my mind."

"'Plots of angels,'" said Christopher. "I like that." He stood and looked out a kitchen window into another gloomy November morning.

Wellington laughed. "Soon enough. When you get to Kinsale you ought learn more…Now, sit."

"It cannot be soon enough. I must get there——"

"But not today, Kipper," said Emily. "Now, as you can see the cook has provided us with plenty and we have been waiting to hear thy story directly from thee."

Tell my damned story? It is time to talk business!

Wellington cracked an egg with a flourish. As if reading Christopher's mind, he said, "After breakfast I shall answer *all* thy questions. But now, the lady of this house has made a request of thee."

Christopher yielded and began relating his tale from the very beginning when the Janissaries crashed through his father's front door. He finished two hours later and pushed himself away from the table, exhausted. He offered a forced smile to his slack-jawed host and hostess, as well as the two cooks, three housemaids, the butler, gardener and the groomsman who had moved ever closer. "Well, many thanks for a fine breakfast. I've not eaten English food for a very long time."

Wellington shook his head in near disbelief. "By the saints, Kipper. My mind is reeling." He wiped his mouth with a napkin. "But I remain worried about the Sultan's agents hunting thee."

Christopher shrugged. He had other things on his mind.

CHAPTER 39

WINSTON WELLINGTON TOOK a commanding seat within the securing arms of a high-back mahogany chair in the parlour. He tapped his finger on the side of his china cup until the servant finished stoking the hearth and left the room. "The story you tell may be difficult for some to believe, and so I must wonder what the court shall say. After all, an Irish muse, corsairs and cannonades, beyliks and pashas, Sufis and Coptic surgeons…to say nothing of the Holy City and Sister Mary, a friend among the Janissaries, the survival of the great siege, a clan of Scots…"

Wellington leaned far forward. "One could ask whether you refused escape with Barrington and Fry in order to extend such an adventure. And now, growing grey and weary, you return to claim what others have earnestly laboured to preserve. What say thee?"

"An adventure?" Christopher stood, angrily. "Are you mad!" He stormed to a rain-splattered window. "If I left an impression that these tales were of sport and daring I have done us both a terrible wrong." He whirled about. "I lost all that I—"

"Sit down, sir. It is not *I* who ask, but you should know that the court directed this precise challenge to Fry who admitted you denied an opportunity to escape."

Christopher seethed. All thoughts of releasing his earthly claims to lofty virtues vanished. "And you, sir, have used the court against me!"

The butler entered the room, bowing. "With pardon, Sir Christopher, but blue or green?"

"What!"

"The clothier wonders whether you might favour a blue or green outer cloak?"

"I do not give a shite."

Wellington turned to the butler. "Tell Mister Featherstone that he needs not come today, but should prepare a proper wardrobe as follows:" He bade Christopher to stand still. "Tell him that Sir Christopher is my height, but has a slender frame." He walked a circle around Christopher. "Tell him we need a brown waistcoat, a green woollen frock—both correctly falling to the knees—unassuming breeches, woollen hose and a buff linen shirt." He scrunched his face. "I think not a periwig after all; it does not suit the man's spirit. But be sure to include a proper English hat—one trimmed in beaver or ostrich—and travelling boots. Also under-trewes and the rest of the necessaries. All billed to my account."

Christopher said nothing more as the butler scurried away. He then put his face close to Wellington's. "Do I or do I not have an estate from which to reimburse thee?"

Wellington took his seat and bade Christopher to do the same. "You mistake me for thy adversary, Christopher."

Still standing, Christopher narrowed his eyes. "Barrington and Fry both said you opposed my interests."

"No wonder you are upset." Wellington sipped some coffee. "That was before they understood. Now sit, please."

As Christopher plopped himself in his mahogany chair, Wellington said, "Even in our days at university you were smitten by Raven O'Morrissey. Remember how you fussed over the damned Irish post?"

Wellington set his coffee to one side. "You look surprised that I remember. I told you then that yours was an ironic tragedy in the making. Now here you are, the heir of promise who suffered the chains of slavery. My prediction was sound."

Taking his pipe in hand, he went on. "I am struggling against the temptation to feel offended by thee. I would never have stolen thy birthright."

Christopher fixed his face on his cousin's.

"Now listen to me carefully: The Crown wanted to confiscate thy estate upon the arrival of Sir Redmond's head, and on account of thy presumed death. Redmond had named no other heir." He paused to pack his pipe with tobacco. "Always believing you to be alive, Aunt Comfort concocted a conspiracy to protect you. I was needed to serve as her foil."

Christopher leaned forward.

"Aye. A conspiracy. Since we share a common forbear—our great-grandfather, William Clive—Comfort suggested that I contest Sir Redmond's estate on my behalf even as she contested it from her side. She knew that as long as two ends of the family created a stir in the courts, the Crown would have difficulty intervening for its own claim."

Wellington lit his pipe with a nearby candle. "I agreed, and so we maintained a very expensive delay. Do you understand?" Wellington drew on his tobacco and released a satisfied puff of smoke.

Christopher blinked, thinking. "So for all these many years you entangled thyself and Aunt Comfort in a game to block the King?"

Wellington shrugged. "To be fair, *she* entangled *me*."

Astonished, Christopher wiped his palms atop his breeches. A wave of shame washed over him. "It seems I owe thee an apology."

"Accepted."

Christopher stood and paced. "This is just...I have no words."

360

"You are most welcome." Wellington chuckled. "If I may boast, when Barrington and Fry learned of this, they thought it was genius."

Still reeling, Christopher stopped in front of a painting of a horse grazing beneath a willow. "I agree." He returned to his seat. "Then how are things presently?"

"Now that you are home, my attorneys shall withdraw all my claims. Barrington is retired, so Fry shall put the Crown's curiosity to rest. I expect thy assets shall be promptly released to you." He sneezed. "Oh, once Sir Redmond's head arrived in its pot, the Crown did at least acknowledge thy inheritance of his title. You are forever 'Sir' Christopher Clive."

Wellington drank some coffee. "I suggest you meet with Fry quickly, however. I sent a messenger yesterday informing him of the good news and requiring an immediate appointment."

Christopher nodded. "I am left speechless. Opposing the royal solicitors, sustaining a ruse against the feigned wrath of my aunt… By God, man, you stood for me well. You must have been slandered a grasping fiend, whilst you were actually denying thyself for me."

Wellington shrugged and drew on his pipe. "Another irony; life is full of them." He watched a puff of smoke fade away, thinking. "There is one thing, though." He shifted in his seat, awkwardly. "Thy presumed death required the transfer of thy seat at the Levant Company. The members offered it to me and I accepted." He leaned forward. "The seat has provided for me well. Will you allow me to keep it?"

⚜

Christopher soon met with the delighted Charles Fry, and in the weeks that followed he began the tedious process to secure his inheritance. Legal fees surrounding Comfort's grand ruse had reduced the huge estate by some, but what remained—despite his willing surrender of his Levant membership to Winston Wellington—was enormous.

In the midst of his legal distractions, Christopher wrote a long letter to Comfort in which he clarified his present state, thanked her with every word he could summon, and told her how all she had once told him was proven true. He then informed her of his pending voyage home, and closed by begging her to write him in regard to Raven. Several weeks later, he received her response in a nearly illegible hand. In it she wrote that she was 'happy beyond human measure' for both his journey and his return, and would dare the angels to take her away before he set foot in Kinsale again.

But the old woman had not informed him of Raven.

Frustrated, Christopher realized that he doubtlessly had written too much for the elderly woman to comprehend, and so she had fixated on his return and not his passion. So he wrote again, this time simply asking of Raven. More weeks passed until the infamous Royal Post in Ireland returned his letter as undelivered. Screaming, cursing and shouting, 'Leviathan!' along Bedford Row, he turned more than a few heads. He tried writing again.

In the meanwhile, the legal matters wound their way from Cork to Dublin to London and so Christopher found himself with little choice other than to pace around Winston Wellington's fine Bloomsbury house through the Advent. The endless days obliged him to attend numerous teas and fine dinners where the 'splendid gentleman of exotic tales' was expected to tell and re-tell his story.

February in the Year of Grace 1684

On a raw morning, Christopher finally stood in Wellington's dining hall with a package in his arms and a grin across his face. He bowed and presented Emily a departing gift—a fine gown sewn by a French clothier in the fashionable west end of London.

Emily hid her pleasure. "Thank thee, and godspeed, sir. This is the day we have all longed to see."

"Aye, indeed," said Christopher.

"We are most especially happy that the Sultan's agents did not find thee here, in this house." She turned to leave.

Christopher's words chased after her. "And I am thankful beyond words for thy patient kindness over these months." Chuckling to himself, he then handed Wellington the flintlock pistol from Taras' tent. "I should like thee to have this as a token of my gratitude. My old Ukrainian friend would have wanted you honoured for such loyalty. It shoots on a line."

Wellington received the gift reverently. "Kipper!" He embraced his cousin. "But now, Aunt Comfort awaits thee…and I surely hope thy Raven is standing on the dock with her. I am sorry you have not heard from her."

Christopher shook his head. "Damned Irish Post." He then clasped hands with Wellington and offered another heartfelt thanks for his heroic efforts at protecting what was his. "Masterful; selfless. The world should know of it."

Wellington blushed. "Fie. Write a poem about Aunt Comfort." He laid a hand on Kipper's shoulder. "But have a care, cousin. I do not want to learn that some Mohammedan carved thy neck along the dock in Kinsale."

Christopher shrugged. "The Sultan shall surely die someday and that shall be the end of it." He then tossed the servants some coins and hurried to his waiting coach. *Spies be damned. I am going home.*

⁃⧓⁃

Wrapped in a wool blanket, Sir Christopher bounded up the gangway on a ship named the *Wayfarer* that was daring the stormy four-day February passage from London to Kinsale via Portsmouth. He directed a steward to stow his two travel chests. He followed with his battered blue satchel slung over the shoulder of his new, green knee-length frock. Once alone in his private berth, he tossed his beaver-trimmed hat atop a tiny table and threw himself upon a wool-stuffed mattress. He closed his eyes.

The journey was bitterly cold and unpleasant for most. But for Kipper Clive the journey may as well have been aboard a dreamy Sunday brit beneath the willows in Salisbury.

He slept well enough on the brief journey, and on the mid-morning that he heard a sailor cry, "Kinsale to starboard," he thought he might fly aboards and dance with abandon. He bounded from his quarters and scrambled on to the ice-slickened deck, heart pounding. Smiling in the cutting winter wind, Christopher gazed through early morning light. Ahead, he beheld the headlands of Ireland reaching for him once again from the grey sea.

"I am home." He reached within his shirt to retrieve Taras' little icon hanging faithfully around his neck. He kissed it. "Thanks be to God." His chin trembled. "And may you be at peace, Taras."

As gulls quarrelled in the rigging above, the *Wayfarer* soon heaved gently into Kinsale Harbour. She passed the star-shaped walls of Charles Fort to starboard and sailed deeper into the small bay. Old James Fort then passed by port and the ship began lowering her sails to slide slowly between the hills now rising like muscled shoulders.

Kipper wiped his eyes.

Finally docked, Sir Christopher Clive nearly fell off the gangway as he charged toward the wharf. His eyes scanned the crowd gathering to meet passengers or unload freight. *Not her; not her; not her.* Grinding his teeth, he finally tossed two young lads a tuppence each. *She's not here.* He pointed the scampering lads to his baggage. "And keep up!" He rushed them around the familiar wharfs— admittedly changed in the past twenty years—and toward the

Clive House still standing proud on the far side of the harbour. "Hurry boys!"

Christopher arrived at the base of the town house steps with his heart pounding. *She may be married to that Healy...or to someone else. She may have moved to Cork for work, or even Dublin? Has she children?* These questions and more had followed him from Vienna but they now shouted at him.

He secured the satchel on his shoulder and removed his hat. He shook his hanging curls like he had done as a boy. He raised his hand to the brass ring. Kipper took a firm hold. *My dear Christ, finally.* He filled his lungs.

He rapped on the door.

Waiting, he licked salt off his dry lips and shifted his weight on his boots. *Fie! Someone open the bloody—*

A young Irish servant pulled the large door inward. It creaked. "Good day, sir. How can I help ya?"

Christopher studied a boy of about thirteen. His hair was black and his eyes were sage green. "I am Sir Christopher Clive," he said, carefully. "This is the home of my grandaunt, Miss Comfort Clive."

"So it is, sir."

"Then let us in." He waved the lads carrying his baggage forward.

Christopher followed the young doorkeeper anxiously into the familiar entranceway and to the parlour where a small fire was burning. He pointed his belongings to a corner and quickly dismissed the panting lads.

The house looked the same; it smelled the same and as such filled Christopher with a rush of familiar feelings. "Where is everyone?"

"Not here, sir."

"What do you mean?"

"Not here, sir."

"I heard thee! Where? Where is my aunt and—"

"She is with the Blackamoor fella—"

"Who?"

"Tattie, the Blackamoor."

"Tattie? The butler? Where?"

"He rents a small house by the sea just past Kinure. She visits him often."

"Where is she, exactly?"

"In the cottage at yer family's former plantation."

Christopher thought for a moment. "Cottage?"

"Metinks one was built where a stable once was."

Grumbling, Christopher pressed. "Why is Tattie living there? He should be here, in this house and answering the bloody door instead of thee."

"He is old and loves the sea, sir, as does yer aunt. The Burroughs' pay him a bit to keep an eye on tings. And I answer the bloody door right well."

"So you say." Christopher looked at the boy. "What is thy name?"

"Brendan."

Christopher took a breath and set his shoulders. "And what is thy surname?"

"Healy."

A cold chill ran through his limbs. "Is thy father Fallon Healy?" He bit down on the inside of his cheek, fearing the worst.

CHAPTER 40

"Why do you ask, sir?"

"Answer me, please."

"He is."

Christopher exhaled and moved to a seat by the fire. He sent the lad to fetch him hot tea and some food. *The boy looks like her.* He let his eyes drift about the familiar room. His fingers tapped atop the arm of his chair until the Irish boy finally returned with tea, biscuits, honey, and a small box.

"The cook is away today," Brendan said.

"Sit."

Brendan obeyed. "Are ya Sir Christopher Clive?"

Christopher nodded with a grunt.

Brendan studied him, wide-eyed. "The whole county tells a story of ya, sir. Ya was a slave to the Mohammedans?"

"Aye." Christopher took a sip of tea but could barely swallow it.

"T'ey cut off yer bollie-wollies but not yer dangle."

Christopher set his cup hard atop the saucer. "How do you know all this?"

Brendan shrugged. "Tat sort of news travels well. And we knows of an old Clive's beheading by rovers—"

"Enough." Christopher grumbled.

"But some strange fellas were asking about ya at the docks not so long ago."

That news startled Christopher. "When?"

"Metinks back at Christmas or so."

"Are they still about?"

Brendan shook his head. "Tey sailed away." He opened the box and offered Christopher a candy.

He stared at some sort of lozenges but had no appetite.

"'Tis pawpaw marmalet," Brendan said. "A friend of Miss Clive sends it from the Virginia Colony every year fer Christmas. Taste one."

"Reginald Burroughs."

Brendan shrugged. "I don't ask."

"A good doorkeeper is supposed to know things." He turned his face away from the candy. He could delay no longer. "Who is thy mother?"

"Why?"

"'Tis a very long story." Christopher braced himself.

"I am not certain it is yer business, sir."

Just like his damned father! "Perhaps not," Christopher said with a rising voice. "But can you not just offer me this simple charity?"

"Have ya a sixpence?"

"By the saints, Healy!" Christopher dug into his satchel and tossed a coin at the imp.

Stuffing the coin into a pocket Brendan said, "Her name is Fiona. Her father was a Murphy from Cork City."

Christopher nearly fell from his chair.

"Does ya know her?"

Christopher shook his head. He gathered himself. His heart rose. "Now two more things: First, does another woman work for Miss Clive?"

The Healy boy crossed his arms.

"Shite." Christopher tossed him a tuppence.

"The lady employs t'ree womens. A fuller and a cook…and a cleaner."

"Their names?" Christopher dug for another coin.

"The fuller be an Englishwoman named Goody Stockhard. The cook is Lily somethin, and the cleaner is Katy."

Christopher's mind was racing. *Then where is she?* He reached into his satchel and retrieved a silver coin. He held it up in front of Brendan's face. "You are a thief in need of a priest. Now here's a question you must think hard about. Are you ready, boy?" He leaned his nose against Brendan's. "And I do not want an answer that you think shall please me! I know ye Irish well."

Brendan nodded.

"What do you know of a woman named Raven O'Morrissey."

The boy puckered his face. "Em...em..."

"If you lie to me I shall have thee beaten."

"By truth, sir, I only overheard some talk of a woman once in slavery...I t'ought her name was a bird's name."

"Aye? And?"

Brendan shrugged. "Tat's all I know, sir." He wrinkled his nose. "Wait. My pa said her bird name once and ma threw an egg at him. I remember 'cause me and m'brothers all laughed."

"Nothing else? Does she visit, does she write....does Miss Clive speak of her?" Christopher began to sputter. "Does she tend old Tattie?"

"I do not believe so, sir. But I only began work here a few months ago—"

"Well, why the devil did you not tell me that in the beginning!" Christopher stood. "Have you a horse in the stable?"

The boy nodded.

"Good. Saddle it, quickly. I must get to Tattie's cottage."

As Brendan dashed out the rear door, Christopher paced about the empty house. He paused before the dining hall to remember a different lifetime. He entered the empty parlour and then walked up the wide stairway, now draughty and cold in the February chill. *Where is my Raven? What has come of her?"*

Brendan called from below. "Ready fer ya, sir."

Christopher descended the stairs, grabbed his hat, coat, satchel and a wool cape. He secured his dagger and stepped out the rear door of the house.

Brendan led a saddled mare out of the small stable in the courtyard. Christopher thought her to look overweight and a bit lifeless. He took a step toward the sleepy mare when he heard another horse snorting from a closed stall. "Who's that?"

"Oh, he's old—"

Christopher suddenly welled. Saying nothing, he pushed the stall door open and ran to the horse now whinnying at him. "Étalon?" He flung open the stall door and wrapped his arms around his old friend's neck. "Étalon! O precious Jesus! Can it be?"

Étalon pawed the earth and tossed his head.

"The lady says he be 'bout twenty-five or so. Miss Clive lets me ride him from time to time. She says he used to roll over the hills like black thunder."

Eyes filled, Christopher nodded and squeezed himself against Étalon's thick neck. He rubbed the horse's forelock and stroked his flanks. "He was mine when we were both young." A lump as large as Étalon's wide eye filled Christopher's throat. He took a quaking breath. "I shall saddle this one and we'll just have to go a bit slow."

By early afternoon, Christopher Clive was walking Étalon east on the snow-dusted Kinure Highway. New farms had sprung up; old ones had burned away. The Kinure Church had many more tombstones. But the land—the quilt of fields stitched by hedgerow and stone fences—had remained magical.

Étalon eventually began to toss his head and whinny. Laughing, Christopher threw himself into the saddle and let his horse set the pace for the final mile until they passed the yet-charred ruins of

Giardín an Croí's house where Christopher stopped. Little remained. Scavengers had claimed what stone Reginald Burroughs had not used to build Tattie's cottage. A web of frozen weeds covered the remaining foundation. In the distance a few lonely thatched roofs dotted the beach where Skeefe once stood.

Christopher looked ahead to the squat, stone cottage standing where his father's stable had been. Smoke poured in a straight column from a squat chimney that poked through a well-thatched roof. With the familiar sounds of a loud kiss, Christopher prompted Étalon forward toward Tattie's hitching rail where he dismounted and pulled the saddle away with a "thank thee, friend."

The low cottage door opened and a squinting Negro with white hair filled the space pointing a brace of pistols. "Halt, else I shoot thee dead!"

Surprised, Christopher threw up his arms. "Tattie? 'Tis me! Kipper Clive."

Tattie had barely lowered his weapons when an old woman pushed her way from behind and leaned a musket on the plastered wall. "I told you that was Kipper and Étalon, you old dolt."

Grinning widely, Christopher received his aunt's embrace. He thought she felt like life itself. "I cannot believe I am home," he choked.

Comfort could not speak.

Tattie wrapped his arms around the pair and led them gently indoors where the three stood before an ample fire. Christopher cast his eye about, seeking another when Comfort distracted him.

"I…have…no…" The woman let the tears fall. "Thanks be to God." She embraced her nephew again. "I always believed, Kipper. I always believed." Weeping, she kissed him once more. "But why did you not write me again from Wellington's?"

Christopher kissed her upon the head and held her tightly. "I did."

"You did?" Comfort scowled. "Damned Irish Post."

"Sit, both of ye," said Tattie. "Sit before the fire. God be praised for such a day as this." He walked carefully to the larder and retrieved bread and fruit preserves, salted pork and a slab of moulded cheese. He then poured three tankards of hearth-heated, spiced rum.

Comfort stared at her Kipper; he stared back. The woman had aged, of course. Now seventy-seven, her weepy eye had closed completely and her other was dull. Her skin was wrinkled like toes abandoned to water. Her hair was white and thin. It hung beyond her shoulders to give her the look of a woodland witch. Yet, her kindness filled the room and she had love resonating from her heart that Christopher was sure could be felt all the way to Dublin.

"You look grand," said Christopher.

"The Mohammedans are the best liars in all the earth." Comfort drank a large swallow of her rum. She then lit her pipe, slowly, as if thinking very carefully. Blowing a cloud of smoke, she then said, "I do not need to hear thy story, dear boy. I already know enough of it and I can guess the rest." She leaned forward. "But I want to know two things before we go on: First, have you taken a wife?"

Surprised, Christopher shook his head. "Nay. But I am not a whole—"

Comfort scowled and raised her hand. "You are a whole man, methinks a better man than when you were taken from us. You'd make a fine husband." The old woman took another long draught on her pipe, exhaled, and swallowed more rum. "So, no wife. Wonderful. Now my last question: Have you turned Turk? I'll love thee no less if you have—"

"Nay!"

Comfort drew on her pipe and released a cloud of smoke. "Good."

Christopher now wanted to ask questions of his own—hundreds of them. "Aunt Comf—"

Ignoring him, Comfort turned to Tattie and slanted her eye to the cupboard from which he returned with a basket. He set it by Comfort's leg.

A clammy dampness covered Christopher's skin. "I am desperate to ask about—"

"Wait." Comfort lifted the basket's lid and withdrew something folded within an oily cloth. She unwrapped it and handed Christopher an old doglock pistol.

He stared at the trigger—an upside down baby covering its ears. He laughed. "My piece!"

Comfort grinned. Tattie found it in the weeds within a week of thy capture. He's kept it clean and firing well ever since.

Christopher bounced it in his hand. "Thank thee, Tattie!"

"But now this," said Comfort. She threw the basket's lid back to reveal a collection of empty boxes. She retrieved one and handed it to Christopher. "Does this look familiar?"

"Aye. Brendan Healy offered me the same this morning. 'Tis pawpaw marmalet from the Burroughs'."

Comfort and Tattie chuckled, knowingly. "If you count the boxes, you'll find fourteen. The one in my Kinsale larder makes for fifteen." Comfort then pointed to a bundle of papers bound in a cord at the very bottom of the basket. "There are fifteen greetings, one for each box of candy."

Christopher's heart sank. *She is gone mad, like Winston said.* He feigned a smile and changed course. "It is most considerate that the Burroughs' remember thee at Christmas with marmalet and greetings."

Comfort wiped ooze from her closed eye. "Fie. Pull thy chair close, y'prating proppet."

Confused, Christopher obeyed.

Then, like a cobra striking, Comfort grabbed hold of Christopher's cheeks with two hands. She spit out her pipe. "The Burroughs'? Nay." She released his face and reached into the basket. She lifted out the bundle of papers and pushed them at Christopher. "All the way from America and still sealed for these many years. Now open one."

Curious, Christopher broke the first wax seal, unfolded the letter and began to read.

———— ✥ ————

CHRISTOPHER DID NOT sleep all that night. Instead he read and reread the letters by candlelight, each written during the early September fruit harvest along the James River in Virginia. He smelled them, he caressed them; he let his fingers follow the loops and jots of his dear Raven's hand.

He read from one of her early letters a fourth time and out loud. "'It seems there really are sea monsters. Perchance we ought fear them after all, if but a little.'" Christopher laughed. "A little?"

Reading from the next, he wiped his nose with a kerchief. *She loves me still. She ALWAYS loved me, and in spite of anything I ever did or was expected to do...* "'We can bear good fruit together.'" He looked up. A sudden chill passed through him. *She must not know of my mutilation.*

Heart pounding, he rose at first light to peer out the window by the door of Tattie's cottage. *Whatever happens of this, it is a marvellous story she tells. And what of that Gaia. And Uncle Finn.* Christopher shook his head in disbelief as he recalled all that Raven had written about the beloved crone, and the way her uncle had been saved.

As Tattie stirred from his bed and Comfort began walking about the loft, he suddenly spotted a horse and rider trotting toward the house. Concerned, he snatched his old doglock and threw open the door. "Who goes?"

A muscular old gentleman dismounted. Christopher thought his square jaw and grey goatee to look familiar. Removing his cavalier's hat, the gentleman said, "Lower thy piece. I am no highwayman."

Christopher kept his aim straight as the stranger studied him carefully. He then watched a smile spread wide across his narrow face.

"So it is true!" The old man offered his hand. "I am Reginald! Reginald Burroughs! I cannot have aged that much."

Christopher lowered his pistol with a joyful laugh. He took his hand, cheerfully. "Ah, Mister Burroughs, come in, come in. What a wonderful surprise."

Burroughs ducked through the door and removed his coat. He greeted Comfort and Tattie who bade him to sit by the fire. Christopher poured him hot tea and offered him biscuits, buttermilk and a slice of cold ham. "I thought you lived in Virginia."

"Some of the time. The rest is spent here or in England. But I soon must make a choice."

"Mister Burroughs, I have no words for how you have helped Raven—"

"Sir Christopher, call me 'Reginald.'" He looked deeply into Christopher's eager face. "It gives me joy to see you, my son. Much has happened since we spoke of Henry Curtis and the horizons of the New World."

"Much indeed." Christopher sat down across the table from him. "As I say, sir, I am in thy debt on many accounts." He looked Burroughs squarely in the face. "Tell me. Is she well?"

Burroughs smiled. "So you read the letters! Wonderful. Aye, she is well. I saw her during the last harvest. I brought this year's pawpaw and letter with mine own hand. When she learns of thy freedom, she shall fly atop the orchards with her angel wings."

Christopher forced a swallow of warm tea over the lump in his throat. "She writes that she waits. How has that been possible?"

"I have no idea. There has ne'er been a shortage of suitors." Burroughs leaned forward. "Methinks it is on account that she *believed*, Kipper. Like thy blessed aunt, she always believed." He stabbed some ham with his knife. "By faith, I have never seen love like this. And then that whole business with Gaia."

Christopher bit his lip. "Does Raven know of my—"

"Acorns? Aye, she does. Seems the whole world knows. Sorry." Burroughs darkened. "The Mohammedans are a scourge of Satan. You know that they are still raiding helpless Christian villages and boarding ships. I do not understand why the Crown cannot protect us."

"But does she—"

Burroughs laid a sympathetic eye on him. "Raven is only a year or so younger than thyself. She has no thought to more children, if that is what you fear."

Christopher faced his food.

"Fie! Look at me, sir. Look at my eyes! If half of what I hear about thy story is true, then you'd be more a man than any I ever knew." Burroughs took a deep breath. "Now, did she write of my propositions?"

"Aye, thrice she wrote of them."

"And?"

"I am left without words. I am humbled and most grateful. It is a true charity, sir. However, what of thy son, Oakely?"

"He lives in Virginia permanently with his family of six. As my heir and partner, he is obligated to embrace the thoughts of Henry Curtis." Burroughs smirked.

"I remember Curtis as well."

"Good! He once wrote, 'A Kindness hath no equal until a persevering Consideration presents itself.' It has been my wish—and that of Oakely—to persevere this consideration out of respect for what you have suffered for our common Cross, and out of love for our dear Raven."

Christopher shook his head. "This is an uncommon thing."

Burroughs waited. "Well, let us not drag this out. Tell me thy heart's desire."

Christopher took a breath. "I accept, humbly."

"Ha! But which offer?"

According to Raven's letter, Reginald Burroughs was prepared to sell Christopher all of Giardín an Croí—including Raven's Cove—or sell him a 1500-acre plantation along the James River in the Virginia Colony near the Burroughs' own huge estates.

Comfort and Tattie leaned forward, four ears cocked.

"It seems from her letters that Raven hoped I might accept the Virginia offer. She says it is most beautiful, even magical like her cove—only vast. She especially loves the orchards covering the bottom land by the river—"

"Aye. She is our fruiter. She loves the pawpaws, but methinks the better profit is in the cherries. Her apples do well, as do her pears, and she oversees the beehives that bring life to them all. She may have told thee that she also teaches children of willing natives. Anyway, to the point, it is my opinion that she loves Virginia."

Christopher nodded. "But she also writes that Englishmen own Blackamoor slaves there."

"Of course."

Christopher recoiled. "Of course? I thought the New World was to break with corrupting traditions."

Burroughs narrowed his eyes. "It is the way of the whole world."

"I do not like it." His fists closed.

"Then you would not prosper there."

"I cannot imagine Raven supports this!"

"Raven does not need to approve." Pausing, Burroughs sat back. "Did she write that we set her uncle free?"

Christopher's hands opened. "I was very pleased to read about it."

"She was very persistent, you know. In the end, Oakley found Finn on a plantation in St. Andrew's Parish on Barbados and bought him for £10. He manumitted him on the spot, and delivered him to Raven in Virginia where the poor wretch lived two happy years. She begged me to bury him in the Burroughs' family plot, which I did."

Christopher relented. "That was a kind thing to do, sir."

Hastening to return to more pleasant conversation, Burroughs said, "So, enough of this business. Now, which do you choose, Ireland or Virginia?"

Christopher turned to Comfort. "Which do you think Raven would have me choose? She loves her cove—"

"I know, dear boy." Comfort whispered into his ear, "*Feel* it. Let the Breath guide thee."

Christopher closed his eyes and imagined Raven in her cove, gliding. He then imagined her along the James River as she had described it in her letters: meadows filled with butterflies, misty summer mornings with the song of croaking frogs; orchards buzzing with bees and heavy with fruit. Finally, he opened his eyes and looked squarely at Burroughs. "If it is possible, I choose both."

"Eh?" Burroughs sat back.

"I should like to buy it all."

Burroughs blinked. "*All* of it? Why?"

"I love this green land that I know," said Christopher. "I would like to see it prosper in ways my father hoped. And yet I also love what I imagine Virginia to be. I can hear the music of both places."

He glanced out of the window. "I do not wish to be greedy, sir, and I shall choose but one if that is thy preference. But I can imagine nothing better than offering Giardín an Croí as a gift to Raven."

Laughing, Burroughs tossed his head at Comfort. "Ha, thy aunt wagered it would be exactly so. And why not?" He stood and lifted a glass of buttermilk as a health. "To Sir Christopher Clive and his angel-in-wait." He stood. "May home be always ready to follow thee, and may thy paths always lead thee home."

Buttermilk drained, the men clasped hands. "Now, Sir Christopher," said Burroughs. "We do have a debt to pay 'afore you sail away." He pointed Christopher to his overcoat and hat. "Let's be off."

Curious, Christopher saddled Étalon and followed Burroughs westward, upslope toward Raven's Cove. Along the way, Burroughs said nothing other than that in a master's absence, Giardín an Croí would need more tenants and a good caretaker.

Before long, the two men crested the low ridge and began the descent toward Raven's narrow cove that was cut seductively between the high headlands. As they drew closer to the sea, Christopher could make out Mitten Rock still standing defiantly against the southern horizon. Étalon instinctively followed the narrowing trail downhill toward the water's edge, finally delivering Christopher to the stony beach and the ruins of the old friary where Gaia once hid.

"Tie the horses here, Kipper," said Burroughs. "And follow me."

A steep, winding path still made its way up the side of the cliff overlooking the edge of the cove—the same path that Gaia once climbed to survey the English raid on Skeefe. Wrapped tightly in his wool blanket, Christopher pulled the brim of his hat low across his forehead and climbed upward through the winter-stiff gorse. His mind filled with memories.

Burroughs stopped to catch his breath. The two men paused to survey the pewter swells below. Christopher smiled. The tossed Irish sea was wonderfully wild, untamed and free.

Grunting, Burroughs climbed another hundred paces uphill and then stopped before a magnificent wooden Celtic cross. "What say thee?"

Christopher stared at the towering cross standing against the bitter wind. He shrugged. "I've not seen this before."

"The men of Irish Town built it from Gaia's old dinghy, the one she rowed everywhere between Kinsale and Dingle." He brushed frozen leaves off a block of granite lying at the base of the cross. "I can't read the Irish, but a fisherman told me what it says." Burroughs began to recite the inscription:

"'Here rests Gaia,
Spinner of Whirlwinds, Bearer of Wisdom.
Invited to dance with the Angels on the Ides of March, 1699.'"

Christopher reflected for a moment. "I never recognized who this woman actually was. I am able to see it now." He looked up at the wooden cross. "Raven wrote that Gaia had saved her, but she said someone should tell me the story 'at her new home,' as she put it. I am guessing that is here."

Burroughs pulled his collar up. "Aye." He wiped his nose, now red from the cold. "Gaia suffered greatly after the raid. She blamed herself for being a party to the trickery and could not sleep. Comfort then delivered her a potion. On that very night Gaia had a dream. In the dream, she saw the book she had spent her life searching for. It was hidden *inside* of Mitten Rock. This was a mystery until she hired two boys from Irish Town to swim to the bottom where they found an underwater cave."

Christopher raised his brows.

"But the cave was black as death. Gaia then met a Chinese sorcerer passing through Kinsale and asked him if he knew how to start a fire underwater. The Chinaman sold her some secret combination of rust and salts and metals.

"She swam into the hole herself, set her magic torch ablaze and discovered the *Libro Mandala* lying atop a stone shelf overhead. She found a buyer for it amongst the criminals in her life who paid her over £4,000."

Christopher could hardly believe his ears.

"Gaia immediately hired Mohammedan spies to find Raven and thee."

"God bless her soul."

Burroughs nodded. "Less than a year after that, the spies reported that Raven was a concubine on the island of Jerba, and that thine own plight was hopeless. Gaia quickly arranged a heavy ransom for Raven through an English broker at Leghorn. In short, our dear girl set foot in Kinsale on 9 July '67. And I remember that date because she said it was thy birthday."

Christopher was spellbound. "Thanks be to Christ...and Gaia."

Burroughs shivered in the cold wind. "So there it is. I should also tell thee that Raven tended Gaia to the very end, and that she held the old woman's head as she died in a soft bed at the Clive House. She refused any thoughts of Virginia until then."

The two men began their descent. "Even after ransoming Raven, Gaia had money left over," said Burroughs. "She paid in advance for her wake—they still sing of it in Irish Town. The rest she left for

Raven." He paused and laid a hand on Kipper's shoulder. "Thy woman is free in the New World, and no more the peasant girl in rags. She works for me but has land of her own."

Christopher faced the sea and laughed. "And she dared wonder about happy endings." He continued downhill. *Ought I send a letter, or surprise her?*

CHAPTER 42

EVERY SHIPS' DELAY in his departure for Virginia nearly drove Christopher mad. But for the rest of that winter, he used his time to learn much from Reginald Burroughs about the climate, crops, and politics of the Virginia Colony.

Christopher further decided that he wanted his father's legacy to be a blessing for the Irish. So he and Burroughs planned a rebuilding of Giardín an Croí as a grand experiment in tolerable land leases, light rents and crops of Virginia potatoes. To oversee the project, the baronet sought out the hard-working—albeit cantankerous—Fallon Healy to offer him the position of overseer. Healy accepted with a short list of unreasonable demands.

Christopher spent his evenings reading to Comfort. Her favourites were the works of Shakespeare, of course, but also John Bunyan and, of late, William Wycherley's *The Country Wife*. Mercifully, the good woman would fall to sleep early, and so he would then hurry to his room and read Raven's letters to himself again, and then once more.

With each reading it was as if Raven's breath warmed his ear. Christopher was certain that he could feel her heart pulse in the imagined hand he held. However, on one stormy night he suddenly realized that an unexpected feeling of separation was rising within him. Troubled, he quickly discerned its cause as two things, the first being something of a petty wedge. *She has experienced the New World and I have only imagined it.*

Shaking his head, he set one of her letters aside. *Child. I am a child!* However, he could not quite dismiss an unexpected sense of injustice of his having been the first to dream of Virginia and her to be the first one there.

Unfortunately, the second point of separation was deeper and when he thought of it, he began to pace. Burroughs was aware of this one, of course, though he had been too gracious to mention it publicly. The matter was in regard to Raven's two daughters whom she had disclosed in the first letter. When she wrote of them, Christopher's heart had first failed him. He could only think of some sweating Muslim having his way with the helpless girl. Now that same monster's pleasures were personified by two living souls.

Working against these feelings, Christopher forced himself into a chair and he lit a pipe. *She loves them,* he repeated several times in his mind. *And they deserve my affections, as well.* He had calculated that Raven's elder daughter must now be about twenty-one-years old. Raven had described her as a dark-eyed beauty whom she had renamed, 'Doon O'Morrissey,' upon their ransom. Young Doon was engaged to be married in the coming Spring.

He estimated the younger to be about nineteen. According to Raven, she was fair-skinned, wise, and aptly renamed, 'Comfort O'Morrissey.' Apparently, she was presently filling the imaginations of many a Virginia lad. Christopher drew hard on his pipe, ashamed of himself for harbouring resentment toward the innocent girls.

All of this became more exaggerated until he finally was able to reserve passage to Jamestown for the last week of March. However, on the thirteenth of that month a messenger stood in the doorway of the Clive House, head hanging.

"Whatever do you mean?" Christopher was cross.

The lad repeated himself. "The carpenter ordered the wrong materials, sir. And the repair is necessary."

"By the saints! How long a project?"

"About a month, sir."

Christopher slammed the door. "No ships to Virginia for months and now this! I should have sailed back to London and then embark from there."

However, the delay proved fortuitous in an odd way as Christopher was able to help Comfort mourn Tattie who died suddenly. The good man was laid to rest in the St. Multose churchyard on 1 April. Much of Kinsale—English and Irish alike—attended his burial. Christopher vowed to remember him, well.

With his passing, the family of Fallon Healy was presented with Tattie's cottage. Thus Christopher was also able to witness the first steps in the renewal of his beloved Giardín an Croí.

⊰⊱

On 19 April Christopher was pitching hay for Étalon when Brendan raced into the stable. "Mohammedans are at the docks."

Christopher chilled and whirled around. "What?"

"They were in front of the Customs House."

He dropped his fork. *They've found me.* "How many?"

"Three."

Christopher bit his lip. "Are they bearded or moustached?"

"Bearded."

He began to pace. *Not Janissaries...* "You are certain there are three?"

"I am."

Christopher's mind raced. He took Brendan by the shoulders. "I want you to watch them closely. Tell me who they talk to and where they go." He released the boy and dug for a coin. "And keep a sharp eye for others."

Near midnight, Christopher loaded a brace of pistols and secured his dagger. He folded his hair under his hat and pulled the brim low to his nose. He then slipped out of the Clive House and made his way through the rain to the Salidan's Head—a tavern of low reputation.

This all must end. He stepped inside. *I shall do whatever I must do.*

The room was smoky and crowded. He quickly surveyed the patrons. Most were labourers, some were sailors. A few of the King's soldiers were about but they were busy with the night's ladies. Christopher pulled his hat lower and shouldered his way through the tavern until he spotted a trio of dark-skinned, bearded men under wool hats. They were slumping over ale and a plate of cheese, laughing. He wiped his hands on his trousers and adjusted the pistols at his belt. Ready, he moved cautiously to a nearby stool where he could hear the men speaking in Turkish. Christopher cocked his ears.

"Evet. The infidels are fools," said one. The others chuckled. "Look at them."

"But ah, their women…"

Christopher thought them to be relaxed, even celebratory. For the next quarter of an hour he listened carefully but heard nothing other than talk of business and women. *Merchants? But are they also sent to spy?*

Heart pounding, he finally stood. *'Tis time.* His perspired hands ran over the smooth grips of his pistols once again. He drew a deep breath and took three long strides to the Muslim's table. "*Selamünaleyküm.*"

Startled, the Turks gawked.

Christopher pulled an empty stool close, keeping his weapons out of sight. He slid his right hand carefully beneath the table and fixed it securely around a pistol grip. With his left hand he then removed his hat and shook his mane loose with a flourish. "I am Christopher Effendi of the family Clive."

Ready, he locked his eyes on the Turks.

One of them belched; the other two stared at him, blankly.

Christopher's face twitched. He nearly fainted in relief. *Thanks be to Christ.* His mind raced. "I…I am here on some old business but am making my way to a new home…in Bristol. Aye, I shall make my new life in *Bristol.*"

The Turks scowled. "Why are you bothering us?"

⌑

22 April in the Year of Grace 1684

Christopher walked into the stable behind the Clive House. Competing feelings filled him. He took Étalon's huge head in his hands. "Today is *the* day, old friend. I have dreamt of this day for two decades and yet it is not without sorrow."

His eyes filled as he took a brush and began to sweep bits of clutter from the gelding's legs. "I hope you shall forgive me." He stopped and watched his friend nibble a lap of hay. "You are too old to survive ten weeks of bad water and a pitching ship."

Tears dripped from Christopher's jaw. He wiped his hand along Étalon's long neck. "I could not bear to see you dumped into the sea." Choking, he then embraced him with all his might before laying his cheek against the horse's face. Looking deeply into his large dark eye Kipper sniffled. "Healy loves you almost as much as I do. He shall take good care of thee." He could barely speak another word. "Thank you for being my friend. Run free for all thy days." He dragged his sleeve across his eyes. "Perchance we shall ride together again. Aunt Comfort says that we cannot even imagine the joys that await us—"

Christopher turned and walked slowly to the house, collected himself and then took a final look about the rooms that had served his family for all these years. With a sigh, he walked out the front door to meet his carriage just loaded with his several travel chests under a broken sky. The most important one contained his writings and gifts for Raven that included a collection of her beloved 'Joy Stones' which he had picked from the sea with his own frozen toes a few weeks prior.

Aunt Comfort and the Burroughs' waited for him quietly as he climbed aboard the carriage. He took a seat by his aunt and took her hand as the coachman snapped his reins. He thought Reginald seemed unusually grave. "The Turks were merchants, but I planted a deception in case they are asked about me. They would report that I shall soon reside in Bristol. I think all is well."

Burroughs sat back. "In Virginia a Turk stands out like a pickle in a Yorkshire pudding. We shall keep watch."

As the carriage jostled through busy Kinsale, Christopher's mind became crowded with layers of emotion. Memories of his early years called to him; images of his father's face then appeared as he passed near the Clive offices. Listening to Comfort humming an old hymn, he closed his eyes.

Arrived at dockside, Christopher stepped from his coach. He turned to help Comfort and Mrs. Burroughs step atop the cobblestones.

Reginald stretched his hand forward. "Godspeed."

Christopher took his hand. "Until Virginia." He then faced his dear aunt. At the sight of her, his eyes filled. He tried to be brave but he could not speak a word.

Frail under a large fur hat, Comfort kissed Christopher tenderly on both cheeks. "Are you ready to soar?"

Christopher saw her chin tremble. He forced a twisted smile.

"Good. Are you ready to dance with abandon?"

He nodded.

"I am happy for it." She wiped her closed eye, slowly. "And have you seen God today?"

Christopher pulled her close. "Aye," he said. "I have." He was glad to feel her yield to his arms. He kissed her cheek.

Comfort then gathered herself with a deep breath. "That is very good." She set her hands flat upon his lapels, sniffled and struggled to speak. "You have always been worth far more than you could ever know." She pressed gently against his lingering embrace. "You are loved, my dear Kipper." Free, she turned. "Now go and love."

Christopher wept.

⁂

The *Restoration* remained at anchor in Kinsale Harbour until the tide was ready. Sometime in the night Christopher opened his eyes to the sounds of a whistle and pattering feet. His berth then pitched gently to one side; wood groaned, rope stretched.

The ship was under way.

Wide awake, Christopher stared at the dark ceiling of his quarters. He recalled watching Aunt Comfort disappear into her carriage just hours ago. Sad, his mind quickly filled with an image of her and Raven performing by the Twelfth Night hearth. His body warmed.

He then began to imagine Virginia. In her last letter, Raven had asked what he might name a Virginia plantation. He had wrestled with that question for some time, but he suddenly sat up. "Of course." he said out loud. "I shall name it, 'Gaia's Ransom'" *And no man shall be a slave there.*

Christopher pictured he and Raven running through green meadows of colourful wildflowers and edged with the pink and white blossoms of cherry trees and pears. He imagined her swimming in some wild Virginia river. *I shall finally toss my boots into the deep and dive naked among the rocks with her!* He smiled and begged the dawn to hurry.

As the first light of a clear day cut a bright line beneath his door, Christopher hastily dressed and went aboards. He stood at the stern rail and licked salty mist from his lips, feeling the gentle heave of the ship as he watched the headlands of Ireland fade behind him.

A strong westerly wind tilted the tacking *Restoration* to one side. Christopher held the stern rail firmly and opened his nostrils wide to let clean air fill his lungs. He looked at all that was behind. He dug into his pocket to retrieve a Joy Stone, smooth and comforting in his hand. He put it to his lips and whispered that for which he was most joyful, kissed it, and held it for a final moment before launching it toward the disappearing silhouette of Ireland.

A shearwater swooped close, abruptly sounding her rhythmic call. He followed the seabird as she flew past him and disappeared over the lifting nose of the ship pointed to the unbroken horizon.

A cool gust tossed Christopher's curly mane off his face as he stared forward. It was then he thought he heard a voice. He cocked his ear. "Eh?"

Sea spray hissed and the canvas sail rippled.

Christopher strained to listen again. He was now certain of what he had heard: "'Look and see how I have made all things new.'" *The Breath*...His eyes filled.

The *Restoration* heaved in the breeze and Christopher held fast. The shearwater rose beyond the spars; a crying gull fastened her wings to a sweeping current of wind. Heart filled to overflowing, Kipper Clive gazed into the boundless blue above and offered his thanksgiving for it all—even for the pursuit of Leviathan.

The End

A Note from
C. David Baker

My Dear Reader,

I didn't want to say goodbye without expressing my appreciation for joining me on this adventure. Writing is ultimately a collaboration between you—the reader—and me, and I'm so grateful for the significant time and attention you invested in this story. I pray you've sensed the shaping of *your own* emerging story through Christopher's and Raven's as have I.

Uncovering this work has been a life-changing experience for me. Above all, I encountered the Spirit so much greater than myself who continues to love, guide and comfort through the most difficult times of life and despite all my shortcomings. My primary hope is that you will continue to grow in experience of this particular love—for a lifetime and beyond.

If this book has meant something to you, please consider telling others. You could post a review on Amazon.com, Goodreads.com, or simply tell a friend. We authors live off the consideration and support of readers, so I would be delighted by your companionship and help.

I invite any questions or comments you might have, and you can connect with me and find my other books at www.cdbaker.com. Until we meet again!

With you for the journey,
C. David Baker

CPSIA information can be obtained
at www.ICGtesting.com
Printed in the USA
LVHW081454040420
652136LV00033B/2950